"SOVIET COMMANDER, THIS IS MAJOR CURT CARSON!"

Carson's voice, amplified by the loudspeaker, boomed out over the burning town.

"We are strong enough to win if we have to fight," he continued, "but we come under a flag of truce!"

Carson knew from experience that he needed a show of strength to convince the commander of the Spetsnaz battalion. At that precise instant, black holes appeared in the starry sky as the lightless Harpies, operating in stealth, topped the eastern ridge and ducked down into the gorge. The thunder of their passage shook the ground.

Carson stood up and pulled a white flag from his harness pack, a flag that signified not surrender but a willingness to negotiate before the killing.

He hoped to God the Soviet commander wouldn't fire the 73-millimeter that was aimed at him. He'd become meat if that happened. No way his body armor could stop that kind of incoming. . . .

WARBOTS by G. Harry Stine

#5 OPERATION HIGH DRAGON   (17-159, $3.95)

Civilization is under attack! A "virus program" has been injected into America's polar-orbit military satellites by an unknown enemy. The only motive can be the preparation for attack against the free world. The source of "infection" is traced to a barren, storm-swept rock-pile in the southern Indian Ocean. Now, it is up to the forces of freedom to search out and destroy the enemy. With the aid of their robot infantry—the Warbots—the Washington Greys mount Operation High Dragon in a climactic battle for the future of the free world.

#6 THE LOST BATTALION   (17-205, $3.95)

Major Curt Carson has his orders to lead his Warbot-equipped Washington Greys in a search-and-destroy mission in the mountain jungles of Borneo. The enemy: a strongly entrenched army of Shiite Muslim guerrillas who have captured the Second Tactical Battalion, threatening them with slaughter. As allies, the Washington Greys have enlisted the Grey Lotus Battalion, a mixed-breed horde of Japanese jungle fighters. Together with their newfound allies, the small band must face swarming hordes of fanatical Shiite guerrillas in a battle that will decide the fate of Southeast Asia and the security of the free world.

#7 OPERATION IRON FIST   (17-253, $3.95)

Russia's centuries-old ambition to conquer lands along its southern border erupts in a savage show of force that pits a horde of Soviet-backed Turkish guerrillas against the freedom-loving Kurds in their homeland high in the Caucasus Mountains. At stake: the rich oil fields of the Middle East. Facing certain annihilation, the valiant Kurds turn to the robot infantry of Major Curt Carson's "Ghost Forces" for help. But the brutal Turks far outnumber Carson's desperately embattled Washington Greys, and on the blood-stained slopes of historic Mount Ararat, the high-tech warriors of tomorrow must face their most awesome challenge yet!

WARBOTS

G. HARRY STINE
#7 OPERATION IRON FIST

PINNACLE BOOKS
WINDSOR PUBLISHING CORP.

PINNACLE BOOKS

are published by

Windsor Publishing Corp.
475 Park Avenue South
New York, NY 10016

First printing: August 1989

Printed in the United States of America

"It has, in our time, been customary to think of war and peace as though these are mutually exclusive conditions, as though you must be at war if you are not at peace, and vice versa. This is hardly self-evident and certainly untrue at any time when war is not total. . . ."

—General Sir John Hackett,
"The Profession of Arms"

Chapter One

The warbot topped the rise.

A burst of shots rang out.

The rounds bounced off the armor of the M33A Jeep, throwing a shower of sparks.

Companion Leader, this is Bucephalus in Companion Jay-One, the warbot dutifully reported via neurophonic linkage to Major Curt Carson who was riding in the turret hatch of his Armored Command Vehicle "Sweet Chariot" fifty meters behind the warbot. *I am taking small arms fire from hidden riflemen on magnetic bearing zero-eight-three, range estimated five hundred eleven meters. I am tracking the incoming rounds by radar and do not have targets on either visual or infrared at this time.*

Curt had heard the incoming and had already started to do something about it. The Washington Greys, the 3rd Robot Infantry Regiment, were still having problems with the new warbots and the advanced Mod 7/11 Artificial Intelligence circuitry, the latest innovation from McCarthy Proving Ground as a result of more than two years of research. Although the upgraded bots were able to do a lot of "thinking" for themselves, their speech circuitry tended to make them somewhat long-winded.

"Grey Patrol, this is Companion Leader!" Curt snapped both verbal and thought commands into his helmet tacomm. "Incoming! We've been ambushed! Take cover! Go to armor in Sweet Chariot or Artie!"

Major Curt Carson was a combat field officer. He didn't like ducking for cover when the action started.

And he didn't like the rules of engagement with which he was forced to operate on this patrol.

The Washington Greys were a Sierra Charlie—"Special Combat"—warbot regiment, the first in an otherwise roboticized United States Army. Curt and his people had developed the Sierra Charlie doctrines and tactics to make the Regiment into a versatile, hard-hitting force capable of dealing with deadly situations that the all-warbot units couldn't handle very well. Over the past several years in a dozen places in a world that never stopped fighting, the Washington Greys had learned the hard way and written the Sierra Charlie book themselves. As a result, they'd organized, equipped, and trained to take the initiative and go on the offensive with high mobility and heavy fire power.

But now they were under orders—rules of engagement— prohibiting them from doing what they were trained to do. And, again, Major Curt Carson and his Washington Greys had to do what soldiers everywhere and in every age have had to do when their orders made no sense in a situation: be versatile, show initiative, and do whatever was necessary to save their asses.

"Companion Leader, this is Deer Arrow!" came the message on the tacomm from Platoon Sergeant Dyani Motega. "I think I see the source of the incoming! Request permission to scout it out!" The young Crow Indian woman was perhaps the best scout in the entire Washington Greys.

Sergeant Sid Johnson riding on the Airportable Robot Transport Vehicle, code-named "Artie," called on tacomm, "Sid Johnnie has visual contact! On the other ridge to the east of the river bed! Behind the rocks!"

First Sergeant Nick Gerard cut in, "They musta been waitin' to nail us coming up the river bed, but we put 'em off-balance when we came up the rise to the south of the river instead!"

"Roger that!" Curt replied, gritting his teeth. "Now take cover! Everyone! That includes you, Deer Arrow!"

"Major, why can't we give 'em the Washington Greys shuffle—hold 'em with fire while we sweep around and kick 'em in the ass?" Nick wanted to know. "Send out Sid Johnnie and Joe Jim with Murphy and Boom Bucket! When they get the two Mary Anns in position and targeting the attackers, we'll move around to the north and work up the easier north slopes of that ridge with the Jeeps!"

"Negatory! Negatory!" Curt snarled. "You all know the goddamned rules of engagement! No assaults! If attacked, we return fire! We counterattack only if we're assaulted! Now get your asses back to armor! Sid Johnny, Joe Jim, leave the Mary Anns outside and establish remote voice command links with them! Everyone else, leave your Jeeps outside to bring the attackers under fire when commanded to do so, but remote-link with the Jeeps and take cover! Repeat: take cover! *Now,* goddammit!"

"Roger, Companion Leader! Sid Johnnie and Joe Jim have Murphy and Boom Bucket in position!" came the tacomm voice call from Sergeant Sid Johnson.

"You may fire when ready," Curt told the Sergeants commanding the two Mary Anns.

Johnson and Watson gave no tacomm reply. Both Mary Anns opened up with bursts from their 25-millimeter M300 automatic cannons using a combination of airburst and smoke rounds. The barren, rocky hillside to the east of the river bed suddenly was covered with the brown dust of Iraq and the black smoke of the Mary Anns' rounds.

Bucephalus, remain outside in your present position! Curt ordered his M33 Jeep by thinking his command into the helmet tacomm unit. The helmet's non-intrusive sensors against Curt's scalp picked up the officer's brain activity and the nanocomputer translated the nerve impulses into electronic signals sent on radio link to the Jeep. *Maintain sensor contact with the enemy! Fire three-round bursts at the enemy every ten seconds! If you get a solid target contact, report that to me and be prepared to go to full-automatic fire on them!*

Roger! Bucephalus has a visual contact! It is a human being that has been hit by one of my rounds! The target jerked erect before falling!

The tactical procedures of the Washington Greys had undergone a major change in the two years since they'd returned from Brunei. Reorganized now as a far more versatile combat team with the new Mod 7/11 Artificial Intelligence circuitry in the warbots, the Greys were now capable of working together in any quickly organized combat unit configuration. Each Grey had a particular specialty, but they'd all cross-trained. The incredibly smart "7/11" warbots — "smart" in relation to how "dumb" they'd been with the old Mod 5 AI — could now act almost independently, doing what warbots do best and leaving human soldiers to concentrate on doing what human beings do best. The warbots had the heavy firepower, the defensive armor, and the ability to serve as "smart light tanks" so humans could utilize their versatility and ability to adapt to unplanned circumstances. As a result of smarter warbots and better communications, the Greys had gone to a more familiar form of address on tacomm, using call code names they'd picked up from their contacts with the Navy and from their new tacair squadron, Worsham's Warhawks. Furthermore, because the warbots were "smarter," they'd also been given nicknames which served as code calls.

Curt noted the location of Sergeant Dyani Motega's beacon on his ACV's tactical display. She wasn't returning to the Sweet Chariot Airportable Command Vehicle. She was already crossing the dry river bed to the north of their position.

"Deer Arrow, get the hell back here!" Curt ordered her via tacomm. "You were ordered to return to Sweet Chariot! So what the hell are you doing out in the boonies with your Jeep?"

"Companion Leader, my return path to the ACV is under heavy incoming!" was her reply. "I'm not attacking, sir! I'm doing what you taught me to do under these circumstances. I'm conducting a reconnaissance in force. The enemy doesn't see me. But I've got them targeted now! I'll call fire for you if need be. I'm wearing my body armor, and if they start shooting at me I'll use my Jeep as cover. Moonbeam has better armor!"

"Damned right! Let the warbot take the incoming!" was Nick Gerard's advice. He'd been wounded several times in combat in spite of body armor. Even with body armor, taking a hit from a 7.62-millimeter round hurt like hell and, if it hit in the wrong place, it would put a person out of action temporarily just from the pain and subcutaneous trauma.

Even wearing body armor, it took a lot of guts to stay in the open under fire. There's always the Golden BB—the round that hits you where your body armor isn't—hands or face, for example. Or hits the body armor at such an angle that the incredibly tough crystalline fiber can't distribute the impact energy over a wide enough part of the body.

"Okay, Deer Arrow, do it! But we don't have a bio-tech

with us today!" Curt told her.

"Yeah, this wasn't supposed to happen!" was Joe Jim Watson's acid comment.

"Anything can happen in this part of the world when you're on patrol," Curt reminded him. "Why the hell do you think Uncle Sammy sends us out here?"

"I dunno, Major. I ain't figgered that one out yet! Sure as hell ain't no vacation!" Nick Gerard told the patrol leader as he slipped through the personnel hatch on the side of the ACV away from the enemy fire.

"Grey Head, this is Companion Leader!" Curt snapped into the vehicle's big tacomm set to report to the regimental command nine kilometers south in the Iraqi city of Mosul.

The voice of Regimental Staff Sergeant Georgina Cook replied, "Grey Head here! Go ahead, Companion Leader!"

"Tell the regimental commander that Patrol Mike Three is under attack!"

A brief silence followed, then Curt heard the familiar voice of Colonel William Bellamack, "Companion Leader, report specifics! We see your beacons and note your location. How many and how serious?"

"Apparently a small unit, Colonel," Curt told him. "No head count yet. Small arms fire. No rockets. No heavy stuff. We're complying with the rules of engagement. We've laid Mary Ann twenty-fives and Jeep fire on them. Request instructions, sir!"

"Dammit, Curt, I don't micromanage your battles!" Bellamack came back.

"Yes, sir, I know you don't! But we're saddled with rules of engagement that force us to just sit here, take incoming, and shoot back. I won't run except under a direct order. What I really want to do is go over and cream those bastards! That would put a searing halt to this goddamned ambush crap!" Curt admitted to his commanding officer. He knew Bellamack, and he also knew that the regimental commander chafed under the ROE that was laid on them from high command.

The Washington Greys were part of a major United States military commitment stationed in the Mideast oil patch for two reasons: (a) to protect vital industrial resources there because the Iraqis had lost three generations to the various

11

Iran-Iraq wars and were thus too weak to do it themselves; and (b) to act as a stabilizing force in the incredibly complex international situations that continued to evolve in the region. Soviets, Turks, Israelis, Iraqi, Iranians, Syrians, and Saudis all had immediate conflicting interests; some of these countries had nuclear capability and missile delivery systems. Those countries with more remote but nonetheless deep investments in the Tigris-Euphrates River Valley, the "Fertile Crescent" of ancient history, included the United States, the European nations, and even the Pacific rim countries, all of whom had the ability to conduct surgical, low-intensity tactical strikes with nuclear, chemical, and biological weapons—none of which had been used so far because of a general fear of the consequences.

So the Americans were on the scene with three regiments of their awesome war robots, the pinnacle of war-making which combined human and machine to produce a force of incredible destruction. (Or so the encouraged belief went, and the United States Army wasn't about to rock the boat.) The motivation on the part of the United States wasn't just to protect the rights and interests of free-world businesses in petroleum—used mostly in the twenty-first century for chemical feedstocks, not fuel—but also the mineral wealth of the Kurdistani mountains and the most precious of all commodities in an arid part of the world: water.

"Curt, my eagles are on the block. I can't override an order from the Joint Chiefs," Bellamack reminded him. "My lonesome bird doesn't stack up against a constellation of silver stars."

"Colonel, this is the third time in as many weeks that one of our patrols has been bushwacked! Probably by the same local tribe of Dervish Kurds. If we go in and cream the bastards now, maybe this fucking harassment will stop!" Curt pointed out.

"You know the rules of engagement."

"Yes, sir, I do!"

"Why the hell don't you follow them?" the Colonel suddenly wanted to know.

"Goddammit, Colonel, I am!"

"And you're the field officer who knows how to find the loopholes in orders?" Bellamack went on, subtly reminding

Curt of the times in the past when he'd given a direct but incomplete order to the field officer, knowing that Curt would dive right through the loophole.

"I can go after the bastards only if I counterattack!"

"So? The ROE don't say anything about provoking a direct assault on your unit, do they?"

"Colonel, say no more," Curt advised him.

"Need tacair support? Cal Worsham is also hot to lay a little ordnance on someone," Bellamack advised. "And if it looks like you're getting into deep slime, we can airlift some stuff in damned fast. You're only nine kicks away. Russ Frazier is his usual gung-ho tactical self.

"Colonel, we're in an excellent position at the moment. Why don't we wait a bit and see what develops?" Curt suggested, a plan forming in his mind.

"Sounds like a good idea! Why don't we do that? Keep me advised. But run your own fracas out there. And, Curt, try to be home by Stand-to and chow-call this evening."

"Yes, sir! Will do, sir!" Curt grinned as he toggled off.

First Sergeant Nick Gerard of Ward's Warriors was also grinning. He'd served under Curt Carson for years, and all the Greys had gotten used to Colonel Bill Bellamack's unique style of command, which often involved looking the other way. Gerard knew what Curt Carson was capable of doing, and he knew that whatever Carson was cooking up would be downright nasty.

"Deer Arrow, Companion Leader here! Can you get an ID on our attackers? Who the hell are they?" Curt radioed to Dyani Motega.

"Major, all these people look alike to me! But they're using the same weaponry that was reported in the other two ambushes," she replied. Like Lieutenant Adonica Sweet and Battalion Sergeant Major Edwina Sampson, her mentor and best friend respectively, Dyani Motega had become a real expert in the small arms and assault weapons of the world. "They sound like old Soviet A-K-Thirteens; I can hear the rattle of the action even here! And see the dust cloud kicked up by the stupid damned vertical muzzle brake the Soviets are in love with. Some sound like old A-K-Seventy-fours. And I hear a few real ancient bolt-action Lee-Enfields — a couple of seconds between shots while someone pumps the

13

action. So my guess is that they're Dervishes!"

That's what Curt wanted to hear. "Good! Stay put! If they don't see you, they won't bother you when they pull off their next move," he told her, then broadcast to his patrol, "Okay, everyone listen up! Sid Johnny and Joe Jim, suspend firing. Repeat: suspend firing, but don't cease fire. Keep your Mary Anns and Jeeps tracking targets, but don't shoot. Everyone stand by to repel a direct assault!"

Curt was not only a field combat officer; he was also a student of military history. He knew what had to come next because of the nature of his adversaries who had fought the same way for fifty centuries regardless of the sort of weapons they used.

What he didn't know then was that he was fighting this battle on exactly the same spot where in 401 B.C. the remote ancestors of these Dervish tribesmen had hassled the Greek general Xenophon and the Ten Thousand on their incredible trek back to Greece.

And these modern guerrillas did exactly the same thing that Xenophon reported.

"Here they come!" Dyani Motega announced.

Chapter Two

Almost silently, about fifty men erupted from the rocks and hollows of the hillside across the shallow river bed. Carrying rifles of various makes and ages, they swarmed down the hillside, dodging from sparse cover to sparse cover and splashing through the shallow, muddy river.

When they were visible, they made tempting targets for the four M33A Jeeps emplaced on the military crest just below the ridge line with their 7.62-millimeter automatic weapons ready, armed, and tracking. The Jeeps had the new Mod 7/11 artificial intelligence circuits that were more than two generations ahead of the old Mod 5 units the Greys had used in Sierra Charlie combat thus far. The new 7/11 Jeeps knew what they had to do and wouldn't miss. The targets were too well-defined both visually and in the infra red. Curt wouldn't even have to use the patrol's two Mary Anns; their 25-millimeter cannons would be gross overkill.

"Hold your fire!" Curt told his patrol and the Jeeps. He knew the enemy's tactics. They were the same throughout the Mideast among the guerrilla and insurgent groups, the same mass human attacks that he'd seen in Zahedan within the Jehorkhim Muslims. These people were religious fanatics who believed they'd go to Paradise if they fell in battle against the infidel. They were using the same tactics as the ancient Mongols . . . except their leaders really hadn't studied those tactics well and hadn't evaluated their deadly consequences when used against modern warbots.

On the other hand, Muslim zealots had come up against warbots in Zahedan, and they'd overwhelmed the old remotely operated bots by presenting a confusing array of targets. But they hadn't tried it against the Sierra Charlies or the incredible 7/11 warbots that combined the best of the magical Mod 7 AI with the miniaturized Mod 11 AI adapted from the megacomputers.

Maybe the ROE prevented Curt from attacking, but it didn't keep him from defending. He'd called to his troopers and warbots to hold fire because he wanted to make damned sure that this ambush force was creamed but not totally wiped out. He wanted the word about the new Sierra Charlies and their 7/11 warbots to get back to the rest of the Dervishes — if that's what they really were — and cause their leaders to re-evaluate making these constant, harassing ambushes.

The discipline of the Washington Greys was excellent. No one fired, although the three NCOs had their Novias poised, aimed over the lips of turret hatches.

Although some of them had faced human wave attacks in other places where they'd fought, none of the Siera Charlies would ever admit to *not* being scared when a human wave assault bore down on them.

"They're not shooting!" Nick Gerard observed, peering over the lip of one of the ACV's turret hatches.

Curt was in the other hatch. "Didn't expect them to," he replied brusquely. "Don't let them scare the shit out of you, troops! Hold your fire! Let them close the range! They're not shooting . . . and they won't start until we do."

"What the hell's the matter with the bastards?" Sergeant Sid Johnson asked in disbelief. This was his first real combat as an "Eleven-Echo" Sierra Charlie. When the Regiment had recently reorganized, Sid Johnson had been given the option of converting his Rated Position Code from RPC 54 Operations to RPC 11E Robot Infantryman (Special Combat), or transferring to another regiment with his old RPC. Sid Johnson did what nearly every Washington Grey had done under the circumstances: he'd elected to stay with his Regiment and comrades, even though it meant being in a position at which he could be shot at and maybe killed. (Actually, he'd been shot at already in several earlier operations because the Sierra Charlies had developed the tradition that *everyone* in the outfit, except the biotechs, would fight if necessary.)

"It's a military secret which I shall reveal when this is over in a minute or so. Just keep a cool stool and a hot pot," Curt muttered calmly in an almost distracted tone as he watched the oncoming horde of ragged men dodging from rock to bush to rock as they closed on the Greys' position. Curt didn't know when they'd break into a mass charge.

Even though he knew from miltary history how these people tended to fight, it utterly amazed him that experienced insurgent warriors would think of making a wild charge in the open into the teeth of the enormous firepower of a warbot unit.

Curt had to admit to himself it was eerie.

He also thought it was the height of military stupidity.

Before the Washington Greys arrived in Mosul a few weeks ago, the guerrillas from the various Kurdish tribes had never come up against Sierra Charlies and MOD 7/11 warbots.

Curt trusted the reports of other regular Robot Infantry regiments with their old linkage-operated neuroelectronic warbots who'd faced this sort of thing in northern Iraq. And the books had reported similar clashes in the twentieth and preceding centuries. So had the classical works of military history.

Sometimes the history books *don't* lie!

At a range of fifty meters as the guerrillas were clambering up the slope from cover to cover, they suddenly seemed to respond to a silent command. They broke cover and began a screaming, yelling charge out in the open against the Jeeps. Curt gave the order, "Commence firing!"

The three M33A Jeeps got the order first through the speed-of-light tacomm. It was a fraction of a second before the three NCOs heard it. The Jeeps were faster to react with their circuitry, and had been tracking the oncoming targets.

The air was torn by the ripping, roaring, thundering sound of their M133A 7.62-millimeter variable-rate automatics. The Jeeps knew enough not to waste ammo, so they'd cut back the fire rate to one round per target. The first volley was fired almost simultaneously. Their on-board sensors, primarily their targeting radars, tracked the outgoing rounds to determine if they achieved "convergence with the target." Most of them did; at fifty meters' range, it's almost impossible for a warbot to miss. Each Jeep then picked a second target and fired, within a second of getting off the first round.

Because of the slower speed of human neural responses and information processing within the human brain, it took nearly seven-tenths of a second for Nick Gerard to get off the first human-fired round . . . and Nick's reaction times were considered to be excellent. By the time the 7.62-millimeter round from his M33A2 Novia rifle reached his first intended target, the man was already hit by a Jeep round and starting to fall.

The two Mary Anns with Johnson and Watson didn't have to shoot. They could find no targets.

Curt didn't even get the chance to get off a single shot from his M33A2 Novia, the improved version which had been given back to the Greys after the abortive M101 Hellcat tryout. And he didn't get the chance to try out the M44A Black Maria assault shotgun which was an awesome close-in fighting tool.

It was all over in seconds.

And it was so startling and bloody that Sid Johnson could only rasp, *"Jesus!"*

Even the experienced Nick Gerard growled, "Godamighty, I sort of hate to grease them *that* hard! They didn't have a chance!"

"You kinda forget, Nick, that they shouldn't have attacked in the first place," Sergeant Joe Jim Watson reminded him. "Stupid bastards, why the hell are they fightin' in the first place?"

"Because they're Kurds and they've been here for about five thousand years and they've been fighting for every one of them," Curt explained. "They want their own country, but they're only tribal. So the Turks, Iraqis, Iranian, and Russkies smash them down by better organization. Anyone left alive out there? Any wounded?"

"Two of them are getting away!" Dyani Motega called in from her hidden scouting position on the other side of the river.

"Your targets, Dyani!" Nick told her.

"No, not unless the Major wants me to waste them," she called back. "Old Crow Indian trick is to let a couple of survivors get away to carry back the story of the massacre."

"Hey, that'll just drive them even more nuts!" Sid Johnson

18

complained.

"No, not at all. You can't stop the real crazies anyway. But somewhere some cooler heads prevail back home," she reminded them. "They'll either withdraw, or they'll change their tactics. If they don't, the crazies among them will be wiped out damned quick."

"Let them go, Dyani, then get back here when you're in the clear," Curt told her. He also knew that the perception of hopelessness on the part of terrorists in attacking the new Sierra Charlies might also lead to either a truce or some talking. He had nothing against the Kurds or any of their tribes such as the Dervishes. He and the rest of the Washington Greys were in northwestern Iraq to keep terrorists from killing oil patch people and destroying equipment because the war-exhausted Iraqis couldn't. He'd been there before as a warbot brainy, and the only reason that a specialized combat regiment like the Washington Greys had been deployed to carry out the boring task of pipeline and facilities patrol was that the 9th Robot Infantry Regiment, the Manchus, had been there for three years and *had* to be rotated out for R&R. And the Washington Greys were the only available regiment at Level One Readiness Status.

Companion leader, this is Bucephalus, came the computer-generated signal from Curt's Jeep outside the ACV. *I have found wounded.*

"Shoot Luke reports another wounded man," Sergeant Joe Jim Watson communicated the findings of his own Jeep.

"Roger!" Curt replied and turned to Nick. "Get on the hooter to Mosul. Wosham's going to get to log some flight time. Get an evac aerodyne in here with a couple of biotechs. If we can save those two Dervishes, maybe we'll learn something."

"Maybe we will, and maybe we won't," Nick unconsciously mimicked Regimental Sergeant Major Henry Kester. "Lieutenant Allen is the only one who speaks Arabic, and he's been having trouble getting any information from wounded prisoners we've brought back so far."

"Yeah, but there's always the outside chance," Curt reminded the First Sergeant of Ward's Warriors. "So get on the horn to Mosul." He toggled the tacomm switch and put out the all-call to his patrol, "Companions all, this is Companion

Leader! Go to ground and let's check the casualties for possible items that might be of interest to Major Gibbon and his spooks. Take your Novia loaded with a clip of tranquilizer fletchettes in case you stumble on someone who's been wounded and still wants to fight. Remember, we're not really here to kill. We're here to patrol and protect, so we bring back enemy survivors if we can."

That order didn't bother the Greys. They had no grudge-hatred thing against the Iraqis or Kurds or anyone else around these parts. They were trained and disciplined voluntary professional soldiers of the United States Army in the twenty-first century, people who liked military life and didn't mind fighting. The Sierra Charlies of the Robot Infantry had their roots in the British Commandos and SAS as well as the American Green Berets and Special Forces, so they fought for different reasons than their enemies.

And therefore a lot more effectively, too.

But, as Curt knew all too well because he'd been right in the middle of the transition from a remotely operated warbot military force to the present Special Combat unit that fought in the field with its warbots, it hadn't been easy getting there . . . and they weren't there yet anyway. The Washington Greys were the guinea pigs who made all the mistakes and reinvented the square wheel, and wrote the field manuals with blood in the process.

That was a source of great pride to a Regiment that could trace its lineage back to the Revolutionary War.

It also helped make the Washington Greys a tightly knit "family" which carried on strong traditions and provided some people with a sense of family loyalty they'd never had as children.

You had to be special to be a Washington Grey.

And its unit commanders had to be even more special.

Curt debouched from Sweet Chariot with Nick, and together they began checking the guerrilla casualties. Sid had already taken care of one of the wounded men by slapping a plastiskin dressing over the wound made by a Jeep's 7.62-millimeter round and giving the man a painkiller that also effectively put him to sleep. Joe Jim was tending to another one.

"This is one thing I don't like about this kind of duty," Nick admitted. "We don't have our bio-techs along on these patrols, and I'm not enough of a gung-ho killer type that I like to go around afterwards kicking at bloody bodies to find out if they're still alive. . . ." He touched a form with the toe of his boot and rolled it over. It had been a young boy in his teens. "Damn! I also don't like bein' a baby-killer!"

"They start them young, Nick," Curt reminded him.

"Yeah, Major, easier to indoctrinate them early," the First Sergeant muttered in distaste. "But indoctrinate them for what? And why? This is pretty damned good farm and grazing land around here, and there seems to be plenty of it for everybody. . . ."

"This is the upper end of the Fertile Crescent, Nick," Curt explained. "People have been fighting about this land for maybe ten thousand years or more. And fighting on it, too."

"Why the hell don't they get busy and farm it, then?"

"They do. And when they do, someone else comes down out of those hills to the north and loots the place," Curt went on.

An older wounded man moved and vented a little groan out of the side of a bloody mouth when Curt touched him with the toe of a boot. "Okay, Nick, we've got another live casualty here. Kick that rifle away from him, then cover me while I get that pig-sticker out of his belt so he can't slash at me."

It was bloody work taking care of casualties in the field, Curt had to admit. Maybe Nick Gerard had a valid recommendation. Maybe each patrol should have a bio-tech along for this sort of thing. The company bio-techs were all trained P.N.s, and they were used to this sort of thing.

Curt wasn't squeamish. Neither was Nick Gerard. Both had seen a lot of personal combat since the Washington Greys had become Sierra Charlies. Combat for them was now on a far more personal level than that of a warbot brainy who lay on a linkage couch in the rear area and operated his warbots by remote control, a form of warfare very much like that of the Aerospace Force where fighter and bomber jocks never saw what happened when one of their bombs or missiles or rounds hit another person. Although the Sierra Charlies had seen a lot of personal combat, they'd never really gotten used to it or gotten to like it. And it did nauseate some of the newer Charlies the first time out of the starting gate.

Within a few minutes, a saucer-shaped aerodyne was hovering over the battle site. It disgorged two of the Regiment's bio-techs when it touched down. Alan Williams and Shelley Hale were experienced medics, so Curt returned to his vehicle and let Al and Shel do their work.

Nick Gerard had picked up some of the guerrillas' weapons and brought them along. The old bolt-action Lee-Enfields were museum pieces now, of course, but Nick knew that Henry Kester and Edie Sampson would be interested in the Soviet AK-13s. They hadn't run up against them before, and Edie was anxious to learn something about the new Soviet assault rifle that was showing up in Iraq. It was a cheap, grungy assault rifle that was even more of a plastic wonder than the M101 Hellcat that Ordnance had tried to foist on the Greys. The Soviets were punching out AK-13s by the millions because it was an expendable rifle that never had to be cleaned; eventually, it just stopped working, so you threw it away and picked up another one.

Since combat was a way of life to Curt Carson, he wondered why he was so damned bushed after this short foray. Insofar as he was concerned, it was time to head for Kabul for a shit, shine, shower, shave, and shampoo . . . along with some good chow and a few hours at the Club with Alexis or Kitsy or whomever. So he toggled the regimental tacomm and called, "Grey Head, this is Companion Leader. We've got things under control here. Request permission to return to Mosul."

"Companion Leader, Grey Head here. The head man didn't authorize a return after the fracas," was Georgina Cook's reply. "In fact, he asked me to remind you to continue the patrol to Zakho, then return by highway."

"Shit!" Curt said under his breath, then told the Regimental Communications Sergeant, "Tell the Colonel that this was a hell of a patrol! We got shot at!"

"The Colonel anticipated your remarks, Major, and he asked me to forward to you the following code groups: Tango Sierra and FIDO! And he wants you to be sure to get back in time for Stand-to at eighteen-hundred hours. Hassan is here!"

Chapter Three

"I'll be go to hell!" Regimental Sergeant Major Henry Kester said with some awe and reverence in his voice. For Henry to speak that way meant he was *really* impressed. "Lieutenant, you sure have changed since we pulled you off that mountain outside of Zahedan!"

"That was five years ago, Sergeant Major," replied Second Lieutenant Hassan Ben Mahmud with a grin. "I see a lot of changes in the Washington Greys. . . ."

"Yeah, we're a down-and-dirty infantry outfit now," Captain Jerry Allen replied. "No more lying on our butts and letting the bots take the incoming! But Henry's right: my God, you've changed!"

It was a special Stand-to in the makeshift Club that had been set up in the casern occupied by the Washington Greys in the Iraqi city of Mosul. A new officer had joined their ranks. And he was a special person.

Years before, during the Zahedan hostage rescue mission, Curt and Henry Kester had brought back a scrawny, ignorant Iranian youth from the recce mission. They had to bring him back or take the chance that the dirty, scrawny, underfed, illiterate youngster might report the presence of the Greys. That young man was known only as "Hassan."

"Well, it was either change or go back to prospecting for gemstones in the mountains of eastern Iran," Lieutenant Mahmud said with a shrug. "You people gave me a chance. I would have been a damned fool not to take it."

"You earned it. You gave us the information we needed to rescue Major Carson and the others trapped in Zahedan," Alexis Morgan reminded him.

"You made it happen," Hassan added. It had taken only a little string-pulling to get Hassan classed as a political refu-

23

gee — if he'd gone back to Zahedan, he might have been killed by the fanatical Jehorkhim Muslims. The former regimental commander, then Colonel Belinda Hettrick, had uncovered some scholarship money to send Hassan to school in the United States.

It seemed to Curt that it had been only yesterday, but actually several years had passed. With the help of modern biotechnology, Hassan had overcome the shortcomings of his youth. "Lieutenant — and I'm amazed that I'm calling you 'Lieutenant' now — you've undergone the goddamnedest metamorphosis I've ever seen . . ."

"Like a butterfly," Hassan pointed out. "I'm told the biotechnologists got to me at just the right time in my adolescence. So I sort of overcame some of the shortfalls of growing up around Zahedan."

The young officer who now stood among the Greys at the Club was still a small man. He would always be short because of both his heritage and the fact he'd gone hungry most of his childhood. But he'd filled out and was now in outstanding physical condition.

"I also remember you when we gave you that first bath," Battalion Sergeant Major Edie Sampson recalled. "But right now, Lieutenant, I'm not sure I'd want to tangle with you even in a friendly little lump session in the martial arts spa."

"Might be fun," was Lieutenant Kitsy Clinton's comment. Curt just threw her a sideways glance because, although Kitsy sometimes sent oblique signals, it was apparent to Curt that she had other things in mind.

Hassan was still Hassan, but he'd filled out with a square, strikingly handsome young masculine face with deep, dark eyes, bushy eyebrows, and a bushy black mustache. Rumor Control Headquarters was already passing the word that Hassan had been pegged as a target by some of the ladies of the Washington Greys.

In the mental area, Hassan wasn't as much of a surprise to Curt . . . although he was still surprising. When Curt had gotten to know Hassan after the Zahedan rescue mission, he'd sensed that the young man had something special upstairs because he'd seemed bright and intelligent.

Hassan's 101 File confirmed this.

His academic record hadn't been outstanding; it had been

24

unbelievable. It was as though he was being driven by the ghosts of his youth to do whatever was necessary to make certain he'd never have to go back to what he'd been. He'd learned English within months and now spoke excellent, unaccented American English. He'd shown a natural talent for mathematics. He was able to grasp new information and ideas readily and meld them into a unique world view. In three years of what would have been exceptionally intense effort on the part of an American student, Hassan had graduated from high school scoring so high on tests that he'd been admitted to OCS after only one year of college undergraduate education . . . during which he amazed the academicians and psychologists alike by learning at an impossible rate, retaining what he'd learned, and performing well at the level of a graduate student.

Hassan could have been a boy-genius scientist, but he would have none of it. He knew who'd befriended him, and he intended to honor their trust and faith in him. So he'd passed up an opportunity to work under a very large grant with some of the best scientists in the world at the California Institute of Technology. And he'd insisted on becoming commissioned as an officer to serve with the Washington Greys.

Although he'd been granted political asylum in the United States and therefore could have gotten United States' citizenship almost for the asking, Hassan had insisted on qualifying for naturalization by taking the necessary tests.

At OCS, he'd graduated at the top of his class. Furthermore, he'd shown physical audacity and aggressive pursuit of winning at whatever he was doing. As a result, he was outstanding in the martial arts, capable of besting even the biggest and brawniest of his colleagues (and instructors, much to their chagrin).

When queried by Major Pappy Gratton, the Grey's Regimental Adjutant who had trouble believing Hassan's 101 File, an OCS instructor commented, "For God's sake, please take him! Maybe you can housebreak him! He wants to serve with the Greys, and maybe that loyalty will temper his drives. Otherwise, this guy is going to end up either destroying the Army or being Chief of Staff at age twenty-five, which will also destroy us! He needs to have his energies channeled by people he likes and respects . . . and those are the people in your Regiment. By the way, tell your women to look out. Hassan is a ladies' man the likes of which I've never seen!"

Major Pappy Gratton hadn't intended that comment to be circulated widely in the Greys, but the Regimental Chief of Staff, Major Joanne Wilkinson, caught it and Rumor Control was quickly buzzing with speculation about this new man whom most of the older Greys remembered only as a scrawny, dirty youngster. It also caused some minor and temporary problems for some of the men in the Greys when their POSSOHs — Persons of Opposite Sex Sharing Off-duty Hours — showed interest. It was rumored that Captain Jerry Allen and Lieutenant Adonica Sweet, two inseparables from the day Sweet first reported aboard, had had their first serious spat only a day or so before . . . and it had been over the new officer reporting aboard.

"You're not drinking, Hassan," Major Joan Ward observed. "We've got servicebots to take care of such things around here. Let me —"

"Thanks, Major, but —"

"Oh, I forgot! You're Muslim. . . ." Joan suddenly recalled.

Hassan shook his head. "Maybe once, but no longer. Over the last few years, I haven't had time to pray five times a day. I may not go to Paradise to be surrounded by beautiful houris as a result, but on the other hand I'm having a little trouble imagining that Paradise could be much better than this. And I didn't have time to learn how to drink, either."

"The latter can be remedied . . ."

Hassan grinned. "Thanks, but I don't need it. Kills too many brain cells, and I may be running on only half as many neurons as the rest of you anyway."

"Judging from your record, that I doubt," Curt observed briefly.

Hassan shrugged. "It was necessary that I work harder than the other students. On the other hand, since my mathematics teachers taught me that the sum of all vices is constant, where the hell's the food around here?"

Joan turned and picked up a bowl of snacks from a nearby table. "Nachos. They can't make them worth a damn around here. Cheese gets green too quick. Taco chips. About all until chow time, Hassan."

He grabbed a handful. "Better than nothing."

"We've got ourselves a real chow hound," Kitsy observed. Hassan looked at her. Kitsy Clinton was one of the few ladies of the Greys that Hassan didn't literally have to look up to. "A mere consequence of my deprived childhood, my dear," Hassan told her smoothly with a smile.

"What else were you deprived of that we might now remedy?" she asked. "You mentioned houris . . ."

"As I said, Lieutenant, the sum of all vices is constant . . ."

"We ask for a fighting officer, we get a philosophical math shark," Curt muttered, well aware of the reputation of the young officer which had preceded him. Curt was trying hard not to let his brass get green, to use West Point slang for jealousy. It had been difficult over the past year or so because he felt that Alexis Morgan was slipping away more and more. And Kitsy Clinton was more of a type who played the field with joyous abandon. Not that Curt had become celibate himself because he'd cultivated outside interests in the form of Colonel Willa Lovell, among others. But he went on easily, "At any rate, we're glad you're with the Greys at last, Lieutenant. Now your education *really* begins! I want to assign you to the second platoon of Frazier's Ferrets under Captain Russ Frazier and Platoon Sergeant Beau Greenwald, if I can find the Colonel to discuss it with him. Where the hell is Colonel Bellamack tonight? Not like him to be late for Stand-to!"

"According to Pappy Gratton, the Colonel had a visitor show up at the last minute," Joan Ward explained in her small voice which always seemed incongruous coming from such a substantial woman. But if anyone would know of the whereabouts of the Colonel in off-duty hours, she was the one. For the past several years, she'd been one of Colonel Wild Bill Bellamack's off-duty companions, Number One among several. He'd been discreet about it, just as all the Greys were about their own off-duty liaisons. The output of Rumor Control was always more one of delight than spite in knowing who was with whom at a particular time.

"Who the hell would come visiting in a Godforsaken place like Mosul?" Edie Sampson wondered.

"Sergeant, in case you may have forgotten," Jerry Allen

piped up, exhibiting his encyclopedic memory again, "Mosul isn't very Godforsaken. We're within a kilometer of the ruins of Nineveh. . . ."

"Wasn't that more of a fleshpot than a holy city?" Adonica asked.

"Depends on the religion."

"Well, although I'm not exactly a religious type," Edie quipped, "I'll repeat that I think it's a Godforsaken place."

"It may be Godforsaken, but it's not general forsaken," was the sudden input from Major Joanne Wilkinson, Regimental Chief of Staff, who overheard the conversation and stepped in. "The aircraft that landed about an hour ago was a five-star TC-39 Sabredancer."

"VIP transport!" Joan exclaimed. "Five stars? Must be CJCS."

"Or someone he loaned his personal aircraft to," Alexis guessed. "By the way, who got Carrington's slot when he retired a few weeks ago?"

"The new Commander in Chief hasn't announced all the shake-ups in the Joint Chiefs yet," Joanne pointed out. Then she admitted, "But the Colonel asked me to delay dinner until he could get here, and my guess is that the Sabredancer brought in some high brass with some answers . . . and God knows what else."

Curt grunted. "Yeah, when something like this happened in the past, it usually meant that someone slipped it to us greasy and we ended up having to do something nasty we weren't prepared for."

"Curt, we haven't done anything nasty since we froze our buns off on Kerguelen Island," Alexis reminded him.

"Except Brunei," it was his turn to remind her.

"Officially, that is," she corrected herself.

"Actually, Kerguelen Island wasn't official. Still classified 'Destroy Before Reading,' " Wilkinson recalled.

"I'm sorry. I don't follow you," Hassan said. "It's going to take me some time to find out everything you've done since Zahedan. . . ."

"Oh, don't worry, Lieutenant!" Edie Sampson reassured him. "People will start telling war stories in about three hours. You'll get goddamned tired of hearing and rehearing all the yarns: 'There I was, cut off from my unit, down to a single clip of ammo, surrounded by ravening savages intent upon my immediate demise, their automatic weapons loaded and ready and their brainwashed fanatical minds primed to assault my position which was the last bastion defending the Free World against the overwhelming hordes in the final battle for the freedom of the world . . . with my chances of survival going from slim to nothing very fast! Then I remembered the secret code to reactivate my warbot, so I took the initiative and unleashed the huge, mighty, invincible warbot which smashed forward and—' Aarrgghh! I can't go on!" she finally said.

"Damned good thing!" Henry Kester muttered.

"Hey, Sergeant, it worked on me a couple of years ago!" Hassan reminded him. "I'm sure Major Morgan and Captain Allen remember showing me that horrible Robot Infantry recruiting tape! It wasn't much better, come to think of it!"

"Oh, my God, I'm going to get blamed for him, too!" Jerry moaned.

"Hey, you're hogging the new man!" exclaimed Dr. Ruth Gydesen who wandered into the growing group around Hassan. The handsome new officer was indeed attracting the ladies, Curt decided. "And even before I've had the chance to give him his Regimental physical exam!"

"What's this about a Regimental physical exam?" Joanne Wilkinson wanted to know.

Major Ruth Gydesen, who ran the bio-tech support company, wasn't a stodgy doctor. She did indeed have a sense of humor sharpened a bit by the earthiness of a professional bio-technologist to whom no physical feature is sacred. Furthermore, Doctor Ruth was a party type when she wasn't being sincerely serious about the work of her unit, which was still unique because the Washington Greys had had to get a bio-tech unit that was more than the sort that accompanied every ordinary Robot Infantry regiment; people in a Sierra Charlie regiment could actually get wounded in combat. "I just decreed it to be necessary," Ruth admitted, then added with a bit of her medical humor, "I need to get to know you by sight. Bend over and let me see your rectum . . ." She took from her pocket one of her bio-tech medical sensors. Quickly, she ran it up and down Hassan's body, but only a green light flashed.

Hassan was both amused and mildly interested. "Excuse me, but what's that?" he asked.

"Virgin detector," Ruth Gydesen told him with a straight face.

With an equally straight face, Hassan fired back, "It must be broken."

Curt choked on his drink, but before he could recover something else happened.

Colonel Bill Bellamack stepped into the room accompanied by two familiar people.

"Ladies and gentlemen of the Greys, please give me your attention for a moment!" the Colonel announced in a loud voice that cut through the hubbub. "We have distinguished guests to grace our Regimental Stand-to this evening! Allow me to introduce the new commanding general of the Seventeenth Iron Fist Division and the new Army Chief of Staff!"

Chapter Four

Colonel Bill Bellamack's announcement brought a sudden hush to the personnel of the Washington Greys in the Club.

Nearly everyone in the room immediately recognized the two people who were with the Colonel. At first, a muted series of cheers went up, then everyone broke into immediate applause.

The VIPs accompanying Bellamack were general officers, one of whom wore two silver stars on her collar tabs now, the other wearing four stars where only two had been a short time before.

Bellamack continued his unnecessary introduction as the brief applause subsided. "I am honored to present to you the new commander of the Seventeenth Iron Fist Division, Major General Belinda J. Hettrick, and the new Army Chief of Staff and member of the Joint Chiefs of Staff, General Jacob O. Carlisle!"

"Ladies and gentlemen of the Greys, the next round of drinks is on me!" Carlisle announced. "Then I want to say hello to each of you personally."

"And I have a few old acquaintances of my own to renew," Belinda Hettrick added. "So everyone please stick around!"

"I didn't think that they'd be able to keep General Hettrick away from a combat command," was Regimental Sergeant Major Henry Kester's *sotto voce* remark to Curt.

"Either that, Henry, or she was too much for them to handle at the Potomac Video Game Company," Curt replied.

"Especially after Brunei," Alexis Morgan added. "I don't think the Army's recovered from that one yet. . . ."

"Nor have you," Joan Ward added.

"I see Colonel Mahathis occasionally. So?" Alexis seemed more than a bit defensive about her on-going relationship with a very rich man.

"Stand at ease, Allie! Allow me a twinge of jealousy, please! So the heir to the throne of Brunei finds ample excuses to visit the Greys to get up to speed on our latest Sierra Charlie activities," Joan said with a smile.

She didn't mention that the Sultana Alzena, the twin sister to the son of the Sultan of Brunei, always accompanied her brother, and often came alone to visit Curt Carson. Curt had confided in Joan that he didn't exactly know how to handle the situation of having a very rich Muslim princess dropping by at her whim, and Joan took it no further than that because of Curt's confidence. Alzena's visits didn't bother Curt except that it caused a bit of a disturbance among the ladies of the Greys who didn't have what the Sultana had either in terms of money or appearance. Insofar as Curt was concerned, he did indeed have a special relationship with Alzena, and he tried to handle it in the same manner that he handled his special relationship with Colonel Willa Lovell, the bio-robotics expert from McCarthy Proving Ground who'd grown close to Curt back in the days of the Zahedan hostage rescue.

Curt reflected that he'd certainly developed some interesting relationships both inside and outside of the Washington Greys, relationships that would have been the envy of other soldiers in earlier times. But times had changed, and the soldier of the twenty-first century United States Army was a lot different from the GI and grunt of the twentieth century . . . and the johnnie of the nineteenth. It was inevitable that social progress would change the Army, and warbot technology had been one of the drivers. But few people expected that the United States Army would actually end up leading much of the social revolution that continued into the twenty-first century, a revolution in which people learned to enjoy the variety of differences in other people rather than fear them. This, in turn, had become possible when most peoples of the world discovered they were rich and in control of most of the forces of nature and had no reason to fear one another any longer.

The big problem of the twenty-first century, of course — and one of the reasons why the Greys and other troops were present in the Mideast — were the peoples who hadn't discovered this yet and who were stuck a thousand years or more in the past.

Although the Washington Greys were a friendly and compatible bunch, they did have their friends and comrades who were closer than the rest, and Curt naturally gathered with them at a table—Alexis Morgan, Jerry Allen, Kitsy Clinton, Henry Kester, Nick Gerard, Adonica Sweet, Edie Sampson, Tracy Dillon, and Dyani Motega. However, Curt, along with Jerry and Alexis, made sure that a new face was made to feel a part of this group because, in a way, he'd also been shot at. Hassan Ben Mahmud might have felt a bit like an outsider at first, but that didn't last.

"Please remain seated," General Carlisle remarked easily as he came by their table. "A Stand-to and formality don't mix well."

Curt rose anyway and told the former division commander respectfully. "General, in your case, it isn't a matter of formality." He paused and turned, "I don't believe you've met our new officer."

Carlisle reached out and offered his hand to an amazed Hassan who still was in awe of high ranking officers. "I haven't met the Lieutenant personally until now, but I do know of him, of course. And I have for many years since Zahedan! Congratulations on your commissioning, and welcome to the Greys, sir!"

"Thank you, General. Serving with the Greys is a wish come true," Hassan admitted.

"Well, be careful what you ask for; you'll get it," Carlisle advised him. "You can be shot at and killed being a Sierra Charlie officer."

"Yes, sir, but that's better than continually starving and being beaten," Hassan reminded him.

"General, you should be congratulated as well for your assignment as the new COS," Curt told his old division commander. "This is all sort of sudden, isn't it? We haven't heard anything, so when did all the changes take place?"

"A week ago," Carlisle explained. "You people out here on the line really don't get much news, do you? Have to see about that."

"That isn't the whole story, General. We've been sort of busy being shot at. Three times this week," Curt explained.

"Sort of doesn't leave much time for things that aren't important to saving your own ass out on patrol."

"Really? Three times this week? Well, we'll talk a bit about that tomorrow morning," Carlisle told him, then went on, "As for the stateside hot skinny, the new President appointed me when General Carrington retired a while back, and the Senate just got around to confirming me last week. General Brooke moved up to CJCS. And the President wanted people on JCS who'd had experience with international military cooperation. Do you remember Len Spencer from Namibia?"

"How could I forget?" was Alexis Morgan's quiet comment.

Carlisle shot her a strange look, but didn't ask what she meant. Instead, he went on easily, "Len Spencer is the President's new press secretary. He told Brooke to reach down to the divisional level and pull my name out of the hat, then he called in a few favors from our new Secretary of Defense and Secretary of the Army. *Voila!* Here I am. So I wanted to come over to the Persian Gulf not only to find out what's going on now but also to thank the Washington Greys for helping me."

"Helping you, general? How?" Jerry asked.

"Captain, if you hadn't done what you did in a lot of places, including the Kerguelen Island, I'd be tending my flower garden in Sun City," Carlisle reminded them. "Somehow I got the reputation of being one sierra hotel high-level commander, especially when it came to joint command. But no commander can hack it at all without damned good troops. Besides, I had to help break in a new division commander . . ."

"General Hettrick will do you proud, General!" Alexis assured him. "We'll see to that, sir! But who takes her Sierra Charlie desk in the Pentagon?"

"Brigadier General Emmett Calhoun," Carlisle explained, "former commander of the Cottonbalers."

"Oh," was Alexis Morgan's emotionless comment. Calhoun had been promoted to a BG at Sixth Army before the Cottonbalers had finished their transition to a Sierra Charlie outfit.

Carlisle nodded, watching her disappointment. "I know.

He's not really a Sierra Charlie because he hasn't been shot at, but he's the closest available person to hold down Belinda Hettrick's OSCAR desk right now . . . and I must have someone there because of all of you out here. But it's temporary, Major Morgan. General Calhoun wishes to retire at the earliest opportunity when I no longer need him. Excuse me, but I want to chat with some other old comrades over at the next table . . ."

"Well," Henry Kester put in quietly, "we don't always have things go a hundred percent our way in the Army. Thank God General Carlisle didn't have to consider some other generals we know who shall remain nameless out of military courtesy. . . ."

"And because of a top kick's common sense not to name names," Nick Gerard said. "At least we're getting General Hettrick back."

"And we've got a Commander in Chief now who's got an appreciation for the military," Edie Sampson added.

"Must have for sure," Nick guessed, "especially to tag General Carlisle as COS after he went ahead over a direct presidential order and saved our butts at Kerguelen Island."

"And he came out smelling like a rose on that campaign, Sergeant Gerard, because of the Washington Greys," General Belinda Hettrick said as she pulled up a chair and joined them. "Damn, I'm glad to be back with you people again! Washington duty is interesting, but I've always been a combat type."

"Also a pretty good military diplomat from what I heard, General," Curt said. "I think you had about as much to do with saving that operation as anyone. You did have dinner with the former President a couple of times, I understand."

She nodded. Except for the addition of a few years, she looked like the Belinda Hettrick of old. Her face had filled out after her prolonged illness resulting from being poisoned by a Bushman arrow in Namibia. And she moved and acted in a way that told Curt she was again physically fit. "Interesting man."

"Well, General, tell us . . ." Alexis Morgan prodded.

"Read it in my published memoirs, Alexis," Hettrick told her bluntly. "What's this crap about you being ambushed three times in a week?"

Curt nodded. "My patrol got it earlier today."

"You don't look any the worse for wear, Curt."

"No, ma'am, and we can thank the seven-eleven bots you finagled for us, plus the fact that the Dervishes fought about the same way the Jehorkhims did."

"They're crazy. Insane," Dyani Motega ventured. "No one in their right mind would try to carry out a direct foot infantry assault on a warbot position. I didn't believe it. Who taught them how to fight?"

"You, young lady, must be the Sergeant Motega I've heard so much about," Hettrick remarked, looking at the Crow Indian girl. "I suspected you'd be a good Sierra Charlie. Spotted your One-oh-one when Curt here complained about having no women squad leaders assigned to the Greys after the Sonoran fracas."

This took Dyani Motega back with surprise. "Uh, General, I'm sorry. I am Sergeant Dyani Motega. I didn't realize that you knew about me. . . ."

Hettrick reached over and shook her hand. "I'm pleased to meet you, Dyani. And, yes, I do know about you. I knew your father. With your name, you could only be his daughter. And your background fit perfectly with what Colonel Bellamack and Major Carson were trying to do with the Sierra Charlies. So I'm going to be blamed for you, too!"

Motega smiled shyly. "Yes, ma'am! I'll try to make you proud of me!"

"So the level of native harassment has picked up recently, eh?" Hettrick went on. "The seven-elevens working okay?"

Edie Sampson nodded. "General, they're the best thing to come along since afternoon sex."

"I figured you'd like them, Sampson, but you always were a gadget freak," Hettrick pointed out.

"General, you act like you've got some hot gee-two about that," Curt remarked because he knew this woman very well.

"I do," she admitted. "Why do you think the Greys were sent over here in the first place? Certainly not just to relieve the Manchus and get bored out of your skulls on pipeline patrols."

"Now we're getting somewhere!" Alexis Morgan piped up brightly "We know you too well, General! You didn't come popping in here with General Carlisle just to pay a social

36

call. What's up? What's *really* up?"

Major General Belinda Hettrick looked around and told them seriously, "We'll get around to an intelligence brief maybe tomorrow. Basically, our spooks tell us this area is crawling with Israeli and Saudi types trying to slit each other's throats. . . ."

"That's nothing new," Curt observed. "I understand they both want their share of the Tigris River water for their desert reclamation projects."

"That's only part of it, Curt," Hettrick told him. "The Russkies are restless again. Looking south once more. Our spooks tell us there's a Soviet Spetsnaz battalion operating covertly up in the hills to the north. The Kurds don't like us very much, but they like the Russkies a whole hell of a lot less. We think that Spetsnaz boys are training and equipping some of the renegade Kurdish tribes, and if so, the Greys are going to have to find out and do a number on the Sovs again. Covertly, of course . . ."

Chapter Five

"I thought so!" was the acidic comment from Regimental Sergeant Major Henry Kester, an old soldier who had almost seen it all and who knew how the Army operated. "The Greys never get sent anywhere except where Big Trouble is brewing."

"Not so, Henry," Belinda Hettrick told him brusquely. "You were indeed sent here to relieve the Ninth Robot Infantry because they'd been out here for three years and *had* to be rotated. My last act at the OSCAR desk was to recommend against your assignment because we've spent the last couple of years configuring this Regiment as a fast-moving, highly mobile, and very versatile unit along the lines of the old regimental combat teams and Special Forces outfits. Obviously, I didn't win that one."

"So here we sit as usual," Curt growled, "the right tool for the wrong job . . . or vice versa."

"Don't be so sure about that, either, Curt," Hettrick replied. "At the moment, the Greys happen to be the right instrument in the right place at the right time . . . and we didn't plan it that way."

"Some day our luck will run out," Edie Sampson ventured.

"You presuppose that we're all issued a luck ration, Sergeant," Hettrick reminded her. "If that were the case, my luck ration would have run out in Namibia. Think about where yours would have petered out. No, in the Army you know damned good and well that you make the best of what you've got, even when it isn't very good to start with. Now, tell me about the fracas you ran into today, Curt. And anything you can about the two others."

Curt shrugged. "About fifty idiots took us on in the open and staged a mass frontal attack against our new seven-elevens. All we had to do was sit there behind armor and let the bots do the work. The ROE don't give us any real choice in the matter."

"High pucker factor," Nick Gerard added. "You just hope to God the warbots are working right!"

"Did they?" Hettrick asked.

Gerard nodded. "It was a massacre, General."

"Then the ROE are correct for what you were doing," Hettrick pointed out.

"General, if the Russkies are training and equipping those people, they're doing a very bad job of it," Dyani Motega said.

"They could be probing our new capabilities, Dyani," Nick suggested.

"Very expensive way to do it," she replied. "But we now know the Sovs are equipping the Kurds."

"Not all the Kurds, just the Dervish tribes," Hettrick explained. "What weapons are they using, Motega?"

"A little bit of everything from old Lee-Enfields up to AK-thirteens."

"Aha!"

"We brought some AKs back today."

"Good! The ordnance types will want to look at them."

"Plastic throw-away toys!" Edie Sampson muttered in disgust. "Expendable guns."

"So?" asked Henry Kester. "So they last for only about a thousand rounds or so. Maybe one of those rounds finds a human target. Then you throw away the gun and grab another one. Yeah, it bothers us old gunmaster types, but I'm happy as hell the Russkies think it's the neatest thing since sliced salami. What's interesting about the Thirteen is that the Russkies copied most of it from the expendable terrorist gun made by the Czechs, the Zastava Vee-zee-ninety-five."

"Henry, you haven't changed a bit," Hettrick told him with a smile. The old infantry rifleman right down to your muddy boots! Well, thank God you taught me and a lot of others how to do the job when we went Sierra Charlie! But, Curt, how about prisoners? Take any?"

"Four, but they were pretty badly wounded."

"How'd the interrogation go?"

"I didn't get back until an hour before Stand-to, General. I understand Jerry handled the interrogation because he speaks Arabic," Curt explained.

Hettrick turned to the new Captain. "Well, Jerry?"

"General, only two of them were in shape to talk at all," Allen reported, "and they wouldn't say a damned thing."

Hassan Mahmud spoke up for the first time, "Captain, let me take a shot at them tomorrow morning. They may speak a dialect I know, and I think I can also be a little bit more persuasive. . . ."

"Persuasive?" Jerry asked.

"Yes, sir! Frankly, the milk of human kindness has diluted the nasty juice you have to use with most Kurds," Hassan explained. "I knew a lot of Kurds who managed to get as far east as Zahedan."

Jerry replied in Arabic to Hassan, who retorted in kind.

"Well, you've got a terrible accent, Captain, so no wonder the prisoners were reluctant," Hassan finally told him in English.

"Hassan, you've got that job first thing tomorrow morning," Curt told him. "If you run into any trouble from Captain Frazier, have him come see me."

"Oh, I won't run into any trouble with him, Major! I'll complete the interrogation by oh-eight-hundred and be on deck to take over Captain Frazier's second platoon," the new officer popped. Curt had to admit that the young man certainly was gung-ho and probably organized to beat hell as well.

"So, Hassan, what are you going to call your platoon?" Alexis Morgan wanted to know.

"I'm not sure I follow you, Major."

"To increase unit morale and cohesiveness now that the Greys can operate in just about any arrangement that suits a given situation, the Colonel is allowing even the platoon leaders to name their units now," she told him.

"I haven't even thought about it, Major."

"Well, it's as obvious to me as calling my outfit Allen's Alleycats," Jerry piped in. "You've got to lead Hassan's Assassins."

Hassan hesitated. "Uh, Captain, I'm not an Assassin. I was a Baluchi. The Assassins were a group of Shiites who

40

believed that the murder of enemies was a sacred religious duty."

"I know," Jerry told him, and the young Captain did know because his encyclopedic memory was legendary in the Greys. "But it sounds right and doesn't mean your platoon are real Assassins any more than my Alleycats are a bunch of raunchy tom cats . . ."

"No, but it reflects well on its platoon commander," was the unexpected comment from Adonica Sweet.

Hettrick roared with laughter. To Curt, it was great to see her back in good health, looking and acting like her old self again. "Lieutenant, Allen has always been an alleycat . . . even from the time the two of you first met on Trinidad!"

"Yes, ma'am, I know. And I'm not complaining about it, either!"

"Some things about the Greys never change, thank God!" Hettrick remarked easily.

"Oh, a lot of things have changed since you almost bought it, General," Henry Kester said with reflection. "A lot of people have come and gone. We've lost some good people. And the Sierra Charlies are a lot different now in the way we're organized, the way we're equipped, and the way we fight."

"You're looking at the person who greased the skids for most of that, Henry," Hettrick admitted. "Takes a heap o' work and scheming to get the Army to change its ways. I hope the new battalion organization works."

"We've still got to find out about that, General," Kester pointed out. "Unfortunately, there's only one way to find out if a military unit's organized and equipped right. We're going to have to go out and get our butts shot at, and we're sure as hell not going to find out very fast around Mosul if we have to continue to play the old game of Warbots On Patrol. It's great for regular warbot outfits but hell on Sierra Charlies."

"General, you said that's going to change," Alexis reminded her. "When do we get to take on this Soviet Spetsnaz battalion?"

"You'll find out more about that maybe tomorrow, but it won't happen until you find out where the hell they're hiding."

"John Gibbon will like that. It keeps the RECONCO busy doing what it's designed to do," Alexis pointed out. "But Ellie Aarts is likely to have some heartburn because it also means a lot of hours linked with birdbots out on recon."

"Ellie will do all right," Adonica insisted, knowing that Captain Ellie Aarts really hadn't relished taking over the new birdbot platoon that was created when the new Reconnaissance Company came out of the regimental reorganization. Ellie didn't want to go back to being a warbot brainy. However, she'd been an outstanding warbot brainy when she'd joined the Greys just before Zahedan but had turned out to be only an average Sierra Charlie. Putting her back in charge of the Regiment's only neuroelectronic warbot unit which ran the remotely controlled birdbots meant giving her the chance to get ahead at something she was good at doing rather than continuing to allow her to try very hard at being something she really wasn't. Bill Bellamack, Curt, and Pappy Gratton had agonized over it for several days during the reorganization planning sessions. Fortunately, all three operated on the principle that everyone is good at something and that the real challenge lies in providing the leadership that allows each person to do what they're best at.

They were fortunate in the reorganization. The Washington Greys contained people with a lot of varied talents which could be meshed together into a new type of Sierra Charlie regimental combat team capable of making the best use of the new Mod 7/11 warbots.

"Think Cal Worsham's people will fly some recon missions for us?" Alexis wanted to know.

Curt nodded. "Cal and his tactical air support people will jump at any excuse to fly those new Harpies of theirs, even if it's just out and back with sensors looking for things."

"Harpies?" Hettrick asked.

"General, the troops don't always hanker for the official names the contractors and tech-weenies hang on the equipment, usually for public consumption," Henry Kester reminded her. "If you recall, the Army insisted on calling our best rifle the Ranger, but the troops never stopped calling it the Novia. Well, when the Aerospace Force reluctantly turned over some of their tacair capability to the Greys — very reluctantly, I might add, because the blue flyboys really don't like the green flyboys — they tried to stick us with calling the AD-forties 'Thunder Devils.' Didn't catch on, General. Worsham's Warhawks started calling them Harpies after a well-known aggressive video news personality whose hairdo looks like an aerodyne in deep trouble . . ."

"By God, the AD-forties *do* look like her damned coif!" Hettrick reacted with delight. "Or maybe it's the other way around. Don't worry, I won't say a word to the top brass."

"Uh, General, aren't you part of the 'top brass' now?" Edie Sampson ventured to suggest.

Hettrick jerked her head around to look at Sampson, then smiled and said, "Sergeant, the day that happens is the day I'll no longer be sitting around a table drinking with all of you at a Stand-to! Which isn't going to happen unless *you* keep *me* out by locking the door before I get here. And just for even thinking that, I ought to make you feel uncomfortable the rest of the evening by asking you to join me for dinner."

"General," Edie Sampson told her levelly, "with all due respect, there ain't a whole hell of a lot you could do to make me feel uncomfortable, ma'am."

"Good! Then I expect all of you to join me for chow! It's been too long since we've had a bitch and brag session, all of us!"

The renewed camaraderie between Major General Belinda Hettrick and the people of her old outfit wasn't lost on General Jacob Carlisle who noticed it from time to time during the evening. He envied her and didn't try to interrupt it. He'd done the same thing himself when he'd been kicked upstairs from the Greys to the Iron Fist command. Then as the responsibilities and pressures of running a division began to grow on him, and as people came and went within the Greys, he'd found that the bonds of comradeship had slowly loosened, leaving only a few cherished friendships within the Iron Fist Division and the Greys.

The higher one went in the chain of command, the lonelier the position became.

Which is why Carlisle envied Hettrick at that moment. The feeling at this Stand-to was "The Battleaxe is back!" Everyone knew that was her unvoiced nickname, but everyone's respect for her kept them from using it even privately.

He knew she'd do an outstanding job commanding the 17th Iron Fist Division, even better than she had in the Pentagon. The OSCAR desk had been only a stopgap measure in her career; she was a combat leader of proven worth, and leaving her in the Pentagon would have been a waste of talent. She belonged at the head of the Iron Fist Division now that her physical stamina had returned.

But the wonderful feeling of "it's great to be back" couldn't last . . . and circumstances quickly transpired to make sure that it didn't.

Chapter Six

"Well, Lieutenant Mahmud, what's the situation?" Colonel Bill Bellamack asked his new officer.

The small room was crowded, even though attendance had been restricted for this preliminary planning session. Bellamack's new short-tailed regimental staff and the three battalion commanders were the only Washington Greys present.

Also present was General Carlisle with his ADC he brought from the 17th Iron Fist Division, Lieutenant Colonel Kim Blythe, who everyone in the Greys knew as the quiet, efficient, omnipresent, omniscient Girl Friday for the General and now with even greater responsibilities handling two other ADCs for him.

General Belinda Hettrick had rated a single lieutenant as an ADC in the Pentagon but hadn't paid any attention to the sequence of dumbjohn staff types that had been assigned to her. And as the new CO of the Iron Fist, she knew she'd need all the help she could get. But she was so new to the position and the TDY to Mosul had been laid on so fast that her new ADCs and division staffers were still at Fort Huachuca in Arizona . . . and she hadn't reported in there yet, either.

A newcomer present was the Commanding General of the Persian Gulf Peacekeeping Command, Lieutenant General Jeffrey Winfield Pickens, former CO of the 50th Big L Division still with three of its regiments in the Gulf and also former CO of the 505th Robot Infantry, the Panthers Regiment. Bellamack knew him, and Pickens knew Bellamack. A sense of uneasy respect seemed to exist between the two men, and everyone in the room sensed it and tried not to notice that it really wasn't quite normal. Pickens had his aide de camp, Colonel Arlo Lusk, with him and it was obvious that there was no love lost between Bellamack and Lusk; the two men sat as far away from one another as possible.

If Lieutenant Hassan Ben Mahmud felt a bit awed by the presence of the high-ranking officers there, he didn't show it. One of his legacies as a child who'd had to survive in the harshest of environments among harsh and wily people was his ability as an actor. *Never let 'em see anything that you don't want them to see* was his creed. "Colonel Bellamack, I wish I could report better success."

"Lieutenant, what do you mean by 'better success?' Either you got some information out of those four prisoners or you didn't," Bellamack told him testily, obviously uneasy himself with people who, but for the grace of God, hadn't gotten caught in the arms scam on which then-Major Bellamack had blown the whistle several years before.

"Sorry, sir! I'll try to be more specific." Hassan replied contritely, then hesitated to go on.

Curt thought he knew what had happened during Hassan's interrogation of the four Dervish prisoners taken in yesterday's ambush. He'd seen where Hassan had grown up, and he understood a little about the young officer's background. From his own knowledge of military history, he knew that "Dervish" was sort of a generic name for a type of Shiite Muslim who used a trance-like hypnotic state to work up a feverish mental attitude for battle, something which turned out to be a suicidal form of motivation against modern military forces with automatic weapons and warbots. The British under Kitchener had come up against Dervish-type Muslims in the Sudan more than a century ago and beaten them then with only slow-firing bolt-action rifles. So he spoke up quietly in a friendly tone, "Hassan, I know what you're up against. These prisoners are Dervishes. I think they're crazy to even try to assault our seven-elevens in the first place. But all the nuts aren't up in the trees around here; some of them are running around on the ground with Soviet assault rifles. Could you get them to talk willingly . . . or did you have to break their arms first?"

That caused Hassan to smile. "Neither, Major. None of the prisoners would talk until I tried the 'good buddy' approach and made like a Shiite myself, and that confused the hell out of them because they didn't expect to find an Arabic-speaking Shiite Muslim in the United States Army. Their mental attitude may be dangerous because at this point they have nothing left to lose. They're whipped and they're scared. They didn't win yesterday and they didn't die in battle. They got captured instead. So they don't think they're qualified for that ticket to Paradise."

"In short, they've blown their chance for immortality," General Pickens put in knowingly from his years of experience in the region. "So they'll either try to suicide, or they'll try to bust out and kill as many of us as they can during the escape attempt."

"Yes, sir, that's possible. Even probable," Hassan agreed. "I wish I could *really* get inside their heads using the neuroelectronic linkage techniques we use with the warbots. . . ."

"That's contrary to the Bonn Ethics agreement," Carlisle pointed out, referring to a protocol developed in NATO not only to make non-warbot types happy—NE techniques could indeed get inside a person's head and was used in that manner for psychiatric purposes as well as some criminal rehab—but also to help control the highly classified nature of the NE warbot control links.

"General, with all due respect, I don't think that ethics protocol would last ten seconds if we got into the Big One with the Sovs," Hassan ventured to opine. "Or with anyone else, for that matter. We're dealing here in northern Iraq with people who are downright mean, nasty, distrustful, deceitful, untruthful . . . Uh, sorry, but English isn't my native language and I've run out of synonyms," Hassan apologized.

"You're doing damned well," Hettrick assured him. "I've got to agree with Lieutenant Hassan. Historically, these are the personality characteristics of anyone who feels a sense of inferiority to an alien but dominant civilization. To what extent can we use NE techniques to break through these qualities and get some good intelligence data?"

"To no extent at all," Carlisle told her firmly, "and it isn't within my prerogative to authorize it. And I'll have to take action if such a thing is reported to me."

"Yes, sir." Hettrick dropped the subject. The message was clear and it was somewhat like the procedures surrounding Rule Ten. Army Regulation 601-10 prohibiting physical contact between male and female soldiers on duty except where required in the performance of official business. Rule Ten was the keystone that supported the mixed-gender Army of the twenty-first century. In some outfits, it was probably honored in the breach. But insofar as any West Pointer was concerned, it was an important appendix to the Cadet Honor Code . . . and anyone learning of a disregard of one of the most important of all Army regulations would be honor-bound to report it.

"Have you gotten any information at all out of the prisoners, Lieutenant?" Bellamack got the meeting back on the subject.

"Only that these Dervishes are also Kurds, and they look upon the American Army patrol forces the same way they've looked upon the Iraqis, Turks, Syrians, Iranians, and all the other people who have occupied their homelands and exercised control over them for the last couple of dozen centuries," Hassan reported almost unnecessarily because that information was something everyone in the room already knew. "What the Kurds have wanted all along is their own land, their own country, their own government—"

"Well, we can't give them that," Bellamack said gruffly. He'd spent a lot of time in the Persian Gulf theater with his former outfit, the Gimlet Regiment. He knew the peoples of the region pretty well. Basically, he didn't really like them because he didn't believe he could trust them.

"Nothing more?" Hettrick asked when Hassan didn't continue.

"Nothing more, General," Hassan admitted.

"Damn!"

"May I be dismissed, General?"

Hettrick looked at Carlisle briefly, then made one of her first decisions as the division commander. She'd never been afraid to make a decision, and Carlisle knew this. He also knew that he was only a high-ranking staffer in this situation. After all, Carlisle was indeed her boss as Army Chief of Staff and Army member of the Joint Chiefs, but General Belinda Hettrick was basically responsible for command decisions within her 17th Iron Fist Division. And, while the 3rd Robot Infantry, the Washington Greys, was in Pickens's bailiwick, he had de facto operational control. It was a fine line of command protocol, and if Hettrick didn't know exactly where she stood, she leaned a little on the command structure until it complained and let her know.

Which was one reason why the staffers in the Pentagon really preferred that she go back to doing something she was good at, combat unit command, rather than continue to rattle cages in the Outer Ring.

"Stick around, Lieutenant," she told Hassan. "This is only a preliminary planning session, and you'll be getting the full dog and pony show briefing with the rest of the Greys pretty soon anyway as soon as we can come up the proper level of ignorance and confusion ourselves. I think your basic knowledge of the people in this part of the world might come in handy in helping us figure out what we're going to do next."

"Thank you, General," Hassan said and quietly took a seat away from the table.

"General, do you have any further specifics on that Soviet Spetsnaz battalion playing in the neighborhood?" Colonel Bill Bellamack asked suddenly.

Hettrick hadn't told anyone except the group at the Club last night. She knew that scuttlebutt is the only form of communication known to travel faster than light, but she'd trusted the people there last night to be discreet about it. So she snapped, "Bill, how the hell do you know that?"

"Rumor Control Headquarters, General," the Colonel replied candidly. "Don't worry. The Greys can keep a confidence. I overheard it last night when you mentioned it at the next table. I got only one word: Spetsnaz. Then things started adding up. I've been wondering where the hell the Kurds were getting all those AK-thirteens. And with all due respect, I had the hunch that you didn't come all the way from the States just to pay a social call."

"After all my years in the Greys and the hitch I just spent at the Pentagon, I should have known better than to ignore the facts of life in the Army . . . and the Greys," Hettrick said as if talking to herself aloud. She turned to General Jacob O. Carlisle. "General, do you wish to give the background brief on this since it's your Op Dir that's involved?"

"Why not? May be the last time I have the chance to brief the troops now that they've turned me into a gilded staff stooge," Carlisle replied easily. He looked around the room. "Jeff, if I say something wrong and make a damned fool out of myself, please break in; you've been on the spot here for years, and you know the territory."

"General, I'll do my best because the monkey's on my back after you fly out of here," Pickens told him without rancor. He'd hoped he'd get a job at least as a deputy chief of staff after all the years of hard service he'd put in out in the Persian Gulf, but he didn't begrudge Carlisle his promotion; he could work with Jacob Carlisle because they went way back together. In fact, most of the general officers in the smaller twenty-first century Army knew each other reasonably well. The Old Comrades' Network was pretty strong.

"Thanks, because I've probably got some news that's news to you, too," Carlisle told him, then addressed the rest of the group seated in the crowded room. "We'll give a full Regimental OSCAR brief on this later today, but General Hettrick and I wanted to dump it on the leadership of the Greys first to see if we'd missed anything and to get some fresh input from the troops in the field getting shot at. Or about to, God forbid . . . because when we're dealing with the Soviets and their Spetsnaz units, someone sure as hell is going to get shot."

Of all the people in the room, Major Curt Carson knew about that first-hand. He was one of the few people in the last twenty-five years who wore the white-edged purple ribbon on his tunic, the signal that he'd been decorated with the Purple Heart for wounds suffered in combat. And some of those wounds came from Soviet Spetsnaz bullets on Kerguelen Island when the Spetsnaz battalion supposedly had been fighting on the side of the Greys.

Curt didn't like the news that Carlisle brought.

Chapter Seven

General Jacob O. Carlisle went on after a short pause, "General Murray at NIA confirms what our spooks at DIA found out several weeks ago. We haven't actually seen open evidence of a Soviet Spetsnaz battalion in the hills of Kurdistan astride the borders between Iraq, Iran, and Turkey, but the reports are solid and hard. And they come from excellent sources, not only field agents but very, very, black, classified, and clandestine *things* best described as 'national technical means.' Which means you shouldn't know about them because you don't have to know about them . . . and this means one less thing that could be wrung out of you if you're ever captured. Jeff, you don't seemed surprised at this revelation. Why?" Carlisle suddenly asked the CIC of the Persian Gulf region.

"Should I be, Jake?" Lieutenant General Jeffrey Pickens replied offhandedly. "Certainly wouldn't be anything new. The situation in this part of the world hasn't improved in centuries. A lot of people who haven't been here seem to think it's all been pretty recent. But this land has been a theater of war for a long, long time. Fifty centuries or more, maybe. And the people here show no signs of quitting. And other people always seem to want to take it. Especially the Russkies. The Brits pulled out of here in nineteen-forty-six, but the Russkies dragged their boots and didn't go until they got a very firm invitation to do so from the UN a year later. Well, as you damned well know, this area's been a powder keg for centuries. These days with primitive nuclear technology so widely available, the Fertile Crescent could easily become the Nuclear Desert."

Pickens needed to say no more. Everyone in the room knew very well what the situation was and why American troops were there in the first place, in spite of various admin-. istrations in the White House which had from time to time professed the philosophy of "bring the boys home" and "no foreign involvement." It was simply a matter of having to keep American Army troops there as a remote form of self-defense. If the Fertile Crescent went up in nuclear smoke, no one was sure what the next step on the ladder of escalation would be because that depended on who got nuked by whom for what reasons. So Americans had to take it in the shorts occasionally to keep the locals from one another's throats. It was easier to dislike the Americans and object violently to their powerful presence than to hate one another and commit genocide with chemicals, germs, or atoms.

If the Fertile Crescent were just old farmland, it might have been different. But the industrialized and post-industrial world knew that the region was still loaded with natural resources. More than two centuries of history had proved that the only way natural resources could be developed was not to let them just sit there under control of men on horseback whose only function was to fatten out-country bank accounts but to get in there with the necessary private enterprise.

Furthermore, the Americans were tolerated because they didn't act like the conquerors of the past. The American attitude, never mind the official policy, was widely recognized; The Americans didn't want the region any more than they'd wanted the Philippines which they gave back when everyone thought they were soft in the head to do so. "Pax Americana" wasn't anything like "Pax Romana" or any other imperial occupation before; the Americans didn't collect taxes or run governments; they just defended industrial activities. A new role was being born here in the old Fertile Crescent for the military forces of a post-industrial nation.

American foreign policy — tested and honed in Germany and Korea — was to maintain stability by military presence, not by military oppression. Which is why down at the roots of it all was the policy of Russian containment inherited from the British. The hungry bear to the north had had its eye on the southern real estate for more than a couple of centuries and, if it moved in, it wouldn't be to just develop the place; the Russkies would dominate it the same way they'd dominated the other peoples and lands they'd scooped into their empire.

"That's a given, Jeff," Carlisle agreed and shrugged. "So what else is new, eh? We can read all about it in the Army foreign affairs journals. Be that as it may, DIA and NIA report the Soviets are down here again for the first time in many years. NIA thinks its because the Sovs see a way to take advantage of the Kurdish situation to get other people to do their fighting for them, which is a pretty slick way of doing things on the cheap if it costs only a few thousand plastic assault rifles, which keeps their production lines open and their subjects busy. But DIA sees some additional factors. The Sovs want to make sure things go the Soviet way down here this time; they screwed up pretty badly in remote-control warfare in Africa recently, so they aren't about to let it happen the same way again. So they've got a clandestine Spetsnaz battalion operating in the hills north of here supporting cooperative Kurdish tribes."

"So why us, General? As if I really needed to ask that question," Bellamack interjected.

"Bill, you know what your Regiment was designed to do and what it's been able to do even when it wasn't specifically organized and tasked for it," Carlisle complimented the Colonel. The General knew the Greys very well. He'd not only been their regimental commander once, but he'd served in the Regiment from the time he'd graduated from West Point. "The real reason why the Greys are in here rather than the First Cavalry or even the Second Robot Armored is simple: first of all, the Greys have come up against a Spetsnaz battalion before; you, Bill, speak Russian like a native—"

"General, the last time I palavered with a Russkie, he told me I had a terrible American accent," Bellamack recalled.

"So? I'll bet his Russian accent wasn't any better when he spoke English!" Carlisle countered with a wry smile, remembering the situation on Kerguelen Island when Bellamack had faced down a Soviet Spetsnaz colonel. "What counts is the fact that you did the job. Secondly, the Greys have spent the last two-plus years reorganizing as a modern robotic version of a special forces unit that can move fast and do unusual things. Among these unusual things is looking like

53

it's a regular warbot patrol regiment under Jeff's command while going out and doing things General Pickens's units aren't allowed to do under his rules of engagement . . . which I understand has given you some real heartburn for the last few weeks, Bill. By the way, Jeff, this whole operational is probably going to give *you* heartburn because you'll have only administrative control. The Greys will be operating under a separate JCS Executive Order. Any problems?"

"Yes, and I told you about them earlier this morning," Pickens remarked sourly. "No commander likes to have an independent unit operating in his area. Especially when I don't know what the hell you're doing and when your fun and games may affect my command!"

Carlisle knew he was going to have trouble with this command situation, but he couldn't allow Pickens to know what was going on at all times. DIA had reported that Pickens's headquarters in Bahrain was compromised and had about as much security integrity as a leaky sieve. Counterintelligence was working on the situation at the moment, and Carlisle couldn't tell Pickens that either. It wasn't just KGB and GRU down there in Pickens's shop; the Saudis and Israelis had ears there, too. And probably a lot of other countries as well.

"Jeff, you will indeed know what's going on because Belinda here is going to be feeding coded reports to Arlo who's to let you and only you see them," Carlisle explained again.

"Still don't like it, General."

"Like it or not, that's what you've got." Carlisle told him for the second time that morning. He turned to Hettrick. "Belinda, the ball is now in your court, so take over."

Hettrick didn't waste a second. "I can't run this operation all the way from Fort Huachuca by long-distance computer link. So I won't micromanage you, Bill. You're going to have a lot of autonomy. So for God's sake don't shoot into General Pickens's goal. If you think you'll be doing something that might conflict with anything General Pickens is responsible for, let me know."

"General, I'll need a full and complete briefing from General Pickens on his force dispositions, contingency plans, and overall theater tactical situation. And will I be able to communicate with General Pickens's staff in an emergency?"

Bellamack asked, wanting to make sure that he didn't have to check in all the way back to Arizona if he happened to need some quick local help to get the Greys out of a slimy situation fast.

"In an emergency, anything goes, as usual," Hettrick reminded him. "Protocol blows away when it comes to saving your ass. Bill, your basic mission is this: go out there, find the Sovs, and convince them it's in their best interests to get the hell back across their border into Armanskaja. By the way, try to do this without tangling assholes with the Turks or the Iranians in the process."

Bellamack sighed. "Tall order, as usual. Typical wide-open operation directive for the Greys." Bellamack observed with resignation in his voice.

"How well I know! While official motto of the Greys is 'First in battle,' it should be, 'The difficult we do immediately but the impossible takes a little bit longer,'" Hettrick reminded him.

"The Army's been doing that for a long time, General. Who are we to change tradition?" the Colonel responded. "General Hettrick, I take it that General Pickens will see to it that our minus-x is covered?"

Pickens shook his shaved head. "Haven't got anything to cover you with, Bill. You'll be mooning to the wind."

"Can we count on *any* help at all if things go to slime, General?"

Again, Pickens shook his head. "You know the sit around here. We're spread thinner than ground meat in a PX hamburger."

"Okay, we're used to operating that way," Bellamack said with a sigh. "Makes us meaner than hell if we get in deep slime, but it's something we can count on. Looks like we're going to have to do a lot of recon and then be ready to move quickly with our airlift capability unless we want to chase guerrillas the hell and gone all over this place. . . ."

"Excuse me, sirs." Hassan had raised his hand in a tentative gesture, not really certain that he should break into this discussion but buoyed by Hettrick's remark about his native expertise. "I may be out of line here, but I think I know a way to carry off this mission that may save us a lot of trouble."

55

"Lieutenant," Bellamack told him frankly, "it'll be a cold day in hell when I won't listen to inputs from my troops. What do you have in mind?"

"Well, sir, I know from my own experience that the people in this part of the world don't have a basic unified national consciousness, if that's the proper term," Hassan ventured cautiously, feeling his way and trying to utilize not only everything he'd soaked up in his American schooling but also what he'd learned the hard way as an indentured child servant in Iran. "Don't mistake what I just said. They are capable of expressing it, and the Islamic Republic of Iran was a good example of that after the fall of the Shah in the last century. But, believe me, it's pretty thin and mostly propped up by religious fervor. Generally, people around here have had difficulties moving out of the tribal era."

"What do you mean by that, Lieutenant?" Carlisle asked.

Hassan shrugged. It was a natural reaction of his, a holdover from his childhood when it was an expression of submission to the ways of the world. Now, it was just a habit. He'd learned from Americans that if you don't like something, you bust your ass to do something about it. "First priority is to yourself, then to your family, then to your village or tribe with the same customs and beliefs you and your family share. Then your religious beliefs, which are mostly Islamic laid over a base of old time religious beliefs. If national pride and consciousness don't get in the way of those things, you go along with the national leaders. But what I'm talking about, sir, is the fact that we shouldn't look upon the Kurds as a monolithic people. The Dervishes that have been assaulting the Washington Greys are only a religious sect of perhaps one or two Kurdish tribes. Other Kurdish tribal groups exist—the Bektashi-Qizilbash, the Yezidis, the Kakai—"

"Lieutenant, are you a Kurd?" General Pickens suddenly asked.

Hassan shook his head. "No, sir, I was a Baluchi."

"That's a thousand klicks on the other side of Iran. How come you seem to know so much about the Kurds?" It wasn't meant to be an embarrassing question on Pickens's part; he felt it was a legitimate question because, after all his years in the area, he didn't really trust the Persian Gulf people. And

Hassan looked like one of them although he wore the uniform of the United States Army.

Hassan grinned. Modern dentistry had repaired years of dental neglect, and his smile was white and straight. "One of the most marvelous things I discovered in America was the encyclopedia. I read it twice once I understood English."

"*Twice?*" Pickens had referred to encyclopedias during his years at West Point, but the idea of actually reading an encyclopedia from cover to cover, even in a data base, overwhelmed him.

"Yes, sir. I was afraid I might forget something if I read it only once."

"You and Captain Allen are either going to get along famously or enjoy some furious arguments," Curt muttered.

"So what are you trying to tell us, Lieutenant?" Hettrick asked.

"That we shouldn't go out in the field and just look," Hassan explained. "That we should ask for help. One of the Kurdish tribes must not approve of the unprovoked attacks on American troops. Or they don't like the idea of the Soviets infiltrating Kurdistan. I would like to suggest that we make some inquiries around Mosul and attempt to find a Kurdish tribe such as the Kakai who could be made into allies. They know the country. They have channels of communication we don't. And the quicker the Soviets go home and things quiet down here, the sooner the Americans will leave, and then the Kurds may have a chance to get their own land back. Or they may see that American support can help the cause of a unified Kurdistan."

"You mentioned that a lot of the tribes around here don't have nationalistic feelings," Bellamack observed.

"The Kurds do, Colonel. It's been the zealous tribes and religious sects among them that have kept them from unifying," Hassan pointed out.

"General Hettrick," Bellamack addressed his division commander, "if there are no objections, I intend to take the Lieutenant's advice."

"I agree, even though I told you this was your show, Bill. I did the same thing in Namibia," Hettrick shot back.

"Colonel, I damned well want to know what you're doing if you go ahead with this!" Pickens objected loudly.

"Sir, with all due respect, I thought the chain of command and communication had already been established," Bellamack replied, knowing that this man really didn't trust him because of Bellamack's background as a whistle-blower who'd caused the cashiering of some of Pickens' friends several years ago.

Carlisle merely looked at Pickens.

Pickens knew that look. He didn't like what was happening in his own backyard, but there wasn't a whole hell of a lot he could do about it right then.

"Curt, coordinate this in your Tac Batt," Bellamack snapped.

"Yes, sir!" Curt Carson knew it wasn't going to be an easy thing to do. The situation was rife with personal animosity, professional jealousy, political tension—and the real commanders were on the other side of the world.

Chapter Eight

"Okay, Mister, it was your idea—and it's a good one—but Bellamack dropped the project in my lap," Curt addressed Lieutenant Hassan Ben Mahmud. "We can't turn a wheel on Operation Sturdy Spectra and go after the Sovs until we get information. What's your suggestion on finding a suitable Kurdish guide we can trust? Who do we talk to? The Mosul police?"

Hassan shook his head and replied vehemently, "No, sir! Definitely not! You can't trust the police here."

It was a private conference in Curt's cubicle off the battalion day room in the casern. The only other person present was Battalion Sergeant Major Edie Sampson, Curt's leading NCO and the person he really counted on to run the Tac-Batt. (See Appendix III, *Organization of the Special Combat Robot Infantry Regiment*.) Bellamack had just finished briefing the Regiment on the new assignment, tagged Operation Sturdy Spectra by some computer somewhere Curt believed, because no naturally intelligent entity would come up with such a screwy code name. To preserve security, the Regiment had been given only the rudiments of the Operation because Curt had yet to work out the initial details of how to obtain good intelligence and guidance so the Regiment didn't spend all its time and consumables running hither and yon around the Mosul region. "So what's the plan? Sure as hell we can't go down to the Mosul marketplace and just ask around to find an honest Kurd guide."

"I had thought about spending a day or so down in the marketplace dressed in mufti—although I've got to admit I don't *ever* want to wear a burnoose or khaftan again! But I don't know how good the Kurd intelligence activity is, and I might be spotted. Sure as hell, I'd be spotted because of my

59

Baluchi accent," Hassan admitted. "I'd also thought about asking Captain Allen to go along with me because he speaks Arabic."

"But with a terrible American accent," Curt said. "Besides, I'm not about to let any Grey go undercover around here. The Kurds could play rough. The Iraqis don't care much about us, and they play rough, too. If the Soviets have agents in Mosul—and I have to assume that they do—then they'll play even rougher if they catch American officers out of uniform. We may not be loved around here, but we're certainly respected and not hated, at least by the general populace."

"True, Major," Hassan agreed. "The Iraqis figure that the Americans will eventually go away just like all the other foreign occupation troops of the past. And the American Army is probably the most benign occupation force to be in here since . . . since, well, since forever, I guess."

"Then why are the Dervish Kurds being super-nasty lately?" Edie Sampson asked, cutting right through as she usually did—but without the tact that Henry Kester had developed over the years and had tried unsuccessfully to teach her. "You don't go shooting at someone unless you got a real, definite dislike for him. And you want to see him either dead or his ass end running the hell and gone out of there."

"Edie, you've had the chance to look at the weaponry the Dervishes were carrying?" Curt asked.

She knew it was a leading question. "Yes, sir. Soviet AK-thirteens. Hell, I knew the answer to my question; I just wanted to make sure everyone else knew what's probably causing the Kurds to show a little lethal irritation all of a sudden. The Sovs are behind it. And, as the Lieutenant pointed out, not all the Kurds are involved, just some of the crazier ones, the ones the Russkies can whip into a lather for their own purposes. But the Lieutenant is also right: we don't go ask the police for references to trustworthy Kurds who could point us in the right direction. And we probably shouldn't even bother the Iraqi Army, either."

Hassan nodded. "That Iraqi battalion that struts around the streets is for show," he agreed. "Helps offset the presence of the American Army here, sort of to give the local Iraqis the idea they're still in charge of their own country . . . which they're not because they couldn't fight their way out of a wet khaftan right now; their fighting age population was practically wiped out in wars over the last fifty years."

"So let's get back to my original question," Curt snapped. "I've got to find some trustworthy Kurds. How the hell do I do it? Apparently, I can't go to the police or the Iraqi Army. Damned if I'll let anyone go cruising the alleyways of the marketplace, in uniform or not. I don't think the local American consul thinks in the terms we do; their job is to get the American oil patch people out of trouble on Saturday night after payday when they bust up a bar somewhere. . . ."

"Major, I think you've just found the answer to your question," Edie told him quickly.

"Oh? Was it something I said?" Curt asked.

"Sure as hell was! I think I know who we can trust to give us an honest answer because we're here to keep them out of the slime," Edie Sampson pointed out. "Let's mosey on over to the local offices of the Iraqi Petroleum Company and find us an American supervisor to chat with."

Curt grinned and remarked to his top kick, "Edie, I knew there had to be a damned good reason why I kept recommending you for promotion all these years! Beside being able to fight, I mean . . . and in spite of the fact that you still insist on toting that goddamned nine-millimeter Beretta toy pistol."

She just smiled and patted the weapon in its holster on her right hip. "Major, a girl has the right to select her own social purpose weapon, and this one has served me very well, thank you. And in these parts, if the stories are right, its presence does produce a modicum of respect."

"Actually, Sergeant Major," Hassan put in, "you could walk around Mosul or any Muslim city in complete safety." He didn't tell her why.

She knew anyway. "Yeah, because I'm not in purdah . . . and a woman not in purdah is a working woman who shouldn't be molested. Otherwise, she doesn't get her work done so that her male master can laze around with the rest of the boys doing not much of anything except fighting or enjoying the ladies still young enough to be in purdah. Thank you, Lieutenant, but I'll pack my heater anyway. As I recall, the goddamned Jehorkhims in Zahedan did some pretty nasty things to the women hostages they held there, including Colonel Willa Lovell."

Curt couldn't help smiling as he told the new officer, "Lieutenant, I know you have an extensive background in the Mideast and the Islamic religion, and I welcome your insights in those matters. However, I should warn you that the ladies of the Washington Greys—officers and NCOs—are a lot smarter than many outsiders think. And they're a tad different from most Islamic women."

It was Hassan's turn to grin with his broad smile and bright teeth. "Major Carson, with all due respect, sir, I was introduced to the mysteries of women by my former master, Mahmud. One of the nicer things he did for me, as a matter of fact. I once found a particularly valuable gemstone which we took into Zahedan and got a very good price for it. Mahmud showed his gratitude by giving me an open account at the local whorehouse for two weeks and instructing the women to teach me well."

He stopped. Edie asked, "And?"

"They did," Hassan said with his broad, sexy smile. "Women are women . . ."

". . . But a good cigar is a smoke," Curt finished.

"Sir?"

"Rudyard Kipling," Curt explained.

"Oh. I haven't read him yet."

"I suggest you do, if Russ Frazier ever gives you any free time once I get finished using you as a temporary intelligence officer. Reading Rudyard Kipling will give you some novel outlooks on the world, especially as an Army officer." Curt turned his chair and tried to call up the local phone directory on the terminal. Nothing happened. He snorted in frustration. "Hell of a place! How do we talk to each other out here? Dammit, they don't even have a telephone data base?"

"Uh, Major, there should be a hard copy of the documentation somewhere in your desk," Edie pointed out.

Curt finally located a poorly bound, tattered volume with the words, "Mosul Telephone Directory" in both English and Arabic on its cover. The date of publication was six years before. He grumbled that he hoped it was still current as he riffled through its flimsy tissue-like pages and found the number for the Mosul office of the Iraqi Petroleum Company, Ltd..

He couldn't access the Mosul telephone system through the Army desk computer, so he was forced to use the telephone handset which must have been surplussed out of someplace on the moors of England because it was old and had a rotary pulse dial. Curt had encountered a few of these in the corners of the American West, so he knew how to work it.

To his great surprise, a female voice answered after three irritating ring signals, " 'Ello, el-Iraqi Petrol Sherka! Sabahil kher!"

Curt was surprised because he'd been told that women in the Mideastern Islamic countries were second-class citizens and normally didn't hold down even an ordinary secretary's job. So he replied very slowly in basic English as he'd learned to do in a foreign land, "My name is Major Curt Carson of United States Army stationed here in Mosul. I wish to speak to the manager or supervisor, please."

The woman replied in excellent English, "Very well, Major. I'll connect you with Mr. Chaney."

Obviously, Iraqi Petroleum Company had a better internal telephone system than the public system owned and operated by the Iraqi Ministry of Guidance because Curt heard no internal system noise from pulse or tone dialing as the secretary quickly located Mr. Chaney, told him who was calling, and connected Curt.

"This here's A. W. Chaney! What can I do for y'all, Major?" The voice sounded like sandpaper going over Texas ironwood.

"Mr. Chaney, I'd like to come over and talk with you for a few minutes at your convenience," Curt told him.

Chaney interrupted, "Well, that's shore somethin' diffrunt! I'm usually the one who wants to talk with you folks! Tell ya whut: I'm needin' to talk at you, too! Why don't y'all saunter on over in the next hour or so and we'll have ourselves a little chat? How many of you coming?"

"Four of us," Curt replied, thinking that it might be a good idea if he took Jerry along, too. After all, the new Captain spoke Arabic and would probably be involved with Hassan

63

in doing the G-2 work required for Operation Sturdy Spectra.

"Fine! Ah'll have the coffee pot hot to trot!"

"What did you have in mind to say to us, Mr. Chaney?"

"What you want to talk to me about, Major?" Chaney countered.

Curt hesitated. He always operated under the assumption that all telephones were tapped. "I don't think we'd better discuss it over an un-scrambled and un-monitored land line, sir."

"Well, if that's the way it is, Major, the same goes here. Tit fer tat, I guess. We'll just keep each other in the dark until we see each other."

Curt could tell that the Texan had a burr under his saddle for some unknown reason. In short, he was pissed off, and probably at the United States Army. That was a hell of a way to start a relationship, Curt thought. On the other hand, maybe it was better that Curt found out what the trouble was before the man lodged a formal complaint higher up the line. "Very well, sir, we'll come expecting the worst, then."

"You better! By the way, pack your artillery, Major. Company rules say you gotta check 'em at the door, but you might be a tad safer these days if you were armed around these oil patch installations. Maybe that will give you some idea what my complaint is all about."

"It does help, Mr. Chaney," Curt admitted with some relief. Obviously, Chaney was upset about the fact that the Kurds were still giving his people trouble out in the boondocks around the various petroleum installations. At least, it seemed like a good starting point for guessing at the nature of Chaney's problem. "And I think what we need to talk to you about may help your situation in the long run, too." He paused for a moment, then added, "And we will come armed in one of our armored vehicles, sir."

"Okay, but better leave someone in it when you park it outside," Chaney warned. "Some of these guys can strip a car in less than thirty seconds. Takes them a little longer to strip one of your vehicles. Maybe about thirty-five seconds."

"Jeez, Major!" Edie Sampson breathed when Curt had hung up. "That used to be such a neat residential area before the airport industrial zone took it over."

"You obviously know the place, Sergeant," Curt observed. "Do we count on your Beretta or . . . ?"

"Major, we go with loaded Novias and extra clips, and a couple of nasty-minded city types like Elliott and Tullis from Lieutenant Clinton's platoon. Maybe, if you want real protection, we oughta take O'Reilly and Moody from Captain Frazier's outfit," Edie Sampson advised, then looked pensive. "Sounds like a part of town you wouldn't go into unless armed to the teeth and ready to use it."

Chapter Nine

For some reason, A. W. "Red" Chaney looked exactly like Major Curt Carson had pictured him in his mind—a big, heavy-set, middle-aged Texan who'd obviously been born in the near-Cajun country of east Texas but raised in the oil patch of west Texas. Chaney had a round, pink face and a shock of thinning red hair that was beginning to turn whitish-red. Something about A. W. "Red" Chaney spelled Good Old Boy, even down to the legendary sunburned neck itself. Curt felt he knew the man's prejudices, and he prepared himself to deal with them. He wasn't wrong in his assessment.

Once the introductions were done—Curt had brought along Jerry, Hassan, and Edie—Chaney settled back into a chair behind his desk, put his hands behind his head, and observed, "I guessed you wanted to talk to me alone without any of the Iraqis around. Or even without the illuminating presence of my chief engineer who happens to be out in the field today surveying some of the damage those goddamned Kurd turds did to my pumping station at Kasik Kopri day before yesterday."

"You've suffered some damage from Kurd attacks?" Curt wanted to know.

"*Some damage?* Damned right! Why the hell do you think I wanted to talk at you, Major?" Chaney snapped. "You Army types are supposed to be over here to protect our stuff. Damned *fellahin* Iraqi bastards can't or won't; I don't care which. They're about as effective at preventin' lootin' and vandalism as tits on a box car. Pardon me, ma'am. . . ." He nodded his head toward Edie.

"What the hell, Mr. Chaney, some of us got 'em and some of us don't," Edie replied, direct as only she could be. "You're talkin' to a combat soldier, so you don't have to mince words around me."

"Yeah, I guess it's tough duty fighting warbots from those air-conditioned vans . . ." Obviously, Chaney didn't realize he wasn't with warbot brainies.

Edie didn't reply at first, and Curt didn't say anything in her defense because he knew she'd handle this little matter in a very effective way.

With a flourish, she pulled a commando knife from somewhere in her cammies and began to clean her fingernails with its sharp tip while she remarked offhandedly, "Mr. Chaney, ever hear of a place called Zahedan over in eastern Iran?"

"Can't say I have. I don't follow war stuff. I got my hands full with oil patch business."

"Well, maybe you remember what happened in Trinidad, which has a pretty big oil patch of its own," Edie went on, eyeing her fingernails professionally as she cleaned them. She didn't look at Chaney. "We're not the usual run-of-the-mill warbot brainies. More like the modern version of the old Special Forces infantry. We fight in the open alongside our warbots. The Major here has been shot at and actually wounded. I've been shot at, but the bullets turn away because I'm so tough and mean. Yeah, I guess you might call it rough duty. But it's rougher on our opponents than it is on us. Major Carson, have you been keeping track of how many men I've killed?"

Curt shook his head sadly. "Sorry, Sergeant, but I lost count after the first hundred or so."

"Okay! So the U.S. of A. is bringing back the old Marines!" Chaney exuded with glee.

"Mr. Chaney, we're Army, not Marines," Captain Jerry Allen pointed out in quiet anger. "The Marines are still stuck as embassy guards and shipboard security. I hope to God they get the chance to follow our Special Combat doctrines. We need all the help we can get! Especially in a place like this. Especially when we've already had our troops shot at, probably by the same people who are tearing up your stuff. And we don't seem to be getting much help or cooperation at the moment even from the people we're supposed to be helping."

"It'ud help if I saw some protection instead of talk," Chaney said with a growl.

"You will, Mr. Chaney. I promise you that," Curt told him bluntly. "Now that the Washington Greys Special Combat Regiment is here on rotation, I think you're going to find that we're a whole hell of a lot different than the warbot brainy outfit that was here before."

"Shit, if warbots can't protect my fields and pipelines and pumping stations against the goddamned Turds, what makes you think ordinary soldiers can?" Chaney wanted to know.

"Who said we're ordinary soldiers?" Curt replied rhetorically. "In the first place, we're not going to stand around waiting for some Kurd to take a potshot at us with a Soviet gun. We're going to go after them."

"About time!"

"Agreed!" Curt told him firmly, then decided he'd probably get further faster with this displaced redneck if he lapsed into the Sierra Charlie equivalent of the man's rough oil patch language. "But damned if I'm going to ask the Iraqis for help. They either don't know their ass from third base, or they're being paid off by the Turds or the Soviets. And I'm not going to go lurking around the bazaar downtown looking for stoolies; even I know that's a goddamned good way to get a shiv between my shoulder blades before the day is out. So that's why we're here today. I can trust what you tell me; you've got a vested interest in our success. And if we can get these Kurds off your back, you can continue business as usual. Then I'm happy. You're happy. The Army high brass is happy. Your boss is happy and his Board of Directors may even give you a raise."

Red Chaney thought about this for a moment, then asked, "What do you want?"

"I want to find out where and when your facilities and people have been attacked," Curt told him without hesitation. "I want to know everything you know about who did it. Then I want your help in finding a couple of trustworthy local or Kurdish types who can serve like Indian scouts for us."

Chaney looked at Lieutenant Hassan Ben Mahmud.

"Looks like you've already got a trained seal."

Hassan stiffened slightly but otherwise didn't move a muscle. He was apparently used to this sort of treatment from some Americans.

Coolly, Curt informed the petroleum supervisor, "Mr. Chaney, Lieutenant Mahmud is a citizen of the United States and an honor graduate of OCS. I expect him to be a valuable asset in this operation, and not just because he speaks Arabic. Even Captain Allen here speaks fluent Arabic."

Chaney was quiet for a moment, then said, "You want a line on a couple of Turds you can trust, huh? Well, I know damned few of them! But there are some. . . . Lemme think about it a while. In the meantime, what the hell are you gonna do to keep those bastards from tearing up company property?"

"You tell me what you want protected, where it is, and what the protection priority is," Curt suggested. "The Washington Greys are a damned fast-moving outfit, both in the air and on the ground. Closest thing the Army's got these days to the cavalry regiments of the Old West. And we've got damned good recon capability. We can keep an eye on things, if we know what to watch. But we're sure as hell not going to send out a combat patrol to check every damned sheepherder in the hills every time he decides to change locations because the sheep shit gets too deep, and we won't come running every time a camel farts somewhere. And you shouldn't give a damn what we do to keep the Kurds from beating up the place any more than I give a rat's ass how you pump that brown gunk out of the ground and shove it down those pipes. You scratch my ass, and I'll scratch yours. If we can have that kind of contract, we might both keep our asses out of a sling or worse. . . ."

Chaney surveyed Curt and his contingent through squinty eyes for a long minute. Curt could almost feel the gears going around in the man's mind. Finally, Red Chaney admitted, "Damn if I don't think I might be able to get on with y'all for a change. You sure as hell talk different than any other fancy Army officer types that have pranced in an' out of this office so far. I think you mean what you say. And I'll admit sure as hell I wouldn't want to tangle assholes with any

69

of you—includin' you, lady—in any Mosul back alley after payday. In fact, I think I'd sorta like to have you alongside when the brawl gets going . . . and they do get going, even with the Brits I got workin' for me. But you act like the friggin' Aussies who don't mind grinnin' ear to ear while they slip it to you greasy between the legs."

He paused. Curt said nothing but just smiled.

He admitted, "Okay, you got a deal. I'll find you a Turd or two you can count on to be more honest than most. . . ."

Curt's tacomm brick on his equipment harness squealed. He punched it and heard Sergeant Jim Elliott report from where he and Sergeant Paul Tullis were guarding the ACV outside, "Tac Batt Leader, this is Conqueror Three! Couple of natives just tried to fire-bomb us with a Molotov cocktail out here! I think I got one of them with my Novia!"

"Convention is over!" Curt snapped and was on his feet along with the three others. "Chaney, get us our rifles!"

"Come on!" Chaney told them and quickly led them out of the room at a dead run.

At the entrance foyer, Curt accosted the Iraqi security guard who was manning the front desk. It wasn't the same guard that had been there when they'd come in and checked their weapons. "Give us our rifles! Now! Quickly!"

The guard looked dumb, so Jerry repeated Curt's command in Arabic.

Now the guard seemed to understand. He shrugged. "*Effendi,* your servants came in and collected them to take to the armored vehicle outside!"

"Dammit, I told Elliott not to leave the ACV!" Curt exploded and keyed his tacomm. "Conqueror Three, this is Tac Batt Leader! Why did you take our Novias back out to the ACV?"

Elliott's reply was quick. "Major, what are you talking about? You took your Novias inside with you! I don't have them! They're not out here!"

The security guard suddenly broke from behind the desk and dashed for the door.

Edie Sampson stuck out her leg and tripped him. As he fell to the floor, she was suddenly on top of him with her commando knife at his throat. He struggled momentarily until he felt the edge of the knife, then became meek and

70

submissive.

Red Chaney moved to stand over them and put his booted foot on top of the guard's face. "All right, you sonofabitch!" he growled. "I don't remember seeing you around here before! You're gonna tell me right now what the hell's going on or I'll kick your damned face in! And maybe the Sergeant's knife will slip in the process."

"*Ana la a fahim! Ana la a fahim!*" the guard tried to say.

Hassan stepped over and began rattling Arabic at the guard. Jerry joined him and added to the crowd around the prostrate man. It took only a moment for Hassan to report to Curt, "He says he doesn't know anything. He's new here."

"If Elliott or Tullis didn't take our Novias, then who did?" Curt wanted to know.

"He says our Iraqi *khaddams*—servants—came in and took them outside to our vehicle for safekeeping," Jerry remarked. "Bastard is either lying in his teeth or he's just plain stupid . . . maybe both. Major, I think we've just lost our Novias. We'll probably find them when someone starts shooting them at us!"

"Conqueror Three, this is Batt One Leader!" Curt growled into the tacomm brick. "Any action on the street out there?"

"Negatory! Want me to call in the bio-techs for the wounded guy?"

"Affirmative! We might learn something from him!"

"That I seriously doubt, Major," was Hassan's comment.

"Three, are you and Four wearing your body armor?" Curt asked his NCO waiting in the vehicle.

"Negatory!"

"Get it on! We'll need you to cover our transit from the building to the ACV," Curt explained.

"Major, everything's copacetic out here now."

"I don't believe that for a goddamned second, Elliott!"

"Tell you what, sir: I'll just back this humper up against the door so you can come in the back ramp."

"Okay, do it! Better idea anyway! Three, did you see anyone leave this building with our Novias?" Curt asked.

"Negatory!"

"They must have gone out the side doors," Chaney explained.

"Damn! Okay, Conqueror Three, let us know when you've got the ACV in position," Curt requested, then turned to Chaney. "Nice people you've got working for you! We've just lost four assault rifles! Damned well ought to send Iraqi Petroleum a bill for them!"

"Goddammit, Carson, I do the best I can with what I've got!" Chaney snarled. "So report it! The IRS will just tack it onto Shellexxo's quarterly tax bill back in the States! But you'll pay hell getting anything out of the international consortium that's operating this nationalized company for Iraq. Dammit, I'm sorry you lost your weapons; you're going to need them around here. I'm even sorrier that they're probably in the hands of the Turds now . . . or will be by evening."

"Uh, Major," Edie remarked from where she was still atop the guard, her knife still at his throat. "I wouldn't worry too much about the Novias right now. We've got replacements. You want I should let this guy live and get up? Or should I finish the job while I'm down here?"

"Let him up. We can't pin anything on him. That's Chaney's worry," Curt told her. "Besides, you're likely to get blood on your uniform, and you know from experience how hard it is to get out unless we've got a good laundry."

Chaney was impressed at last. "You weren't shitting me about being different troops, were you? Yeah, I think you may do okay in Mosul. I sure as hell don't want to get on your shit list! Let him up; I'll take care of him . . . maybe."

"Sergeant," Curt addressed Edie, "what do you mean, 'Don't worry too much about the Novias'? Do you like fighting your own equipment?"

"No, sir," Edie replied, getting to her feet and sheathing her commando knife. "But how the hell is anyone going to use them? We unloaded them after we came inside here, remember?" She pulled a clip from her equipment harness and held it up. "Those Novias were empty. And they don't shoot worth a damn without ammo. And only the Sierra Charlies have the seven-millimeter caseless ammo for the Novias and the Jeep guns. If you remember our warbot brainy days, Major, the only seven-millimeter caseless ammo we had was the short rounds for the old Hornets, and that won't fit in the Novias. At the moment, we've got a trump card; the Kurds or whoever stole our Novias will try to steal the ammo next, and we can be watching for them. When they do, we'll either blow their lips off or get our Novias back, or both."

Chapter Ten

"I won't *ever* turn *anything* loose around these parts unless I don't want to see it again!" promised Major Curt Carson as he looked over the replacement M33A2 "Ranger" assault rifle that Captain Harriet Dearborn handed him.

The commander of LOGCO looked at him and told him with mock seriousness, "Better not! It's going to take you a couple of months to pay for the one you lost!" she kidded, although it didn't sound that way.

"Oh, my God, you're not docking our pay for the Novias that were stolen from us, are you?" Captain Jerry Allen asked in horror. "Hey, listen, a Captain's pay isn't that great in the first place!"

"Tell me about it," she replied, flicking one of the two silver bars on her shoulder tabs.

"We were requested to turn them in when we entered a civilian facility, Captain," Edie Sampson complained.

Dearborn winked at her. The others didn't see it. "Someone's got to pay for losing government-issued equipment. I think I'm still being dunned for the old tacomm brick I gave to that anthropologist before the Strijdom Airport battle in Namibia. He went off into the boonies and never returned it."

"As temporary regimental commander at the time, I distinctly recall telling you to show it on the records as expended in combat," Curt reminded her as he checked the action on the new Novia.

"Oh, I know you did, and that's exactly what I did. The problem is that when I pull your leg, it sometimes comes off in my hand. Actually, I just wanted to see you sweat for a change," Dearborn admitted to them. "I'm forced with doing some real sweating on this tour. I've got to be *real* careful

74

accounting for damned near everything, thanks to those clowns in the Gimlet Regiment who 'expended,' stuff on 'combat patrols' when they were actually selling it to the Iraqis . . . before Colonel Bellamack stepped in and blew the whistle on them."

"Hell, that was years ago, Harriet," Curt reminded her. The Gimlet Regiment was withdrawn in disgrace and re-organized from scratch at Fort Leonard Wood. The former officers who were involved got Dishonorables. Bellamack had been promoted and given command of the Washington Greys Regiment when Hettrick was wounded and out of action. "So what's the trouble today?"

"Major," she told him flatly, making a final entry on her terminal keypad, "when something like the Gimlet arms scam happens, the regs don't get changed but a lot of new policies and procedures are put into place, and those are damned hard to get rid of! Maybe at some future date the procedures will slowly be forgotten and fall into disuse, but they'll still be on the books in case someone wants to cream some poor brainy for losing a bot. So all of us logistics types are going to have to live with it for the rest of our careers." She closed down the terminal cover and smiled at them. "In the meantime, this AI won't have to be reported for a couple of months during which time you may find the lost Novias. And if past experience is any guide, you'll go out and honestly expend some stuff in combat — not that I want to wish death and destruction on any of you in the process because that *really* creates paperwork! So in the meantime, please don't lose any more Novias; I had to draw these down from our limited combat replacement stock."

Curt's tacomm brick squawked. He toggled it and said "Tac Batt Leader here!"

A warbot voice replied, "Tac Batt Leader, this is Marauder Jeep Delta at the main gate guard post. Two English-speaking Iraqis are here. They ask to see you. They state they were sent by Mr. A. W. Chaney of Iraqi Petroleum Company, Limited. They have no identification documents. I am requesting instructions, please."

The new 7/11 AI modules almost made the warbots seem human. They were a lot smarter than the old MOD 5 AI warbots, but the Greys knew the 7/11s were only about as

75

bright as retarded children; you had to be very careful what you said to them and how you gave them commands. (But you couldn't hurt their feelings because they didn't have any.) And then you usually had to follow up to find out if the bots had gotten into trouble.

The new 7/11s were a joy to work with, at least in the war games conducted during train-up and during the three skirmishes with the Kurds thus far. The new bots didn't have to be constantly monitored, but they did have to be watched. Henry Kester described them best by pointing out they were like the stupid farm boys who used to make up the bulk of the conscripted European infantry armies of the nineteenth century and before, and had made up most of the Union and Confederate armies during the Civil War.

In fact, many Greys were hanging human nicknames on their new bots, although the bots continued to report by their official designators.

But, unlike the conscripted low-quality human cannon fodder of the past, the 7/11 warbots wouldn't break and run from a battle. They were machines, not cowards; they couldn't be routed. In fact, they had to be ordered to retreat or withdraw.

This created another problem that was unique to warbots and that hadn't been solved yet at McCarthy Proving Ground where all the advanced AI work was going on: 7/11 warbots, like their Mod 5 predecessors, had only elementary survival instincts in the form of built-in programming. Work was still progressing on finding the delicate balance between survivability and machine cowardice so a warbot wouldn't lock-up into immobility.

No one had the slightest idea of how to tackle the biggest problem with warbots: machines really don't give a damn whether they win or lose. They depend on humans to provide that part of the game equation.

Colonel Willa Lovell had told Curt that Captain Owen Pendleton was getting there, for which Curt was grateful. The Greys had put up with a lot of grief because of Pendleton's little experiment on learning why soldiers fought. It had saved their asses on Kerguelen Island, but only because the experimental equipment had been used for biological monitoring, a function it was never intended to perform

So Curt instructed the Jeep via tacomm, "Marauder Jeep Delta, this is Tac Batt Leader. Obtain visual images of the two men. Then contact Regimental Staff Sergeant Georgina Cook. Ask Sergeant Cook to contact by video circuit Mr. A. W. Chaney of Iraqi Petroleum Company, Limited. Sergeant Cook is to request that Mr. Chaney confirm the visual identity of the two men. Do not allow the men to have access to the casern. Do not allow the two men out of your immediate vicinity or your visual range. Lieutenant Mahmud will join you at the gate in a few minutes, and you will then respond to Lieutenant Mahmud's orders. Report that you understand these instructions."

"I understand your instructions. Do you wish a read-back?" the warbot's voice asked.

Since Hassan would be going down to the gate, it wasn't important to get a read-back at this time. "Negatory! Execute your instructions now!"

"Roger! Executing!"

Curt turned to Hassan and flipped his hand in the direction of the main gate. "Lieutenant, shag down to the main gate, confirm all this, and then escort the two men to the regimental day room. I'll see them there."

Hassan rendered an unnecessary salute and slung his Novia. "Yes, sir! Looks like Chaney came through on his promise to find us two Kurdish guides. On my way!"

"Jerry, stick with me," Curt told the younger officer. "I want you around when we talk to these characters. Maybe you'll get a chance to brush up on the Kurdish language."

"Major, the Kurdish language is different from Arabic," Jerry pointed out, calling up his encyclopedic memory. In some ways, this could be a pain in the ass to Curt because Jerry could get pedantic on occasion. If Jerry hadn't been such a good combat officer, he would make an outstanding military academician at West Point or some other military school. Jerry didn't parade his knowledge, but he could get tiresome. This threatened to be one of those times. "Arabic is a Hamitic language, but Kurdish is Indo-European. I'm not sure I can follow Kurdish. The language structure is different."

"Save me the linguistics lecture, Jerry," Curt said wearily, cutting off the monologue early. "When it comes to different language structures, you really haven't had the course until you try to learn something as totally different and alien in structure as Chinese."

Jerry nodded, aware that he'd mildly irritated his former company commander who was now his battalion commander. "Yes, sir, that's why I opted for Arabic. I didn't have the guts to tackle one of the inflective Asiatic tongues."

One reason why Curt had selected Mandarin Chinese as his second language at West Point wasn't because it was difficult but because he thought it might be far more useful in the long run than Russian or even Arabic. And in his plebe year, he'd really gotten the hots for a fellow female plebe, a Chinese-American Medal of Honor legacy who'd been unapproachable but had suggested that Curt might have a better chance if he'd learn how to think like she did. Later, it didn't matter; she found someone else and he found Chinese to be a challenge. Military history and small unit tactics were his favorite subjects, but Chinese had trapped him because of the fascinating and highly different way he had to think in order to understand and speak it, which, in turn, had helped him learn how to express himself better in his own language.

Hassan showed up with two men — one a bearded youngster with bushy black hair and intense dark eyes like Hassan, the other an older man with eyes that were almost blue and an unbearded face that reminded Curt of one of his grandfathers. Both men were surprisingly light-skinned, even in comparison to Hassan who was a little darker. And both men carried Iraqi Petroleum hard hats which they now held in their hands, leaving them bareheaded. Apparently, their association with the Americans and British operators of Iraqi Petroleum had taught them Euro-American manners and mannerisms.

The Lieutenant was obviously very happy. Curt didn't find out why until Hassan had introduced the two men. "Major, Marauder Jeep Delta did what you told it to do, and Sergeant Cook had a double-check with Mr. Chaney by the time I got down to the gate. So everything's copacetic. And these two gentlemen speak excellent English as well as Arabic and Kurdish. Turns out the Kurdish language is similar to Baluchi, so I'm stumbling along reasonably well. This

78

man is Mustafa Sahab, a Jaf Kurd who's been working for Iraqi Petroleum for sixteen years."

The older man smiled and nodded. "I am pleased to know you, Major Carson," he said in a high-pitched voice that slightly cracked but was without appreciable accent. His grip was firm and his hand was leathery when Curt shook it.

"And this is Haji Somayeh, a Shakak Kurd who is a second-generation employee of Iraqi Petroleum," Hassan went on, introducing the younger man with the beard.

"You must like oil field work if you followed your father," Curt remarked as he shook hands with him. The younger man's hand wasn't as work-hardened as Sahab's.

Somayeh smiled briefly, showing white teeth that were the result of Iraqi Petroleum's company medical and dental programs. "It's a good job, sir. But my uncle on my mother's side got the job for me. I was born and raised in the hills north of here."

"Did Mr. Chaney tell you why you're here?" Curt asked.

Sahab shook his head. "No. Have we done something to upset the American Army?"

Somayeh was also shaking his head. However, unlike the older man, his face showed a mixture of confusion and wariness. Curt spotted that and thought he knew the reason why, so he asked, "Mr. Somayeh, how long has it been since you left your home in the hills north of here and came down to work for Iraqi Petroleum?"

"Five years, sir." Somayeh wasn't sure why Curt asked, but the Kurd did know that these people had enormous power in their computer machines, power that involved obtaining and storing knowledge. Somayeh believed that Curt probably knew everything about his background. Was the American officer trying to trip him up by getting him to say something that wasn't in the computer information? Somayeh didn't know, but he figured he'd better play straight arrow right then. His own experience with Iraqi Petroleum told him that these Americans with their computers could catch him lying almost at once.

"Well, I didn't ask Mr. Chaney to send you here. I asked him to recommend a few good, reliable, trustworthy Kurds who worked for him. He chose the two of you. So don't worry; you've come here with outstanding recommendations," Curt explained.

The look of relief on Somayeh's face was immediately obvious.

"We were asked by Mr. Chaney to put ourselves at your disposal," Mustafa Sahab explained. "How may we be of service to you, sir?"

"We need you to tell us about the Kurds in the hills north of here," Curt told them, being careful not to reveal any of the details of Operation Sturdy Spectra at this point. These two Kurds would first have to prove their trustworthiness before he'd do that. "We also need people who know the hills and can guide us into that territory."

"*Effendi*, do you intend to take your soldiers into the hills to make war on the Kurdish people there?" Sahab asked directly in his cracked voice.

"At this point, I can't discuss our plans and intentions," Curt replied with equal bluntness.

"I know nothing about what is going on in the hills to the north!" Somayeh suddenly blurted out. "I cannot give you any information. It has been five years since I have been in Kurdistan, and everything has changed so much that I cannot be of help to you as a guide!"

Chapter Eleven

Curt suddenly realized he'd made a colossal blunder.

While attempting to be general and not reveal military information that might be leaked to the Dervish Kurds who were chivvying the Washington Greys, Curt knew he'd given the impression that the powerful Robot Infantry of the United States Army was planning to foray into the hills of Kurdistan in a general offensive.

These people had been subjected to that sort of thing for fifty centuries. Distrust of strangers and fighting foreign invaders was a way of life. It was natural that Sahab and Somayeh would immediately conclude that they were being asked to betray their own people by providing information and guiding these powerful American soldiers in a war.

The young Somayeh asked, "May I be excused, sir?"

The older Sahab sat passively. He wasn't as impulsive. He knew he was in no danger from these Americans. If he remained, he might learn something more.

If what he learned caused him to believe he'd be betraying his Kurdish colleagues in the hills, he could still walk out as Somayeh now threatened to do. In that case, he knew the information would be very valuable to the Dervish and other militant anti-Iraqi tribes, and he knew how to pass the information along through covert channels so that these powerful Americans could never trace the leak to him. There was no money in it for him; the Kurds might later reward him in other ways if a Kurdish nation could ever be established. The militant anti-Iraqi Kurds weren't making any headway toward this long-term Kurd goal; in fact, Sahab knew they were now part of the problem. If clandestine guerrilla warfare hadn't been successful for centuries, and since the situation seemed to have changed, maybe a new approach might work better.

With that in the back of his mind, Sahab wanted to find out what Major Curt Carson and these Americans had in mind. Their plans might be different. They were by far the most powerful—yet benign—foreign troops ever to occupy this region. He knew from his own experience that Americans were generous and rich. So they had a habit of behaving in unfathomable ways. If the Americans planned surgical strikes—Sahab didn't think in that term, of course—that succeeded in blunting the effectiveness of the fanatical Dervish and other Kurdish factions, then the cause of Kurdish nationalism might be advanced if the militants were out of the way.

If the Americans also planned to counter the covert Soviet troops Sahab knew were up in the hills now, that would also help. And he was well aware of the fact that the Americans and Soviets seemed to act toward one another the same way that his Kurdish friends acted toward Turks, Iraqis, Iranians, and Syrians who occupied portions of Kurdistan.

It was in Sahab's best interests at the moment that Somayeh not create a scene. He knew the young man, but not well. He also knew that young Kurds—like young, idealistic men everywhere—tended to have short fuses, quick tempers, and knee-jerk reactions to things that triggered their emotions. He sighed because these traits of youth were needed to counterbalance the conservatism of older men such as he. Knowing how to handle such youthful zeal was something he'd worked on for years as a pipeline terminal supervisor.

So he put his hand gently but firmly on Somayeh's arm as the latter started to get up. Although he knew that Lieutenant Mahmud understood Kurdish, he spoke to Somayeh in their native tongue, admonishing him, "Haji, remain seated. Don't jump to conclusions. Let us learn what this man wants."

Haji Somayeh may have been mercurial, but he'd also been taught to respect elders. With merely a look, he relaxed back into the chair.

Sahab continued, speaking in English to Curt, "I believe this young man thinks you may be planning to do what so many other armies in the past have done: attempt to wipe out the Kurds because they are a nuisance. What is the term you use? Genosis? Gen-ah-side?"

"Genocide," Curt said. "Of course not! International agreements have outlawed genocide. In any event, Americans don't do that sort of thing!"

Curt knew he was wrong when Sahab reminded him, "I have heard stories about the way the American Indians were treated . . ."

"I stand corrected, sir," Curt admitted, then pointed out, "but those were different times."

"Times don't change the way people behave," Sahab replied.

Curt knew he was talking to someone who, in spite of being able to work with Euro-Americans and their technology, was still in the past and still thought of existence in terms of "tomorrow will be exactly the same as today because today is exactly the same as yesterday." With a belief in a world of Again and Again contrasted to the outlook that generally brought Americans awake in the morning with the feeling the new day would be different or that it could be made different, Sahab and Somayeh couldn't be expected to believe that America of the twenty-first century was indeed different from America of the nineteenth century.

But in an attempt to drive this point home, Curt said, "Times have changed the way we think and behave, Mr. Sahab. An American Indian woman serves as a responsible platoon sergeant in our Regiment. She has been decorated for bravery and valor. And I must assume that you and Somayeh have noticed that American soldiers and even petroleum workers aren't all of the same race." He didn't even try to explain that the twenty-first century American attitude was one of appreciating personal differences rather than ridiculing or hating them.

Sahab nodded. "I have noticed. I do not understand it. But you're right, Major."

"Took us a long time to get used to it, too, Sahab. I like to think we're different, but maybe time will tell," Curt admitted, then got back on the subject. "Now, as I told you, we'd like to retain your services. We're not planning to go

83

into the hills of Kurdistan to kill, loot, and burn. You already know — and if you don't know, I'll tell you in great detail — that troops of our Regiment have been ambushed and attacked by Dervish Kurds in the past ten days. We think these same Dervishes have been the ones that also attacked the Iraqi Petroleum Company's facilities and people. Mr. Chaney told me that Iraqi Petroleum Company has suffered casualties — dead and wounded people, maybe some of them were your friends — and had some of their equipment damaged by Dervishes. We're here to protect you and to stop this sort of killing and destruction. To do that, we're not just going to sit here in Mosul and conduct patrol operations. We're going after the Dervishes who are doing this. We know that the Dervishes and perhaps some other Kurd tribes are being supported by the Soviets. In fact, we know that a battalion of Soviet soldiers is up in the hills right now. We want to go up there, find the Soviet soldiers, and convince them to go back across the border to the Soviet Union and leave the Kurds and the Iraqi Petroleum Company in peace."

Curt paused. Neither Kurds showed the slightest sign of emotion. They sat and listened. So he went on, "We don't want to fight the Kurds. We want to stop the Dervish Kurds from doing what they're doing. We want to stop the Soviets from supporting them and from occupying Kurdistan. We have no intention of staying in Kurdistan. It's Kurd land; we have our own land. The reason we want your services is to keep us from accidentally and unknowingly attacking, hurting, or killing any friendly Kurds. Do you understand what I'm saying?"

Sahab looked at Somayeh. But the younger man shrugged. "Perhaps Sahab does; he has been with Americans longer and understands English better. You are talking about some very complicated ideas. I am not sure my English is good enough to understand all of them."

Sahab began to speak rapidly in Kurdish to Somayeh. Hassan joined in, often speaking haltingly. Then Jerry Allen entered the conversation, speaking Arabic.

Hassan told Curt, "Let Captain Allen and me find out if we can get these ideas across to them. We've decided to speak in Arabic since that's one language all of us understand."

Curt sat back and listened to the flow of words that were largely unintelligible to him. So he let his two officers run the show. Jerry was certainly fluent in Arabic. And Hassan had a basic understanding of these people. Something was bound to come out of it.

It did.

"I'm not sure that I really believe what I am being told," Somayeh finally told Curt in English. "But Sahab says it is the way you Americans do things. I am willing to talk to you about being a guide for you."

Mustafa Sahab added, "We have no problem with helping you now."

"But will you help the Kurds in their desire to have their own nation?" Somayeh wanted to know.

"I don't know. I can't promise you that," Curt admitted to them. "That's beyond my power. The Washington Greys Regiment is here under very specific orders that keep us from doing many things. What we can do and what we want to do is what I've told you."

"Then perhaps it is not worth it," Somayeh decided.

Sahab said something to him in very sharp tones.

Hassan told Curt, "If I understood that, Sahab basically told Somayeh that our operation in Kurdistan would get rid of the Soviets and might produce a situation that might make it easier for the Kurds to get their own nation at last."

"I've got no control over that," Curt said honestly. "After we've stopped these guerrilla raids and gotten the Sovs out, what the Kurds do up there in the hills of Kurdistan is their business. Bellamack sure as hell isn't going to let us get involved on any side in a war of independence. In the meantime, what do you want for your services?" Curt wanted to get into the haggling segment of the meeting. He knew from experience in the Arab world that these two Kurds would bargain sharply and shrewdly. He was prepared for it and knew that he'd have help from Hassan.

Sahab surprised Curt by suddenly stating flatly, "We are being paid by the Iraqi Petroleum Company."

Curt was ready to accept that. But Hassan wasn't Nei ther was Jerry. Curt didn't understand why at first

Hassan shook his head. "That is not satisfactory to us."

Dammit, Hassan, what the hell are you trying to do, cost the United States Treasury more money? Curt thought savagely. He almost interrupted Hassan at this point.

But Jerry continued at once, "If you are going to work for us, we are the ones who should pay you, not Iraqi Petroleum Company!" He shifted into rapid Arabic.

Sahab smiled. "How can one argue with that ancient wisdom? Very well, what is your offer?"

"What is your current pay at Iraqi Petroleum?" Hassan countered.

"Ah, why should we tell you and therefore be the first to set our price? You can certainly find that out with your magic computers!" Somayeh reminded him.

Curt decided to sit back and listen to this. He wasn't a good haggler.

Hassan certainly was. Curt remembered how a much younger Hassan had bargained with him before. Hassan knew what he was doing. He'd grown up in a culture that haggled and bartered. And he'd survived by doing it.

On the other hand, Curt also remembered how naive Jerry Allen had once been in this regard, in spite of the young officer's knowledge of the Arabic language. He listened with a certain amount of pride to Jerry whose experience in the world since then — and especially in Brunei — had indeed been broadened by his close relationship with Adonica Sweet who had grown up in the culture of the Caribbean where bargaining was far more prevalent than in the United States. Jerry was developing a definite smooth and sophisticated gloss on top of his youthful enthusiasm and gung-ho attitude. Part was due to the fact that Jerry had been blooded in combat and had had to face the realities of life and death. Part was due to the fact that his emotional needs were being more than fulfilled by his relationship with Adonica, and this had channeled the sexual river that flooded through all young men (and even those who weren't quite so young any more, like himself, Curt decided). And part was due to Jerry Allen's incredible memory which he'd learned how to call upon and use.

After about twenty minutes, it was settled. Jerry had used what he'd learned from Adonica when she'd served as a "third lieutenant" native guide in Trinidad. Hassan used what he'd learned in his own haggle with the Americans that had resulted in his eventual commissioning in the United States Army. The deal was straightforward. The Greys would match the Iraqi Petroleum pay rates of both men plus twenty-five percent additional for "hazardous duty." Sahab and Somayeh had to take leave of absence from Iraqi Petroleum and give up the salaries there while working for the Greys. If something happened to them, their pay would go to their families. The Greys would arm, armor, feed, clothe, quarter, and provide medical care and treatment for them as "third lieutenants."

And it was lunch time. As they broke for chow, Curt asked Jerry, "What was that bit of wisdom you quoted to Sahab, Jerry?"

"I told him, *Nothing knits man to man like the passage from hand to hand of cash.*"

"Omar Khayyam? Or the Koran?"

The young Captain grinned and said in a low voice to Curt, "Neither. Jerry Allen. I needed something that sounded profound, so I made it up out of bits and pieces!"

Curt laughed. "Jerry, you'll come to a bad end one of these days!"

"I certainly hope so, sir! Only the good die young!"

Chapter Twelve

"Carson, *you're* the sonofabitch who's responsible!" The booming voice came from a large, heavy-set man with a shaved head, large sunglasses, and a huge handlebar mustache. He always spoke as if every other word was emphasized. And there was no question that he was a pilot; he wore leathers—which weren't required these days but which were the classical attire of hot pilots—and a set of wings not only on his jacket and shirt but also alongside the Washington Greys badge on his blue tam.

"I usually get blamed for a hell of a lot of things, Cal. What are you trying to dump on me this time?" Curt asked, looking up from where he was having lunch with Major Alexis Morgan in the Regimental Mess.

Major Calvin J. Worsham, commander of the Regiment's AIRBATT, tossed his head toward the person following him. "*Her*," he said cryptically. "She just reported aboard. So *I'm* going to impose upon you and join *you* for lunch!"

The person following him was a trim, pretty blonde woman whom Curt knew. "Hi, Major! Both of you!" she chirped.

"Nancy Roberts! I'll be damned! You made it!" Curt said in recognition, rising to his feet.

"Yes, indeed, she made it!" Alexis added. "With silver bars to boot!"

Lieutenant Nancy Roberts had once been a Sergeant in Captain Elwood Otis's Maintenance Company. A private pilot, she'd done such an outstanding job flying a Mexican drug lord's commandeered aerodyne in Sonora that Curt, with Bellamack's help, had pushed to get her into Army pilot training. Naturally, she'd made it with honors. And through OCS as well.

"Indeed join us! I can put up with Cal if two ladies are present to stomp him unmercifully when he gets out of hand. Welcome back to the Greys, Nancy! And congratulations!" Curt told her.

"Thank you. I'm glad to be back. Sure been some changes made in the Greys, too," she replied as she sat next to Worsham.

"Mostly as a result of what happened in Sonora and on Kerguelen," Alexis remarked.

"Kerguelen?"

"Oh, yeah, you probably haven't heard about that one," Curt recalled.

"You mean Cal hasn't bent your ear about it?" Alexis asked in surprise. "Don't worry. He will. He was a hero."

"You'd *better* believe it! And the Warhawks got the decorations to *prove it!* But we didn't get any for Kerguelen!" The CO of AIRBATT stabbed a finger at a ribbon on his chest. All flyboys wore their decorations on their shirts under their leathers not only because they didn't have to wear cammies but also because the ribbons were "bragging strips." Army aviators tended to sulk in the shade of their more glamorous counterparts in the United States Aerospace Force; as a result, Army aviators had become boisterous exhibitionists in an attempt to overcome the appellations of "chain gang rock busters" and "bot chauffeurs," as USAF pilots derided the Army pilots' missions of close support tacair and tactical airlift.

"Yeah, it was a black operation some of us would rather not remember real well," Curt muttered, recalling the incredible cold and terrible wind. He'd decided he was a desert rat at heart, and he much preferred the warm, dry climates of the world. He was glad the Greys were permanently stationed at Fort Huachuca in Arizona and, on this rotational shift, had been sent to Mosul. Of course, there was something to be said for the warm, lush, laid-back tropics or the stimulating alpine high country of the mountains. But those were for leave and relaxation, not places for active duty or even combat where you had to get down and dirty in the actual environment itself.

"So, Cal, why the hell are you trying to blame me? And for what?" Curt asked the Regiment's Air Battalion chief. "Nancy's a damned good pilot. She flew a badly overloaded AeroBianchi aerodyne into the Sierra Madres at night . . . without encountering rock-filled clouds, I might add."

"Well, *you* sure as hell wouldn't be here now if she had," Worsham growled. "She's probably a *pretty* good pilot. She'd *have* to be to make it through Fort Rucker. But, then, *all* the girls who've been assigned to AIRBATT are good. So I can blame *you* for that!"

"I can't figure out if you're bragging or complaining, Cal," Alexis pointed out. "But then I never could."

"Come along with *me* for an aerodyne ride so I can get *you* qualified for the One-Kay Badge, Major," Worsham said with a leer. "Then you'll find out *for sure!*"

Alexis shook her head. "No way, flyboy! I've read the Op Directive that circulated about that. You just want to find some innocent girl so you can get requalified!" She was referring to a humorous and very unofficial "Destroy Before Reading" document denying Army Aviation's request for suspension of Rule Ten to permit its pilots to qualify or requalify for the legendary 1K Badge. The Badge didn't exist in reality—although Cal Worsham did indeed have a bogus 1K Badge which he wore on his shirt alongside his wings when he was feeling rebellious at the Club. It was another bit of aviation folklore which supposedly honored those who had managed to engage in sexual intercourse in an aircraft flying at an altitude of 1,000 meters above ground level.

"Hell, I'll accept the blame for the girls in your squadron," Curt admitted, using Cal's preferred aviation nomenclature for the Air Battalion; the AIRBATT people thought that calling themselves a "squadron" was a little classier than "battalion" which was a term applied to a group of gravel crunchers. "But if that's all you've got to bitch about, Cal, something's wrong. Maybe you ought to check with Ruth Gydesen and get a physical . . ."

Worsham was assaulting lunch, but he stopped long enough to remark, "What I'm really blaming you for is encouraging *this* woman to go for pilot training in the first place. She's not here *five hours* before she starts nagging me about why I won't assign her to the Tactical Air Support flight."

"I wondered why your head wasn't shaved," Alexis said to Roberts.

The new pilot officer had an edge on her voice as she replied, "I fought with you all in Bisbee and Sonora. Got shot at. Shot back. Now the Army says that just because I'm a pilot officer instead of a lowly tech sergeant, I can't fly anything but the unarmed Chippewas. Now I can be shot at, but I'm not allowed to defend myself."

"Look, Lieutenant," Worsham told her firmly, "I *can't* do a damned thing about it. That policy is a hold-over from the time when *all* tactical battlefield aviation *except* the old choppers was an Air Farce responsibility. When the Army *finally* got its hot little hands on tacair at long last, some of the Aerospace Force policies came with it. Air Farce *won't* allow women to fly combat aircraft. *Not* like the Navy where a commander can use *everyone's* talents as required. Figure yourself damned lucky in the first place, because it wasn't until *after* Kerguelen that the Army relaxed policy enough to *allow* women pilots in their squadrons in the first place!"

"What would you do if you had a choice, Major?" Roberts was certainly persistent, and Curt was worried that she might cause Worsham to toggle over.

But she didn't. Worsham seemed to be permanently toggled over to begin with. "I don't *have* a choice. Let's not worry about what *might* be. We're going to have our hands full with what's *going* to be . . . if Rumor Control is right. And *that's* what I wanted to talk at you about, Carson! What the hell is this fucking bot flush I hear about *us* having to go out and play *manned birdbot?*"

"Hell, Calvin, that's part of AIRBATT's mission," Curt reminded him. "When you're not creaming someone on the ground or hauling us around in airportable mode, you're supposed to help out by being eyes in the skies."

"Well, shit, I know *that!* Tell me something I *don't* know, Carson!" Worsham fired back, finishing his main course, shoving it aside, and starting on dessert.

"Like what?" Curt wanted to know. He and Worsham

were both Number Two in the Regimental pecking order, both being batt commanders along with Major Wade Hampton who ran SERVBATT—although Curt was de facto second-in-command as the senior combat-rated officer in the Regiment. He also knew he had to work with Worsham, which hadn't been any real problem in the past once Curt had let it be known to Worsham in no uncertain terms that he wasn't going to dump on Worsham and wouldn't put up with Worsham dumping on him. Curt didn't mind Worsham's diamond-in-the-rough attitude; that was the man's image and always had been. But Worsham had a history of pissing off prissy staff stooge types who believed that a person who was certified as being an officer and a gentleperson had to behave that way at all times. However when it came right down to the lickin' log, Curt knew that Major Cal Worsham was one brave man as well as being someone he could count on when things went to slime. Cal Worsham was perfectly capable of being polite, respectful, and mannerly with high brass and VIPs when he had to be. But he let it all hang out when he was among the people he worked with. He was telling the world to accept him as he was—which included being one hell of a shit-hot tactical aerodyne driver.

"Hell, *recon* means replacing ordnance with sensors and recorders," Worsham reminded them. "That's S-O-P! Well, I've got news for *you*: A 'dyne is a big fucking target, *especially* for a Baby Sam or a Wasp! I am *not* anxious to take a Golden BB and *not* be able to retaliate in kind against the bastard who shot it at me!"

"Major, welcome to my world!" Lieutenant Nancy Roberts pointed out.

"Yeah, I *know!* I flew Chippies for *more* hours than I care to remember, including some that were *goddamned* cold and dangerous! Doesn't mean I *like* it, by the way!" Worsham grumbled. "Reason *I'm* pissed is that Rumor Control says we're going into search and destroy mode. Search means *us* in recon mode. Since it's S-and-D, it means *someone* out there doesn't like us and is going to be shooting at us *every* chance he gets. But I haven't heard *Word One* about any change *whatsoever* in the S-O-P Damned if I want to tell *my* tacair pilots to go out there and snoop like the regular pipeline patrols and *not* be able to shoot back if we find some juicy target!"

"Cal, I think you've got the Garbled Word," Curt told him frankly. "You ought to know better than trust Rumor Control! Our job is to go out there, find the Kurds who are giving us shit, go after the Spetsnaz batt that's reportedly in the area, and cream the whole outfit."

"Yeah, so I'm told! I *was* at the OSCAR brief!" Worsham admitted. "*But* S-O-P from Gulf Command *still* requires us to go into recon mode with our ordnance *replaced* by stuff that doesn't go bang. I don't *like* it, but damned if I want to get *my* ass in a sling with General Picky Pickens by disobeying one of *his* directives!"

"Does the Colonel know about this restriction on you?" Alexis suddenly asked.

"I don't know," Worsham replied flatly.

"Well, tell him Major!" Nancy Roberts put in. "I've served with the Colonel before, and I know he's the sort of man who goes to bat for his troops. Some time I'll tell you about the Great Fort Huachuca Latrine Battle which proved to all of us that Colonel Bellamack is always willing to let his troops have their head." She smiled impishly.

"*That* was a goddamned poor pun, Lieutenant! A dozen more like *that* and I'll restrict *you* to the Club in off-duty hours!" Worsham warned her.

"Yes, sir! The punishment would fit the crime."

"Cal, will the Harpies hack both a recon pack and ordnance?" Curt asked.

"Damned right! We put in our *full* load of twenty-five millimeter ammo and take out only *four* of the Em-one-hundred rockets and slip the recon packs right into the tubes. Leaves us with *eight* smokers to use if we have to," the AIRBATT commander explained. "Plus the *two* guns which can hose a *lot* of jackets into the sand if we need to do it."

"Let me get this straight, Cal," Alexis said in a questioning tone. "Gulf Command directives say that our tacair goes out on recon with no ammo and no rockets. Yet you need only four of your twelve tubes for the sensor and recorder gear. What's the reason behind that? Or is there a reason? Or is it just policy?"

"Naw! Cheap Army *bean counting!*" Worsham exploded. "If a Harpie fires its rockets or guns when carrying *sensors* too, the rocket exhaust can either *smear* an exhaust deposit on the sensor windows or even *burn out* the i-r. When we fire the twenty-fives, the *vibration* can shake the shit out of the recon gear, which causes it to *quit* so it has to be sent back for Level Two maintenance. So it costs too damned much *money* if we go armed to *defend* ourselves or *cream* a target of opportunity!"

"Gawdamighty, Cal, Alexis is right! That sort of crap has got to stop!" Curt himself exploded. He pushed back his plate and started to get up. "Come on, let's go see the Colonel about this."

Worsham didn't prepare to leave with Curt. Instead, he said, "What makes *you* think that a mere *colonel* can get a *three-star* to change his mind?"

Curt grinned and so did Alexis. "Not only because we've got some cosmic magic orders, but mainly because Wild Bill Bellamack is one hell of a convincing managerial type. Me, I'm just a combat type, but the Colonel can and has sweet-talked full four-stars out of their shorts to get what we want. By the way, Nancy, if you're finished, come on over and say hello to the Colonel; he'll be glad to see you again!"

Chapter Thirteen

"So we just sit on our asses here and wait!" Kitsy Clinton complained.

"Well, I hardly think that's what you're doing, my dear," Curt pointed out. "Besides, my research confirms the fact that you really don't have very much to sit on anyway, although you do indeed make the best of what you've got in a very satisfactory manner. . . ."

She propped herself up on an elbow but didn't roll over. She didn't have room to do that. Army beds don't have much room for more than one person comfortably. But in off-duty situations, comfort sometimes isn't Number One priority. "I'm very glad you qualified that, sir! If you hadn't, I would have been forced to do something about it to prove you were hasty in your judgement and that your data stinks. By the way, how much longer are we going to be on this three-shift patrol schedule? When are we going to go out and clobber the bastards?"

Curt shrugged his broad shoulders. "We maintain the current procedure until Jerry and Hassan report back. Sahab and Somayeh said they'd lead them right to the proper Kurd chief."

"This is the second day they've been gone. I'm worried," Kitsy admitted.

"They're armed. They've got tacomm and a report-in schedule," Curt reminded her. "So far, everything's copacetic."

"So we won't go chasing off into the boonies until we have someone to chase, right?"

"Right!"

"So we stay here and suffer eight-on and sixteen-off with

a rotation every few days to break the monotony?"

"Suffer? Monotony? You? Am I loosing my touch, Kitsy?"

"Not that I've noticed, but I need to reconfirm my data occasionally. Very occasionally, I might add. My own research program is proving that it's just as good on a warm afternoon," Kitsy replied softly. "Let's conduct some more research!"

"I'll go along with that!"

"You'd better! I fight when I'm insulted or ignored."

"I've noticed."

"I want you to notice some other things now. . . ."

And, as usual, it happened again. The comm unit in Curt's room chimed.

"Damn! Again!"

"Better get used to it," Curt advised her. "The Army way of life."

"I'll never get used to it. Some day, I'm going to go AWOL—Absent Wishing Occasional Loving."

Curt answered the comm without keying the visual, a commonplace response in the Washington Greys which didn't automatically mean that one was with one's POSSOH. Personal privacy was zealously guarded in off-duty hours. And even with the general acceptance of relaxation nudity, some people preferred to be seen only while properly attired in the proper uniform. "Carson here!"

It was the duty officer, Captain Ellie Aarts. "Hate to disturb you, Major, because we all need our rest, but . . . Yankee Alert, and Colonel Bellamack wants to see you ASAP. Papa session."

"Ellie, you imply that rest means sleep, and you ought to know better," Curt told her frankly. "I'm on my way. Fifteen minutes."

"The Colonel says make it ten minutes," Aarts told him. "The recon team has reported."

"Ten it is!"

And ten minutes it was.

But not without problems because Curt had rushed things.

"Your fly isn't velcroed," Bellamack pointed out quietly

as Curt walked in. No one else in the room even snickered. It had happened to them. And in some cases, it had almost happened on this very occasion.

"Sorry, Colonel, but I wasn't informed what the situation was, so I wanted to be ready for anything," Curt replied easily, saluting and taking the seat Bellamack indicated.

Colonel Bill Bellamack didn't say anything more but appeared to be waiting. Curt glanced around the room. Everyone normally present for a Papa or plans session was there except Captain Russ Frazier. Curt steeled himself to be on the receiving end of a reprimand from Bellamack because, as ASSAULTCO Bravo commander, Frazier was Curt's responsibility. But Bellamack said nothing.

Frazier dashed in, somewhat disheveled, two minutes later.

Saluting, the company commander said quickly, "Sorry, Colonel! I was inside a Mary Ann!"

"Hell of a cramped place to be with a woman on a warm afternoon," Bellamack remarked dryly. The regimental commander knew that his people were in a de facto standdown situation except for running the usual and compulsory patrols up to the border every day, so he didn't wear his martinet hat under these conditions. However, he wasn't happy when someone was tardy, perhaps because of the laid-back possible pre-combat situation when Rule Ten wasn't in effect. So he said sternly to Russ Frazier—although his words were also directed to others in the room who might run afoul of his ire, "Captain, when I request that you do something within a given time period and I do not receive a rational assessment from you concerning the possibility you may not be able to meet the time constraint, I expect you to be where I want you to be when I want you to be there! This is especially important in a combat situation! I will not allow the discipline of the Washington Greys to slip even a little bit just because we happen to be in a very boring pre-operation situation right now! Consider that I've given you a verbal ass-chew, so sit down, shut up and listen!"

Frazier sat down, didn't say a word, and listened. Something had Wild Bill jerked off, and this was no time to piss around with him. Frazier knew he'd gotten off easy.

Bellamack turned to his regimental communications staffer. "Sergeant Cook, please reestablish contact with Recon Team Alpha."

Regimental Staff Sergeant Georgina Cook was one of those who'd come up short a slot in the reorganization of the Washington Greys into their new, streamlined, versatile TO that had been tagged the "Ghost" configuration because everyone was and could be anywhere in the table of organization at any time, depending on the situation. Everyone in the Regiment was cross-trained into another job with the exception of the high-tech specialists. But everyone had received combat training and field experience in war games. History had shown that everyone in a Sierra Charlie regiment had to be prepared to engage in personal combat. It was one of the consequences of putting human beings back on the battlefield alongside the warbots instead of sitting back in the rear area running warbots by remote linkage. It was a natural for the Washington Greys who became the "Grey Ghosts."

But, since it was Army policy under the regimental system to keep people in their units for as long as possible not only for unit morale but unit efficiency and, even more important, the tradition of the Washington Greys to take care of their own, Bellamack and Gratton had given people the opportunity to change Rated Position Codes and thus remain with their units. If that couldn't be done for any reason, or if a high-rated and high-ranked NCO would lose points or perks by changing, special "semi-temporary semi-permanent" slots were found or made for them.

Regimental Staff Sergeant First Class Georgina (NMI) Cook was one of those whose long term in grade and many years of service resulted in a staff slot being created for her in the new TO&E. She was outstanding at C^3I. especially the C^3 part. So she was now handling nearly all of the regimental communications, an extension of her former job under Captain John Gibbon in the now-defunct Headquarters Company commintel unit. She was a quiet, competent, older woman who could have taken early retirement, but she didn't. "What am I supposed to do? Go back to Georgia, sit on the porch, and sing songs in the twilight? Not me! This is my life!" she'd stoutly maintained, and stayed.

"Recon Alpha, this is Grey Head," Cook intoned the call-up in the standard format. "Acknowledge, please."

It took only a few seconds for Jerry Allen's voice to come back, "Grey Head, this is Recon Alpha! Go!"

Cook nodded to Bellamack who took over. "Jerry, I've convened a Papa session. Give me a verbal download of the information you've picked up thus far."

Except when the pressures of battle or the need for precise communications demanded them in giving and confirming orders, formal comm procedures were usually tossed aside by the Greys who knew one another well and also knew enough to ask for clarification if something was misunderstood. "We're meeting with the leader of a group of Kurds known by their tribal name, Ahl-i Haqq. The boss man is Sharaf Massoud Qazi. We've established good rapport, but they don't really trust us all the way yet. We must be surrounded by about a hundred Ahl-i Haqqs. The ladies of the Regiment will be interested to know that about half of the Ahl-i Haqq guerrilla personnel are women. The Kurds don't seem to have any compunctions about allowing their women to fight. Or going unveiled, for that matter. At least this group, anyway."

"How are they treating you? Are you being accepted or viewed with suspicion?"

"A little of both," Allen replied. "They've been fighting for so long that they're naturally suspicious of any soldiers. But we have a leg up on them. We're talking in *their* language! I can follow them okay when they speak Arabic. However, Sharaf Qazi has taken a real shine to Hassan because Hassan's knowledge of Baluchi lets the two of them talk together. Except Hassan says it's like speaking with someone having an atrocious accent."

"Okay, so much for the background report for the benefit of the rest of the Greys present here," Bellamack observed, then prompted him, "You said earlier that you were dickering with them about helping us. So what's the deal? Have you come to any agreement yet?"

"Negatory, Colonel!"

"What's the heartburn there?"

"Sharaf Qazi doesn't believe us."

"What doesn't he believe?"

"Number One: that we won't roll in here with our warbots and simply crush them. Number Two: that we're Americans who are brave enough to come out from behind armor and fight with them down and dirty on the ground," Allen's voice explained. "Colonel, I don't blame them. From what I've been able to piece together, the American warbot regiments that have been here before were dedicated strictly to patrol and guard functions; they never went on the offensive against the Dervish tribes or the Sovs, and both have been giving the Ahl-i Haqqs and the other Kurd tribes a lot of grief over the past few years. It doesn't seem to faze Sharaf Qazi that the Robot Infantry troops were merely following orders and trying to stay out of local conflicts. The Kurds perceived and still perceive the Americans as being cowards who are afraid to do anything except protect foreigners and foreign facilities around here."

"Do they realize that's what the standing orders have been? That it's because of international agreements with the Iraqi government? That we haven't been able to move because of UN pressures?"

"They do. And they consider us to be cowards who are afraid to do anything except patrol and protect," Jerry confirmed, continuing his report. "Sharaf Qazi is pissed off that the Americans haven't come up into the hills here and taken care of the basic problem: the militant Kurds and their Soviet supporters. As a result, his tribe along with others has had to fight other Kurds as well as the Iraqis, the Turks, the Syrians, and Iranians, and the Armenians. I really don't know if we can get any help or support out of Sharaf Qazi and the Ahl-i Haqqs at all. At the moment, Sharaf Qazi doesn't consider us to be any real factor in the local equation; we're just someone to be tolerated because we can't be whipped in a fight and driven out of northern

Iraq."

Bellamack turned to Sergeant Cook. "Get Georgie on line and let's have some holographic topography here. I need to see where Allen and Mahmud are right now."

"Roger!" Cook signaled crisply, keyed her control console, and sat back. She knew her regimental commander so well that she didn't need to ask him what he wanted to see just then.

By means of a complex data link of satellites, fiber optics, tight laser beams, very low frequency earth-resonance, and other channels which were so classified that even Cook didn't know about them, Georgie, the megacomputer of the 17th Iron Fist Division underground half a world away at the Army maxicomp center under Diamond Point, Arizona came quietly on line, quickly building a ghostly three-dimensional map of the area north of Mosul in the holo tank of the Grey's snake pit.

Playing her keypad like a piano, Cook entered other commands and linked the Regiment's computer, "Grady"— so called because someone once referred to the much smaller and less capable computer as equivalent to a dumb female regimental whore and quoted Kipling about "Judy O'Grady;" however, the ladies of the Greys quickly perverted that to the masculine "Grady" and the male members of the Regiment decided they'd better quit before they lost too badly.

The location of the two beacons of Jerry Allen and Hassan Mahmud flashed onto the holographic map.

"Tell me distance between Mosul and those two beacons," Bellamack instructed the computer.

"Distance one-one-niner kilometers. Bearing zero-three-niner," was the reply from Grady's vox circuit.

"Damn!" Curt breathed. "They're right up against the Turkish border!"

"No real border up there, Major," Edie Sampson pointed out. "In mountainous terrain like that, borders don't exist. Borders are only lines on maps."

"Like Brunei," Henry Kester added with some distaste in his voice.

"Recon Alpha," Bellamack addressed his remote scouting

101

team, "will Sharaf Qazi allow us to fly in a contingent for further parley? We need to show him we're different from the Robot Infantry he's seen thus far. And I need to convince him that we are indeed going on the offensive, especially against the militant Kurds and the Sovs."

After a brief silence while it was obvious that Allen and Mahmud were talking with their Kurdish host, Allen came back on, "He says bring as many people and warbots as you wish. He's not afraid of you, he says. He also says he and his Ahl-i Haqqs can whip the whole Regiment if he wants to."

"Tell him I'll be coming in with an airlift of an assault company," Bellamack replied quickly. "We will be armed, but we will maintain a cease-fire. We will also be prepared to demonstrate to him how we fight. We'll lift off from Mosul as quickly as we can. Hold things together there while we're mounting up. I'll inform you when we lift off from here. Shouldn't be more than a couple of hours."

"Major, that could mean you'll get here at twilight or even in the dark," Jerry observed.

"So? We can fly at night if we have to. And we can fight at night if necessary. But we don't intend to fight. We'll bring some chow and I'll invite Sharaf Qazi and his Ahl-i Haqqs to have dinner with us. If that's acceptable to him?"

After a brief pause, Jerry replied, "Roger, but he won't accept your hospitality without reciprocating. He says they'll have time to butcher a lamb or two for us."

"Good! Tell him we'll garnish it with field rations! I'll get back to you!" Bellamack turned to the assembled Greys. "It should be obvious from the conversation what we're going to do. We're going up there to show them who we are and how we operate. We'll probably do a little Sierra Charlie demo while we're there. We'll go prepared for combat with one hundred hours of consumables, plus our Jeeps and Mary Anns in airportable vehicles. Major Carson, I want you to join me along with Morgan's Marauders. Major Worsham, I want airlift for myself, Majors Carson, Wilkinson, and Atkinson, Sergeants Kester and Sampson, and the Marauders with their warbots and support vehicles. Carson, how quickly can you get the act together?"

Curt looked at Alexis who merely held up a finger. "We're hot to trot and good to go! Have been for days! One hour, Colonel," Curt promised.

"Major Worsham?"

"Same in AIRBATT. When Carson is ready, we'll be spooled up and hot to lift!"

"Okay, we're good to go! Move it!"

Chapter Fourteen

"Load 'em up! Move 'em out!" Colonel Bill Bellamack called to Major Curt Carson.

It was almost a redundant command. Morgan's Marauders had already loaded their 2 ACVs and 4 ARTVs into the brace of Chippewa Assault Transport Aerodynes on the floodlit tarmac of the Mosul casern.

Curt was a little worried that Kurd agents might see all this activity and report it. It was unusual for the American Army to mount a night patrol of this size.

But they were moving fast, and Curt hoped it would be faster than any espionage data could move.

Besides, the Chippies weren't flying unprotected. Cal Worsham had decided to lay on 4 AD-40C Harpies as "cover." Out of earshot of Lieutenant pilots Nancy Roberts and Timothea Timm who'd volunteered to fly the lift, Worsham had remarked to Curt, "Just want to make sure the gals can count on someone to hose a little ordnance around if anyone decides to mistake their aerodynes for clay pigeons. And, Carson, I want you to understand that I accepted Roberts and Timm because of you! Dammit, you were the one who encouraged both of them to go for wings!"

"Wouldn't also have something to do with the fact that both of them are shit-hot pilots, Cal? Or that they're both rated nine-counters on a scale of ten?" Curt asked the AIR-BATT commander.

"Maybe, but angels they're not," Worsham remarked.

"I always thought angels were beautiful ladies with wings. Seems both of them qualify," Curt observed. "Or have I been reading the wrong books?"

"Okay, angels they are," Cal admitted . . . and that was the origin of that nickname for women Warhawk pilots.

At Bellamack's call, 16 people filed through the cargo doors at the lips of each 'dyne.

Lieutenant Tim Timm was in only partial linkage with her Chippie. The new 7/11 AI didn't require tight linkage to fly the Chippies. This allowed the pilot to pay more attention to system management, including supervision of the nav gear. "Howdy, Major! Welcome aboard! My first nonpatrol semi-combat mission, so you're honored!"

"I am indeed, Tim. Can I rock on the front porch with you on the fly in?"

"Be my guest. It'll keep me company. Gets lonely and a little scary up here over unfamiliar terrain at night, especially when we may get shot at," she admitted while at the same time checking the status of her Chippie.

"Lieutenant, it's always scary doing what we do, whether we think we're going to get shot at or not," Curt reminded her. Then he added with a grin which was barely visible in the glow of the red cockpit lights, "But quit sniveling! This is what you said you wanted when we first met in Wiesbaden and you were bitching about not being able to be a pilot."

"I guess I should have kept my mouth shut. On the other hand, this job has its definite benefits and perks beyond that of a crew chief who only gets to sit on the ground and worry." She looked distracted for a moment, and Curt knew it had to be data pouring in through the loose-fitting linkage harness that was installed in her leather helmet. Vocally, she responded for the benefit of Curt although her thought impulses went directly into the Chippewa's 7/11 AI and thence to its flight control computers and squadrons comm net, "Roger, Air Batt Leader! Tiny Tim is ready to lift!" Then she toggled a switch by passing her hand over a lighted portion of the panel. "You might like to eavesdrop on the comm net, Major."

"By all means."

The cargo door swung down, sealing the peripheral lip

of the aerodyne, and Curt heard turbines begin to spool-up.

One of the problems of listening to the comm was that Tim's command channel was also patched in. Thus, he heard her verbalized commands to the ship's autopilot as well as the ship-to-ship comm. But because she thought so much faster than she or the vox processor could speak, the system's spooler had to buffer the output and string it out in slower sequence. Thus, Curt heard commands long after the response took place.

The aerodyne, "Tiny Tim," broke ground, hovered momentarily in ground effect while its computers sought out the proper stability parameters for the ship's load and weight distribution, then continued its lift in a stable fashion.

Alongside, Curt saw the other Chippewa, code call "Fancy Nancy," as it, too, broke ground, and then continued lift.

Above the ship and through the canopy, Curt could see the position lights of the four AD-40C Thunder Devils, otherwise colloquially known as Harpies by the AIRBATT, hovering in cover.

It was nice to know they weren't totally unable to defend themselves if something should go to worms out there in the hills during the fly-in and recovery. The Harpies, under the command of Cal Worsham, would be scanning with their sensors, identifying potential targets, and calculating optimum attack modes. Worsham didn't expect to be interdicted from the air, but he was prepared to go after ground targets. As he remarked to Curt once, "Put a million guys out there with assault rifles and tell them to fire up in the air in automatic mode whenever they see or hear a 'dyne, and your chances of encountering the Golden BB are definitely increased!"

The lights of Mosul passed beneath them and they headed out over open farm land toward the hills to the north. Suddenly, it was very dark below. Unlike the United States where one flies at night with an almost unbroken carpet of starry lights below—except in the Rocky Mountain regions — Curt could see only a few isolated lights, most of them deep orange indicating they were small cooking or heating fires. It reminded him of the times he'd flown into Zahedan in eastern Iran back when the Robot Infantry warbot brainies also operated their own aerodynes, before the assault transport aerodynes became big, expensive, and complicated enough to require dedicated human pilots.

Since there wasn't very much to see outside, Curt turned his attention to the instrument panel of the Chippewa. It hadn't changed very much since Kerguelen, and the UCA-21C version of the Chippie was merely an upgrade of those Worsham's Warhawks had flown back in Operation Tempest Frigid. From numerous field exercises and war games over the past year, Curt had grown to know the Chippie panel which, to a person not in linkage with the aerodyne, told him a lot.

An instrument panel in a robotic aerodyne flown with neuroelectronic linkage is, of course, a redundancy. But backups had been a way of life with flying machines for more than a century. Pilots were understandably reluctant to trust their lives to single systems that could fail. Murphy's Law — named after a man who was a mechanic on the early rocket sleds at Edwards Air Force Base — says that "anything that can go wrong will." So nearly all airborne systems had at least one standby or another parallel system that would perform the same functions. "Single point failure modes" were something that engineers tried to avoid and test pilots — and often other pilots — uncovered when the engineers missed. Airborne systems also had to have some protection against incoming fire.

The Chippewa being a tactical transport craft, it was liberally equipped with backups and redundant systems as additional insurance against the legendary Golden BB, the random small-caliber from ground or air fire that somehow always seems to find the critical place to hit. The Chippie was armored, of course. But even with twenty-first century lightweight armor, there was a limit to how much weight can be allocated to protection. Curt knew he

107

wouldn't get the Golden BB up his ass; the ship had enough armor around the flight desk to stop that sort of light stuff. But a Chippie was a big craft, and it was impractical to armor the whole thing.

Besides, the UCA-21C was also configured so that it could be flown manually with ordinary controls if all the automatic systems went tits-up. You had to have instruments for that sort of thing.

However, some of the instruments were designed on the principle of "don't call me, I'll call you." The pilot could call up the readings for turbine bearing temperatures, for example, if an overheating engine was suspected. Other instruments were displayed at all times; these were the critical flight gauges such as altitude, forward airspeed, vertical airspeed, artificial horizon, and compass heading. Pilots were still taught to fall back in an emergency on the classical "needle, ball, and airspeed" instruments; the needle and ball had, of course, been replaced with far more human-oriented, ergonomic readouts.

Some of the electronic countermeasures — ECM — readouts were also redundant and constantly displayed. Although Tiny Tim could alert Lieutenant Timm at once if the ECM gear detected any potential threat, the visual indicators were flashing lights, classical backups that reinforced the linkage system warnings which sounded in the pilot's brain.

A yellow light on the ECM monitoring panel started to blink. The boxed alpha-numeric readout alongside it reported:

AD-40C formation radar.

Warhawk Leader, Warhawk Mark.

Touch DSPLY 1 for range/bearing.

Suddenly, a second light began to blink red. The readout announced:

Possible Iranian air defense.

Signature: French Nightingale.

The Iranian border wasn't that far away, and the Islamic Republic of Iran zealously watched its airspace. It didn't bother Curt until he saw another red light and boxed

108

alpha-numeric:

Super Rafael search radar.

Monopulse mode.

No immediate threat.

The Islamic Iranian Air Force was aloft in their old French Super Rafael interceptors, just in case. Curt wasn't worried. The Super Rafaels couldn't stay up very long; they were very old, they were fuel hogs, spare parts were hard to come by, and the Iranians weren't renowned for their maintenance abilities. No one in the Arab world was because most men in these cultures had a strong aversion to working with their hands. And they hadn't grown up surrounded by technology as Americans, Europeans, and most of the people of the Pacific rim nations had.

Another reason Curt wasn't worried was because four Harpies were flying cover for them that night.

Timm came out of deep linkage to relax and let Tiny Tim do the work. The new Mod 7/11 AI was a godsend in that regard. No longer did Worsham's pilots or Gibbon's birdbot operators have to stay in constant control of their robotic equipment. She smiled and pointed at the ECM display. "We've been spotted," she announced unnecessarily.

Curt nodded. "Milk run," he commented.

Just as he said that, another light came on with the observation:

Tin Cup search radar pulse.

"Not tonight," Timm replied and went back into deep linkage.

The airtac net was suddenly alive with comments. Since the computer was transliterating them from neuroelectronic commands, the banter lagged what was actually happening.

"Tiny Tim, Fancy Nancy. Did you get a make on that Tin Cup pulse?"

"Got a light. No range/bearing."

"Warhawk Leader here. We got its specs. We're primed to catch its location on the next pulse."

"Soviet Wasps?" That was the English translation of the Soviet designation *Ohssah* for the SA-77 SAM.

"They use the Tin Cup," was the reply.

"Watch for the i-r boost flare!"

"Wilco!"

"The Spetsnaz batt?"

"Negatory! The Sovs have exported the shit out of that old SAM. Much better than the Strela Three."

"Could be anyone down there. Kurds?"

"Maybe. Have the gravel grinders strap down for evasive maneuvers."

Tim Timm's voice came over the Chippie's speaker system, its frequency response limited so it cut through the roaring noise of the aerodyne. As a result, it made her normally pleasant female voice sound sharp and harsh. "Tiny Tim riders, strap it down! Possible SAM evasion!"

Curt toggled his tacomm. "You heard the lady! Buckle up! Now! No one's shot anything at us yet, but we've picked up a search pulse! Someone has a Wasp or two down below!"

"Tiny Tim, this is Fancy Nancy! I'm going down to nap-of-the-earth."

"You really trust your sensors, don't you?"

"I've done this before," was the reply from Lieutenant Nancy Roberts. And indeed she had, flying a commandeered AeroBianchi into the Sierra Madre mountains of Mexico without any terrain avoidance avionics at all. "Follow me, Timothea!"

"Thanks! I'm a rather devout coward. I'll let you find the rocks first!"

Out of the corner of his eye in peripheral night vision, Curt caught a flash of light-heat below and in front, then something coming up from the ground.

Another flashing red light appeared on the Chippie's ECM visual display accompanied by flashing red alphanumerics:

WASP LAUNCH.
Bearing 024.
Range 1745.
Closing.
Probable miss.

110

"Smoky, Smoky! Coming up! Get on the deck, gals. Go stealth!"

"Against a Wasp? Warhawk Leader, give us some decoy cover!"

"Fancy Nancy, it's on your case!"

"I see it heading for Fancy Nancy!"

The sky overhead erupted with several bright white diffuse clouds. Cal Worsham had apparently launched several decoys intended not only to spoof radars but also infrared sensors.

"Okay, Warhawk Mark has bloomed for you! It's locked on the spoof!"

"Warhawk Mark, can you catch the Tin Cup side-lobe?"

"Got it! Wasp is responding to azimuth spoof!"

The sky lit up with the flash of an exploding warhead.

Because of the delay by the computer in processing the NE communications into audio, the announcement followed, "Warhead Leader has Smoky on intercept. We'll SDI it! Rolling in!"

Seconds after the warhead burst came the call, "Fancy Nancy to Warhead Leader! Nice shot! And thank you!"

"Any more Wasps?"

"Negatory! Warhawk Mark is going down to cream the launcher now!"

"I'm seeing you, Mark! Warhawk Leader will cover your right flank and go behind you on the pass!"

Curt wished he could see what was happening. But he knew what Cal Worsham and his wingman, Lieutenant Bruce Mark, were doing. Mark had spotted the launch point and was rolling in on it. Worsham also had the location coordinates from the data link and was swinging around in a wide curve to the right to take the site from another direction with the tacair pass only a few seconds behind Mark.

In the pitch darkness, the hills of Kurdistan lit up as M100A tube rockets hit the ground. The Wasp launcher, if it was still there, didn't fire again and couldn't have survived that two-pronged attack.

Curt's tacomm suddenly erupted with Captain Jerry Allen's excited voice, "Companion Leader, this is Recon Alpha! Call it off! You're putting fire into friendlies! That attack was less than a hundred meters from us!"

Chapter Fifteen

"Goddammit, Jerry, who the hell just shot that Wasp at us?" Curt suddenly wanted to know. "If it's that close to you, did some of your Kurds get itchy trigger fingers or what?"

"Companion Leader, that's not exactly what happened!" came Captain Jerry Allen's reply. Curt could hear the concern in the young officer's voice. "These people . . ."

"Sons of bitches aimed that humper at the aerodyne I'm riding in!" Colonel Bill Bellamack broke in from where he was riding in Fancy Nancy. And he was pissed. One did not shoot accidentally at Colonel Bill Bellamack and get off easily. "Tell them that the next one they fire at us means we turn around and go home! And I'll leave you and Hassan to figure out your own way to save your ass and get back to Mosul!"

"Yessir! I've passed the word. So has Hassan. But why didn't Warhawk Leader see my locator beacon?" Jerry wanted to know.

Worsham was monitoring the tacomm net as well as the tacair net "Because, Mr. Dumb John, I was up to my asshole in Wasps trying to blow my shorts off! Looks like my seven-eleven didn't spot it or didn't report it to me if it did spot it! This seven-eleven stuff is still full of maggots!" That didn't answer the question, and Curt knew Bellamack would hold an informal inquiry later and ask the inevitable embarrassing question of Major Cal Worsham concerning why the Warhawk Leader's AI system had failed without Worsham detecting it. Thus far, the new Mod 7/11 AI equipment had performed with very few bugs and worms, and most of the ones that had surfaced were immediately spotted and overridden by smarter human beings—as it should be, which is why surviving humans never turn over everything to a robot, especially when their pink bods are involved.

"Colonel, it isn't the seven-eleven gear. It's just . . ." Allen began and was again interrupted because the aerodynes were getting very close and prelanding chatter began to fill the frequencies.

"This is Tiny Tim! I have Recon One's locator beacon now! My seven-eleven had not been preprogrammed to look for it," Curt's pilot admitted.

"There's always someone who doesn't get the word. . . ." came an unidentified voice. It might have been Nancy Roberts. But Curt knew who the patsy was; the accusation could not be made by a subordinate officer. Cal Worsham had either forgotten to pass the word or had overlooked it in the heat of the Wasp attack. Either way, it was Worsham's responsibility, and he'd damned near caused the regimental commander and an assault platoon to be wasted as a result. Whether or not Bellamack had words with Worsham, Curt decided he'd have to chat with the AIRBATT commander himself. Worsham was a guy you could count on, but he did have a tendency to toggle over to hyper-combat mode to the exclusion of all else. In some ways, Worsham was like Captain Russ Frazier of Frazier's Ferrets: outwardly unafraid of a fight because that bravado covered gnawing, almost consuming inner fear of being killed or maimed due to lack of aggressive approach. In other words, keep from being hit by hitting first. It was a perversion of the basic Patton doctrine by which the Washington Greys fought as Sierra Charlies: *Hold 'em by the nose with fire while you kick 'em in the ass with movement.*

"Roger! Fancy Nancy has the beacon, too!"

"After you, Nance!"

"Roger! Watch my lights!"

Curt saw the brilliant white beams of Robert's aerodyne landing lights come on, illuminating the ground in a wash of light that seemed as bright as day.

114

Tiny Tim then lit up, too, and Curt could see that they were flying over semi-forested rolling foothills with broad meadows. Groups of huts and hovels dotted the landscape below as they came into the bright beams of the landing lights.

If anyone wanted to shoot at two very prominent targets, now was the time, Curt thought.

That part of the mission had been choreographed in advance. The Chippie carrying Colonel Bellamack was to land first, followed immediately by the one carrying Curt. The four Harpies would continue to orbit, providing cover, then go to ground in standby ready-scramble mode to keep airborne targets to a minimum and also eliminate the possibility that the meeting site might be located by the Soviets or Dervishes.

But what Bellamack didn't choreograph and what no one expected was the reception they got.

Tiny Tim touched down about twenty meters from Fancy Nancy once the dust from the downwash of the first aerodyne had dissipated. Once both 'dynes were on the ground, the cargo doors on both opened simultaneously. Bellamack debouched first. When Curt saw him step out of the other 'dyne, Curt stepped out.

Both were followed by Sierra Charlies of Morgan's Marauders.

Following the Marauders were the Jeeps and Mary Anns.

Bellamack did not debouch the ACVs and ARTVs. They were overwhelming and looked too much like futuristic battle tanks. Curt had suggested to Bellamack that this should be a people-to-people meeting but with the warbots present as well in the background as a signal of the additional power of the American Army.

It worked in one way but didn't work in the other.

Bellamack should have paid attention to Jerry Allen instead of becoming engrossed in the matter of being shot at by a Wasp SAM.

The landing area was surround by armed men and women clad in the loose-fitting clothes and headgear of the

Kurds.

All of them—more than two hundred were standing in a circle around the grounded 'dynes—were armed with a collection of Soviet AK-17s and AK-74s, American M16s and Hornets, British Sterlings and Webley-Fosburys, and German HK-26s.

And they just stood there.

Over the tacomm came Hassan's neuroelectronic "voice," *Grey Head, this is Recon One Bravo. I recommend that you order the Greys not to unsling their Novias and that the Jeeps and Mary Anns do not bring their guns out of travel position . . . no matter what happens!*

What the hell is going on here, Mahmud? Allen, explain! Bellamack snapped on tacomm.

Colonel, I tried to warn you before you landed, but you were pretty busy with the SAMs . . . which are a part of this whole affair! Jerry's neuroelectronic "voice" replied. According to doctrine, he was verbalizing his reply into the NE circuitry of the tacomm to keep everyone around him from hearing him.

As I asked, what the hell is going on here? Bellamack persisted.

It's a sort of a welcoming ceremony, Colonel, Hassan's NE "voice" cut in. *Sharaf Qazi wants to test you before he lets down his guard.*

Test me?

Sharaf Qazi will try to provoke you, Hassan tried to explain. *He will try to learn whether you're a man of honor or a man of emotions.*

What the hell is he planning to do?

Neither of us knows, Jerry replied. *Just remember: don't flinch! He tried to provoke us when we found him, and Hassan kept me from shooting the guy's lips off! So please stay cool, Colonel! Sharaf has us outnumbered even with our warbot firepower! And let Hassan do the translating rather than working an interactive translation channel with Georgie. Computers are magic jinn to these people!*

Curt knew something about the enduring Islamic belief in jinn and devils in spite of the teachings of the Koran.

116

And the disembodied computerized voice of the 17th Iron Fist Division's megacomputer, Georgie, back underground in Arizona, would certainly be magical to these hill people in northern Iraq.

From out of the gloom beyond the carpet of light from the two 'dynes strode Captain Jerry Allen and Lieutenant Hassan Mahmud, accompanied by a tall, weatherbeaten man who had the aura of a chieftain and leader. A young woman, shrouded in the Kurdish version of the Arab burnoose, was with them.

Curt walked over and joined Bellamack, alert and on his toes now because he didn't know what to expect. However, if Jerry and Hassan had survived a provocative welcome by keeping their cool, Curt would try to do the same and would also do his best to keep Bellamack from losing it. However, Curt knew the Colonel could be a very cool character when necessary, although he did become excitable when combat was imminent.

The two groups stopped less than a meter apart. Sharaf Massoud Qazi seemed impassive and imperious. He spoke and Hassan translated. "I welcome you to my presence! I have invited you to come in peace. Your emissaries have indicated you came in peace. You show much power. So I will see if you indeed come in peace."

And with that, he rapidly drew what looked like a long, curved kris whose shiny blade reflected the lights of the aerodynes. In a smooth movement, he quickly brought it alongside Bellamack's throat, edge to the Colonel.

Bellamack didn't flinch. He was wearing body armor, and it would take more than a sharp knife to cut through the Krisflex armor fabric that surrounded his neck in a skintight skein. "We come in peace," Bellamack told him coolly. "So why do you threaten me?"

Sharaf Qazi reached out with his other hand and patted Bellamack softly on both cheeks without moving the blade a fraction of a millimeter. The Kurd chieftain then smiled. "Because you threaten me with your warbots." The word *warbot* came out in English because the Kurd language had no word for a war robot. "I know about the American warbots. American Army Robot Infantry soldiers have been here for many years with their warbots. Warbots are powerful but can be defeated. But they are used to threaten!"

Bellamack didn't move and told the man, "My warbots are like your soldiers whom I see all around us. My warbots are servants to my soldiers. I see your soldiers threatening me with their rifles. But my soldiers and my warbots do not have their weapons ready to use. I come in peace to talk. Let's do that!" And he extended his right hand.

Sharaf Qazi could not take Bellamack's proffered hand without taking the kris blade from the Colonel's throat. He did so, then, replacing the weapon in its scabbard at his belt. As he took Bellamack's hand, his smile was broad and genuine.

When the surrounding Kurds saw this, they raised their weapons skyward and let off a fusillade of small arms fire. The din was deafening.

The discipline of the Washington Greys held. No one even twitched in a way that might indicate a Novia was being unslung and brought around into firing position.

"We will save our ammunition for the troublemakers around here who are giving us both sleepless nights," Bellamack promised Sharaf.

"We have other causes of sleepless nights." Hassan had a little problem translating this remark by Sharaf Qazi.

The Kurd chieftain motioned his companion forward. "You should know that we have women warriors just as you do in the American Army," Sharaf Qazi pointed out. "This is my valued subordinate, Shariat Khani."

The woman let her burnoose fall around her shoulders, revealing feminine features that, while soft and young, had nonetheless seen far too much of the harsh environment of the hills of Kurdistan. Yet her eyes were bright, and she had a sense of purpose and competence about her.

Major Morgan, front and center! Bellamack ordered over the NE tacomm circuit. "Then you know that we too have women who fight alongside us. But they're not like the women warbot soldiers you've seen in the American Army in the past. Our women now also fight with us in the field."

When Alexis reached the group, Bellamack told her, "Take off your helmet, Major."

"Sir, we're in a potential combat situation here," Alexis tried to point out.

Bellamack shook his head. "No, that was just Sharaf Qazi's form of welcome. Take off your helmet and meet another warrior, Shariat Khani."

The two women, worlds apart in terms of cultural differences, stood and looked at one another. Alexis was bigger, but Curt wasn't sure whether she could prevail against Shariat Khani in hand-to-hand. The young Kurd woman also looked as hard as nails.

Alexis extended her hand. "I'm Major Alexis Morgan, Shariat Khani. Looks like we're both real-life Amazons."

In perfect English, Shariat Khani told her, "Where do you think the Greek legends about the Amazons came from, Major?"

"It's obvious you haven't spent your whole life in these hills," Alexis observed.

"I was well-schooled by Englishmen in Baghdad," Khani explained. "But unlike the American Army, in the Ahl-i Haqq tribe, we maintain the old tradition. We're not allowed to marry until we've killed a man in war. Now that you're allowed to fight in the field, is that also true for you?"

Alexis smiled. "Not exactly. Different rules. We still have to fight to get a mate, but usually it's against other women! And that sort of fight rarely gets physical. However, I qualify under your rules! Shariat Khani, I think the women in our Regiment will get along fine with the Amazons of the Ahl-i Haqq!"

Chapter Sixteen

"So why did you fire a Soviet Wasp at us?" Colonel Bill Bellamack wanted to know. They were meeting now by the light of several dim oil lamps inside an incredibly old house made of baked clay bricks. It looked like it should have fallen to the ground a couple of centuries ago, but it was apparently well-built and was also the headquarters for the Ahl-i Haqq high command. "Didn't Captain Allen and Lieutenant Mahmud tell you we were coming on a friendly mission?"

"They did," Sharaf Massoud Qazi replied in good but accented English.

Bellamack and Curt had surmised that Qazi was both shrewd and distrustful. The Kurd chieftain kept his cards close to his chest at all times, revealing nothing to these strange Americans except as it became necessary to do so.

"One does not always believe everything one is told by soldiers, even soldiers of the American Army," Qazi went on.

"My officers are men of their word," Bellamack insisted.

"That may be so, but I did not know that. And it still remains to be proven, although you and your officers have shown you can be trusted . . . thus far." Sharaf Qazi was exhibiting what both Bellamack and Curt had come to know as the typical wariness of the Mideast tribesman. But this fiercely independent chieftain had more of this wary distrust of strangers than anyone either American had come up against in their years of service in the Persian Gulf Command. "By launching a Wasp, we

120

learned of your tacair aerodynes, and we lost nothing because we moved our people and the launcher away before they counterattacked the launch site. You lost nothing because you were prepared for such a thing and moved to avoid being hit. You learned that we take nothing for granted. We learned that you are fully prepared to fight back and defend yourselves. Not all American forces stationed here have behaved that way. You are not cowards."

"And if we had not shot back?" Bellamack asked.

That was an unnecessary question. "The hired Kurds who brought your officers here would have been properly dispatched. Your two officers would have been returned to you with a few—ah—modifications to indicate we were not afraid of you," Qazi replied smoothly, a slight smile twitching over the corners of his mouth in the flickering orange light of the oil lamps.

"Colonel, the ancestors of these people were the Assyrians," Jerry pointed out. "The Assyrian Empire was built on the principle of terrorizing the populace with no quarter given to enemies. The Assyrians never took prisoners . . . or if they did, the prisoners didn't live very long."

"I know. I read Ferrill's classic on the origins of war. Which is why I want the Kurds on our side in this thing," Bellamack admitted, then turned again to Qazi. "May I ask where you got the Soviet Wasp? Are you being supported by the Russians?"

The response was sudden and emphatic. Qazi spat out "No!" in two languages. He glared at Bellamack. "We have Soviet Russian rifles. We have Soviet weapons of all sorts. We were not given these weapons. We took them as part of the spoils of war. A weapon is a weapon, and we don't care where it was made as long as it is useful. We also have some of your American weapons, but not your new rifles and none of your war robots. We would like to get your new rifles."

"Our Novia rifles can't use the Soviet ammunition," Curt advised him.

"Once we have rifles, ammunition is not hard to steal

because it is smaller and not so closely accounted for," Qazi reminded him. "I would like to have some of your rifles and ammunition."

This was something both Bellamack and Hassan understood: barter, bargaining, cutting the deal. Curt sat back and listened to the haggle.

"What are you willing to trade for our guns?" Hassan asked, opening the discussion.

"What do you need from me? You obviously need something from the Ahl-i Haqqs. If you did not, you would not be here tonight," Qazi observed quietly.

"As my guides and officers have told you, it's my mission to stop the guerrilla raids that have bothered us and to get the Soviet military unit to return to their country," Bellamack explained again.

"Soviet Russians? Here in Kurdistan?" Qazi acted surprised.

"I'm sure you know exactly what we mean, Sharaf," Jerry Allen interjected quickly. "When I explained this to you earlier, you gave me the impression that you knew of the Soviet Spetsnaz battalion and are as anxious as we are to get it out of these hills."

"Suppose a Soviet battalion was in the hills," Qazi retorted. "What do you intend to do to get them to retreat to the Soviet Union?"

"Find them first," Bellamack outlined his mission plan. "Then try to convince them to go home. We'll also broadcast the information that the Soviets have troops in Iraq contrary to international agreements. Once this news is out, the Soviet leadership in Moscow will either abandon this Spetsnaz battalion or recall them. Either way, we want to get them to go back to the Soviet Union without having to fight them."

"You don't wish to kill these Soviet invaders?" Sharaf Massoud Qazi seemed very surprised at this announcement.

"We may have a different view of war than you do, Sharaf," Curt entered the conversation again, trying to explain and get through the man's obvious cultural mind

122

block. The Kurds had been fighting for centuries. They hadn't changed their fighting policy, even though it hadn't succeeded in getting them national status. Maybe they knew no other way. Maybe Qazi might understand that there was another way of fighting and winning. "We've learned that it's sometimes possible to win without fighting and killing. Sometimes it's possible to shame an enemy into retreating if he can withdraw without losing honor. Sometimes it's possible to arrange things so that both sides appear to win."

"How is that possible?" It was Shariat Khani who spat out the words defiantly. "If you don't kill an enemy, he comes back another day to kill you!"

"Not always," Alexis Morgan said for the first time in this conference. As the commanding officer of Morgan's Marauders and as a woman soldier, she'd been asked to participate in the conference. Thus far, she'd seen no role she could play in the negotiations between Bellamack and Qazi. Now she did. "Sometimes it's possible to make a friend out of an enemy if it's to his advantage. Then you've got an ally against other enemies."

"That's possible only if you buy off the enemy! You Americans can afford to do that because you're rich!" Khani replied to Alexis. "You give away your wealth! You're the biggest suckers in the world because you'll give away everything you own in the hope of making friends and allies!"

Alexis laughed. "Shariat, you don't understand. Sure we're rich. But we can't possibly give away everything. So we give gifts to friends. Believe me, it's a lot better to live with friends around you than to be surrounded by enemies!"

Shariat Khani snarled, "*You're* the one who doesn't understand, Major Morgan! You can't buy the Ahl-i Haqq!"

"Who said anything about buying the Ahl-i Haqq?" Alexis fired back.

Curt knew he had to step in here, even at the cost of incurring the wrath of Alexis and possibly a verbal asschew from Colonel Bellamack. Shariat Kahn was right:

Alexis *didn't* understand. He wasn't sure that Bellamack did, either. Most Americans wouldn't. They didn't understand what it meant to be poor, really poor, with little or no hope of things getting any better.

When Curt was an Army brat, he'd always resented a very wealthy uncle, his mother's brother, who had things the Carsons could never afford because Army pay was never enough. His uncle had delighted in giving them gifts they usually couldn't afford even to use. Curt had never succumbed to the belief that his uncle should share his wealth or that other rich people didn't deserve what they had. Curt did object, however, to being treated as a poor relative. And from his own military experience in Africa and the Persian Gulf, he knew that same feeling was behind Shariat Khani's remarks.

It's a feeling of hopeless inferiority. When you have to treat someone as a superior whom you can never equal in any way, you end up hating yourself as a result.

Curt hadn't understood that until his overseas military service. Now, he understood it all too well. He'd quit hating himself and taking it out on other people when Henry Kester had been the NCO of his first command, a platoon in the Washington Greys. He would always thank Henry Kester for subtly redirecting Curt's energies away from an inferiority feeling and toward the personal concern a leader must exhibit for his own subordinates, many of whom might think that way. It was Henry Kester who'd shown Curt that he had to give subordinates hope of progress and advancement that would make them strive for it. So Curt knew that the self-hate born of hopeless inferiority is usually the sand of social friction that causes heat when people meet.

He had to turn it around here before it got out of hand and screwed up the whole operation.

It wasn't Alexis's fault for bringing it up. In fact, Curt resolved to thank her later for doing it.

"Shariat Khani, it isn't a matter of giving you gifts or buying your honor," he said firmly, taking command of the situation by leaning forward where he sat on the dirt

124

floor of the room and thus putting himself slightly ahead of even Colonel Bellamack in the circle. "We want something, and we've told you what it is. We think what we want is also something the Ahl-i Haqqs and the Kurdish people want. We may look powerful and we may actually be powerful, but we use our power with great care. You have power of your own that's different. Now, let's see if we can reach an agreement where we get what we want and you get what you want. If you can't help us get what we want or if we can't help you get what you want, we'll go back to Mosul."

Bellamack reached out and laid a hand on Curt's arm. Curt merely replied in a low voice, "Colonel, let me cut through some crap here."

The Colonel knew that Curt was a leader whereas he was the organizer and manager. This had become patently clear during the years the two men had worked together. Bellamack just wanted to make sure that orders were carried out — and returning to Mosul empty-handed at this point wasn't part of the orders. As regimental commander, Bellamack was the one who had his ass bared to the breeze if he came back with nothing. Curt's response to Bellamack's unvoiced question confirmed that he knew what was going on. And also that the rapport between the two men was still strong and working. So Bellamack was willing to step back a bit and let a man with expertise carry the ball. The coach can't be the quarterback, too.

"We can't give you our Novia rifles," Curt went on. "We don't have enough of them to give away. In that regard, we're poor. And Colonel Bellamack would get into trouble. Do you remember the arms scam in Bahrain a few years ago when American Army officers were caught dealing in American weapons with some Arab tribes?"

Sharaf Massoud Qazi nodded. "We tried to get some of those weapons. But the Arabs wouldn't deal with us. We still want American weapons. We want your Novia rifles."

"I can't give them to you," Colonel Bellamack put in, knowing that he would be in deep slime if he tried. He'd been one of the officers who'd blown the whistle on superiors who were carrying out that scam. As a result, a lot of the friends of those who'd been caught were still out there, waiting for him to make a mistake so they could get him. He wasn't about to let that happen. And because of that, he wasn't about to ask General Pickens for any weapons to trade with the Kurds. And he'd be in trouble with Pickens if he asked Carlisle at JCS. This was a sticky situation, and Bellamack didn't know whether or not he and Curt could come to any sort of agreement with Qazi under the circumstances.

Qazi shrugged. "Then we have no basis for an agreement. You go your way and we will go ours."

"Why do you want more weapons?" Curt suddenly asked. He knew the answers, but he wanted Qazi to come up with the answers.

"To continue our fight for freedom and our own land, Kurdistan," Qazi replied in a straightforward manner.

"How long have you been fighting for this?"

"As long as the Kurds have been a people."

"Fifty centuries. Perhaps more," Shariat Khani added.

"Did you ever stop to think that after all those years of failure maybe you were doing something wrong? That maybe you should try something else?" Curt persisted.

"American, what else can we do when Kurdistan is occupied by Turks, Syrians, Iraqis, and Iranians? When they send out tax collectors to demand tribute from us? When they send armed soldiers with the tax collectors? When they use force to put down our efforts to gain freedom?" Qazi wanted to know. "You live in a dream world! It is not our world!"

"We want guns to shoot the tax collectors and their soldiers," Shariat Khani explained.

"They'll just send more. They always have," Curt reminded them. "Ask yourself what you have that they want. Certainly it isn't money. Or grain. Or sheep. What do you have that's valuable to them and to others?"

Qazi laughed. "Nothing! Our land is worthless to them! But they take what little we have in order to keep us from growing and progressing!"

126

"I don't think your land is worthless, Sharaf Qazi," Curt continued. "And I think you have something they want. Otherwise, the Iraqis, Turks, Syrians, and Iranians wouldn't waste their time hassling you. It's not worthwhile to expend the time and effort to hassle you otherwise. Especially since they also know you're tenacious and will fight to hold what you believe is yours."

Curt didn't realize at that time that he in turn was looking at the situation with the unique perspective of one who has grown up in a complex world of international economic bartering, a world where time is considered to be money and where the principle of the "cost-benefit ratio" reigns supreme.

But he didn't have time to pursue it further.

Neither did anyone else there.

The unique, warbling, zipping sound reached their ears. It was something like someone tearing open a very long Velcro seam.

But everyone in that ancient room in that ancient building knew what it was.

"Incoming!" was the sudden call from Henry Kester.

But he didn't have to give warning. Everyone had moved fast.

Two huge explosions rocked the hovel.

Chapter Seventeen

Someone had fired three 100-millimeter Chinese S-220 rockets at them from the surrounding hills.

They might have been made in Burma, or they might have been Soviet copies of the Chinese weapon system, but no one mistook the distinctive sound of their approach and arrival.

Curt slammed his helmet back on his head, got to his feet, and ran into both Alexis and Jerry in the narrow doorway to the outside.

No one wanted that fragile old building to collapse on them.

But if the attackers had planned on the infrared seekers of the S-220s to do the final job of targeting, they hadn't counted on the fact that the old i-r sensors in that weapon system deteriorated quickly and badly without special storage facilities.

The three incoming S-220 rounds missed the neat heat target of the building with its infrared plume of smoke rising through the smoke hole from the fire within.

But even when an S-220 misses, it carries enough explosive in its 100-millimeter diameter to cause more than a little nastiness when it arrives.

Only two of the incoming rounds detonated. The third, the closest one, didn't; it merely plowed a rather large hole in the rocky soil.

Lack of quality control, poor design, sloppy field treatment, and the general shortcoming of the S-220 saved their hides. The weapon had been primarily designed to counter Soviet T-110 Main Battle Tanks, and the Soviets had discovered it would also take out nearly any armored vehicle possessed by its potential enemies; it had seen widespread production in spite of its shortcomings. When it turned out to be a poor anti-tank weapon, it was relegated to use as a guerrilla light artillery piece, and that's what it was that night.

Curt didn't waste any time, and neither did Bellamack. "Colonel, we'll hit 'em on the ground with the Marauders! We need to get the Harpies up for tacair! And the Chippies the hell out of here so they don't take a Two-twenty!"

The night was suddenly filled with small-arms fire punctuated by an occasional incoming S-220. The small-arms fire was nearby, which told Curt that he was hearing the Ahl-i Haqqs firing at possible targets. But the occasional incoming S-220 also told him that the assaulting enemy was possibly more than a kilometer away because of the high incoming trajectory angle of the rockets which were being used as artillery.

There's nothing quite as unnerving as an unexpected night assault. You don't know at first who's out there shooting at you, or how many of them are out there, or how many others are just waiting for the fight to develop before they pitch in and get nasty. Curt was pissed off that the Ahl-i Haqqs had such damned poor security that such a night assault could even be mounted against their high command. He and Bellamack hadn't worried about that sort of thing, assuming that Sharaf Qazi would naturally cover his ass with all sorts of security in the form of pickets and sentries all around the meeting place. That assumption had apparently turned out to be wrong. The Ahl-i Haqqs may have had the reputation of most Kurds for being a fighting bunch, but Curt was beginning to wonder if maybe the reputation had been enhanced somehow. After all, if the Kurds hadn't won in fifty centuries and were still vulnerable to an unexpected night assault on the headquarters of one of their tribal chiefs, maybe they just didn't know they were doing something wrong. Maybe they hadn't won in five thousand years because they hadn't been doing the right thing. In warfare, you either learn damned fast or you don't survive to learn. Maybe the Kurds hadn't learned but had been hardy enough to breed fast enough to cover losses.

The Kurds might have some modern technology in the form of smart rockets which sometimes didn't work very well, but they were in the classical situation of soldiers who are forced to fight at night, something many commanders in the past had flatly refused to do.

Fortunately, the twenty-first century Washington Greys were equipped to fight at night using highly sophisticated and very accurate infrared sensors; invisible ultraviolet target designation and ranging lasers; chemical sensors capable of picking up the unique smell of human beings as well as the vapors from vehicle exhausts; and computers that were fast, artificially intelligent, and capable of laying guns, giving people information on their tactical helmet displays, and generally using technology to overcome the fact that humans can't see in the dark.

"Roger your assessment!" Bellamack snapped. "Shift to November Echo tacomm!" *Marauder Leader, this is Grey Head! Debouch your vehicles and warbots! Go to ground! Tacair Leader, get your Harpies up and looking for targets! And get your Chippies up and away before they take incoming!*

Grey Head, this is Conqueror Leader! came Kitsy Clinton's "voice." *We have a make on the source of the incoming! We have a target! Bearing zero-seven-three! Range two-point-five-zero klicks!*

In the blackness that now enveloped the Kurd village as a result of the incoming fire, Curt heard four aerodynes spooling up. Worsham was wasting no time getting the AD-40C Harpies up. *Roger, this is Tacair Leader! We're up and we'll move a little mud in that area! Fancy Nancy and Tiny Tim, spool-up and lift out of there as soon as the vehicles have cleared your ramps! Withdraw three klicks south and go to ground and cover with turbines spooling and stealthed for i-r!*

Damn! No GUNCO! was Jerry Allen's comment. As the top heavy artillery expert in Major Joan Ward's gunnery company, he not only had charge of 4 75-millimeter Saucy Cans in their LAMVA vehicles, but he also had the responsibility for targeting. But all the Saucy Cans were back in Mosul because this was supposed to be a fishing expedition to seek help from friendly Kurdish tribes. The mission had sufficient firepower to protect itself, but to Jerry's mind it would have been better to have some "heavy stuff" just in case. *Marauder Leader, this is Alleycat Leader! You ought to be able to reach them with the twenty-fives on your Mary Anns!*

Just barely! was the reply. *That's out where the rounds don't have much energy left! So I'll order airburst just to scare the shit out of them!*

This sort of communication went on very rapidly because it was subvocalized by each person and picked up by the skin pads of the neuroelectronic equipment in each combat helmet. It was more than twice as fast as verbal communication, but it took a lot of training to be able to filter out one's personal thoughts and keep stream of consciousness thinking out of the communications system. Everyone had had some regular warbot training, though, and some had been warbot brainies before becoming Sierra Charlies.

The exception was Lieutenant Hassan Ben Mahmud, and the NE tacomm channel was suddenly jammed with his undisciplined thoughts in the Baluchi language.

It suddenly came to a halt, and Curt saw through the gloom of darkness well enough to learn what was going on.

Captain Jerry Allen had grabbed Hassan. A brief scuffle ensued before Jerry yelled. "Hassan! I've got to turn off the November Echo equipment in your helmet! You're jamming the tacomm net with your thoughts."

"What the hell do you mean?" In the heat of taking incoming fire for the first time in his career, Hassan's Baluchi background had almost overwhelmed his American-imposed military discipline.

"Go verbal, goddammit!" Jerry shouted, found the switch point on Hassan's helmet, and activated it. "You'll have to talk your communications now! No time to explain more! I'll give you the course in Battle Comm One—

oh-one when we get back to Mosul! Okay, you're off-line!"

Good work, Jerry! Curt transmitted to his former subordinate.

Art-Vees are on the ground! Mary Anns and Jeeps coming out! reported Alexis Morgan.

Spool-up and shag out, Fancy Nancy and Tiny Tim! Bellamack snapped.

Curt checked the tactical display on his helmet visor by looking up at its dull red night vision presentation. The disposition of the Washington Greys company and additional people showed up clearly. The fast-moving targets were tagged as the Warhawk Harpies, and the large moving blips were noted as the Chippies moving south and away from the action for security. *Where are the Alley Hacks?* Curt asked no one in particular, using the phonetic nickname of the Ahl-i Haqq tribe the Greys had unconsciously adopted that night.

This is Puma Leader, was the comment from Lieutenant Lew Pagan, one of the new platoon officers who'd been promoted up from the NCO ranks because of past performance as a Sierra Charlie. *I've spotted some i-r signatures that seem to be Alley Hacks firing back at the intruders. And I've got some additional i-r targets that may be small-arms fire from the enemy!*

Put it on the tac display! Curt told him, *Okay, I've got it! Alexis, transfer control of all Marauder Mary Anns to Pagan so that the Pumas can form a fire base! Everyone else will join the maneuver team! I don't know where the hell the Alley Hacks are, but we'll use our usual tactics: Hold 'em by the nose with fire while we kick 'em in the ass with movement! Allen, I want you and Hassan to find Sharaf Qazi and stick on his ass as our communications link with the Alley Hacks!*

Curt didn't stop to think that he'd basically taken over the tactical command in this fight. He had such a solid and well-honed contract with Bellamack that it seemed natural for him to step into tactical command. However, he was brought up short by Bellamack's remark, *Carson, you run the fight, and I'll work the Alley Hack coordination with the help of Allen and Mahmud!*

The sharp muzzle blasts of the 25mm M300 automatic cannons on the Mary Anns told Curt that Pagan had commenced fire on the rocket site targets. The new officer was doing the right thing, putting single shots in at maximum range using airbursts against potential nonarmored ground troops. His radars were following the shots, spotting the burst points, and then his computers were relaying the guns for the next shot closer to the i-r targets.

Grey Head, this is Tacair Leader! We have multiple targets! was the call from Cal Worsham aloft with the 4 Harpies. *We've pinpointed the rocket launch sites and we'll go for those. Otherwise, our i-r and chem sensors indicate about a hundred men dispersed between you and the rocket sites. Whup! We've just gotten a make on another group off to the west, to your left! Different i-r and chem signatures, and they seem to be holding position and not firing!*

Small-arms fire had increased now. From the sound of it, the Greys weren't involved yet because Curt didn't hear the distinctive sound of Novias or the 7.62mm M133A automatics on the Jeeps. The Ahl-i Haqqs apparently had engaged the enemy, judging from the i-r displays on Curt's helmet visor.

Grey Head, this is Assault Leader! What I would like, sir, is for the Alley Hacks to mount a frontal assault on the initial dispersed force and rocket launch sites that Tacair Leader has pinpointed, Curt remarked to Bellamack. *We're going to go flankers left up those hilly slopes with the Jeeps in the van and the Charlies following the Jeeps. We'll sweep the gullies with sensors as we go so we don't get bushwhacked. If we run into this bunch on the left and they turn out to be nasty, I'd like TACAIRCO to help us pinpoint targets and bust a few rocks for us. In any event, we'll try to make contact with the flanker group and either blow their shorts off or have TACAIRCO discourage them while we nail the first ambush party from their right flank. Got any heartburn with that, sir?*

Negatory! Sounds workable! Go get 'em! And keep me advised! I'll be following you on the tac display! his regimental commander told him.

Marauder Leader, this is Assault Leader! Curt called to

Alexis. *Henry and I will be right with you on this flanker move. But you call the micromoves!*

Companion Leader, unless those targets up ahead have night vision equipment, I think we've got it made, Alexis replied, using the old and familiar code call she'd grown used to when she was a platoon leader in Curt's company, the Companions, which was now the TACBATT. *The Kurds don't seem to have much high-tech night vision equipment, so I think we're pretty safe unless they get an actual visual on us . . . which is going to be pretty damned hard to do as dark as it is!*

Don't bet on it, Alexis! Curt warned. *We don't know who the hell is out there ahead of us now.*

"Might be smart, Major," a quiet voice came to him from his right side, "if we had TACAIRCO stand by to lay a little ordnance on them and discourage them if they turn out to be nasty."

Curt looked and saw Regimental Master Sergeant Henry Kester about two meters to his right. Curt just nodded and motioned to the old soldier to stay with him, which was unnecessary because that's exactly what Kester was going to do anyway and had always done. His battalion sergeant major, Edie Sampson, was following to his left. The Greys had recovered from the initial shock of a night attack, had it together, and were reacting properly according to doctrine and their training.

Curt found Alexis's beacon on his helmet display and moved to merge the plot.

Night vision equipment made it possible for them to move together almost as well as during the daytime. Once having joined up with Alexis, they all began following the eight Jeeps moving ahead up the rolling terrain in a line of skirmishers. No one fired. There was no need to fire. At this point, they needed to move rapidly without drawing a lot of attention and to conserve ammo against future confrontations.

But they hadn't gone more than two hundred meters before one of the Jeeps reported, *Marauder Leader, this is Conqueror Alpha. I have ten targets ahead of me. Visual analysis indicates they are military personnel, not guerrillas or insurgents.*

134

They are wearing berets and . . . Incoming! Incoming!

Sparks flew as jacketed rounds ricocheted off the armor of two of the Jeeps ahead.

Chapter Eighteen

From the sound of the impacts, the bullets that hit the Jeep were 7.62-millimeter high-velocity rounds.

The Jeep asked, *Orders?*

It was Kitsy Clinton's Jeep, but it was also programmed to respond to the voices of other people in the TACBATT. So Curt snapped, *Conqueror One, can you identify the source of the incoming? Who's shooting at you?*

The reply was immediate, but three more rounds bounced off the Jeeps' armor even in the millisecond time period it took for the neuroelectronic communications to go back and forth, *Human soldier, armored, helmeted, identity unknown. He is shooting a Chinese A-ninety-nine assault rifle of the bullpup configuration developed by the Soviet Army.*

That was a surprise to Curt. He'd counted on running into only fanatic Kurd tribes out here, not well-armed and well-equipped modern infantry units. He didn't want to believe what they might now be up against. They were woefully undermanned.

Alexis Morgan's thoughts were running in the same vein. *My God, have we encountered the Soviet Spetsnaz battalion this soon?* was her incredulous question.

If the target was indeed a member of the Spetsnaz battalion Curt knew was in these hills, it meant the man was armored in the same fashion as the Washington Greys. A well-placed 7.62-millimeter round from one of the Jeeps might put the soldier down, but it wouldn't kill him. So Curt ordered, *Open fire on any target that fires on you!*

The response from the Jeep was instantaneous, but it fired off a three-round burst before it replied, *Fire on anything that fires on me! Roger from Conqueror One!*

Companions all, this is Companion Leader! Curt immediately communicated with his single-company battalion. *We may have encountered the Soviet Spetsnaz battalion! Grey Head, we may need you over here on the left flank to communicate with the Russkies!*

Roger, Companion leader! Grey Head is coming! Warhawk Leader, hold fire on the unknown unit on our left flank, but be aware they may be Soviet Spetsnaz troops with anti-air capability! was Bellamack's response.

Curt's Jeep was up ahead alongside Kitsy's. Curt had nicknamed it "Bucephalus" not only because that had been the name of the sturdy warhorse of Alexander of Macedon but also because the word also meant "bull-headed," which is why that legendary horse was named such in the first place. *Companion Leader, this is Bucephalus! The target fired upon by Conqueror One has disappeared from visual, infrared, lidar, and chem sensors! I see no further targets in the area!*

"What the hell?" Curt said aloud.

Lieutenant Kitsy Clinton was now beside him but maintaining battlefield discipline at a distance of about three meters. Over the continuing din of the firefight going on to their right between the Ahl-i Haqqs supported by the TACBATT's Mary Anns and whomever had bushwhacked them, "I don't pick up anything on my sensors, either."

"Kitsy, you're not a warbot," Curt told her, alluding to the fact that even the Jeeps had a better sensor suite than any of the individual human soldiers. The Sierra Charlies simply couldn't have handled the weight and bulk of the sort of total sensor package mounted even on the little Jeeps.

"Thank you for reminding me, sir. I've sometimes wondered about that since there have been times lately when I haven't gotten even the attention of a warbot!" she shot back without rancor. Sometimes when the going got shitty

137

in combat, Kitsy had the tendency to be rather sharp and brittle, especially with a superior officer she knew as well as she knew Major Curt Carson. "But, Major, whoever was out there is *gone!*"

Warhawk Leader, this is Companion Leader, Curt called up to Cal Worsham aloft in his AD-40C Harpie and conducting surveillance when he wasn't busting rocks during ta-cair assaults on the site where the S-220 rockets had been launched. *Do you still have a make on all those targets here on our left flank?*

Affirmative! But they're dispersing rapidly to the northwest! They haven't shot anything since that initial series of bursts at your Jeep.

Companion Leader, this is Grey Head! I'm coming up on your five o'clock position, range about thirty meters! What the hell is going on over here, Curt? Colonel Bill Bellamack sounded about as confused as Curt was at the moment.

Whoever was out there took a couple of shots at one of our Jeeps then got the hell out once the Jeep returned the fire, Curt explained.

Curt saw Bellamack approach through the night vision scope deployed from his helmet visor. Lieutenant Hassan Mahmud was with him. The conversation continued over the neuroelectronic tacomm channel although the two men were now close enough to one another that they could have conversed verbally. Staying in NE tacomm mode meant that others on the tacomm net could hear what was going on. And in a confusing night battle such as this, both communications and sensing were key to keep from being wasted.

I intend to continue the original advance, Curt decided. *Sorry you came all the way over here, Colonel, but I thought for sure we'd encountered the Spetsnaz boys.*

You might well have, Bellamack told him. *A Spetsnaz unit might have been out here waiting to either flank us or move in behind us and go after the Alley Hacks left down there in the hovels. It's my guess that one of their riflemen panicked when he saw the Jeep, opened fire, and was immediately told by the Spetsnaz commander to shit and git because the unit's stealth*

138

security had been compromised. In other words, the Spetsnaz unit is outta here. That's the way they work.

Curt might have been the tactical leader of the team, but he deferred to Bellamack's expertise on Soviet tactics because the Colonel read, understood, and spoke Russian. Thus, the regimental commander knew how the Soviets tended to fight, especially in the Spetsnaz teams which were their equivalent of the British SAS Paras or the French *Legion Etrangere Especials.*

Except that the Soviet Spetsnaz units could be drawn from the ranks of the KGB troops and usually were. The KGB was still a very enigmatic, secret organization. As "The Sword and Shield of the Party," the KGB was one of the reasons why JCS and NSC still didn't totally trust the Soviets.

I want to leave four Jeeps here to cover our rear, Curt told his unit. *Clinton, you're in charge of them! Just make sure you holler loud and clear the instant you think someone has come back and may be getting ready to hit us from the rear.*

Yes, sir! Must be my day to get all the shit details!

FIDO! Soldier, shut up and soldier! Curt used the expression Henry Kester had taught him many years before when it was snivel time. He knew that Kitsy was gung-ho and tactically eager; she wanted to be where the action was. But he needed someone to cover their asses while they made the flank assault on the enemy who'd fired the S-220 rockets at them. Kitsy would do the job fine. She'd be all alone with four Jeeps, and Curt knew she'd be scared shitless and overly sensitive to anything that even so much as moved out where the unknown unit had disappeared.

Yes, sir! I think I'll also go out there and check to see if my Jeep hit whoever fired on it. I bore-sighted Conqueror One pretty good, and it should have nailed that guy dead nuts.

Okay, but keep an eagle-type eyeball peeled for the rest of the outfit, Curt reminded her unnecessarily. He knew she would. *Companions all, this is Companion Leader! Continue our planned flanking maneuver! Move it! Allen, I hope to God you've still got our beacons on your displays!*

139

I won't let the Mary Anns shoot into you, Major! came the quiet reply.

Grey Head will stick with you, Companion Leader. But I'm sending Mahmud back to continue to serve as communications with Sharaf Qazi, Colonel Bellamack advised. *No sense in me going back when we'll all be converging on that hill within a few minutes anyway. Mahmud, shag your ass back to where the Sharaf is.*

"Sir, he's about to lead the Ahl-i Haqq assault up that hill," Hassan pointed out.

So you get back there fast and tell him to hold off until we hit 'em from the left side. Otherwise, he's going to lose a lot of men in the assault! Bellamack warned. *He can't afford to lose men. He hasn't got enough in the first place!*

That sort of tactical error had probably been made many, many times in the past, Curt thought, which was perhaps one reason why the Kurds had been fighting for five thousand years without success. Maybe the Greys could teach them something about winning tactics.

While this neuroelectronic conversation as going on, Curt kept moving as planned. The Companions battalion—what there was of it, just one company plus some Jeeps and some of the regimental leadership—turned the right flank of the enemy position and began to move in on them.

It was always eerie making a night assault in total darkness with only sensors to substitute for human eyesight and show the way. The Jeeps were better at it than the Sierra Charlies; they should have been because sensors were the only means the Jeeps had for seeing where they were and where they were going in the first place. The human soldiers had to switch from their natural sensors—eyes—to the artificial ones of infrared, lidar, radar, and chem units. Infrared was most useful for spotting obstacles, while pulsed lidar was great for ranging because of its high accuracy. Radar was useful only in the doppler mode to get approach rates toward obstacles already identified by i-r and ranged by lidar. At this stage, chem sensors were pretty well useless because they were more or less a recon and surveillance tool than a movement aid.

And no one shot at them as they made the flanking maneuver.

If the attacking force up on the hill more than two klicks from the Ahl-i Haqq village had any night vision sensors, they weren't using them to scan the countryside for possible flanking attacks such as the one the Companions were carrying out. Curt set his helmet computer to monitoring for any active lidar or doppler interrogations from the enemy position; he couldn't detect passive infrared sensing, of course. If the enemy had any night sensors, they were concentrated to their front, not to their flanks. Which made Curt wonder what kind of tactical dummies were involved in this skirmish. He could put up with the gung-ho nationalistic fervor of Sharaf Qazi and Shariat Khani; he might be able to teach them something they could use if the deal went through—which it hadn't yet. If the Ahl-i Haqqs were regularly up against the sort of primitive guerrilla operations exemplified by the rocket attack that night, it wouldn't take much training in modern tactics for Qazi to end up being top dog of the Kurds around here, Curt decided.

Medic! Medic! came the sudden cry. It was Kitsy. *This is Conqueror Leader with the four Jeeps! I need a medic right NOW!*

Bio-tech Sergeant Ginny Bowles, the Marauder's bio-tech, answered before Curt could get on the net. *Conqueror One, this is Marauder Medic! Ident your beacon so I can find you! I'm following Marauder Leader, so I'm not very far away!*

You've got the ident, Ginny! Make it fast! I told you I'd bore-sighted Conqueror One for close-range operations! It performed right to spec! Got this guy twice with a seven millimeter, once where he wasn't protected by his body armor! Kitsy reported. *He's bleeding pretty badly, and I can't stop it! Make it fast! I don't want this guy to die. In fact, the Colonel won't want him to die, either.*

From what Kitsy had just said, Curt had a pretty good idea who she'd found. *Conqueror Leader, this is Companion Leader! Sounds like you've identified the victim. Tell me who and what.*

Her computer-vocalized voice immediately replied, *He's*

141

wearing no insignia, but that's commonplace even for us when we go into combat. But there's no mistaking the fact that he's Soviet! He's wearing Sov equipment, carrying Sov weaponry, and made the mistake of carrying those godawful Russian cigarettes in one of the pouches of his equipment harness.

Curt then knew that the man had to be Soviet! No one else in the world would even think of smoking Soviet cigarettes, even people in the poorest developing countries who'd become addicted to nicotine in all its plant leaf forms. The Soviets couldn't grow decent tobacco even when they'd tried to steal good germ plasm and grow good stock; their climates and soils weren't right. So Soviet citizens couldn't get anything but the horrible *pahpeerohsah,* and they were scared to smoke non-American cigarettes normally found in this part of the world for fear of additional hallucinogens that might be mixed in. As the American Army had learned its lessons with regard to mind-altering substances in Vietnam, so the Red Army had learned in Afghanistan back in the twentieth century.

Curt had never smoked. It just wasn't done in America any longer. Americans weren't prudes; that particular fad cycle had peaked and waned, and Americans were now involved in far more sophisticated "nasty habits" because, as one of his West Point fitness instructors had once pointed out, "The sum of all vices remains constant." But Curt couldn't understand why people in Europe and especially in developing countries would willingly become addicted to nicotine, hashish, pot, or the so-called "hard drugs." But they did.

Bellamack broke in, *Save that guy! If I can get him to talk, he's damned important!*

I always do my best, Colonel, was the quiet reply from Bowles.

Curt knew she would; she was a competent bio-tech. Excited as he was over actually capturing a possible Soviet Spetsnaz trooper, however, Curt knew he had to carry through and finish the job of making the flanking assault on the guerrilla position.

They had only another hundred meters or so before

142

they got close enough to be a factor.

Thus far, the flanking maneuver hadn't been detected. Suddenly, it was.

Chapter Nineteen

Curt heard the snap of the bullet's shock wave as it went past him. Since you don't hear the shock wave unless the round misses you, that didn't bother Curt. But the adrenalin level in his blood immediately increased dramatically as a result. Someone up on that low, rolling, rocky hill had probably heard the warbots coming, although the Jeeps were very quiet machines.

But whoever was up there didn't have infrared sensors or laser targeting. Otherwise, that round wouldn't have missed him. Or the Jeep.

So whoever was up there was shooting at shadows, spooking at sounds, or snapping off a round Just In Case. However, in so doing, the sniper had given away his position.

Companions all, open fire when you have a target ahead! he passed the order along to his troops immediately, then added, *Companion warbots, open fire on any target ahead of you that fires upon you!*

Orders to humans had to be a little different than those given to warbots. In spite of the sophisticated Mod 7/11 artificial intelligence circuits in the Jeeps, they were still pretty damned stupid when compared to the highly trained Sierra Charlie soldier of the Washington Greys.

He was mildly surprised by the rapid response from the Jeeps. Three of them opened fire at once, squirting off short bursts from their 7.62-millimeter M133A heavy-fire machine guns. That was one of the advantages of a warbot; it responded quickly and its fire was absolutely deadly.

All the Jeeps responded via neuroelectronic tacomm, which was quick because their on-board 7/11 AI and computers didn't have to transliterate human thought patterns to electronic impulses; they just sent digitized computer responses which were identical to NE verbal responses and so-recognized by Curt's helmet tacomm equipment.

The Sierra Charlies with him on the flanking movement waited until the Jeeps had responded. That was doctrinaire because of the slowness of human thought formation and the nanoseconds that were required for computers to shift the messages into electronic transmission format.

I don't have any target yet, was Alexis Morgan's response.

Hang in there, Major! was Henry Kester's advice. *You'll have plenty of them pretty quick. We don't have to go looking for trouble this time out of the box. It's up on this hill and it'll let us know where it is damned quick!*

Trouble with you, Henry, is that you're so damned encouraging! was her light response, typical of Alexis Morgan going into combat as she tried to cover her fear with humor, a typical infantry soldier's reaction. *It would help if you'd tell me I'm not going to get my ass shot off.*

Major, that already happened in Brunei.

Yeah, but no Purple Heart, Henry, since it was caused by so-called friendly forces, Alexis reminded him.

Please don't make a second try for it, ma'am! I know the medal has our regimental coat of arms on it, but it ain't worth what it costs to get!

Although Curt didn't like to interrupt combat chatter on the tacomm because it provided an emotional outlet, especially in this sort of dark battleground where no one could see either friend or foe without i-r sensors, and although he knew he usually got a lot of incoming combat information in the chatter mode, he had to lay out some other orders. So he snapped, *Break it off for right now! I've got orders to give! Report when you need help or have multiple targets you need additional fire support to nail.*

Rog! was Kester's brief response, so brief that it told

145

Curt that Kester suddenly realized he was hogging a command tacomm channel in the opening minutes of a fracas, a period when things are fluid and dicey.

Alleycat Leader, this is Companion Leader! Curt called on tacomm to Jerry Allen. *We've made contact from on your left! Exchange of fire has started! Give us some fire support from the Mary Anns! Do you see our beacons?*

The helmet tacomm was strangely silent.

That shouldn't be, Curt knew. Jerry Allen had enough discipline to monitor the proper tacomm channel. Was Curt's tacomm busted or not putting out a signal strong enough to reach back to Jerry? Taking his right hand from his Novia nestled against his hip, he did what anybody does when a piece of gear may have stopped working. He smacked the side of his helmet hard, following the old truism, "If it don't work, kick the shit out of it first!"

Nothing.

Marauder Leader, this is Companion Leader. Tacomm check. How do you read? he transmitted a test message to Alexis.

Loud and clear, Companion Leader! Got problems?

Can't raise Alleycat Leader, Curt admitted.

That young stud probably got the Mary Anns targeted in and went chasing Shariat Khani. No one could have made that remark about Captain Jerry Allen but Alexis. Jerry had been one of her plebes; in spite of the intervening years, a shadow of that original West Point relationship still lingered between the two of them although they were now close friends.

I'll have his hide for a doormat if he did!

That's nothing compared to what Adonica will do to him!

Major, try again. He could have misread the code call, Battalion Sergeant Major Edie Sampson suggested. She'd started assuming Henry Kester's mantle as the unit's bunker tech, the NCO who could figure out what to do with warbots and weapons and comm gear. She'd always had a natural affinity for high-tech things, but also understood some of the shortcomings inherent in any form of human communication, including face-to-face exchanges.

146

Curt followed her suggestion. *Alleycat Leader, this is Companion Leader! Jerry Allen, where the hell are you?*

Alleycat Leader here! I thought you were calling Hassan with Sharaf Qazi and the Ahl-i Haqqs or Alley Hacks, came Jerry's reply at last.

I was calling you, Jerry! Greys all, attention to orders! Hereafter, the code call 'Alley Hacks' is not to be used to refer to the Kurds under Sharaf Qazi! It can be confused with Captain Jerry Allen's company code call! Okay, Jerry, we need Mary Ann fire support! Do you see our beacons? Curt wanted to know.

Affirmative!

Okay, give us a walking barrage of AP rounds about twenty meters ahead of us! That should put us outside the effective range of the shrapnel!

Wilco! Jerry was now being strictly tactical, knowing that he'd screwed up by assuming the code call was for Hassan and Qazi. Fortunately, battlefield NE tacomm was so rapid that the whole affair had consumed less than thirty seconds.

Curt now had his Novia nestled against his shoulder and was peering through its i-r sensor and associated laser rangefinder, looking for targets.

The image of a boulder appeared as he scanned the rifle's display. Although he was walking rapidly in a semi-crouched position, the stabilizer in the Novia sight kept the image steady. The i-r sensor showed the dim image of a man's head above the edge of the rock and the hotter image of a rifle barrel.

A touch to the ranging button sent out an invisible pencil beam of laser light from the scope's lidar element, and a sensitive electro-optical sensor on the sight picked up the light bounced back from the target. Very accurate electronic timing circuits measured the picoseconds it took for the laser beam traveling at a speed of 300,000 kilometers per second to get to the target and be reflected back. That told the sight what the range to the designated target was. The data caused the sight's computer to automatically adjust the images of the sighting reticule and sight post on the Novia's sight display. The sight then informed

147

Curt with a flashing red symbol that it had a good, firm target and that the range was not ambiguous. In other words, if Curt decided to shoot, the Novia knew where the round should go and would put the bullet exactly where Curt aimed. So he had only to align the pips and make the decision to fire. He did. The Novia bucked against his shoulder.

This was all standard targeting technology for the M33A2 "Ranger" rifle—which the Washington Greys affectionately called by its original Mexican name, Novia or "sweetheart." But Curt had never before used the full night targeting capabilities of his Novia. Even in the darkness of the Brunei rain forests during their deadly "R&R" on Borneo, there had always been some light somewhere. But on the hills of northwestern Iraq that night, it was pitch black. And Curt needed all the help he could get from technology.

Technology alone doesn't win battles, as Curt well knew. The user has to indeed use the technology to help him, but he should never depend upon it. Curt's training of the Washington Greys over the past two years in their revision of organization and operations to a modern special forces regiment had stressed that. The Greys could go into action throwing rocks if all else failed; such a move would be far more dangerous and costly than using the high-tech warbot weapons, but the Washington Greys knew that battles are fought by people against people. When the warbot goes tracks-up, the human has to continue to fight or possibly be killed or captured. And some of the people the Greys had fought against were the kind you wouldn't want to surrender to even if tradition permitted it . . . which it didn't, at least not in the Washington Greys.

Curt didn't get to see the man he'd shot. It was too dark, and too many other people were now shooting at the advancing Greys. The battle scene was lit brightly at rapid but random intervals by the air bursts of the 25-millimeter Mary Ann rounds breaking 10 meters off the ground ahead of them. It was as if the whole world around them were illuminated by strobe flashes. It allowed

Curt to get a rapid glimpse of things that his i-r sensors didn't pick up or didn't discriminate completely.

On the other hand, the flashes of the bursting Mary Ann rounds also allowed the enemy to see the warbots and Sierra Charlies advancing up the hill toward them.

And for the first time in a small unit action, the Greys had their own close tactical air support. And it was working well. Cal Worsham and his four Harpies were aloft; they had somewhat larger and better night sensor suites, so they were hovering outside of rifle range and laying 25-millimeter rounds in on the hill just like the Mary Anns under Jerry Allen's command. It was almost unnecessary for Curt and his advancing Sierra Charlies to shoot. In fact, Curt was having more and more trouble finding live targets that the 25s hadn't gotten first and that the 7.62-millimeter automatics of the Jeeps hadn't polished off.

Occasionally, a Harpy would break out of hover, climb into the darkness, roll into delivery mode, and put some heavy ordnance on a target that had refused to be silenced otherwise.

There was no question about the fact that the Washington Greys with one company of Sierra Charlies and their warbots, plus four Harpy aerodynes, completely overwhelmed the enemy with incredibly superior firepower.

The enemy seemed to be armed only with personal weapons—rifles, some pistols, and perhaps one or two light machine guns. No more rockets were fired. Curt was delighted that they received no incoming mortar fire because that stuff was deadly.

It was quickly apparent that the guerrillas who'd tried to ambush them in the village had counted on the Washington Greys being regular Robot Infantry troops who fought by means of warbots guided by means of neuroelectronic linkage, and had neglected to take into account the additional factor of the Warhawks and their Harpy attack aerodynes being present as well. The Washington Greys were, after all, the first Sierra Charlies to be garrisoned in the region. The combined arms tactic of warbots, Sierra Charlies, and Harpy aerodynes was totally new. Perhaps it was an overkill situation, because it didn't take long to carry out the assault on the hill.

The guerrillas were obviously unprepared in all respects for what happened. Maybe they were just slow to learn, Curt surmised, because in spite of the few patrols that had been ambushed, the word about the Americans who now fought alongside their warbots with close air support hadn't gotten around all the way yet.

The attackers, now aware that something had gone wrong and that these Americans fought a lot differently and a lot more effectively against guerrilla forces, didn't surrender. They tried to break contact and retreat.

That was tough to do now that the Greys had them targeted. And spotted from the air.

We got 'em! We got 'em! came the excited call from Cal Worsham aloft in his Harpy with a good overview of the battlefield. *They're breaking to the north! Lots of them! Perfect targets! Colonel, do you want us to go after them and cream them real good?*

Negatory! Let them run! was Bellamack's decision.

Hell, Colonel, we can load up the Chippies and get out ahead of them! was Alexis Morgan's excited comment. *We can cut 'em off at the pass and mow them down for good so they don't bother us again!*

Curt suddenly got the impression that Major Alexis Morgan was becoming almost as aggressive as Captain Russ Frazier . . . and one company of gung-ho aggressors in the Regiment was plenty. Or maybe it was just the excitement of combat that had made Alexis react this way. If so, it was the first time that Curt could remember. Alexis as changing. She'd started when she got her own company. The change hadn't stopped. Curt wasn't sure it was for the good. He'd trained Alexis to be a cool-headed, calculating, shrewd small unit commander; now it seemed that his training was coming unbonded.

I said negatory! Bellamack snapped. He listened to his subordinates, and he was always open to their suggestions. But there were times when he made a firm decision and expected his troops to do what he said. This was one of

150

them. But he did go on to explain, *I want them to get away! I want them to spread the story of what happened tonight! I want them to tell others that we fight in an aggressive new way. Maybe that will help stop these goddamned ambushes!*

That made sense to Curt. He didn't exactly relish the idea of chasing off into the hills of Kurdistan at night trying to outmaneuver some tribal guerrillas who might pick up additional strength from other groups who might be out there. And he didn't like the idea of doing it when it was obvious that the Greys had been shadowed during this fracas by a Soviet Spetsnaz unit. Well, if the bio-techs were good, they might be able to save one of the wounded members of that Spetsnaz unit, and maybe they'd learn more about the situation. Curt was happy to break it off right then and figure out where they went from here, especially since they hadn't come to any workable agreement with Sharaf Qazi. It would be better to have the Ahl-i Haqqs working with them. Curt sure as hell didn't want Qazi loose and free in their rear when the Greys had to go up into the hills after the Sovs.

Breaking off the battle might have made sense of Curt, but not to others.

Grey Head, this is Assassin Leader, was the tacomm call from Hassan Mahmud back with Qazi. *I'd suggest you get back here quickly, sir! I've passed your no-hot-pursuit order to Qazi, and he's more than a little unhappy about it. And with us!*

Chapter Twenty

"Why did you not pursue the routed enemy, the hated Qadiri?"

Sharaf Massoud Qazi's command of English might have been limited, but no one around him had any doubt that the man was livid with rage. Curt wasn't really sure what the man might do. He thought the Kurd chieftain might pull the short knife from his waist band at any moment and attack either Colonel Bellamack or even him. So Curt was on personal alert, ready to move quickly at any instant. His Novia rifle was cradled in what appeared to be an easy position in the crook of his right arm, but Curt could actually bring the weapon to bear on a target and shoot from the hip within a fraction of a second, firing with only his right hand grasping the hand grip if necessary.

Curt knew he'd probably have to shoot if something happened because he felt he might not stand a chance in a hand-to-hand with Qazi. Curt probably wouldn't get the opportunity because the Grey officers were surrounded by Ahl-i Haqq tribesmen, whose dark faces were somber in the firelight of the burning old building in the village. In spite of the intensity of the engagement, the Kurds apparently suffered only a few casualties. Some had bandages over what might be minor wounds, but that sort of thing didn't seem to slow them down very much and actually made them seem a bit more formidable. Anyone who could stay vertical and conscious with a badly wounded leg or arm had to be one tough son of a bitch, Curt decided.

On the other hand, the Washington Greys and their warbots were also there, positioned all around the village, deliberately prominent. The Greys, of course, had taken no casualties, primarily because of their body armor and the enemy's lack of night fighting technology. Very few of the enemy rounds had even hit the Greys, and bullets that had hit the Jeeps easily bounced off the tough warbot armor shell.

Curt decided that Qazi would probably keep himself under control since he was surrounded by a group of tough Sierra Charlies and their deadly, accurate warbots, but it was obvious that the man was pissed off.

"Several reasons, Sharaf," Bellamack explained. "First of all, I've got no reason to pursue them; they're not the Soviet Spetsnaz troops that I really want to clean out of this region. . . ."

Curt noticed that Bellamack was speaking as if the Washington Greys were his personal troops, and this was totally different from the manner in which he usually spoke of the Regiment. Curt realized that Qazi probably wouldn't understand the concept of a military force that wasn't like his own, loyal to him and only to him. Bellemack's previous experience in the Persian Gulf Theater was obviously paying off here.

Qazi interrupted Bellamack with a wave of his hand. "So? I know that! But the men who attacked are Qadiri who are our enemies and yours as well! We want to pursue them and kill them!"

Bellamack shrugged. "So go ahead and do it. I'm not preventing you from chasing and annihilating them."

"I want your help to do that," Qazi suddenly admitted. "You have excellent ways of seeing people in the dark. Your warbots shoot straight and accurately. They do not miss what they shoot at! And I have discovered that your regiment does not fight like other American soldiers. You fight like we do. Together, we will have much better success against the Qadiri and Naqshbandi terrorists."

"Sharaf, before the battle, you told me in no uncertain terms that what you really wanted from me were our new

153

Novia rifles," Bellamack reminded the Kurdish chieftain.

"That was before I saw how you and your soldiers fight with your warbots. You have new kinds of warbots I have not seen before, and you fight with them in the field, not from some protected truck where you're safe. You are *soldiers* and you fight very well! Even your women fight as well as our women," Qazi admitted in a straightforward manner. His basic attitude, while still angry, had changed as a result of the fracas. He knew now that these Americans were real fighting troops, not the technological wimps he'd met before, people who looked like soldiers and wore uniforms but who were soldiers in name only because they depended upon their technology to eliminate danger and their indomitable warbots to do their fighting for them.

"Well, if you want to go after the Qadiri, if that's who they are, I certainly won't try to stop you," Bellamack advised Qazi. "But I make the decisions for my Regiment, and I've decided not to send my soldiers and warbots in hot pursuit of an unknown enemy in the dark through unknown territory. On the other hand, if you want my help in stopping or even winning future battles with them and with the Soviet Spetsnaz battalion that we now know is somewhere around here close, that's another matter. But no matter what we do or what agreement we come to between us, you should realize that you're going to benefit from the fact that I *didn't* chase the Qadiri tonight even when I could."

Curt knew exactly what Bellamack was up to. He'd spent enough time in North Africa as a warbot brainy to understand what was going on. The Colonel was dickering again, and now he had a much stronger position from which to bargain. As a result of the fracas, Qazi had seen what the Sierra Charlies of the Washington Greys could do in a very difficult combat situation: in the dark of night against an unknown foe with unknown numbers and unknown weapons. And, in the process, the Greys had succeeded in intimidating a Soviet Spetsnaz unit into withdrawing surreptitiously after making only minimal combat contact. Bellamack had used the chieftain's perception of the fight to defuse the issue of giving the Ahl-i Haqq any of the Novia rifles that Qazi had originally demanded. Qazi now realized that the Washington Greys and their commanding officer were a force that had to be dealt with in a different manner than the American Army troops who'd been in the region before this.

Curt also noticed that Hassan was grinning from ear to ear, which meant that the new officer who'd grown up in Iran was essentially sprinkling holy water on Bellamack's approach. Hassan's very survival had once depended on dickering.

What surprised Curt was the fact that Major Alexis Morgan was smiling in a knowing fashion as well. Then he remembered that she'd grown up at Fort Bliss and had learned at a tender age how to deal in the *mercado* in the Mexican border city of Ciudad Juarez right across the Rio Grande River. Alexis was a dickerer, a barterer, someone who, if she hadn't already been an outstanding combat officer, could probably make a very good living selling used cars.

"I will benefit from the fact that you did not chase and destroy the Qadiri who attacked us?" Qazi asked Bellamack in disbelief, then shook his head sadly. "I have never understood you Americans, and this is one reason why! You do not choose to destroy your enemies when you have the chance! Yet to you this isn't considered to be a weakness! And you think it will be an advantage to you and to me! Please explain this to me."

"Sharaf, if those Qadiri guerrillas are from the same Dervish tribes that have been harassing the Iraqi petroleum facilities and attacking my patrols, I *want* them to return to their leaders with the news they've been beaten by a new American force of overwhelming strength," the regimental commander of the Washington Greys explained carefully.

Then Bellamack quickly and smoothly added, "That isn't what actually happened, of course, because you and your Ahl-i Haqq soldiers had a very strong role to play in

155

defeating them. But the Qadiri will never admit they were beaten by you or even by ordinary American robot infantry units! Instead, they'll make up a story of fighting valiantly against vastly superior forces that outnumbered them ten to one and overwhelmed them with terrible firepower! And the next time either of us run into them and other groups who've heard the story they dream up to cover their asses and to excuse their defeat, they'll be a whole hell of a lot more cautious!"

"Ah, yes! I begin to understand you now! You fight with your minds as well as with your weapons! That is interesting!" Shariat Khani suddenly interrupted, nodding her head which was no longer covered by her shawl. In the flickering fire light, Curt saw that she could be a very attractive woman indeed, if she were dressed in more than the near-rags of the typical Kurd and could take advantage of some modern hygienic facilities. Living for months at a time out in the wilds of Kurdistan wasn't the cleanest of life styles. In fact, living "naturally" was the pits, as Curt knew many of the "naturalists" and outdoors types had discovered once they'd been out in even the American wilderness for a week or more. Curt wondered what Khani would be like if she were in Mosul. She certainly knew about civilization from her educational upbringing by the English in Baghdad. Shariat Khani was also an experienced guerrilla fighter because, with a knowing look on her face, she went on, "So in the future they may not attack you at all because they fear and respect your strength. They will not have great enthusiasm for attacking the new American warbot troops!"

"You're quite right, Shariat," Bellamack told her diplomatically. He recognized her as a tough, battle-hardened fighter, and he guessed she must have some influence on Sharaf Qazi because she seemed to be with him most of the time. So he stroked her ego with words. "Your knowledge of how they fight can be combined with the zeal of Sharaf Qazi's soldiers. You have been fighting here for a long time; you know how to do it, and it's a way of life for you. Sharaf, I propose that your Ahl-i Haqqs and my

Washington Greys should fight together as a team. Together, we'll be able to knock down some of the dissenting tribes, run the Russians back across their borders, and give you the opportunity to become the Number One leader of the Kurds. In short, we might help you become the Kurd chieftain who finally unifies his people after fifty centuries and creates a Kurdish nation."

Goddammit, Bellamack, that's an audacious concept to lay out in front of this guy! Curt thought to himself. Bellamack was either setting up Sharaf Qazi to become the George Washington of Kurdistan, something these people needed after all these centuries of divisive fighting, or he might end up creating the biggest totalitarian dictator in the region since Cyrus the Great put the Persian Empire together.

Curt sensed that Colonel Wild Bill Bellamack was becoming more self-assured and therefore considerably more devious and shrewd in his dealings with locals. That told Curt that the man's self-esteem had finally returned, although it had taken a couple of years in command of the Washington Greys and about two years of low intensity non-combat activity in Brunei and Fort Huachuca while the Greys rested up at Level Three combat readiness, slowly working up to Level One again as the Regiment's people recovered from the chronic fatigue of nearly constant combat in Trinidad, Namibia, Mexico, Kerguelen, and Brunei.

Sharaf Qazi thought about this for a moment. It was obviously a deal too good to turn down because Bellamack had appealed to the Sharaf's self interest. There had been no talk of Novia rifles in Bellamack's proposal. It was a matter of "you scratch my back and I'll scratch yours." Qazi could understand that approach, and, furthermore, he could buy it without losing the respect and awe of his position that he knew he had to maintain in order to remain the Ahl-i Haqq chieftain.

"I like your ideas, Colonel Bellamack!" Qazi suddenly roared with a broad grin. He took his hand off the knife at his waist. And to Bellamack's great surprise, the Ahl-i

157

Haqq chieftain stepped up and embraced him.

Colonel Bellamack went along with this and tried to keep from wrinkling his nose. Qazi hadn't had a bath for a very long time. None of the Ahl-i Haqqs had. Although it was a little cooler in the hills of Kurdistan north of Mosul than it was down in the Euphrates River valley, people tend to get a bit ripe after several weeks with no bath. Like most Americans, and especially Major Curt Carson, Bellamack was perhaps overly sensitive to odors. After all, America is a pretty clean place thanks to modern twenty-first century public health and private hygiene.

With a typical Kurdish expression of friendship, Qazi patted Bellamack on the cheek following the embrace and shouted, "We shall talk more about this tomorrow! But right now, we have fought a great battle with you and we have won it! It is therefore necessary to prepare a feast! Let us celebrate together both our victory tonight and the victories that are to come because of our new friendship with the Washington Greys!"

Chapter Twenty-one

Curt reflected that most people in the world liked a good party and would use any excuse to have one, even if they were poor and hard-pressed to scrape up the fixings for one. In fact, it seemed the poorer the people, the wilder the party. Somehow, people everywhere managed to find the means to have a good time although the food might be rather boring (although somehow there usually was lots of it) and the alcoholic beverages rather strong and sharp.

However, he'd also discovered that all warriors shared the same post-combat urges. Part of that was the great relief at having survived combat without being killed or mutilated. Another part of it was the great joy of discovering that friends had also survived.

Thus, the meeting broke up, and Curt found he was, as usual, pretty horny as a result of the fight.

But he was now a battalion commander. He had responsibilities that came before his personal desires. He had to see to it that his battalion—the company under Alexis Morgan—was all right. In spite of the fact that he was no longer directly in charge of people as he had been when he was a company commander, the old habit of looking after the troops hadn't gone away.

He found Kitsy Clinton, Edie Sampson, and Sergeant Charlie Koslowski guarding Alexis's ACV. They were carrying their Novias at the ready, and they were actively scanning the surroundings with their helmet-mounted i-r sensors.

"Halt! Who goes there?" came the classic sentry's challenge from Sergeant Charlie Koslowski. There was a catch in his voice. The man was antsy, spooky, hyped-up. Something other than the recent skirmish had him scared because this wasn't the typical reaction to a fracas.

So Curt was very careful. "I don't know what the hell the fucking password is, Koslowski, because there's always some poor, dumb bastard who doesn't get the word . . . and tonight that's me! Major Curt Carson approaching, and if you shoot my ass off, I'll hang your balls on the wall in the Club!"

There was immediate relief in the sergeant's voice. "That can only be Major Curt Carson. Approach and be recognized, sir!"

"What the hell's going on here, troops?" Curt wanted to know as he stepped into the lights of the ACV so he could be seen. He suddenly discovered that his voice sounded tired even to him.

Edie was quick to reply as she shifted her Novia from the ready to a more comfortable carrying position in the crook of her right arm. "The goddamned Ahl-i Haqqs found out we'd captured the wounded Russkie. They wanted to cut his balls off and do other nasty little things to him."

"We knew Bellamack would want to talk with him once Ginny got him stabilized and in a condition to talk," Kitsy continued. "So I had to post a pretty strong guard detail out here to keep the Kurds away. Damn, they can be pretty fucking mean when they want to be."

"Yeah, they're tough people, all right. But their ancestors did worse things to captives," Curt reminded her. "One of the favorite sports of the Assyrians after they'd won a battle was to flay the captives they couldn't sell off as slaves."

"Well, gettin' beat with a stick doesn't sound too bad," Koslowski remarked. He was a city boy, and out in the wilderness like this he felt very much out of place. As a result, he was a very good sentry; his eyes flicked furtively around, checking into the darkness outside the circle of the ACV's lights.

"Uh, Kos, I said 'flay' not 'flog,' " Curt pointed out.

"There's a difference?" Koslowski asked innocently. The man really didn't know.

"A slight difference," Curt told him and went on to explain, "The Muslims may still flog men as a punishment—a hundred lashes across the butt in the public square. Gets to be pretty bloody, hurts like hell, and is probably more embarrassing than permanently damaging. But when you flay a man, you take him while he's still alive, strip his skin off like dressing out a fur-bearing animal, then nail it up beside where you've nailed the rest of him to the wall."

Koslowski made a sick face. "Jesus, what a way to go!"

"Remind me to get sick all over the next Kurd bastard who tries to get through us to the Russkie," Edie snarled. "I can hold what's left of my lunch until then."

"Play it cool, Sampson," Kitsy Clinton advised her. "The Kurds are a tad more civilized than the Assyrians were."

"They've got to prove it to me!" Edie muttered. "They were getting pretty mean and nasty before they discovered they couldn't push the Lieutenant and me around."

"And I presume you and my battalion sergeant major handled the matter properly, Lieutenant Clinton?" Curt asked unnecessarily.

Kitsy nodded. "We took care of the bastards. Seems they're scared shitless of women soldiers. I don't know why. But Sampson and I made use of it. Poor Kos here was about to piss in his pants when the Kurds pulled knives on us. But Edie has a couple of pig-stickers hidden away in her cammies, and she convinced the Kurds she not only knew how to use a knife but also knew where to start cutting first. Like between their legs." When she was in a combat situation like this—and it was obvious that she considered it a combat situation—Clinton no longer looked cute and pubescent; she acted small and mean like a fox terrier.

"How is he?" Curt asked.

"The Russkie? I don't know, Major. Why don't you

barge in and ask?" Kitsy suggested to him. "I presume, however, that you're not thinking about cutting his nuts off. Or are you? These Kurds are mean, and it rubs off . . ."

"I've got no use for his," Curt explained, and slung his Novia muzzle down over his shoulder by its carrying strap so he could bring it into action quickly if needed, then relaxed by leaning against the side of the ACV. These Greys were jumpy. They were tired and hyped by combat, and they shouldn't have been standing guard duty at night in the middle of a bunch of tough Kurds. But TACBATT was out there in the Kurdish wilderness with minimal personnel on what had started out to be only a small show of force to back up the Colonel's negotiating team. Curt tried to defuse the situation a little bit by behaving in a laid-back manner. "And I have no urge to send him back to his Spetsnaz unit as a horrible example of why you don't want to get captured by the barbaric American soldiers who are the hired lackeys of the running capitalist, imperialist dogs. I was just curious about the Sov. I don't want to interrogate him. So I'd better wait for the Colonel. Besides, I don't speak Russian."

"I don't think he's Russian, Major," Kitsy suddenly said. "He may speak Russian because most Spetsnaz troops do, but some Spetsnaz soldiers are drawn from the Asiatic tribesmen. I think the guy is maybe Uzbek or Kazakh. From what I could see of his face through all the blood, he didn't look European like most Russians. And he was screaming and yelling in a language that sounds a lot like what Hassan speaks."

Bio-tech Sergeant Ginny Bowles stepped through the aft hatch of the ACV. "Major," she said when she saw Curt, "you'd better get some air evack for our Soviet guest."

"Is he going to be all right?" Curt wanted to know.

"Not unless we can get him back to Mosul where Major Gydesen and her doctors can help him, sir. That Jeep was bore-sighted real well. It put one round through the left side of his neck just above the line of his body armor. Missed the carotid artery, and I got the venous bleeding stopped. The other round went through the fleshy part of his neck just below his right ear and missed most of the critical stuff there. But the secondary damage due to the bullet shock and energy transfer sort of tore things up around his mastoid and inner ear. I've run out of things I can do for him. I'm just not used to handling bullet wounds. . . ."

That was no shortcoming on her part. Robot warfare had all but eliminated the need for field medics because no one got shot in the Robot Infantry. When the Sierra Charlies went back into the field alongside the warbots, they suddenly discovered they could be wounded and even killed in combat. Bio-techs were hurriedly recruited and added to the regimental TO&E, along with a mobile field hospital. But it was tough to get bio-tech recruits with the proper background and experience; the best places to look for them were in the emergency rooms of big urban hospitals. And it was tough to get them to leave the ERs and go to war because, as field bio-techs, they could be shot at, which wasn't a threat in the ERs. The Army finally had to offer commissions to RNs who worked in the field hospital, and special hazard pay NCO ratings to PNs who turned out to be the best field medics. The best sources were those people who needed financial help to get through school and were therefore willing to mortgage a few years of their lives to serve in the Sierra Charlies after graduation. Happily, only three regiments were Sierra Charlies, and therefore only a few dozen people were required. So the Sierra Charlie bio-techs were indeed special people.

"I'll get right on it," Curt promised. "Come on, Edie. We've got a piss pot full of work to do to get this guy evacked. Since we didn't expect intense combat, we've got to get our replenishment pipeline flowing before we run out of things that go bang for us."

"Yes, sir! Somebody's gotta do it, or we may get kinda hungry in a day or so, to say nothing about not having anything to shoot!" Edie Sampson said with a sigh as she slung her Novia. "I think I can gin up enough computer power and network channels over in the other ACV, if it ain't already full of Sierra Charlies trying to either get some sleep or some recreation."

"Rule Ten is in effect," Curt reminded her.

She looked at him. "Major, if I see it, I'll report it. But I'm not going looking for it."

"Fair enough," was his tired comment. "With the kind of party the Ahl-i Haqqs are throwing, I won't be looking either. As for myself, the Sharaf's sheep are safe tonight."

The two of them got to work. Curt didn't like military administration. He wished he had a staff, but staffs were the luxury of regimental commanders and higher forms of life. As TACBATT commander, he was essentially in charge although Colonel Bellamack was on hand as regimental commander. But Bellamack was busy being diplomatic with the Sharaf. And the regimental staff was back in Mosul.

It wasn't an easy job because Bellamack didn't know at that point whether or not the unit would stay in the hills to be joined by the rest of the Regiment tomorrow and then continue its mission with the help of Sharaf Qazi's Ahl-i Haqqs, or whether the unit would go back to Mosul tomorrow. Thus, Curt found himself faced with the problems of reprovisioning ammo, food, and fuel that evening to handle the contingency that they would indeed proceed further north with the rest of the Regiment joining them.

He expected Alexis to drop by and stick around until he'd finished red taping, but strangely enough she didn't. This bothered him in one corner of his mind; Alexis was growing more distant. Curt expected people to change, but he also couldn't understand why Alexis was allowing their long relationship to change, too.

Lieutenant Nancy Roberts volunteered to take the Soviet casualty back to Mosul in the dark and be on hand in the morning in case additional airlift was needed from

Mosul. Curt made a passing remark to her about being able to operate pretty well in the dark, whereupon she got huffy with him and stomped off to her aerodyne. She was on edge after combat, and Curt realized she'd misunderstood his remark. But she was relatively new to combat flying, and she was undoubtedly still a little shaky over being shot at that night.

He missed the feast with the Ahl-i Haqqs. He was needed where he was, doing what he was doing. He and Edie grabbed some hot heatable field rations. He was pissed off at the whole affair by 2330 hours, and so was Edie.

"Dammit, Edie, if this is what higher command involves, I'd just as soon stay at company command level!" he groused at one point.

"Major, I'm the one who's faced with this sort of thing as my future in this man's Army," Edie reminded him. "You officers can always pass the buck to us and go do something else. It's always been up to the senior NCOs to run the Army!"

"I'm not passing the buck to you on this one," he reminded her.

"Yes, sir, I know, and I thank you for it, because I know what we're both missing. . . ."

At one point, Kitsy Clinton stuck her head into the ACV. Curt knew what she had in mind. But his job wasn't finished yet. "Later, Kitsy, later," he told her rather sharply, then wished he hadn't because she disappeared.

Some time after midnight, Curt and Edie finished their administrative tasks. Go hit the snore shelf, Major. I can finish up here in about fifteen minutes, and you look like something a bot ran over."

The outside air was almost cold in the hills of Kurdistan. As he was stretching muscles that had become cramped from hours at a terminal, he heard the sounds of the feast which was just about finished. A huge fire now flickered in its dying hour, and the silhouettes of people still seated around the flames cast long shadows over the hills around them. The place smelled of people who had lived there too long without proper sanitation and hygiene. He was ready to hit the hammock in the ACV when someone came toward him in the dark.

He knew it was an Ahl-i Haqq. He could tell by the smell.

And he was surprised when it turned out to be.Shariat Khani.

She stopped not two meters from him, dropped the shawl from her head to reveal her long, dark hair falling around her shoulders.

"Good evening, Major."

"Good evening, Shariat."

In a direct and outspoken manner, she announced to him, "I killed three men today. I killed them for you."

"Pardon me?"

"I could ask for any Ahl-i Haqq I wanted tonight because I killed three men," she went on. "But I noticed you when you first arrived and I decided that the next time I killed it would be for you."

Holy shit, what a weird spin they've put on post-combat sexuality! Curt suddenly realized. But he couldn't. Not with her. Not that night.

Even though he was dirty and stank of sweat and combat, so did Shariat Khani. She might have been a very beautiful woman without the ragged clothing, and she was probably terrific in the sack. But at that moment, Curt simply couldn't face the fact that she smelled far worse to him than he must to her. And he didn't exactly know how to handle the matter diplomatically.

"Shariat, my apologies, but we'll have to put it off until later. Maybe in Mosul when we can both get cleaned up a bit. In addition, I'm in command here, and our rules say that I can't make love to you under the circumstances," he lied.

She stiffened. "Others in your unit don't feel that way!" she snapped.

"Maybe others don't have the responsibilities that these entail," he pointed out, tapping the gold oak leaf on his collar tab.

166

Shariat Khani wasn't used to being denied. Curt realized she must be one of the best female soldiers Qazi had, a modern Amazon who was a vicious killer, a woman who met men on her own terms, but in a much different way than the ladies of the Washington Greys met their men. Thus, he was shocked when she snarled at him, "I shall shit upon your dead body on the battlefield, if I do not kill you myself first!"

And she was gone.

Curt shook his head and was sorry he'd done so. He had to laugh at himself in spite of it all because at the moment he had a splitting headache, a malady usually reserved for the other sexual partner. But he realized that he'd made a horrible blunder with Shariat Khani.

He hoped it wouldn't come back to haunt him . . . or worse.

Chapter Twenty-two

"You wounded and captured a *what*?"

Major General Belinda Hettrick sat straight up in her chair before her terminal in the headquarters of the 17th Iron Fist Division at Fort Huachuca, Arizona. She really wanted to be with the Washington Greys in Mosul in Operation Sturdy Spectra, but her new duties as division commander meant she had to keep the wheels of the Iron Fist turning. She had four regiments to think about now — the Washington Greys, the Cottonbalers, the Wolf-hounds, and the Can-Do. She'd done a good job at the OSCAR desk in the COS office in the Pentagon, but she'd lusted again for a combat command once she'd gotten her strength back. She'd forgotten about the old Army warning, *Be careful what you ask for because you may get it!* The Powers That Be had told her she was too good a combat commander to be wasted on a Pentagon desk, even though she was the best qualified general officer for the new Sierra Charlie human-warbot doctrine. Mainly, they wanted her out of the way right then because, in her intense manner, Belinda Hettrick had discovered where too many bodies were buried and had no compunctions about using that information as leverage to get what she thought was best for the country. When the new President was elected and the usual shake-up occurred in JCS, she'd lost the most powerful friend she had in Washington as well as those on JCS and Army COS who'd gained a grudging respect for her. As with most other large organizations, both the good and the incompetent go on to other things or retirement.

Now she was frustrated because, if what Wild Bill Bellamack was reporting was true — and she had no reason to doubt his integrity — it meant that Sturdy Spectra was turning into the usual sheep screw in which the Greys always seemed to get involved.

"General, in our regimental field hospital is a seriously wounded *starshiy serzhant* of what I believe is a KGB Spetsnaz battalion," Colonel Bill Bellamack reported via satellite link. He looked very tired. It was 0300 in northern Iraq, but it was 1700 in Fort Huachuca. Hettrick was getting ready to pack it in for the day, but she realized that Bellamack had probably been up all night, which he had. "He can't talk yet, one of our Jeeps put two seven-millimeters through his throat. But he made the mistake of wearing his Soviet ID tags according to international law. The Sovs always follow international law to the letter; makes it easier for them when they get caught. His name is Kondrati Stephanovich Pugachev which, along with his general facial features, tells me he's a Kazhak or Cossack. Bound to be one mean son of a bitch. My big question right now, General, is real simple: what the hell do I do with this guy and how can I keep him long enough to wring him out?"

"You haven't told General Pickens yet?"

"No, ma'am. You're my immediate superior and commanding officer," Bellamack pointed out unnecessarily. "When I tell General Pickens down in Baghdad, I know precisely how he's going to react to this; he's going to want to give the *serzhant* back through the Soviet embassy in Baghdad as quickly as he can in order to keep the Big Bear happy across the border to the north. Pickens won't want to rock the boat although he knew we were out here to contact the Soviets. Well, we found them, I think. And got one of them by accident. I don't want to give this *serzhant* back right away."

"Well, we have to do it, Bill. We can't hold the Sov as a prisoner. No state of war exists with the Soviet Union," Hettrick explained.

"I know that. But how do I keep General Pickens and

his people away from Pugachev right away? I want to have the chance to talk to Pugachev before anyone else gets to him," Bellamack admitted. "I speak his language pretty well, and the Greys saved his life out there in the hills. So I may be able to get some information out of him if I can talk to him before Pickens's Gee-two people get their hands on him and cause him to clam up. But if I know Pickens—which I do because he was three classes ahead of me at the Point and a bird colonel in the Five-Oh-Fifth Panthers stationed in Kuwait when I served in the Gimlets over here—he'll react fast. Within hours. But Ruth Gydesen tells me Pugachev probably won't be in any position to talk for days. Maybe weeks. I can't keep him to myself that long."

"Hell, Bill, have your BIOTECO commander declare the guy to be in critical condition, unable to see visitors," Hettrick suggested. She understood Bellamack's concerns, but she couldn't understand why the man seemed to be out of his depth at this point. He'd certainly shown himself to be a strong regimental commander, and a man who would take a stand on principle. Why, then, was he apparently shaky on this issue? Why didn't he stand up to . . . ? She had the sudden flash of insight and understanding. She remembered being told why a warbot brainy who wasn't a Sierra Charlie had been picked over Curt Carson to command the Washington Greys after she'd been wounded and unable to exercise command.

Hettrick knew what she'd do if she were still in command of the Greys and was faced with this situation. She'd take the initiative. But she was no longer top Grey. And as division commander of the Iron Fist, she couldn't issue the sort of order required to put her initiative into action terms. She had to do it by suggestion and with the careful caveats indicating she wasn't giving a direct order. So she thought black thoughts for a moment before she finally replied, "Bill, how much of a brass-plated bastard are you?"

"You have to ask that question of a former Major in the Gimlets?" Bellamack replied by asking her a question.

He'd been labeled a brass-plated bastard because he'd blown the whistle on his regimental commander and several light colonels in the Gimlets, the 21st Robot Infantry Regiment, when he'd caught them "expending" firearms, light machine guns, comm gear, ammo, and other "expendable" government property and selling it to clandestine international arms dealers in Bahrain.

That remark confirmed Hettrick's suspicions about why he was acting this way in this situation. "Yeah, but this is a different deal than the one where you qualified for your original rating as a BPB," Hettrick told him without rancor. "If you recall, the United States never signed the Toronto Accords. It would have meant we'd have to reveal some highly classified NE warbot linkage technology. Well, as best we could, we've tried to follow its principles anyway. But the Soviet Union never signed it either, you know, for different reasons than we did."

She was referring to the international accord about twenty years old between nations that were working at the time on neuroelectronics, a technology which held literal mind-blowing potential, if misused. The Toronto Accords prohibited neuroelectronic mind probing without the consent of the probee or another responsible close individual. American neuroelectronic researchers, having an open window to the brain and mind for the first time, thought it was too early to put that sort of restriction on an emerging technology where research needed to be done to show what could and couldn't be pulled out of a person's mind. NE technology wasn't there yet, of course, because a person could block what NE surface probes were permitted to pick up. But the use of neuroelectronics in electro-psychiatry, especially in criminal rehab, did have the capability of getting pretty deep into a person's mind. The Americans were right in taking the stand they did, of course, although it brought the wrath of civil libertarians down on the US and resulted in American NE researchers being shunned or even refused registration at many international NE conferences. As a result of not being restricted, the United States now led

171

the world in the application of neuroelectronics, and no one had been hurt in the process.

It was Bellamack's turn to pause before he asked, "So you think I should go into linkage with Pugachev because I can communicate with him in his language and thought patterns?"

"I can't tell you what to do in this one, Bill. But that's about what I had in mind when I suggested it to you. Want to try it?"

"Not really. I will if I have to. But I'm not sure Gydesen will permit it."

"If she balks, remind her about her brother," Hettrick suggested.

"What about her brother, General? She's never told me anything about a brother. What's important about that piece of personal information?"

"Did you ever wonder why such an outstanding physician and surgeon opted for the Army Medical Corps when she could have been pulling down ten times the money with a lot less hardship and red tape and living in country-club luxury as a civilian doctor?" Hettrick asked. "Golf or tennis on Thursday afternoon. Whole weekends off. A Mercedes and a Caddie in the driveway of a six-bedroom home on ten hectares. Don't you think she could have had it all by now?"

"No question about it. And, yes, I have wondered about why she's in the Army, but all of us have personal reasons for holding our commissions in the service of our country, so I never asked her. She does an outstanding job and tends to keep her personal feelings pretty much to herself, even when we've been alone together in off-duty status." Bellamack had been known to play the field rather broadly when Rule Ten wasn't in effect, but, following the lead of Hettrick and other regimental commanders he'd known, he'd been very discreet about it when he became a regimental commander himself. The only item that Rumor Control ever got its fangs into was the more serious relationship that flowered for a time between Joan Ward and himself.

"Well, sometimes we girls will tell each other things we would never let on to the rest of the outfit," Hettrick admitted. Bellamack knew from his own experience in the mixed-gender twenty-first century Army that this was so, and even the men did similar things. "I found out about it one very drunken night in the Club when I was evaluating her to lead the Greys' new medical team, and she let down her hair with me like she hasn't with anyone since, I'm told. Later, I checked on what she said in a rather tearful episode during which she spilled a lot of grief on me. I'm breaking a confidence here because it won't hurt Gydesen for you to know and she didn't ask me not to pass it on at my discretion. In fact, if you know, it may help both of you in many ways. But you never heard this from me, Bill. Understood?"

"I can have a very short and/or selective memory when I want, General," Bellamack promised her.

Hettrick looked down and said in a low voice, "During the German Reunification brawl, Captain Fred Gydesen came out of warbot linkage and left his armored command vehicle when the NORTHAG made contact with the Sovs around Wulfsburg. Unarmed and unarmored, walking in the open, he tried to personally intervene and get a KGB barrage battalion to stop killing retreating GDR troops because the shooting had supposedly stopped."

Bellamack nodded. He knew about the KGB barrage battalions whose job was to make sure no WarPac troops retreated. Their personnel were political zealots or those who did what they did because the KGB held their families as hostages at home against the proper behavior of these KGB troops in the field.

"Well, this KGB barrage batt didn't get the orders in time or decided to ignore them temporarily," General Belinda Hettrick went on. Bellamack could detect the frustrated and quiet anger in her voice. It was obvious that she considered these Soviet barrage battalions to be non-humans, mere military animals. "So they shot down Captain Fred Gydesen while he was walking toward them

173

unarmed and waving a white flag of truce. If there'd been a medical wound trauma unit in the Robot Infantry then, her brother might have lived. After we learned the hard way in Trinidad that we needed such a unit in the field at the regimental level and put the call out for volunteers from the Medical Corps, Ruth personally came to visit me from Fitzsimons and asked for the job. When I wanted to know why, she told me her story. And with considerably more emotion than she displays in a professional capacity, I might add."

"I don't think I'll trigger unpleasant memories for her," the regimental commander of the Washington Greys finally spoke up. "But I may have to be a little careful myself that I don't let emotions get in my way when I link with Pugachev."

"Just consider that Pugachev is just another Sov soldier unless you learn otherwise."

Bellamack nodded. "Just hope to God, General, that what I find inside that paranoid Soviet mind doesn't cause me to decide that hanging's too good for him and cause me to revert to Assyrian methods, of which I was reminded today by my regimental encyclopedian, Captain Jerry Allen."

Hettrick forced a smile. "Yes, Jerry does tend to get a bit pedantic because of that photographic memory of his, doesn't he? But he's a good officer, a good fighter, and a good man to have around."

"Lieutenant Sweet thinks so, too."

This did cause Hettrick to chuckle. "Ah, my, that relationship still flowering, eh? Well, I can understand why. She's a beautiful girl. And the relationship dates back to Trinidad, too." Abruptly, she changed the subject. "Now that you've got some Kurd allies and two reliable Kurd guides, what's your next move, Bill?"

"Go back to Mosul and mount a proper operation based on the best Gee-two I can get," the regimental commander told her without hesitation. "Sharaf Qazi won't come with me; seems he may be afraid of losing his position to some young upstarts if he leaves. But he's agreed to send his Number One, Shariat Khani, with us if I leave Lieutenant Hassan with him."

"Not a bad deal, and the sort of thing I'd expect. An exchange of hostages, so to speak," Hettrick mused, then asked, "But why go back to Mosul and regroup? Why not bring the rest of the Regiment up from garrison and continue from where you are?"

"Simply because I'm not organized to do so, General," Bellamack admitted. "This foray wasn't intended for combat but for recce and contact with a potential native ally. I've got only Morgan's Marauders with me. And I would rather regroup and concentrate in the relative safety of Mosul than out here in the hills with a Spetsnaz battalion around somewhere. Carson's my tactical expert, and he doesn't want to stick around here in a potentially defensive mode—without a suitable defensive and defensible position either, by the way. I agree with him. The Washington Greys are configured as an offensive strike outfit, not a guards unit. So I want to get set up and conduct a suitably offensive operation."

"Well, Bill, I won't micromanage your operation from halfway around the world. You're the organizer type, and you'll be thorough when you put it together. Just don't forget that you can over-organize yourself into a position where you can do nothing."

"You read our team real well, don't you, General? Well, I make no bones that it's a team. The hammer and the anvil. And that's how we're organized, too. And led as well. It's going to be a real challenge for me to meld the Ahl-i Haqqs into this operation because I don't intend to get involved in a war against the Kurds. I'd rather go to war with them instead. And against the Soviets. And we may teach the Kurds something about how to fight effectively for what they want. If they want to use the knowledge to get what they want, that's up to them. Actually, I hope they do. Otherwise, we'll never get any peace in this part of the world. . . ."

Chapter Twenty-three

"Nothing? We're doing *nothing*?" Major Curt Carson was astounded at the announcement from Colonel William Bellamack.

The regimental commander didn't look happy, either. Furthermore, since he'd gone into neuroelectronic linkage with the wounded Soviet soldier Pugachev, Bellamack wasn't acting just right. Curt didn't know exactly what it was, but Bellamack wasn't quite Bellamack any longer. The Colonel seemed moody and somewhat furtive.

"What the hell do you want me to do, Carson?" Bellamack snapped, and this was uncharacteristic of the man, too. "Yes, we're facing a Soviet Spetsnaz battalion up there in the hills of Kurdistan! Yes, the Sovs are there on a clandestine mission! No, Pugachev didn't know what the mission is! He wasn't told! He can't read maps because he was never taught to read maps because that wasn't part of his job as a soldier, so he doesn't really know where he is or where the Spetsnaz battalion is! He was in charge of seven other Kazakhs who were riflemen with the additional task of disabling any M-22 assault bots or M-55 fire support bots they ran into."

"Those old warbots?!" Curt exclaimed.

Bellamack nodded. "That's all we've had in the Persian Gulf command until the Greys showed up with our Sierra Charlie warbots."

"If that's the case, I'm beginning to wonder, Colonel, if the Soviets were the ones who salvaged our Mary Anns and Hairy Foxes from the Cook Glacier on Kerguelen Island a couple of years ago," Curt mused.

"You don't understand the Russians! You don't think Soviet style!" Bellamack insisted. "Even if the Sovs did steal our old warbots with the Mod 5 AI in them, we probably won't see the Soviet counterparts in any of their forces for at least another three to four years. Their production would have to be worked into their latest five-year plan. They're so goddamned short of resources that they have to operate with a 'short blanket' economy—when the shoulders get the blanket, the feet get cold. And they'd need another few years to train troops to work with them. So it's no wonder a mere Spetsnaz *serzhant* hasn't been briefed and trained to recognize and attack any of our recent Sierra Charlie warbots. The latest information the Soviets may have gotten from the Kerguelen warbots hasn't filtered through the system to Pugachev's level yet. Remember, that damned political system operates on obsessive secrecy . . . Thank God! Otherwise, the bastards would be able to steal our technology and use it against us much quicker than they already do!"

Curt knew that Bellamack didn't like the Soviet system and, because he spoke Russian, didn't like the way those people even thought, much less how they viewed the world.

But as commander of TACBATT, Curt was concerned about what he'd be called upon to do next, so he asked, "Colonel, if we're not going to proceed vigorously with Operation Sturdy Spectra, then what the hell do you want me to do? What do you want me to be planning for?"

"I don't know at this point!" Bellamack was strangely uneasy. He usually had some sort of tactical plan in the back of his mind. It was odd that he didn't seem to have such a plan.

And this bothered Curt. Insofar as Curt was the basic tactical brains of the team, he knew that they had enough information in hand at the moment to begin some scenario forecasting as the precursor to actual operational planning. The Greys had orders to make contact with the Soviet Spetsnaz unit and get them to go back to the USSR. They'd been authorized to obtain help from native guides and to organize whatever cooperative measures they could with Kurdish leaders. Communications had been established and an initial working agreement had been made with the Ahl-i Haqqs. Initial contact had been made, however briefly, with the Soviets in the field and they had a wounded Spetsnaz soldier who Bellamack had mind-probed with neuroelectronic techniques. Curt didn't say so, but he believed they should now be thinking about what the hell they were going to do to carry out Operation Sturdy Spectra in a timely fashion.

So he took the initiative and confronted Bellamack right then and there in the privacy of the regimental commander's office where the two of them could yell at one another if necessary. This sort of private conference had always worked well in the past because the two men had a contract with one another. Curt respected Bellamack for the regimental commander's integrity and ability to effectively command a unit as unique and highly motivated as the Greys. Bellamack had, in the past, respected Curt's grasp of military history and its relationship to tactical planning as well as the battalion commander's ability to exercise strong leadership. Neither had any intention of shooting into the other man's goal. And this contract had been tested to the extreme in the past. Curt expected it to withstand whatever was bothering Bellamack at the moment.

"Colonel," he began, "I understand the fact that you're satisfied with the arrangements we've made with the Kurds and that you now wish to sit and wait for developments before taking any further action. I agree that we've lost contact with the Sovs and we can't waste our energies and supplies by going out in the field and attempting to make contact, especially since it's apparent from the recent fracas that the Sovs don't want confrontation with us at the moment. Otherwise, they wouldn't have gone retrograde when we made contact. But I'd like to suggest that we don't just sit here in the passive mode and wait for something to happen."

"If you agree with me that we shouldn't chase all over the goddamned Tigris River valley and the hills of Kurdistan, then what the hell do you think I should do?"

This statement surprised Curt. Bellamack didn't use the collective "we" terminology of a team leader but the "I" approach of the lonely commander. Curt was no psychiatrist, but he did know the man well enough and he did understand people to the point where he recognized this as a reflection of concern and even distrust of those commanded and those commanding as well.

"The Washington Greys will do whatever we want, Colonel, on the bounce, sharp, and willing," Curt reminded him, deliberately shifting the slant of the conversation back into the "we-as-a-team" approach. "We certainly have the support of General Hettrick and General Carlisle above her. Neither the Greys or Hettrick or Carlisle have ever let us down. However, the Greys are going to get antsy and spooky if we sit around Mosul waiting for something to happen. Morale may start to slip, and we'll have a hell of a time maintaining it out here so far away from Huachuca on what everybody senses is a temporary posting so we can piss on this Spetsnaz brushfire."

"As I said, what the hell do you want me to do?" Bellamack hadn't shifted his thinking.

"We've got to continue our pipeline and facilities patrols," Curt reminded him. "Otherwise, the Sovs will know something's up. More than that, they might even believe that their encounter with us scared us off because we don't want to tangle assholes with them."

"That isn't what the Sovs think!" Bellamack insisted. "Those bastards are masters of deception. We could be dealing with several Spetsnaz battalions operating in such a way that they appear to be one. Their objective is probably quite straightforward. They're here to probe us again, to find out whether or not they could get away with reestablishing themselves in Iraq, covertly or by brazenly moving troops south. They'll make as much trouble

179

as they can, and I have no way of figuring out where and what they'll do next!"

"Well, sir, let's try to find out!" Curt insisted. "Because of the reorganization, we've got outstanding reconnaissance capabilities now, something we've lacked in past operations. That was why we set up RECONCO as part of TACBATT when we thrashed out this reorg over the objections of the high-level warbot brainies who'd never fought except on their backs on a linkage couch. Gibbon has some resources to work with now: an expanded birdbot platoon under a goddamned good officer, Ellie Aarts, who's been in combat and knows what to look for; an outstanding scouting platoon under Adonica Sweet; plus the fact that we can use AIRBATT in the recce mode, too. Sure, Cal Worsham doesn't like to chase rabbits, as he calls recce. But a recon pack hung on a Harpy or even installed in a Chippie could give us some good long-range data out beyond where our birdbots and scouts can operate. Furthermore, we can combine the recce with our regular patrol activities. . . ."

"I've got to think about that," Bellamack grumbled.

"Think about? Colonel, it's part of our mission! We just go do it!"

"We'll burn up fuel and other consumables. . . ."

"Colonel, all the fuel we need comes out of the holes in the ground around here that we're supposed to guard! It goes to Abadan where they turn the goop into gunk which they send back here and we use."

"I've got other things that concern me," Bellamack finally admitted.

"Hell, Colonel, if I don't know what they are, I can't serve as a good second-in-command, much less your trusted tactical advisor."

Bellamack got up from his desk and wandered over to the window of the casern that looked out over the Tigris River toward the ruins of the ancient city of Nineveh. "I'm worried about timely replenishment of our consumables, including fuel. Why? Because I'm getting zip cooperation from the Persian Gulf Command," he finally admitted.

"General Pickens?"

"You mentioned the name, not me."

"I take it that's because you two tangled assholes over the Gimlet affair?" Curt and his regimental commander had talked at length about the whole affair in the past. Curt felt no heartburn about mentioning it as a possibility behind the Colonel's problems with General Pickens.

"Not really, General Pickens wasn't involved in the arms scam at all. But some of his close buddies were. He might have had a distant role in it, but nothing that I knew about. Most of the officers in the Persian Gulf Command probably had some minor part in it. It's kind of tough to make millions of dollars worth of arms and ammo disappear and be able to write it off as 'expended in combat.' " The Colonel turned to face Curt, "I don't want to get the Greys out on a limb here and have them suffer because of something I did out of conscience before I assumed command here."

"Does General Hettrick know about this?"

"She will. I doubt that she can do very much about it. She has no command authority over Pickens."

"She does with General Carlisle! Either Hettrick or Carlisle can call in the IG and leave you in the clear on this one with Pickens. But he sure as hell will know even if there's nothing he can officially do about it."

Bellamack shook his head sadly. "Hell, I called in the IG once in my career already. And it damned near ruined me! Would have if I hadn't done some very quick dancing." Then he dumped his problems on Curt. "Pickens is aware of Operation Sturdy Spectra, as you damned well know. He doesn't like it because he isn't in command loop over me where he'd very much like to be. He'll get none of the so-called glory that may wash off this operation, and he can't do what he really would like to do to me. So he simply replies to COS that he's doing his job and properly supporting us here in Mosul. And he'll have documentation to prove it. What won't be evident is the fact that nothing gets expedited. Pickens has

181

instructed his staff to do it by the book. So requisitions are being procesesd precisely according to regulations, and if any problem shows up like a misplaced comma or a misspelled word or an incompleted form, the request gets turned around and shoved back through the chain of processing until it lands back on Harriet Dearborn's terminal a week or so later. Or something gets screwed up down in Bahrain and a decimal point gets misplaced or a glitch in the goddamned local power supply causes a computer to hiccup and we get twenty thousand rounds of seventy-five millimeter ammo instead of twenty thousand rounds of seven-point-six-two stuff, and no one thinks to check where the hell we expended twenty thousand rounds of Saucy Cans ammo and no Novia ammo. Curt, if someone in the system decides to work against you by using the system against you, it's pretty damned hard to do anything about it."

Curt didn't say anything for a moment, but finally spoke up, "Colonel, I suggest we take Captain Dearborn and even Major Benteen out of the direct loop of doing something about it—"

"My God, Curt, Benteen runs VETECO and Harriet's my Ess-Four!"

"I know," Curt told him, holding up his hand. "They should continue doing their assigned tasks and requisitioning things according to the good book. Got to keep up appearances and stay legal. But you know who runs the Army, right?"

"The NCOs."

Curt nodded. "If official channels don't get you what you need, I learned as a platoon leader how to let my NCOs dicker for it on swaps with other outfits. If I were you, I'd simply inform my Regimental Sergeant Major of the problem. Don't give him an order, but ask him if he can do something about it. I'll bet that Henry Kester will get together with Joan Stark and Manny Sanchez, and they'll call buddies in other outfits and in the ant hill down in Bahrain . . . and they'll surprise you by getting us what we need when we need it."

182

"Touchy if someone gets caught and Pickens calls the IG in on me!"

"You'll be clean. So will Benteen and Dearborn. Henry Kester and our other top NCOs know how to bury cat shit on a glass table top without getting themselves dirty and leaving a smell! How the hell do you think we won all the wars the United States has gotten involved in? Besides, Colonel, by the time the IG might get around to showing up, we really will have expended our consumables if we go out on active recce, find the Soviet bastards, and close on them! But not if we sit on our asses here in Mosul."

Bellamack was quiet himself for a moment, then replied, "Curt, if logistical problems were my only worry, I wouldn't sit in Mosul, either. But our little fracas in the hills brought a visit from a guy by the name of Colonel Sven J. Ohllsson."

"Who he?"

"He's Swedish Army and the UN monitor here in Mosul. Don't forget, we're here not as an occupation force but to protect petroleum facilities. We're not supposed to go charging off into the hills, according to the UN."

"So we shouldn't sit around. We go in, do our job, go home, and let the diplomats argue with the UN."

"The diplomats are already involved. I also got a visit from an asexual little bitch from the State Department, one Amy McPherson-Abelard, US consul in Mosul," Bellamack groused. "I don't mind going up against the Sovs. We've done that before. But I don't like to fight two people at once, and now the Turks are goddamned unhappy with us, too!"

Chapter Twenty-four

"The Turks?" Major Joan Ward asked in disbelief. "Why the hell are the Turks upset with us? They've been our allies since the end of War Two! Fought with us in Korea, too! And kindly kept their fingers out of the mess in North Africa when it looked like it was going to line up on the score card as Christians versus Muslims in a sort of twentieth Crusade."

The Club that had been set up in the Mosul casern was certainly a far cry from the one in Fort Huachuca. It was far older. The Greys had once thought that the 200-year-old building at Fort Huachuca was ancient when they took it over for their Club—not an O Club or an NCO Club, but a Club that was for all Greys. But this one in the ancient Iraqi city of El Mawsul or Mosul was far older. Someone said it was part of a fortress built in 641 A.D.. The Greys, for whom anything more than 300 years old was ancient, simply ignored that and did their best to turn it into a twenty-first century Club.

And, as usual, the place was busy in the evenings for several reasons.

First of all, it was the Club. It was where everyone was. It was the place where everyone saw everyone else in a relaxed atmosphere. It was a place where the food was different and cheap, although not always 100% American because of the difficulty of teaching local cooks to prepare genuine American dishes, but it was "close enough for government work," as the saying went. Furthermore, the Club was an antidote to barracks boredom which has always been the bane of any soldier's existence.

Secondly, the Club was cool. The ancient seventh century Islamic engineers had built well, but twenty-first century American engineers had brought air conditioning to the building and made it comfortable. The Tigris River valley was a fertile swath of river bottom land that slashed through desert and semi-desert from the mountains of Asia Minor to the Persian Gulf. It was a hot place. The presence of the river and tilled land created a climate that was far more humid than the surrounding desert. The Club was the refuge from that as well.

"Major, there were only seven Crusades. Officially, that is," Jerry Allen reminded her. "We're probably the eighth . . . if anyone is still counting."

"Or the twentieth if no one's been counting, Mr. Britannica," Joan persisted. She was not above poking a kidding finger at various personality attributes of her colleagues, but no one took her seriously except when she wanted to be taken seriously, and when that happened she let you know.

"Hell, I can't help it if I'm an encyclopedic synthesist," Jerry remarked.

"A what? Say that again," Adonica Sweet remarked with a smile. Whether she was attired in the baggy cammies of combat or leisure clothes, she was still an all-American beauty. She had a way of wearing the desert khakis that turned a plain set of light tropical cottons into a fashion statement. Only those who knew her well also knew that beneath her breath-taking wholesome beauty lay a vicious fighter who was a stalker and a killer . . . with a radiant smile on her face while she was doing it. Adonica was a sweetie, but she was also a very complex young woman.

The same might be said of all the Greys, although they all weren't killers at heart. They were professional military people, a manifestation of the twenty-first century's recognition of the fact that some people *like* the military life and *like* to fight because of some abstruse genetic trait the scientists hadn't pinned down yet. For some Greys like Curt Carson or even Dyani Motega whose ancestors had served well and honorably for generations, it was indeed in their genes, and they probably would have been either very miserable in the civilian world, probably becoming aggressive industrial or financial managers.

"Take it any way you want," Jerry told her.

"I have and I did and I do," was her cryptic reply whose meaning was lost on no one there because from the very first day she'd appeared in the middle of the road in Trinidad, she and Jerry had been like oppositely charged particles.

"So why the hell are the Turks upset with us?" Joan picked up the thread again.

"They found out we're talking with the Kurds," Curt explained.

"So?" Adonica asked.

"So the Kurds have been a thorn in the side of everyone in these parts for fifty centuries," Curt reminded them. "The Kurds want their own nation. They don't realize that they don't have to have a separate country just for them. That they can be a nation within a nation or nations."

"Sort of like the Crow Indians," Dyani Motega put in quietly. "Or some of the other tribes who have their own laws and have exploited their own natural resources."

"Before a group of people can get to that point, Dyani," Joan reminded her, "the nation where their minination exists has got to agree to keep hands off and to respect the tribal laws. Hey, it took us a long time to learn how to do that in America."

"Yes, but the Kurds have been at it for fifty centuries with very little progress," Adonica put in quickly.

"They almost had their own country right after War One when the Treaty of Sevres was signed," Jerry put in his bit of encyclopedic knowledge. "But the Turks and the Iranians screwed them out of it and refused to follow either the Treaty of Sevres or the more definitive one that followed it, the 'Treaty of Lausanne."

"I think it's their own damned fault," Curt observed with candor. "After fifty centuries of fighting, they apparently haven't learned enough to take control of what they consider to be their own land and defend it against the Turks and Armenians and Iraqis and the rest. They're doing it all wrong. And the first thing they're doing wrong is that they're fighting wrong. Look around the world. The Kurds must be the only people who haven't fought a successful war of liberation in the past hundred years."

"So the Turks have smelled something in the wind here and think maybe the United States Army is about to either come in and help the Kurds or train them in modern tactics?" First Sergeant Nick Gerard of Ward's Warriors put in. Nick was very happy with his new position as chief NCO for Joan Ward's heavy fire company, GUNCO. He'd always liked the big LAMVs and their 75-millimeter Saucy Cans guns.

"Nick, everyone around these parts hates everyone else," Edie Sampson reminded him. "That's what makes it such a wonderful place to be stationed. You don't know who's going to shoot at who next. Or at you, too."

"Yeah, these people hate each other," was Regimental Sergeant Major Henry Kester's quiet observation, "And they've been doing it for fifty centuries or more. You can build up a hell of a lot of hate in that period of time. We don't really understand that."

"We used to hate each other pretty intensely," Kitsy Clinton put in. "You damned Yankees were pretty hard to forgive after you beat us down with sheer numbers in the War of Southern Independence instead of fighting by the rules like true Southern gentlemen did!"

"Why, Kitsy, I never knew you were a Southern belle!" Joan exclaimed.

With a pixie grin, Kitsy slipped into an overdone drawl. "Mah ever-loving granddaddy was seduced by one of them smart Yankee mathematics gals who came south in the last century to help us Southerners industrialize the place. Seems she also tricked him into marrying her six months before mah daddy was born. Then mah daddy beat the Southern accent out of me at an early age because he told me it would retard mah progress in whatever Ah did, especially in the Army which used to be an honorable haven for Southern gentlefolk."

"Yeah, Kitsy, but no one hates you any more!" Joan kidded her with a smile. She turned her attention back to Curt. "So what the hell, tac boss? Are we going to cave in to the Turks?"

"We've got our orders, and it's not in our job descriptions to play the international diplomatic game here. Amy McPherson-Abelard gets paid to worry about that as American consul here. And the Colonel's the one who's going to be saddled with all the problems handling her," Curt reminded Joan.

"I could handle that peace-loving broad in thirty seconds," Joan Ward estimated with a scowl on her face. "She thinks she's got bossing privileges over the military around here. Well, maybe she could get away with it when the warbot brainies were lying around here, but this is a different sit. Problem with trying to get something done here is too many chiefs and not enough Indians, if you'll pardon the metaphor, Dyani."

Dyani Motega shrugged and smiled slightly. "You should hear how we Crow Indians used to express a similar feeling."

"So are we going to sit on our asses and then go into panic mode the next time the Qadiri or the Sovs raise a little hell?" Jerry Allen wanted to know.

"I doubt it. The Colonel isn't here tonight because he's conferencing with Hettrick and contemplating his belly button," Curt told them. "He's in horseshoe mode right now—between the hammer and the anvil."

"He hasn't been right since he did the linkage bit with the Sov earlier today," Joan Ward pointed out. She, of all those present, should know because while Curt was close to the man professionally, Joan Ward was close to him personally. What had started out as an interpersonal attachment when Rule Ten wasn't in effect had slowly grown to the sort of brother-sister relationship that Curt and Joan had had for years—and this wasn't totally to Joan's liking because beneath her Valkyrie exterior lay a very romantic person.

"Any news for Rumor Control?" Kitsy asked.

Curt nodded. "Nothing official yet, but I'm willing to lay a small bet on the fact that we have an OSCAR briefing in the morning and activate some intense, long-range recce. We'll probably go looking for the Sovs with RECONCO and anything else we've got. And we'll put Qazi and the Ahl-i Haqqs to work out in the hills because they know the territory."

"Orgasmic!" Jerry exclaimed. "Hassan doesn't like the idea of staying out there with Qazi as 'liaison officer,' more like a hostage. But, on the other hand, Shariat Khani came back with us as Qazi's liaison. So the sooner we get moving on something, the happier the troops are going to be on both sides of the hill."

"AIRBATT isn't going to like recce for rabbits," Joan warned. "They like to either haul us into action or move rocks around. Worsham's as aggressive as Russ Frazier!"

Curt shrugged. "Before they can haul warbots or bust rocks, we've got to locate an objective," he reminded them all.

"Good evening, Greys!"

Major Alexis Morgan walked up to the big, round table. She had someone with her. Curt didn't recognize Shariat Khani for an instant.

"I'm sure you remember Sharaf Qazi's Number Two, Shariat Khani," Alexis went on. "Sorry we were late getting over here, but it's been Beautify Shariat Night."

And indeed it had been, Curt decided. Alexis had obviously taken the Kurdish Amazon under her wing for a general cleanup once they'd gotten back to Mosul earlier in the day. "It has been a long time since I've enjoyed such luxuries," Khani put in as the two women took seats at the table. "We do not have such good facilities in the hills. But we do not have to have them in

189

order to fight. Happily, Alexis has helped me do again some of the things I learned in school in Baghdad."

Alexis had apparently gotten Captain Harriet Dearborn to issue some khakis that fit Shariat's hard, slender figure, and Alexis had helped the Kurdish girl apply some subtle cosmetics and fix her long, dark hair in a soft cascade down her back. Shariat's gaunt face with its high cheeks and slightly aquiline nose had been softened with a little eye makeup and cheek blush. Her thin lips had been enhanced by Alexis's careful application of lipstick in just the right manner to also soften their usual hard lines.

Shariat Khani was now a remarkably attractive woman. She didn't have the robust sensuality of Alexis, the sheer wholesome beauty of Adonica, the earthy attractiveness of Joan, or the playful pixie quality of Kitsy. She was exotic, which is the best word Curt could come up with to describe her at that moment. She was different in a group that enjoyed and even rejoiced in personal differences.

Now Curt felt a certain excitement when Shariat Khani glanced at him with a predatory look.

He hoped she had better manners than to attempt to haul him away in front of the other ladies of the Washington Greys because such an act would certainly cause something more than just hard feelings; Curt was worried that Alexis might attempt to retaliate and Kitsy certainly would if Allie didn't. He wasn't sure whether or not either of them could prevail in a hand-to-hand with Shariat Khani, if the others in the Club let it get that far before breaking them up. Shariat Khani looked tough as nails and at least in as good physical shape as the combat ladies of the Greys. It might be interesting, however, he told himself.

On the other hand, he tried to regain his perspective and had to laugh at himself for even thinking that way. Maybe he'd had too many drinks on an empty stomach after a hard day's work. Why was he so goddamned egotistical as to think that he was some sort of sex symbol for the Kurdish girl? She'd cursed him pretty strongly out in the hills last night for rejecting her direct and unsophisticated advance and invitation. Maybe that look she was throwing at him wasn't predatory but merely pure hatred.

But Shariat Khani remembered her manners and was properly polite during dinner which Alexis bought for her. She was decently pleasant to all the Greys she met that night. And she threw Curt no more of those looks.

Curt dismissed the possibility that she was still stalking him. Her actions had probably been the Kurdish equivalent of the post-combat syndrome that the Greys felt and that Rule Ten was designed to keep under control. So he left the Club early with the remark that it had been a long day and they all better get some sack time in case they were treated to an 0800 OSCAR briefing in the morning, which he rated as a very high Rumor Control possibility.

Besides, his own post-combat syndrome had leveled off and he was downright tired.

But he was wrong about Shariat Khani.

When Curt sacked out from fatigue, he slept the sleep of the dead. He suddenly awoke to find someone in bed with him.

"Allie?" he muttered sleepily.

"No, but you can thank her for taking away the excuse you used last night!" was the muttered reply. "All right, Yankee, let's see if you're the equal of my Kurdish comrades!"

Curt never had the opportunity to find out because Shariat Khani was a strong, powerful, and demanding bed partner. She did things he never thought a woman would do. Or could do. She was incredibly primitive and a total handful. But no matter what he did, he couldn't really control her or seem to satisfy her.

For some unknown reason, Curt found himself comparing Shariat Khani to the other women in his adult life, and discovered something about each of them as a result.

Alexis was a tender and caring companion who was an independent woman eager to make her own way in the world and yet unwilling to proceed without male companionship.

Kitsy was full of the fun and enthusiasm of a woman who enjoys virile men.

Colonel Willa Lovell was an older woman of great intellectual brilliance who was, underneath, a frightened child and needed Curt to remind her that she was still a woman.

The Sultana Alzena of Brunei was the ultimate in sensuality, a woman educated in all the ways to please who gave love in full measure and therefore received it in return.

But Shariat Khani was all raw sex and totally unbridled. Curt had never had a woman make love to him with the violence and passion Shariat Khani did that night. She put herself in control of the situation from the start and gave no quarter. She left no question in Curt's mind: she was indeed a sexual animal of the sort that excited most young men. Battles and even wars had and probably would be fought over a woman like Shariat Khani among men who wanted to possess a woman like her and perhaps needed that as an excuse to break the incredible boredom of their everyday lives.

But, for some strange reason, although Shariat Khani was certainly a desirable and exciting woman, and although she was as erotic and experienced as any he'd known, and although she physically satiated him and begged for more, Curt himself wasn't satisfied in a strange and undefinable way.

As for himself when he had the time to think about such things that night, Curt wondered why this woman, as well as the others, excited him and were in turn attracted to him because he was no muscled superman with a hairy chest and a macho unshaven chin. He was a soldier pledged to carry out a contract and ready to accept the unlimited liability clause in that contract.

When dawn broke its first light over the ruins of the

192

ancient fleshpot of Nineveh across the Tigris River from
the Mosul casern, Curt knew that the Greek legend of
the Amazons probably had been based on reality.

Chapter Twenty-five

"What the hell is eating you, Cal . . . as if I didn't know?" Major Curt Carson confronted Major Cal Worsham in the high-ceilinged hallway of the Mosul casern. "You're stomping around like you're about to spit seven-millimeter slugs yourself. What's the matter? Nervous in the service or something?"

Major Cal Worsham glared back at Curt and the ends of his long, bushy, handlebar mustache quivered. He ran his hand over his shaved head—AIRBATT pilots still had to fly their 'dynes by direct linkage with the autopilots even with the Mod 7/11 AI installed. "*Shee-it*, Carson, I might as well go out and fly around the fucking *flagpole* for all the good we've been doing lately! When the *hell* is this goddamned fucking *recce* crap going to *stop?*" Cal wasn't one to mince words with anyone, and he'd gotten worse about it lately. He was like Russ Frazier; he needed a fight every once in a while. Bellamack had made it very clear to him that all the fighting was going to be done with the Shiite Kurds and maybe the Soviets, not in the Club and certainly not in Mosul. Things were taut enough with the Iraqis anyway because they didn't like the idea of American troops in their country in the first place. However, the Iraqis couldn't do much about it since their own military vitality had been pretty much drained by the protracted warfare with Iran over the past decades.

"We'll stop it when we find something to attack, Cal. I don't like sitting on my ass here in Mosul either. But if we go charging off into the boonies without an objective,

194

we might as well be pissing into the wind." When talking with Cal Worsham, Curt had discovered it helped to be just as surly and foul-mouthed as the frustrated Air Battalion commander. Curt didn't like the boring activity of reconnaissance either. But if the Greys didn't know where to go to take on the Kurd guerrillas or the Soviet Spetsnaz battalion, it was senseless to wander around the countryside, even with Mustafa Sahab and Haji Somayeh as guides who knew the lay of the land and the Qazi Kurds as an allied military force who knew how and where other Kurds would fight.

Curt wanted action, too. Sitting in Mosul was a drag. Hassan was bitching and sniveling because he had to stay out in the field with Sharaf Qazi. And Curt was more than anxious to get busy doing something because the presence of Shariat Khani was causing some of the women of the Washington Greys to get a little upset themselves.

In a closely knit unit such as the Greys, it's tough to keep a secret. Alexis knew that Shariat Khani had stalked Curt and bagged her prey. The commanding officer of ASSAULTCO Alpha reacted by assuming a cool aloofness toward Curt but a continued friendly attitude toward Shariat Khani, which Curt didn't need just then, much less understand. As for Kitsy Clinton who also got the word from Rumor Control, she just acted like a hurt little girl and turned off her bounce and perkiness around Curt. Even Joan Ward cluck-clucked at him one day in mild disapproval.

It wasn't that Shariat Khani had bragged, but she had assumed she'd been allowed into the camaraderie of the Greys, and no one was allowed membership in such an exclusive club without the acquiescence of the Greys themselves, especially a potential troublemaker like Shariat Khani was revealing herself to be.

"Well, on these *goddamned* continual recce flights, we're just burning up *fuel* and running out the TBO on our *engines*," Worsham bitched.

"Hell, you're not paying for it," Curt reminded him.

"I'll *pay* with my pink *hide* if we run out the useful *lifetimes* of the time-critical *parts* in my 'dynes," Worsham reminded him. "Then I'm likely to find my *ass* sitting on the fucking *desert* somewhere a zillion goddamned *klicks* from anywhere with nothing but *camels* for transportation! Do you know how *tough* it's been to get spare *parts* in this fucking backwater?"

Colonel Bill Bellamack poked his head out of a doorway. He looked unhappy. "I thought so! No sonofabitch in this Regiment swears like the two of you bastards when you get together! Shag your asses in here! *Tyehpyehr! Nyeh-myed-lyen-nuh!*" he snapped at the two of them.

Curt nudged Worsham. "I've got news for you. When the Colonel snaps at you in Russian, whatever he says means 'right now with no more sniveling!' "

Without another word, the two men stepped into the regimental commander's office. Curt knew this was serious official business, so he snapped a serious official salute. Awkwardly, Worsham followed suit, which was unusual; Army aviators had unconsciously adopted the relaxed protocol of the Aerospace Force which had been spun off from them after War Two.

Bellamack returned their salutes and muttered, "At ease, gentlemen. I couldn't help but overhear your conversation in the hallway. Hell, no one in the building could help overhearing it! Cal, one of these days go see Ruth Gydesen and see if she can't turn down the gain on your vocal cords a notch or two." He didn't sit down behind his terminal desk but walked over to where he had a huge 1:100,000 three-dimensional topographical map of northwestern Iraq up on the wall. "How quickly can we move out?"

"Where are we going, Colonel?" Worsham asked in return.

"And what do you want us to do?" Curt followed at once.

"If we have to haul out of this immediate region, I'll have to update my navigational data bases and file the international flight plans," Worsham went on.

"If it's a minor skirmish, I'll have to work up the MRE lists differently than for a prolonged major field operation," Curt added. "And it may take an additional hour or two to get TACBATT configured for the mission. But no sweat, Colonel. What's up? Did one of our recce teams make contact?"

Bellamack had let the two of them report and ask questions until they got to the one Bellamack wanted to answer. "Lieutenant Mahmud just reported to me that Sharaf Qazi and the Ahl-i Haqqs made contact with a Qadiri guerrilla group moving south. They appear to be accompanied in support by what seems to be the Soviet Spetsnaz battalion. This was reported in this area here." Without resorting to calling up the megacomputer of the 17th Iron Fist Division, "Georgie," Bellamack pointed toward a spot on the huge map. "Unless you two have a better idea about where the Qadiris are headed, I think their objective is the master petroleum pipeline distribution and pumping center at Ain Zalah."

Curt reached for his pocket tacomm brick. "I'll check to see if we have a birdbot aloft over the area where Hassan reported the guerrillas."

"I can have a Harpy flight over them in thirty minutes or less," Worsham added, also reaching for his tacomm.

Bellamack waved his hand. "While you two were out in the hallway bitching about how boring this whole operation is, I went around you and did just that. Gibbon reports he'll divert a pair of birdbots from surveillance flights near Mangezn; they'll be over the target in fifteen minutes and we'll have data on the bus then. Worsham, I want you to hold your Harpies on the ground right now. The birdbots can be operated in a clandestine mode; they won't be noticed. But a Harpy is a pretty damned big hole in the sky. And if this Qadiri outfit has any Soviet Wasps, I don't want to take the chance of losing a Harpy at this early stage of the operation. We'll need all we can get later."

"Hell, Colonel, we've *got* suitable countermeasures against Wasps," Worsham insisted.

"You do and you don't. Even if it's one chance in a hundred that a Wasp will get past your countermeasures and you manage to get some good reccé data on the flight, I don't want to waste the chances I've got. I'd rather that you have all hundred chances when Curt calls on you to bust a few rocks. But get AIRLIFTCO ready for hauling and TACAIRCO ready to Wild Weasel for them." Bellamack looked again at the map and stated flatly, "We're going to ambush them tomorrow morning."

The three men were now standing side by side at the map. Curt found this planning procedure quite different from using the usual horizontal holographic map generated and projected by Georgie. "That's goddamned close to the border up in Hell's Corner where the Iraq, Turkey, and Syria borders have a common point," he remarked. "That doesn't give us a whole hell of a lot of room to maneuver. Airspace tight for you up there, Cal?"

"We ought to be able to do *our* thing without violating anyone's airspace," the AIRBATT commander commented. "Or being violated with something our selves . . ."

"It will be tight," Bellamack declared. "The Syrians or the Turks could reach you with their SAMs with your 'dynes that close to their borders. They may not like tacair activity operating so close to them. They're likely to shoot. Don't forget, the Turks are damned unhappy with us at the moment."

"Fuck 'em! The Turks have American Smart Farts," Cal pointed out, using the soldier's nickname for the M-100A (FG/IM-190) tube rocket that also armed the Greys. It had picked up that sobriquet because of its "smart" guidance system and the distinctive sound its short-burn boost rocket made when the projectile left the tube. "Colonel, let me tell you that *my* 'dyne drivers would be sort of reluctant to flit around over even a training maneuver with friendlies if we hadn't worked out a perfectly *acceptable* way to protect our asses against the Smart Fart. It ain't *easy* and it means we have to break off being nasty while we're doing it. But when someone fires one of those at you, you either shit and git or send out one of your own Smart Farts to get rid of it. A *hell* of a waste of perfectly good ordnance, but better than going down in pieces."

"In any event, I want AIRBATT to be goddamned careful at all times when you're within ten klicks of the border!"

Curt could tell that Bellamack was under pressure of some sort. He guessed it might have been partly due to the rather touchy situation with General Pickens. Maybe it was a consequence of Bellamack's neuroelectronic linkage with the Soviet Spetsnaz soldier, Pugachev, because no one really knew yet about all of the consequences of such an electronically achieved mind link. Warbot brainies did it all the time, and Bellamack was a former warbot brainy. But such NE linkage through warbots implied that everyone on the net had the proper training which permitted one to block off areas of consciousness that weren't pertinent to running and fighting warbots. Going into linkage with an untrained person was suspected as being somewhat risky. Even the neuroelectronic psychiatrists were just nibbling away at using full NE mind link for clinical and therapeutic purposes. Bellamack had known these risks before he'd linked with Pugachev. And Bellamack spoke Russian so he knew how the other man thought. But something may have rubbed off on the Colonel from Pugachev's more primitive and paranoid way of thinking.

"Hell, Colonel, it's damned *tough* to stay more than ten klicks from a border around where three countries come together!" Cal complained loudly. Curt guessed that the man's loud voice was partly caused by the pilot's chronic loss of hearing which came from too many years in an aerodyne. "If we get into a fracas closer than ten klicks to a border, do you want me to hold off any tacair support until the battle moves out to *eleven* klicks?"

"Dammit, no! That's not what I meant, Worsham!" Bellamack snapped. "Just be careful when you're within SAM range of anything!"

"We do that anyway, Colonel. It's *our* pink bods strapped into those flying machines!"

Bellamack waved his hand impatiently. "Okay, but you're going to be going into a situation like that because here's what we're going to do."

To Curt's amazement, the Colonel indicated on the map a completely planned series of movements, explaining as he pointed. "Cal, I want you to airlift RECONCO without BIRD plus ASSAULTCO Alpha and Bravo to this point here where you, Curt, will ambush the main force of Qadiri near Asi on the river after they've crossed Highway Two. Since we haven't got the capability to lift more than the ASSAULTCOs and RECONCO in one sortie, I'll be coming up Highway Two in vehicles with GUNCO and as many of SERVBATT as I can use. I'm going to order Sharaf Qazi to stalk the guerrilla forces on their north side. After they cross Highway Two and get down in the river bottom lands near Asi, we'll nail them. Curt, you'll hit them from their left flank at a place of your choosing where the Tigris River gives you the best tactical advantage. Then I'll cut off their retreat path and hit them from behind with the Ahl-i Haqqs. Worsham, I'll need tacair support from your Harpy squadron once we get the guerrillas between the hammer and the anvil down by the river. It's my intention to trap this Qadiri and Spetsnaz force and then call for their surrender. When the Soviets discover they've been stalked, surrounded, and outgunned, they'll fold because they certainly understand when they're outgunned and outmaneuvered."

Curt was dumbfounded. "Colonel, where did this ops plan come from?"

Bellamack snapped his head around to look at Curt. "I worked it out. I want you two to do the staff work on it so we can move out and pull it off tonight!"

It was totally uncharacteristic of Colonel Wild Bill Bellamack to simply present a tactical operations plan to his people in full-blown form with no previous discussion. For a long time now, Bellamack had been the organizer and Curt had been the tactician. Field operations had been worked out between the two men. When Cal Worsham and his Warhawks had been permanently reassigned to the newly reorganized Washington Greys following Brunei, Worsham had been included in the planning because of the additional element of tacair support and airlift which his AIRBATT supplied.

"Colonel, may I voice an opinion?" Curt asked tentatively. He wasn't sure at this point what Bellamack's answer might be.

"What's the problem?"

"This is an outstanding operational plan for a brigade of two regiments," Curt remarked easily but with concern in his voice. "Or even a three regiment operation with one regiment being held in reserve. But this plan proposes to break up the Washington Greys."

"So?" There was a hint of defensive hostility in Bellamack's sudden interjection.

"We've reorganized as the Sierra Charlie equivalent of a World War Two regimental combat team," Curt pointed out.

"And you don't think we should break up the team? Why not?" Bellamack asked, but it was almost a rhetorical question for which the Colonel didn't expect an answer because he went on at once, "After all, part of our training was intended to make us flexible because everyone is cross-trained in someone else's job. We can work outside of the normal platoon and company structure."

"Sir, the plan is too complex and requires exceptionally good communications in order for it to work right," Curt persisted. "If I run into trouble or if you're delayed or if Sharaf Qazi breaks what little discipline he might have when it comes to combined operations—I don't trust the Kurds yet because we haven't worked with them and they appear to be impulsive . . . Well, the plan has no slack if things go to slime. Cal, I don't mean to imply that your Warhawks aren't the best and that you don't run an outstanding air operation—we expressly wanted the Warhawks for our AIRBATT when we were reorganizing—but you know as well as I do that things can screw up the way they did on Kerguelen, and the way I know they can get fucked up like Zahedan. . . ."

"Yeah, I agree with you, Carson, but we try to keep the unexpected variables out of the equation if we can," the airman replied, his voice strangely quiet because he knew that Curt was essentially challenging the Colonel over a plan Worsham didn't exactly like, either, although he didn't know why.

"What do you want me to do?" Bellamack suddenly asked Curt.

"Maintain regimental team integrity. Go in there together. Let the Ahl-i Haqqs be the anvil while we're the hammer. Hit the guerrillas on their left flank while the Ahl-i Haqqs take them on their right."

"Airlift operation?"

Curt nodded.

"Can't get the whole Regiment out there in one eight-'dyne sortie," Worsham pointed out.

"You can sure as hell get the ASSAULTCOs and GUNCO out," Curt pointed out, "and we'll let RECONCO stay on the ground and do their thing there. SERVBATT can follow up on the roads as a possible reserve," Curt suggested.

"Is that it?" Bellamack suddenly asked.

Curt nodded. "In brief, Colonel."

Bellamack shook his head. "I don't trust Qazi to carry through and be a good anvil for your hammer. He's got to have me there to keep him under control. I've spent a lot of time in this theater of operations; I know these people." He paused, then stated, "I expect you to fill in the details of my plan and proceed. I've thought this through, and we'll follow my ops plan."

"Colonel . . ." Curt began.

Bellamack merely looked at his battalion commander and said coolly, "Make it so, Major."

Chapter Twenty-six

"I don't like it! I don't like it one damned bit!" Curt growled as he and Cal Worsham left Bellamack's office.

"Hell, *I* don't like the fucking tactical plan, *either*, Carson, but an order is an *order!*" Worsham shot back. His face was grim, and the tips of his handlebar mustache were quivering.

"Yeah, it is. I don't like that, either. But you're absolutely right. An order is an order. We've made our inputs. The Colonel's mind is made up. So we go do it!" Curt growled. He'd had to work under some ROEs that had damned near cost him his life, and he couldn't argue those because they usually came down from on high. And he'd gotten lots of orders which he hadn't liked at the time because he'd considered them to be unduly hazardous or even downright stupid. But he'd carried them out anyway after pointing out to his superior officer that he thought various things were wrong with the order or the plan.

Curt grimaced and reluctantly said to Worsham, "Cal, you were with us on Kerguelen Island which was one of the times that Colonel Wild Bill Bellamack made his name to shine. This is just between thee and me, and if you ever turn it loose in Rumor Control I'll figure out how to do something real nasty. I'm worried about the Colonel. Something's wrong! He's acting damned strange! Dammit, I've been with him in a lot of operations, and sometimes the pressures of command were even greater. He didn't blow his neurons then, and I'm not saying it's happened to him now. But I wonder if all the stress has pushed him pretty damned near the edge. I've never seen him act the way he did in there!"

Worsham reached out and put a hand on Curt's shoulder. It had just enough pressure to cause Curt to stop striding down the hallway and turn to face the air battalion commander. "Carson, dammit," Worsham said in a very uncharacteristically low and personal voice, "are you suggesting that the Colonel's got some jellyware problems?"

Curt nodded. "Cal, that's a brilliant deduction! You read me five-by!"

Worhsam shook his head. "That's a damned serious thing for you to be thinking about, Carson!"

"Yeah, probably. But the Colonel has *never* worked out a tactical plan all by himself before and then presented it as the final plan with no arguments allowed. He's always called in his officers. And sometimes he's even done the planning with the whole Regiment in a sort of freewheeling OSCAR brief. He used to know he's not the world's greatest tactician, and he's even said that to me a lot of times. Now he's come up with this plan that flies against even the most elementary principles of warfare! It's sure as hell going to lead to a monster sheep screw." Curt didn't like saying what he felt he had to say. It bordered on indirect insubordination. The Navy might tag it "incitement to mutiny."

"Are you thinking of overriding . . . ?" Worsham began.

Curt knew what the man was thinking. "Not only no, but hell no! The Colonel and I have a contract. You ought to know what that means, Cal!"

"Yeah. I do."

"Besides, I've never been overtly insubordinate in my whole career, and I have no intention of starting now!"

"I'm glad you qualified that by eliminating the covert times. Otherwise, I'd have to call you a liar. We've all been given stupid orders, saluted, and gone out and done what was necessary, if that counts as being insubordinate."

204

"It doesn't, or the whole damned Army would have been court martialed long ago. And we would have lost a lot of wars." He clapped Worsham on the shoulder, breathed a sigh of resignation, and told him, "So we go do what has to be done, Cal! Let's figure out some worst-case consequences so we can play CYA and save our troops when the whole thing becomes a sheep screw. In the meantime, it is indeed my duty to bring my concerns to the attention of our regimental medical officer."

"Or maybe even the chaplain."

"Thanks for reminding me. I'll ask Nellie Crile to drop by for a chat with the Colonel. Maybe he'll get some insight that we don't have." They came to a stairwell and Curt turned to go down, saying to his fellow battalion commander as he did so, "Cal, I wonder if that NE linkage session the Colonel had with the Sov somehow pushed the wrong buttons."

"Well, we sure as *hell* don't know a lot about *that* sort of thing yet, Curt." Worsham used Curt's first name for the first time that Curt could remember. "Would Doc Gydesen know?"

"Another good idea, Cal. I'll go ask her. It's probably my duty to tell her what I suspect, anyway."

"Yeah, it *would* tend to cover your ass."

"Speaking of CYA, Cal, we'd better do it ourselves for this forthcoming sheep screw. We need to develop the sort of contingency plans any commander should have when things go tits-up. Why don't you have John Adam check with Edie Sampson in about an hour, and let's get our heads together on the mission contingency planning."

"Ah, yeah! The way the Army *really* gets things done: turn it over to the top NCOs!"

Curt knew that once he got started on the work of preparing for the mission he wouldn't have time to do much of anything else, so he detoured on his way to his TACBATT command office to seek our Major Ruth Gydesen who was down in BIOTECO operations.

"How's the Sov?" he asked her as an opener.

Ruth looked up at him over the top of her terminal. She shook her head. "You can't see him. If I let you in there, I'll have to let in the vultures from General Pickens's Gee-two staff who've been hanging around here for days. Or that stupid woman, Amy Mac-something-dash-something who considers herself to be America's gift to downtrodden humankind and the personal deputy of the Secretary of State."

"I don't want to talk to Pugachev; I don't speak his language anyway," Curt advised her. "I want to talk to you."

"Well, that's different! What did you have in mind? Lunch, perhaps? I'm not on duty this afternoon." Ruth had a professional side and a personal side. The personal side was all woman, as Curt had discovered on several occasions.

"This is a personal and private discussion on the professional level, Major," he told her, sending the signal right at the start.

She reacted properly. "Very well, Major, what's your problem?"

"It's not mine. It may be ours, the Washington Greys."

Ruth raised her eyebrows at this. "Some of your troops been playing around in Mosul again? Does it hurt when you urinate?"

"None of the above. Have you seen or talked to the Colonel lately?"

"Not since he did the NE linkage with Pugachev. Why? Something wrong?"

"In a single word, yes," Curt admitted. "I'm here in an official capacity as the second-in-command. I'm concerned about the well-being of our commanding officer. I wish to bring this officially to your attention and request confidentiality. I may be overly concerned and nothing may come of my worries. I have no intention of going any further in the matter. After I talk to you about it, I'm going to obey some rather incredible orders Colonel Bill Bellamack just gave to Major Worsham and me."

"Oh-oh!" Ruth Gydesen muttered. "Do you mind if I

206

record this for the professional record?"

"Not at all! Please do so!"

"Roger, recording! Say all that again for the record, Curt."

So Curt went through the prologue again. "The Colonel is acting strangely," he went on. "He and I have been good friends since he assumed command of the Washington Greys. We work together very well, as the record shows. I have no intention of doing anything more than report what appears to me to be strange and unusual behavior on his part. He seems to be insecure, sensitive, defensive. Perhaps a little bit paranoid . . . although I'm not a psychologist and therefore unqualified to make that diagnosis. I hadn't noticed this different behavior of his before he undertook neuroelectronic linkage with the Soviet Spetsnaz soldier, Pugachev. But now this personality and behavior change is apparent to me, and I consider it to be highly unusual because I've gotten to know the man very well from the Battle of Bisbee onward. Major Cal Worsham was with me just now in the Colonel's office and can confirm everything I've said about the unusual nature of the Colonel's actions. I'm concerned enough about it that I'm taking the option of reporting it to you as the regimental medical officer."

Curt went on to describe what had happened.

"What do you think, Major?" he finally asked her.

Ruth Gydesen sat there in silence for a moment. Finally, she put the tips of her long surgeon's fingers together, stared past the steeple she'd thus created, and told him, "It would be inappropriate at this time for me to comment as the regimental medical officer. However, I have recorded it and will hereafter keep it in mind. End of recording." She passed her hand over a switch on her terminal desk, then got up and stared out the window at the bright sunlight reflecting off the tiled rooftops and white stucco walls of Mosul. "I think you're right about asking Father Crile to chat with him. I'll have Nellie give him a call because you're going to be busy. And I'll pay special attention to the Colonel without being obvious."

"I'm worried as hell about the Colonel," Curt admitted. He was also worried about the continuation of Operation Sturdy Spectra, but that was something over which he could perhaps gain some control by careful planning and figuring out contingency measures for the various ways the operation could go tits-up. He couldn't do anything about the way his superior officer and friend was acting. "Could that NE linkage session have had anything to do with how he's acting, Ruth?"

She nodded. "Possible. Probable. We know so little about the human mind. Neuroelectronics has helped us a lot in the last twenty years. The neuroelectronic psychiatrists work a lot more slowly than the military technicians who developed warbot linkage. The military always moves fast on weapons systems. 'Technology pull,' they call it. They try to pull the technology along. Sometimes it works. But I don't mean to imply that the military R&D types put people unduly at risk ˙ with warbot linkage. Certainly nowhere near the same level of risk as Sierra Charlie military commanders have to deal with in sending people out into the field to get shot at. Different situation. No analogy at all." She sighed and sat down behind her terminal desk again. "The people who drafted the Treaty of Toronto were probably right: we shouldn't be using NE technology to probe people's minds yet. Particularly *different* minds. People who grew up speaking different languages and therefore with different thinking patterns. The human mind is complex."

She arose from her desk and walked over to the window as though getting a view of distance and depth would somehow help her thoughts get perspective as well. She went on, "The human mind is also highly suggestible, as hypnosis has shown for centuries. I have no idea of the extent to which thinking processes might have been exchanged on a sort of two-way or duplex channeling when Bellamack linked with Pugachev. No one does. But from what you tell me of the Colonel's behavior, he appears to be acting like a Russian within the framework of the English language which is his mind's basic operating system, to put it in computer terminology. I wouldn't go so far to say that his mind's operating system has a bug or two in it; I don't know that. But a program glitch may have been introduced. We'll never know if Bellamack affected Pugachev in a reverse manner; we have no base line data on Pugachev so we don't know what he was like before Bellamack linked to him. The Colonel may be a little confused now; maybe Father Crile can get that important piece of data. Whatever it is, it may be temporary, transient."

"God, I hope so! Ruth, it could screw up the whole Regiment," Curt warned.

She shook her head. "No. Not a chance. The Colonel's got a good mind, and it's full of feedback circuits and circuit breakers that will keep him from going over the edge. He was a warbot brainy with warbot brainy training. That doesn't leave any loose nuts rattling around upstairs."

"Except in very unusual cases," Curt recalled, "but I won't name names because those people are no longer with the Regiment."

"Curt, the same rationale holds true for the Washington Greys, both as individuals and as a unit, which is the reason you and I are sitting here talking right now," Major Ruth Gydesen pointed out, turning to lean against the window jamb with her arms folded before her. "The organization of this Regiment has too many feedback loops and too many circuit breakers of its own of a different type. You and the rest of the Greys will not allow the actions of one man to screw up the Regiment. You'll act to bypass the malfunctioning element, and you'll cover it up so that no one will ever know you did it. The Washington Greys will survive. The Regiment has survived since seventeen-eighty-four. After all, Curt, this outfit is a very complex organism all by itself! It has to be because it's made up of very complex organisms such as you and me and Colonel Bellamack."

"So?"

"So go do what you were ordered to do and do what

you have to do, and I'll keep an eye on the Colonel and try to cover your ass . . . and everyone else's, too," Ruth promised him. She was a good trooper, and she'd just volunteered to shoulder a lot of Curt's concern. She didn't have to, and, if anything went wrong, she might be held up to criticism for inciting insubordination herself.

Curt grinned. He did feel better about the matter. It looked like something he could handle now. "I know you won't take this the wrong way, Ruth, but I probably could have gotten the last part of that inspiration lecture if I'd gone to see Nellie Crile. . . ."

And she smiled back. "Of course! Both Father Crile and I do the same thing most of the time, except we do it a little differently because we've got different Rated Position Codes. And, of course, he's certified by a higher authority than I am!"

Curt left knowing he'd done what he could within the bounds of military regulations and concern for a friend. He also knew that Ruth Gydesen had done a little job on him, too, mostly in the area of attitude adjustment.

Still, Curt didn't relish what lay ahead of him.

Chapter Twenty-seven

"I still don't think this ops plan makes a goddamned bit of sense!" Alexis Morgan complained.

Curt had had it, and he wasn't about to listen to any more bitching or sniveling at this point. He'd spent all day working on the details of Operation Sturdy Spectra Phase II, Bellamack's split regiment plan of catching the Qadiri Kurds and the Soviet Spetsnaz battalion en route to the major petroleum pipeline center of Ain Zalah. The deeper he got into the planning with both the regimental staff and the combat unit commanders, the more he began to worry about the wisdom of the plan. He'd worked hard with everyone trying to come up with a detailed order of battle that would compromise the integrity of the Regiment the least. It hadn't been easy, and a couple of units had had to be split. Everyone knew why, but no one was really very happy with the results. Nor were they happy with the overall plan, either, because it was complex and therefore very sensitive with many failure points.

So Curt coolly told Alexis, "Major, we've been given orders. We've worked out the details. Now we go and carry out those orders."

"We're splitting the Regiment again," she continued to complain. "Didn't we learn *anything* about that in Brunei?"

"I thought we did," was Curt's reluctant reply, then he glared at her, "But I'm forced to repeat something to you that I was once told myself: soldier, shut up and soldier!"

Curt's Battalion Sergeant Major, Edie Sampson, grinned a little at hearing that. She was the one who'd used that phrase on a reluctant non-com a long time ago. But she hadn't been happy about having to do it, and she knew her CO wasn't happy about repeating it.

Alexis sighed. "In other words, Alexis, FIDO, old girl! Well, I guess I deserved that! At least you succeeded in keeping most of the old Companions and the experienced combat teams together this time," she muttered darkly as she watched the Northern Attack Group, NORTHAG, depart Mosul in a column of 36 vehicles which disappeared into the darkness with only their infrared pilotage lights on so their vehicle autopilots could track the vehicle ahead in the column.

It's difficult to hide the movement of so many large military vehicles, even on a paved road. Dust and dirt get kicked up by a column of vehicles moving at 50 klicks per hour. Therefore, Bellamack had decided that NORTHAG, his group that had to move on the ground because not enough Chippies were available to airlift the entire Regiment, would move out under cover of darkness that night in order to be in position where they could maneuver in behind the Qadiri and Soviets tomorrow.

NORTHAG was basically the anvil of the operation, heavy in artillery firepower with all the Regiment's LAMVAs and their Saucy Cans guns, plus all of the vehicles in SERVBATT with their 15 millimeter automatics. Overhead when the battle was joined, AIRBATT would concentrate all 8 of the AD-40C Harpies to move mud and bust boulders.

NORTHAG would be joined at dawn by the 147 irregulars of Sharaf Qazi's Ahl-i Haqqs. They were basically light human infantry armed with a wide assortment of assault rifles, old American M224 60-millimeter mortars, and Chinese S-220 multi-purpose rockets.

At least that was Bellamack's plan for NORTHAG. Lieutenant Hassan Mahmud, the Washington Greys liaison officer still with Sharaf Qazi, expressed some reservations about the Ahl-i Haqqs being able to meet such a critical time deadline and be at a critical point when they were expected.

Shariat Khani, Qazi's liaison with the Greys, had no such reservations. "We will be where we are supposed to be when we are supposed to be there . . . and we shall fight and kill alongside you!" she maintained. She was never one to mince words or to do things in a halfway fashion. Curt knew much about this. "A victory at Asi will help Sharaf Qazi consolidate command over the rest of the Kurds. It will be the beginning of the first unified campaign the Kurds have ever waged. If other nations have denied us our own country in the past because of diplomatic maneuvering, and if we have been unable to take it ourselves because of divided forces, now perhaps we have the chance to begin anew under the leadership of Sharaf Qazi!"

It wasn't lost on the Greys that Shariat Khani's enthusiasm belied a personal motive: if Sharaf Qazi ended up being the de facto King of the Kurds—or whatever they decided to call their national leader, their George Washington and Simon Bolivar—Shariat Khani would certainly end up being the First Lady or queen.

Curt wasn't as upset about the split force as he'd been earlier in the day. He'd helped plan things so that Bellamack was adequately supported by subordinates Curt knew were the best.

Regimental Sergeant Major Henry Kester would be at Bellamack's side, and Curt and Kester had worked together so closely for so long that they almost had a private communications channel established between them . . . provided the tacomm didn't crap out and communications could be maintained.

Major John Gibbon would be running recon from NORTHAG, and Captain Ellie Aarts's birdbot platoon was with them in order to provide Bellamack with recce. Ellie was an old trooper who knew how to shoot straight, and Curt knew she wouldn't go into panic mode and would thus help keep NORTHAG on a level course if things started to go to slime.

The one Curt was counting on to level out NOR-

THAG was Major Joan Ward and her GUNCO of experienced Sierra Charlies who'd decided it would be a little less stressful to sit back a klick or two and send high explosive greetings via the Saucy Cans. But she and GUNCO could get down and dirty in person-to-person combat if necessary.

The various units of Major Wade Hampton's SERV-BATT were part of NORTHAG as well. Curt didn't like to send support troops into combat, but the people of SERVBATT continually reminded the rest of the Greys that they, too, were Sierra Charlies and expected to have to go physical when circumstances required it. Well, circumstances required it for Sturdy Spectra Phase II. Curt couldn't shake his conviction that this was really a brigade operation; the Greys needed everyone for it since they'd be going into it as merely a regiment.

Major Ruth Gydesen's BIOTECO wouldn't be in either group although it was attached to NORTHAG. The Bio-tech Service Vehicles bearing their big red crosses and (special in the Persian Gulf Theater, the red crescent as well) would remain several klicks clear of the action but close enough that the combat medics could get any wounded troopers evacked quickly to Gydesen's mobile field hospital in the BSVs.

NORTHAG was heavy with vehicles and short on warbots. The Regiment now had only Jeeps, Mary Anns, and LAMVAs as a results of the reorganization; other warbots types were too big, too heavy, too slow, and carried far too much fire power for the sort of operations the Sierra Charlies had been involved in. Thus, most of the Jeeps and Mary Anns were with Curt's DIRAG, the Direct Attack Group.

DIRAG was about as lean and tactical as could be with both ASSAULTCOs and the SCOUT platoon. They were going to fill up all 8 Chippewas. And they wouldn't depart until 0400 since they wanted to be on the ground near Asi at dawn and ready to take on the Qadiri and Soviets at first light, which was always a good time to make contact and get combat going when on the offensive; regardless whether the enemy had continued through the night on a night march or had bivouacked overnight, it was a time when they'd be sleepy and just getting their biological clocks started for the new day.

Dawn assaults nearly always worked, even when the enemy was in a defensive position and expecting them. Most of this was due to the fact that human beings have a surprisingly accurate 24-hour internal biological clock and are very responsive to diurnal cycles.

The "wee, small hours of the morning" are very real indeed.

Curt knew that, and the 0400 hours load-up of the Chippies would come too soon insofar as he was concerned. So he looked at his Battalion Sergeant Major and asked her, "Edie, is everything hot to trot?"

She nodded and replied. "Yes, sir! We're tactical! And good to go! Bots are aboard the Chippies, checked out, powered down, armed up, and put away for the night. All we have to do is stuff in cannon fodder and lift off."

Curt couldn't help but grin. Edie Sampson hadn't replaced Henry Kester; no one could do that. But she'd molded the job of Curt's Number One NCO in her own way, and she was just as good as Henry Kester but in subtly different ways. Curt expected that. She was often a mercurial redhead and certainly didn't have the cool and couth of Kester, nor the decades of combat experience. But no one in the Greys had the years of experience that Kester possessed.

It is often said in the Army that "there's one in every outfit." Usually, this applies to Private Zero; it also applies to people like Henry Kester without whom the Army wouldn't exist at all. But that's been true from the days of the Roman centurions anyway, except that the centurions were both top sergeants and company commanders rolled into one.

"Okay, Edie, everyone is off-duty until 0300," Curt told her. "I suggest you pass the word for people to get some sleep tonight. Tomorrow's going to be a rough day with a lot of metal jackets flying around."

Curt looked at Alexis. She looked at him. "You shouldn't have done that, Major."

"Why not, Major?"

"Because I am indeed going to bed to get a good night's sleep," she admitted.

"Command jitters?"

She nodded. "Yes and no."

Curt shrugged. "Okay," was all he could say. Alexis Morgan had always been her own woman. From the early days of their relationship when she was a brown-bar in his company up to the time she'd gotten her own company, Morgan's Marauders, she'd been a young and eager officer . . . for everything. Company command had slowly and subtly changed her, and she was far less impulsive now. It had been even more pronounced since the Brunei operation. Colonel Ahmad Mahathis, the son of the Sultan of Brunei and the commander of the Royal Brunei Legion, often visited the Washington Greys on liaison and training missions now, ostensibly to stay up to date on the latest innovations in American Sierra Charlie doctrine because Brunei was slowly integrating warbots into the jungle fighting units. Mahathis always showed up as the pilot of a Royal Brunei Air Command Sabre-dancer M6. And he always saw Alexis Morgan. Well, Curt had decided, if Alexis wanted to play that one for all it was worth, she'd found herself someone who was not only rich but also outranked her.

Lieutenant Kitsy Clinton had no such inhibitions. Furthermore, she was far more direct in her pixie-like way. She simply stopped him as they headed back into the casern and stated flatly, "I'm glad you declared us all off-duty. On the night before, I need you and you need me. I may be Number Two, but good enough is the enemy of the best."

But when the two of them let themselves into Curt's quarters, the shower was running.

Curt immediately knew what was about to happen. "Kitsy, maybe you'd better leave for the moment. I've got trouble."

"And I know who she is, and *she's* got trouble, not you!" Kitsy snapped with fire in her eyes.

"Uh-uh! No! She'll tear you limb for limb!" Curt insisted, putting his arm in front of her to keep her from charging into the bathroom.

"I may be Number Two, but I don't give in to Number Umpteen-hundred with grace and beauty! Not when she sure as hell is no lady . . . and I am a lady, sir! And I am about to do something intentionally rude as a lady!"

At that point, Curt decided the best he could do was to stand by and try to staunch the flow of blood. He sure as hell didn't want to get between these two women!

Kitsy picked up a wastebasket, marched into the bathroom, turned on the water in the sink, and began to fill the container.

"Curt?" came Shariat Khani's voice from the shower stall. "I wanted to be certain that I am all clean and pretty for you!" The sound of running water stopped as she turned it off.

As Curt watched, Kitsy hoisted the wastebasket of cold water, flung back the shower curtain, and dashed about 8 liters of ice-cold water on the naked Shariat Khani in the shower stall.

Shariat Khani screamed when the cold water hit her then shouted a stream of invective in Kurdish.

Quickly, Kitsy grabbed a towel and stuck it under the still-running cold water tap of the sink, getting it thoroughly soaked as she squeezed and twisted it into what every West Pointer knows as a "rat-tail."

Standing there with her wet rat-tail, Kitsy said in a hard voice, "It's about time I threw some cold water on this relationship! Now get your ass out of here before I smack it with this and turn it real red!"

"You bitch! You can't . . . !" Shariat Khani began.

But Kitsy wouldn't even let her get started. "Grab your shawl and go over the wall! Right now! Or, so help me God, you'll be standing up tomorrow when you could be sitting down!"

217

Shariat made no move to grab her clothing that was in a heap on the bathroom floor. Instead, she made just the slightest move toward Kitsy.

And Kitsy let fly with the wet towel.

And caught Shariat just above what is commonly referred to as the "triangle of Venus."

The snap was loud. So was Shariat's yelp.

"No ifs or ands . . . or it's your butt!" Kitsy persisted. "Pick 'em up! Get your ass out of here!"

Shariat lunged at Kitsy.

But Kitsy got off another snap with the rat-tail, this time across Shariat's breasts.

Hitting a woman in the breasts is like kicking a man in the testicles. Kitsy knew that. She'd been hit with 9-millimeter rounds in the breasts in Mexico. She knew how badly it hurt.

And that took all the fight out of Shariat Khani who'd never come up against that sort of sophisticated aggressive behavior from any woman before.

She collapsed to the floor, moaning in pain.

Kitsy turned to Curt. "Help me get her out of here."

"I'd better call the MPs," Curt suggested.

Kitsy shook her head. She was suddenly in command of the situation, a position Curt had never seen her occupy before. "Not while you're the senior ranking officer in the casern! And she's not permanently injured; I know something about that. She'll be okay in a few minutes. And when she's okay, I want her to be in the hallway outside with her clothes, and the door locked so she can't get back in! I'll even leave her this towel to wrap around her until she manages to get dressed. She's going to be embarrassed enough as it is. No sense in making her any madder than she'll be. Come on! Give me a hand!"

It took them only a minute to drag the moaning Shariat Khani to the door, deposit her in the hallway outside, and drape the towel over her. Then Kitsy closed and bolted the door once she and Curt were back in his quarters.

"Goddammit, Kitsy," Curt exploded, "I've got to work with that woman as our liaison with Sharaf Qazi tomorrow! She'll—"

"She'll be a little easier to work with, believe me," Kitsy said with fire still in her eyes. Then she went all soft and pixie-like again, looking and acting like someone's teenaged daughter who couldn't possibly get angry at anyone. She stepped up to Curt, pressed against him, looked up at him, and began to open the seam on his wet shirt front. "In the meantime, nothing like a good fight to get the juices flowing! As we were saying before we were so rudely interrupted . . ."

Chapter Twenty-eight

It was time to go get shot at.

Or, if Curt and his colleagues had done the proper scheming in their "contingency planning" sessions the afternoon before, maybe the Qadiri and Soviets would be the ones to take it in the shorts.

The Greys hadn't disobeyed orders by developing these contingency plans in the face of what they considered to be a bad plan on the part of their regimental commander, but they'd carefully structured Operation Sturdy Spectra Phase Two so they had a higher probability of winning and creaming the enemy if and when the Colonel's personal plan went down the tubes. Curt simply didn't want the Greys to be left with their asses bare to the breeze without Plan B if Plan A went to slime, as it often did and as, in Curt's opinion, this was almost certain to do.

It would have been easier if they'd known more about the "enemy." The best intel they'd gotten was from their two guides, Sahab and Somayeh. However, Curt didn't know how far to trust the info they'd provided because it seemed soft, sparse, scanty, and elusive — the sort of thing you'd look for in women's lingerie but not what you really needed in the way of combat intelligence information when your life and those of your comrades hangs on its timeliness and accuracy. More G-2 had come via Hassan who'd spent the last several days as liaison officer with Sharaf Qazi and the Ahl-i Haqqs, the ostensible allies of the Washington Greys in this campaign. Curt trusted Hassan, but he wasn't sure he trusted Qazi who was wily, shrewd, devious, and impulsive . . . like Shariat Khani.

Curt still didn't really understand Shariat Khani except that he now knew the woman had an insatiable appetite for both sex and violence.

Which is why he was more than a little concerned when the Direct Attack Group, DIRAG, mustered to load the Chippewas on the military ramp of Mosul aerodrome in the wan half-light before dawn. He might have two battles on his hands that day. The one with the Qadiri and Soviets was something he was trained to fight, and had experience in handling. But the one that might have erupted last night between Shariat Khani and Lieutenant Kitsy Clinton—clearly the winner in the Battle of the Bathroom because of a superior weapon system—was something he didn't know how to cope with. When men fought between themselves, they were violent, strong, brutal, and often honorably forgiving once the enemy was down and beaten. On the other hand, when women fought, they were more violent, more vicious, and far more intense; far-reaching grudges could result, and to hell with forgiveness!

That early morning, Kitsy was, of course, in great shape with high morale. She should be, Curt decided.

Strangely, when Shariat Khani showed up, dressed in the cammies and battle helmet loaned to her by Captain Harriet Dearborn of LOGCO but without body armor which Shariat refused to wear, the Amazon seemed none the worse for last night.

Curt took the chance and spoke to her. "Good morning, Shariat. I hope last night didn't leave you unprepared for today." It was a roundabout remark because Curt really didn't know what else to say, but he had to say something because he was DIRAG commander and she was his liaison with Qazi, but he wanted to stay the hell out of the line of fire in the Clinton-Khani campaign insofar as possible.

She smiled at him. It was the first time he'd seen her really smile. In the wake of the Battle of the Bathroom,

Curt thought this was highly unusual. "Oh, yes! I wa[s] rescued in the hallway by two of your gallant Harpy pilots who treated me very well indeed. I think I migh[t] have been hasty in selecting you on an exclusive basis Major." With that, she said no more about it.

Curt didn't know whether he'd been insulted or not but he didn't really care at that point. She'd gotten o[f] his back . . . or his stomach, as the case might be.

Maybe Shariat Khani was becoming semi-civilized, h[e] decided.

If so, it probably took two flyboys to start the process

And it was something else he didn't have to worr[y] about today, or at least for a while.

Lieutenant Kitsy Clinton wasn't so sure. "Major," sh[e] told him formally, "I intend to keep an eagle-type eyebal[l] focused on Shariat Khani today . . . and you know why I hope you won't get antsy if I maintain a high level o[f] readiness when I'm in her sight, or her sights, if it come[s] to that."

"It may have been the best thing to happen to her in [a] long time, Lieutenant," was Curt's cryptic answer. "I'll te[ll] you about it when this fur ball is all over with or mayb[e] she'll even sit down with you and discuss it woman-to-woman."

"Well! Really?" Kitsy was surprised.

"Yeah, I was surprised, too. But let's concentrate o[n] what we've got to do today, and maybe we'll pull this of[f] without taking the Golden BB."

In spite of the fact that Captain Roger Hawley was th[e] flight leader of "Hawley's Haulers," the AIRLIFTCO Curt had asked that Lieutenant Nancy Roberts's Chip[-] pewa be used for the airlift involving him, Edie Sampso[n] Shariat Khani, Haji Somayeh, Curt's ACV, and his tw[o] M33A2 Jeeps. Nancy had also volunteered to lift Sweet'[s] Scouts with the SCOUT ACV and Jeeps. This put he[r] slightly over maximum gross weight, but she said she wa[s] used to handling 'dynes that were overloaded. Curt kne[w] she was right; she'd done it before in the Sonoran opera[-] tion. Besides, the Chippie design was conservative and s[o] were its published performance limits. The Chippie could be pushed like any really good aerospace design.

It was no hassle loading the Chippies. The Greys had practiced it until it was almost boring. With the ACVs and warbots having been preloaded last night, it took the Sierra Charlies less than ten minutes to carry out the final "ingress" because they knew which 'dyne they were riding in and had already stowed some extra stuff they thought they might need.

As usual, Curt exercised the perk that permitted him to ride up on the bubbled flight deck with the pilot and flight engineer rather than in the spartan and often uncomfortable cargo bays where you couldn't see out.

It was tense. It always was before going into combat. And especially when no one knew exactly what was out there because the recce reports hadn't started to come over the regimental data link yet from Ellie Aarts's birdbots. Except on patrols around Mosul, this was the first time the Greys had gone into action together since they'd reorganized the Regiment. The new units were well motivated and had shown they could work together. But there was still the air of newness and still the same feeling of being scared shitless because you didn't know what was waiting out there for you when the cargo bay doors opened onto the real, nasty, deadly world outside.

Just before the turbines began to spool-up, someone started to sing to relieve tension. Others joined in until the song was drowned in the whine and roar of lift turbines:

Old, fat Chippie
  Liftin' off the strip,
Sierra Charlie
  Gonna take a little trip.
Stand up, power up,
  Dash to the door,
Run right out
  And shoot some more.
If I die

> *In a combat zone,*
>   *Put me in a box*
>   *And ship me home.*
> *Put my tam*
>   *Upon my head,*
> *Tell my folks*
>   *That I am dead.*
> *Gory, gory, what a hell of a way to die!*
> *Gory, gory, what a hell of a way to die!*
> *Gory, gory, what a hell of a way to die!*
> *But you'll party when I'm gone!*

Nancy Roberts lifted the Chippie off the Mosul aerodrome in the pre-dawn gloom and headed at once to the northwest.

Curt knew that Kurd spies had probably watched the operation. They couldn't have missed the departure of NORTHAG in its vehicles last night. With all the activities at the aerodrome last night, the spies certainly must have been alerted for this dawn patrol, too. Haji Somayeh assured Curt that the clandestine espionage ring in Mosul couldn't possibly get the word out to the Qadiri or anyone else before the Chippies reached their landing zone 90 kilometers away. The flight time was too short.

And Hawley's Haulers flew nap-of-the-earth all the way in order to be there and gone and thus avoid any possibility of taking a Wasp SAM. Curt and Roger Hawley had decided to disregard the fact that the downwash from the Chippewas would kick up a huge cloud of dust when the 'dynes passed over dry ground. A quick recon of the area had shown that most of the land was tilled and planted with neowheat, rice, sorghum, and soybeans. The Fertile Crescent had been made fertile again as a result of the twenty-first century biotechnology revolution and its impact on agriculture everywhere. The crops would prevent the dust cloud.

Now there was silence in the Chippie. Nancy had patched the vocalized air-to-air communications through the panel speaker, but little if anything was said between the aerodynes of Hawley's Haulers as they sped northwest toward the landing zone. And no communication came through Curt's helmet tacomm from NORTHAG, which was a good sign because, even with frequency-hopping tacomm which was theoretically impossible to snoop, radsec was still a good idea when you didn't know who or what you were going up against.

The red-lit panel showed Curt their location coordinates on the positioning and navigational readouts. But he kept his peripheral vision attuned to the EW panel which would report radar, lidar, or infrared targeting of the Chippie. It flashed briefly a few times until the equipment identified the signal's signature as either the Iraqi civil air traffic control radars or the Iraqi air defense sensors. Operation Sturdy Spectra Phase II had been cleared with both, requesting a clear block of airspace within 100 kilometers of Mosul to be in use by the Persian Gulf command (no unit designators given or courses identified) between the hours of 0100 and 0700 that day. Standard operating procedure. The Iraqis didn't exactly like the idea that they couldn't grant or deny permission for such airspace usage, but they were really in no position to do very much about it. If the Iraqi government wanted to continue to enjoy the tax and royalty income from the petroleum and other natural resources of northern Iraq that were being protected by the Persian Gulf Command because the Iraqi defense forces couldn't do the job, the Iraqi politicians and bureaucrats simply had to swallow their egos as they groused all the way to their favorite Swiss or Singapore bank.

Curt mentally shrugged. That was the way the world ran. International relations and the financial power games weren't his game. He was doing what he was doing voluntarily. He wanted to. Let the others play their games; he'd play this one which he understood.

But there were times, like right then, when he sometimes wondered why he hadn't chosen a different profession. He began to understand what Henry Kester meant

225

when the old soldier sniveled, "I'm getting too old for this kind of crap!" This kind of crap, of course, was the condition of being too scared to piss in your pants and too damned proud to run. And, as Curt grew older and more experienced and took on more military responsibility, he found himself leaving behind the gung-ho West Point cadet that he'd been and adopting more of the knowledgeable but war-weary ways of Henry Kester. Or Belinda Hettrick. Or even Jacob Carlisle. But, he reassured himself, he wasn't yet to Kester's point where retirement and a flower garden at Fort Bragg were only a few years away. In spite of its shortcomings—like being scared shitless—this *was* an exciting way of life in a century when it was also possible to be bored out of your skull!

Flight time was scheduled to be 22 minutes. Just long enough to be uncomfortable and just short enough to give no time to settle into a comfortable niche in the Chippie's cargo bays.

On schedule and on cue according to the ops plan, Nancy announced through the autopilot vocalizer circuits, "Two minutes to landing. I have the landing zone in sight."

Curt toggled his neuroelectronic tacomm so that the ambient noise of the Chippie wouldn't interfere with his message. *Grey Head, this is DIRAG Head! We are two from going to ground!*

This is Grey Head. Roger, came the cryptic reply. *We are deployed and ready. Please keep me advised.*

Grey Head, DIRAG Head, any birdbot recce data yet? Anyone here?

BIRD is airborne at this time but nothing yet. Cook will put it on the data bus when it starts coming in.

Roger! We'll go in blind in scout mode! Curt fired back.

What the hell are you doing, DIRAG? Bellamack hadn't been totally informed of this contingency plan on Curt's part, a maneuver which involved putting all Chippies down with turbines still spooled-up for immediate lift and Adonica's SCOUT platoon being deployed first. If the

226

enemy was out there waiting in ambush, Adonica and her experienced scouts would find out very quickly.

Covering my ass by putting out SCOUT first for a quick look-see. I don't want to debouch the Chippies into an ambush! Curt explained.

Very well, DIRAG, proceed! But after this, clear your movements with me first! the Colonel told him in tones of command.

Curt then knew that something had indeed rubbed off on Bill Bellamack when he'd gone into direct mind-to-mind neuroelectronic linkage with the Soviet Spetsnaz sergeant. Bellamack may indeed have gotten some data from the Sov, but it hasn't been worth it. The Colonel's statement on tacomm told Curt that the regimental commander wasn't thinking in his usual way.

Bellamack was an organizer and manager of operations and had always in the past allowed Curt to run the leadership department in a fracas. Bellamack's style of command had always been to let the troops know what had to be done then sit back, solve problems, and permit his troopers to exercise their own good judgement and initiative in overcoming their tactical problems. Now, however, Curt recognized that Bellamack was using Soviet-style direct downward command doctrine that permitted no deviation from orders without high command approval.

Bellamack was thinking in a Soviet or Russian manner.

This might come in handy when they had to figure out what the Soviet Spetsnaz battalion was up to or would do next, but it was going to be pure death to the Washington Greys if Curt allowed Bellamack to prevail.

When the Chippie grounded, Curt knew he would probably disobey his Colonel in this operation.

Chapter Twenty-nine

Adonica Sweet put her two Jeeps out the cargo ramp of the Chippie first. Their special rodded sensors were tuned to maximum sensitivity, especially the chem sensors that could quickly detect the unique body odors that the Greys had learned were distinctive signatures of the Kurds. Some data was available on the Soviets, and Ruth Gydesen had been more than cooperative in providing data she'd gotten from Pugachev.

Thus, the Jeeps knew what to sense for, and they could discriminate between Kurds, Soviets, and Americans. All people have different body odors because of what they eat. This was perhaps the most positive means available for sensing and discriminating in this particular situation because the landing zone was surrounded by petroleum facilities, mainly the slowly nodding mantis-like beam pumps of an active oil field. It would be occupied during the day by Iraqis, Kurds, Arabs, Americans, British, Dutch, and Japanese oil field workers and engineers.

Curt hoped to hell those oil patch people knew enough to get under cover fast when the shooting started. He didn't want to hurt the people he was supposed to be protecting. All too often, soldiers automatically assume that they are the exclusive population of a battlefield. Curt knew differently from Trinidad, Namibia, Sonora, and Brunei. He would never forget some of the images of hurt and killed women and children in those places, noncombatants and innocent bystanders whose only bad decision was to be accidentally in the path of the conflict.

228

Confronting uninvolved and innocent people in combat was part of soldiering he didn't like.

DIRAG Head, this is SCOUT Leader! Lieutenant Adonica Sweet's neurophonic voice came to him. *The Jeeps have no targets and have drawn no fire! SCOUT is going to ground!*

Since the Jeeps with their armor had drawn no fire from any potential hostiles, speed and mobility were the next essential tactical elements. Adonica and her four sergeants erupted from the Chippie on PTVs at high speed, spreading outward in a fan formation moving to the north. Their objective was to get themselves out on a dispersed scouting patrol as quickly as possible and then to find the leading elements of the Qadiri or Soviet columns moving southward toward Asi and crossing the Tigris River on their course toward Tall Abu Dhahir and Ain Zalah.

The brilliant orange disc of the sun rose over the low, rolling Iraqi hills to the east as SCOUT erupted from the Chippie.

The plan was working well in its early stages. Now was the time to get the main assault forces on the ground quickly so they could move rapidly behind SCOUT.

Marauder Leader, Ferret Leader, this is DIRAG Head! Go to ground! Deploy! Deploy! Move out your Mary Anns as skirmishers to the north! Follow with your ACVs! Curt snapped into the tacomm. *Hauler Leader, stay spooled-up! Just because we haven't been shot at yet doesn't mean that no one's out there ready to shoot!*

Ready, DIRAG Head! Hauler will stay on dirt until ordered to move to safe haven site, came the reply from Captain Roger Hawley. The Chippies would stay where they'd landed until either the DIRAG troops and warbots had moved forward to the river bottom 2 klicks north or had stopped to dig in for ambush.

In the first case, the Haulers would stay where they presently were in case DIRAG had to get the hell out of there fast.

In the second case, the Haulers would move back

about 5 klicks so they'd be out of the potential FEBA and still be close enough to provide rapid evac.

Curt wasn't being chicken; if DIRAG got into deep slime, this precaution with the Chippies could preserve its mobility by withdrawing all or part of its forces to the Chippies and thus redeploying quickly via air to a better position where the enemy could be flanked or even interdicted in the rear.

Curt knew the engagement was going to be primarily on the shoulders of DIRAG; NORTHAG was basically going to be able to do nothing much more than cut off any potential northward retreat of the Qadiri and Soviets *if* those units walked into the trap Curt was setting and Bellamack knew nothing about. It had been dicey to set up the operation so that the Colonel, in his present paranoid and confused condition, wasn't aware of the *real* tactics behind what Curt was doing and yet continued to believe that the original flawed tactical plan was being carried out.

The only wild card was Sharaf Qazi and his Ahl-i Haqqs. If the chieftain would do as he was told and didn't get impulsive, Curt felt the Greys might carry this one off and shut down the continual harassment of Iraqi facilities by renegade Kurd tribes instigated and supported by the Soviets.

"Let's go!" Curt snapped to Edie, Shariat, and Haji Somayeh. "Nobody's shooting at us at the moment, but make sure your personal weapon is loaded and on safety."

Curt noticed that his young Kurd guide seemed to be fumbling with the M333A2 Novia rifle he'd been issued for personal protection. "Haji, you've got some trouble?"

"I can't select full-auto fire," Somayeh complained with the patience of a teenager, which he was.

"You won't need it. And don't try to jimmy the gun to shoot full-auto. It's got training wheels attached," Curt explained. Henry Kester had disabled its full-auto capability because untrained shooters tended to set the Novia on full-auto in a fight. That caused them to squirt off all their ammo within the first few minutes and left them

230

with a high-tech club in their hands. Modern combat was enough of a logistics nightmare anyway without the supply people having to continually run ammo up to Sierra Charlies on the line in the sort of open combat style they used. Warbots could and did haul a lot of ammo with them, one of their advantages. But no human being could carry all the ammo—even the light-weight caseless rounds—that a full-auto rifle could hose away in an hour of intense combat. And no light assault rifle made, even with modern materials, could hold up to that heavy-fire usage.

"Pardon?"

"Never mind!" Curt snapped. He didn't have time for an explanation of American slang right then. He slapped Somayeh on the shoulder. "Let's go! Into the ACV! Move it!"

Curt's ACV, nicknamed Philip for the ancient king of Macedonia who was Alexander the Great's father, trundled down the Chippie's ramp to the ground with Curt, Edie, Shariat, and Somayeh aboard.

The terrain was mainly irrigated fields of soy beans and reminded Curt of the American Midwest . . . except, of course, for the nodding oil pumps. He checked his helmet display. The Tigris River should be straight ahead about 2 kilometers north. It made a huge loop, flowing first to the north, then making a one-eighty turn in a hairpin curve and flowing back again to the south. Recon and reports from Hassan indicated the Qadiris would be moving south to cross the river at the nothern-most part of the hairpin turn where the little village of Asi was located.

The ACVs and ARTVs of DIRAG stuck to the road which was a good road for Iraqi—a dirt track which wound through the soy bean fields and around the oil wells. The Mary Anns and the Sierra Charlies, on the other hand, were deployed on both sides of the road.

It would be slow going, Curt knew, because of the yet-unsolved tactical problem of speed differentials between the Sierra Charlies and their mechanical tools—the warbots and the vehicles. Pushing hard, Sierra Charlies could move at only about 5 kilometers per hour while Mary Anns could triple that speed and the vehicles could move at ten times the pace of the humans who ran the operation. SCOUT was well out ahead and moving fast because Adonica and her sergeants were riding PTVs. The other Sierra Charlies had to proceed mounted on nothing more than combat boots.

It had been impossible to gain Pentagon approval of PTVs for every individual trooper in the ASSAULTCOs when the reorganization had been implemented. Curt knew that the inability of the Sierra Charlies to move as fast as modern technology would permit, especially in relatively open country such as this, was a tactical problem that could be addressed and corrected only when actual combat revealed it to the Pentagon staff stooges as a real rather than a perceived problem.

"Somayeh, are you sure this road crosses the river up ahead?" Curt asked as the path dropped over the edge of a small bluff and proceeded down to the immediate flood plain of the Tigris. River bottom vegetation now obscured the road. Short trees like the salt cedars and tamarisks that clustered along American rivers, sending their tap roots down into the watery soil, were prevalent. Curt could see the cluster of huts that must be Asi on the bluff to the north, which had to be on the north bank of the Tigris.

"Yes, sir! The Tigris is wide and slow-flowing in the bend, and the road actually fords the river," the guide pointed out.

"No bridge?"

"No, sir. It would be washed out every year during the regular rising of the river. So a new ford is created when the waters subside."

Curt understood this. A similar situation existed around Fort Huachuca and elsewhere in Arizona. The rivers, streams, and creeks were seasonal or intermittent, channeling flowing water only following rainstorms in the area. Since these flash floods were unpredictable in tim-

232

ing and intensity, bridges were rarely built. When they were, the flash floods either took them out or created new flow channels where the bridges weren't. The typical river crossing in the American Southwest was a road that simply ducked down into the dry river bed and up the other side; it was cheaper to lay down fresh asphalt following a flash flood than it was to build an expensive bridge structure.

However, the Tigris River was a major waterway and flowed constantly. It could be quite wide or quite deep, or both, depending on the channel flow rate that day. Curt knew then that his force was going to get wet. It didn't bother him. The ACVs and ARTVs were semi-amphibious, capable of floating—just barely—and being propelled by their wheels in the water because of the design of the tires. The Mary Anns would have to ride the ARTVs if the water was deep. The Sierra Charlies always had the option to ride if the water was over their heads.

SCOUT, this is DIRAG Leader! Report when you reach the Tigris River. I want an evaluation of the river crossing at the north end of this bend. I've just learned it's a ford, not a bridge. We'll need to know the river width and depth. We may have to remount the Mary Anns to get across the ford, Curt called up to Adonica Sweet ahead.

Roger, DIRAG Leader! Be advised the going is difficult ahead off the road. The vegetation is thick and the ground somewhat squishy. I recommend keeping the vehicles on the path. And I'd get the Mary Anns off on the shoulders of the road. This was very familiar to Adonica who'd grown up on the Caribbean island of Trinidad; the terrain here was very much like the swampy river bottoms on the western marge of Trinidad, a place where the Greys had almost bogged down once and where movement had been confined to the roads. Curt couldn't forget; that was where enemy artillery had targeted him and where Captain Samantha Walker had taken a shell fragment, died in his arms, and become another tragic name added to the Honor Roll of the Washington Greys.

233

I would also suggest, Major, that one of the ASSAULTCOs remain on the bluff behind us to the south so they have an overview of this terrain in case something jumps out of the puckerbush at us while we're restricted in our movement down here. A little twenty-five millimeter air-burst fire might do a lot to discourage anyone who might be down here ahead and waiting for us, Adonica added, calling up her own experience gained in growing up and fighting in similar conditions. *At least, if I were going to ambush a warbot outfit, this is where I'd try to do it!*

Curt was pleased at this evaluation and tactical analysis from her. It told him that his training methods and emphasis had been correct over the past months. This sort of feedback was important because he'd been plowing very fresh ground in an unenviable task: taking old and well-proven infantry tactics and merging them back into an outfit that was part grunt infantry and part high-tech warbots. And you never know, he'd told himself, whether or not you're doing things right until someone starts to shoot at you, and then it's too late to discover lethal mistakes.

Marauder Leader, this is DIRAG Leader! Pull in your warbot skirmishers to the edge of the road and your Sierra Charlies in to where they can move faster, he called to Alexis Morgan. *We need to move as rapidly as possible through this river bottom where our mobility is restricted. We need to get to the high ground on the north bank as fast as possible. Ferret Leader, please do the same, except that I want you to detach your rear platoon and have them remain on the south bluff to overlook this area until we get the lead Marauder platoon up on the north bluff. We may need some Mary Ann fire if someone jumps us down here.*

Roger from Marauder Leader! Conqueror Leader, proceed ASAP following SCOUT. Cross the river and make best possible time to the north side bluff.

Roger from Conqueror Leader! None too soon for us! These thickets are pretty damned thick! came the response from Kitsy Clinton.

Assassin Leader, this is Ferret Leader. Halt your platoon at the edge of the south bluff and maintain your position until I pass the word for you to move forward. Unlimber your Mary Anns and their twenty-fives. Be prepared for indirect barrage fire on target coordinates that will be passed to you on the data bus, Russ Frazier told the temporary commander of Hassan's Assassins, Captain Jerry Allen.

Roger, Ferret Leader! Curt knew that Jerry hadn't been too happy about taking over an assault platoon again because he was very proud of Allen's Alleycats, one of the light regimental artillery platoons in Joan Ward's GUNCO. But, on the other hand, he'd confided to Curt that in this operation he'd rather be involved with the active assault group than with the more passive NOR-THAG that would act as the anvil for Curt's hammer to work against in pounding the Qadiri.

DIRAG Leader, this is SCOUT. We've reached the river. It's about a hundred meters wide and slow-flowing, but we're going to have to cross it in vehicles because one of my Jeeps almost went under just now, even in the shallow ford portion!

SCOUT, wait until Conqueror Leader catches up to you and can cover you with Mary Anns and Jeeps before you go to an ACV and find yourself a Class A target out in the middle of the stream with nowhere to go, Curt advised.

Sir, except in very special circumstances, I never leave my ass uncovered! Adonica replied quickly.

Forward movement was slowed to a crawl along the track as the various units moved their Mary Anns and Jeeps in and repositioned their Sierra Charlies. Curt watched his tac display as SCOUT began the river crossing.

DIRAG Leader, this is Assassin Leader. Jerry Allen was breaking command protocol by going around Frazier and communicating directly with Curt, but Curt knew it was old habit on Jerry's part. *Suggest you check the tac display. The river is now on three sides of us, and we're in the middle of this hairpin bend it takes.*

I see it, Assassin Leader, Curt replied. His careful visual scan of the area had detected no human movement, and the hazy air was reasonably clear this morning. Gibbon had his birdbots aloft with NORTHAG, and Curt hadn't received any alarming recce information from that source. This didn't mean that no guerrillas were in the area, and it certainly wasn't any reason for him to let down his guard. Especially since DIRAG's position in this river bend wasn't the best tactical position.

And indeed it wasn't.

This is SCOUT! My Jeep has a make on chem sensor! Kurds!

This is Marauder Leader! Incoming! Incoming!

Chapter Thirty

The tacomm frequency was suddenly alive with calls and reports.

Some people stayed in voiceless neurophonic mode.

Others in the heat of the action forgot and lapsed into vocal mode.

Just light rifle fire! Body armor stops it!

"Light, my ass! Intense! Concentrated!"

DIRAG Leader, this is Marauder Leader! We have back-track on some of the incoming! Looks like it's originating from atop the bluffs on the north bank!

Assassin Leader confirms Marauder Leader! But we now have i-r makes on targets all along the north bluff around the hairpin! Where do you want the twenty-fives to go?

SCOUT is back in ACV! I've got our Jeep in tow! I'll have to abandon my PTVs! Alexis, pick them up before you cross!

"What do you mean, pick them up! Dammit, we're under fire here! Damned if I'm going to cross that river under fire!"

Curt was too far back from the river to see what was going on. Philip was still among the salt cedars and other tall vegetation, and neither Phillip or Curt had a clear field of fire in any direction. This was one time he was going to have to behave like a battalion commander and run the battle remotely instead of up at the FEBA.

His first order of business was to contact NORTHAG and inform Bellamack. *NORTHAG, this is DIRAG Leader! We are taking incoming fire in our present position! I suspect we may have encountered an ambush!*

Roger, DIRAG! This is NORTHAG! Press the attack! I am

237

in visual contact now with elements of the main body of Qadiri and have them under surveillance. *If necessary, I can press the attack on them to relieve you!*

NORTHAG Leader, DIRAG Leader will let you know if we need that support! Curt was hoping that Bellamack wouldn't suddenly decide to change the operations plan on the basis of this fragmentary report. He might be up against only a scouting party or an advanced line of skirmishers. The ops plan shouldn't be changed on that basis. In fact, Curt didn't want any changes until he knew what he was up against.

But he had to get the enemy under fire at once, so he called Jerry. *Assassin Leader this is DIRAG Leader! Pick your targets on the north bluffs and fire at will!*

Roger, DIRAG Leader! Cavalier Leader, can you see my targeting data on your display? Can you handle the target groupings on the right? Jerry Allen's recent training in GUNCO was showing. He was calling for coordinated blind targeting fire from Hal Clock's platoon just ahead of him and not quite yet all the way into the river bottom vegetation.

Hal Clock, who'd joined the Ferrets shortly after Frazier took over the company, was basically Russ's right-hand man and second-in-command of the company. Although Jerry was on temporary assignment leading Hassan's Assassins because Hassan himself was with the Ahl-i Haqqs, Hal Clock was a disciplined young officer trained-up by Frazier. When the crunch was upon him, as it was then, he had no heartburn taking orders from Jerry because Frazier hadn't given any yet. Frazier was down in the vegetation with no overview of the terrain, something which Jerry had up on the bluff. Hal maintained NE tacomm discipline. *Roger, Assassin Leader! Gotcha! My first salvo is going to prune a few trees around here. I, my first salvo doesn't do the job, the second one will!*

The sound of 25-millimeter shells from the Mary Anns filled the air over Curt's ACV. Although the M300 cannons on the Mary Anns weren't considered heavy artillery and were intended for prolonged heavy automatic fire mostly against soft-skinned vehicles and stationary targets, in a pinch they could be pressed into use as heavy artillery. This was a pinch. Jerry and Hal Clock had obviously passed instructions to their Mary Anns to maintain single-shot mode at the range they were shooting to. And Curt could hear the muffled reports of the air bursts of the 25-millimeter rounds as they detonated in the air over the targeted enemy positions.

Conqueror Leader, this is Marauder Leader! Kitsy, button down in your vehicles and get across the river behind Adonica! Alexis passed the word to her Alpha Platoon leader, then called to her Bravo Platoon commander, Lieutenant Lew Pagan. *Puma Leader, I'll stick with you in crossing behind the Conquerors! Kitsy, if you can get a clear field of fire when you get on the other side, commence firing against the targets Jerry has designated! We'll cross under your fire cover! Marauders, when you get on the north side of the river, go to ground with your bots and use the cover over there to close on the snipers on the ridge!*

The Greys were getting things back under control following the initial shock of being ambushed. The neuroelectronic tacomm discipline was back again. People were checking the situation on their tactical displays and playing things by ear, working together to bring their mobility and firepower to bear in solving the little tactical problem of people shooting at them.

Cavalier, when you can do it, start moving forward to keep the gap closed behind DIRAG Leader! Russ Frazier instructed. *When we get to the river bank, deploy out along it and keep those positions on the bluff under intense fire! Alexis, if you're going to ground over there, you'll need my covering fire because you're fighting an uphill battle going up that bluff! We'll try to make them keep their heads down while you do it!*

It was this kind of cooperation that Curt had struggled hard to develop within TACBATT. He knew now that he had it. But what frustrated him a little was that his company commanders were calling the shots. Except for the overall orchestration of the engagement, he felt as useful as tits on a turret. Well, maybe that's the way a battalion commander was supposed to feel in a fracas when his people apparently had things in hand. In that event, he told himself, his main job had been carried out days and weeks and months beforehand in training TAC-BATT.

Roger that, Ferret Leader! Thank God those bluffs aren't more than about ten meters high at the most. Just enough to give them a slight advantage . . .

And just high enough to make them good targets, too! was Jerry's observation. *DIRAG Leader, as your battalion artillery commander at the moment, I wish to report that we originally had about fifty targets up on the bluff. We've silenced about twenty of them. I-r and radar from this vantage point indicates that about twenty of them have taken off to the north, breaking cover. I'll put airbursts over them out to the maximum range of the twenty-fives. But you've got only about ten snipers up on that ridge to the right of the ford. Cavalier Leader, if you can swing to the right a couple of mils and lay your fire on that set of targets, I'll send some presents after those who are retreating.*

Thank you, Assassin Leader! SCOUT, when you gain the top of the bluff, go into scout mode again unless you're still under fire. Curt wanted to get his recon unit out in front of him again. This ambush hadn't been planned. He believed he'd run into the advance scouts of the main body of Qadiri. They'd seen DIRAG approach the southern bluff, quickly deployed along the northern bluff, and made the mistake of shooting too quickly. Thus, Curt knew they couldn't be from the Soviet Spetsnaz battalion; that sort of tactical behavior wasn't Soviet. It was Kurd-ish—impulsive, aggressive, and largely ineffective against the firepower, mobility, and discipline of the new Sierra Charlies. It might have worked against the warbot brainies of the old Robot Infantry, but it wasn't working now.

DIRAG Leader, I'd like to spread out behind the snipers left on the bluff and take them from the rear, Adonica told him.

That's Marauder's job, SCOUT! We need you out in front on recon. The main body can't be very far beyond Asi! Curt pointed out.

Come on, Princess, shag your tail! That was Alexis, breaking tacomm protocol because she was pressed hard. She used Adonica's nickname, the one Alexis herself had given her and the only person in the Regiment who used it. She had a sister relationship with Sweet. *I'm coming up the road behind you in one hell of a hurry, and if you stop to shoot a few of those bastards, I'm going to run you over with my ACV! Get out in front where you're supposed to be! I'll clean out these sonsofbitches!*

Curt let the breach of tacomm protocol slide past. In the heat of combat, it was a minor matter. What was important was that DIRAG had run into opposition and fire in a very difficult tactical location. Yet because of discipline and cooperation and superior equipment—a combination of all because any one of those alone wouldn't have worked—they'd broken the ambush.

Furthermore, they'd done it as a combat team of battalion strength with Curt merely orchestrating and directing activities, redirecting actions here, initiating movements there, giving suggestions, and holding things together as a battle coordinator. He hadn't even been shot at, hadn't taken incoming fire. He'd been in the thick of it halfway down the DIRAG column. He realized he'd led without being in the lead.

It was the first time he'd ever done that.

He wasn't sure he liked it. But it was the way he should have run the engagement as a battalion commander. And the way he'd have to run things someday as a regimental commander, too.

Marauder Leader, this is Assassin Leader! If you're in position to move in behind the targets on my left atop the bluff, I'll lift my Mary Ann fire and move down into the puckerbrush in the river bottom!

Roger, Assassin Leader! You can lift your fire now and we'll move in on them! I was about to suggest that anyway because it isn't healthy to attempt mop-up underneath a Mary Ann A-P airburst barrage!

Cavalier Leader will keep it up on the targets on the right!

Roger! This is Conqueror Leader! We'll swing right when he tops the bluff, and I'll let you know when we start moving behind those targets so you won't be shooting at us!

Curt felt a welling sense of pride in the Washington Greys of DIRAG. They were a fighting outfit. Even with their regular administrative units broken up—SCOUT being detached from RECONCO and Jerry Allen taking over Hassan's platoon for this operation—they still worked together as a team. Curt recalled the words of General George S. Patton: "Never tell people *how* to do things. Tell them *what* to do and they will surprise you with their ingenuity."

By God, it had worked!

The dictums of "Old Blood and Guts," now nearly a century old, still held true! But then again, Patton had only rephrased what military leaders had been saying for centuries; he'd put the principles of combat into modern language that soldiers could understand.

"Well, Edie," Curt remarked to his battalion sergeant major, "how does it feel now to be the big NCO and sit back where you don't get shot at?" Curt asked his sergeant with a grin.

Edie Sampson didn't crack a smile. "I was scared even more shitless than usual," she admitted. "It didn't seem right! I was just waiting for some Kurd bastard to climb up the side of our ACV and drop something in on us. I would have felt better outside the way Shariat Khani and Somayeh did."

Curt looked around the cramped inside of the ACV. Both his liaison with the Ahl-i Haqqs and his Kurd guide were gone.

"What the hell? Where did they go? When did they bug out? Why?" Curt asked, confused. Had he been *that* engrossed in monitoring the fight that he'd completely ignored what had gone on in his own ACV?

"When the shooting started, both Shariat Khani and the young Kurd went out the aft hatch like a shot," Edie reported. "You were too damned busy doing other things, and by the time I realized what they were doing, they were gone."

"Both of them?"

"Both of them!"

242

Curt shook his head sadly. "Great! I've probably blown any and all cooperation from Sharaf Qazi for letting his woman get out and probably killed."

"Yeah, she was an aggressive little bitch, wasn't she?"

"You've got no idea, Edie."

"I might. Rumor Control, you know." That was all Edie said. She didn't have to say any more than that. But the way she said it told Curt that his sergeant major had probably heard about Kitsy's run-in last night but not about earlier episodes.

By the time Philip had transported Curt and his battalion command to the Tigris River, the fighting was all over. The Marauders had cleaned the last ten snipers off the low bluffs ahead of them, and the Ferrets were behind Philip and ready to cross.

A small form in baggy cammies without a helmet dashed toward Philip. Before the 7/11 AI equipment in the ACV could compute a verbal warning to Curt, the person was clambering up the stirrups on the side of the vehicle. Edie had seen it on the video monitor which had immediately switched when it detected the movement toward the vehicle. She started to bring her Novia up to cover the open turret hatch when Russ Frazier reported, *DIRAG Leader, your Ahl-i Haqq liaison officer just came back!*

Shariat Khani dropped into the ACV. "You move too fast with your vehicles and warbots!" she complained. "I couldn't get across the river in time to do anything about the Qadiri snipers on the other side!"

"Is that who they were?" Edie asked.

"Where the hell did you go, Shariat?" Curt insisted on knowing.

"When fighting starts, I am not accustomed to sitting in an armored vehicle. It is my nature to go where the fighting is!" she maintained.

"The next time, you damned well better tell me first! I might have needed you!"

"For what? For a little ambush? I was of more use outside!"

Curt shook his head. "You're not assigned to me to be

243

a combat soldier. You're supposed to be a liaison between me and Sharaf Qazi to tell me how he's going to do something because of what you know of him."

Shariat Khani shrugged. "Sharaf Qazi attacks. That is his way. That is what I tried to do. What else is there to tell you? But I should report to you that Haji Somayeh tried to run away when he saw that he had led you into this trap. I shot him."

"*What?*"

Shariat Khani shrugged again. "He was running away. I shot him along the road about a half-kilometer back."

Edie toggled Philip's tacomm unit. "Ferret Leader, this is DIRAG Major! Debouch your bio-tech and go looking for our Kurd guide. He was shot alongside the road about five hundred meters back," she said into her helmet mike without bothering to use the NE mode.

"We just found him, DIRAG Major! Juanita has just signaled me that he's just wounded in the arm, not dead. But he did a good job playing dead! Who shot him?"

"Shariat Khani. She says he was running away."

"Oh."

Curt glared at the Ahl-i Haqq woman. "Goddammit, now we don't have a guide!"

She shrugged again. "I can do that job."

She would have to, Curt decided, because the tacomm speaker came alive, "DIRAG Leader, this is NORTHAG Leader! Move as rapidly as possible through the village of Asi and press your attack on the objective ASAP!" Colonel Bill Bellamack's voice roared at them alive with excitement. "I have the Qadiri unit in full view in an outstanding position to attack and annihilate them! I am commencing my attack at once! Move forward and strike!"

the way

Chapter Thirty-one

"Oh my God! The Colonel sounds like he's toggled
over into semi-spasm mode!" Battalion Sergeant Major
Edie Sampson blurted out, then realized what she'd just
said and quickly added, "Sorry, Major, I didn't mean
that!"

"You're probably right, Edie! That didn't sound like
the Colonel Bellamack I know!" Curt told her quickly.
He was as surprised as she was. It was totally unlike
Colonel Bill Bellamack to make a major change in an
operational plan without letting Curt and the other officers of the Washington Greys know about it beforehand.

Yet he'd apparently made a unilateral decision to attack a column of Qadiri Kurds NORTHAG was tracking
somewhere north of Asi. This was totally at odds with
the plan — flawed as Curt believed it to be — that Bellamack had laid on Curt and the other Greys yesterday
afternoon.

"Colonel, what are you doing, sir?" Curt asked him via
tacomm, so surprised that he used voice mode instead of
the more rapid NE mode. "What are your intentions?
How do you want me to change the tactical plan here for
DIRAG? Are you attacking with the Ahl-i Haqqs in
support? I can't figure out anything from the tactical
display on my data bus!" The information on the tactical
data bus was quite clear to Curt, but he wanted to make
sure Bellamack was looking at the data and getting the
same inputs that Curt was.

Curt was not only upset about Bellamack's sudden decision, but he was a little scared. NORTHAG was not

configured as an assault group. It was made up of the troops of SERVBATT whose people weren't normally expected to be assault troops although each of them was armed to defend themselves and could act as an emergency reserve. With the exception of BIOTECO, the medical company, SERVBATT could shoot and had done so in the past. Bellamack had the heavy guns, the Saucy Cans of Major Joan Ward's GUNCO and the eight tacair Harpies of TACAIRCO commanded by Cal Worsham. But that didn't make NORTHAG an attack unit.

NORTHAG was intended to be a base of fire, and Curt's DIRAG was the attack group intended to drive the Qadiris and hopefully also the Soviet Spetsnaz battalion against NORTHAG as a hammer strikes an anvil.

However, now the anvil was trying to strike, and it didn't have what Curt considered the basic capabilities necessary to strike any sort of a blow.

"I've got the Qadiris in a position where I can open fire with the Saucy Cans and Jeeps . . . and drive them right into you!" Bellamack replied.

"Where are the Ahl-i Haqqs?"

"I can't count on them! They're undisciplined irregulars! I think they're moving southward on the right flank of the Qadiris, but I can't count on them! I have a chance to take the initiative here, so I'm going to attack!" Bellamack was obviously trapped in some sort of circular logic of wishful thinking or bogged down in mental confusion—perhaps both. Again, his statement was totally unlike him.

"Colonel, NORTHAG is a fire base unit! You've got only six Jeeps and eight Saucy Cans!"

"Major, you forget that I also have eight Harpies aloft as airborne artillery! And the fifteen-millimeters mounted on all my vehicles! And I'm up against only dismounted riflemen with no vehicles! And irregulars at that! I intend to throw all the Jeeps and vehicles at the Qadiris in a concentrated frontal assault and then maximum Saucy Cans and Harpy fire against the Qadiris' weakest spot, the point where the most successful NORTHAG assault takes place! Always concentrate your support on the strongest and most successful part of your forces in the assault, Major! Always!"

And that didn't sound like Bellamack, either.

Curt had studied Soviet tactics. Bellamack sounded like a Soviet officer!

Standard Red Army tactics were based on the doctrine of the offensive regardless of the makeup of the unit. They required that commanders attack quickly and with as much force as could be brought to bear on the enemy. When the enemy began to weaken and one of the assault units became more successful than the others, firepower was to be concentrated to support success while other units that might be in trouble and calling for help were to be ignored; in a typical Oriental approach, the units in trouble didn't warrant support and they had no right to call for it. Force had to be applied quickly and in massive amounts where it would do the most good. Since the Soviets had lots of manpower, they could afford to adhere to this powerful and aggressive doctrine, but it was wasteful of manpower. American doctrine, on the other hand, emphasized conservation of trained manpower and the utilization of technology to offset sheer numbers.

"I will be leading the assault!" Bellamack finished.

Curt honestly believed for the first time that the man had gone insane.

He didn't know what had pushed Colonel Bill Bellamack over the edge. Maybe he had come out of linkage with the Soviet Spetsnaz sergeant too quickly. Maybe some important item on the check list had been overlooked either going in or coming out. After all, Ruth Gydesen had admitted that no one knew a whole hell of a lot about it yet.

So what the hell was Major Curt Carson going to do about it?

According to the tactical display on Philip's projection screen, DIRAG was at least ten kilometers from NORTHAG at this point.

247

Curt knew he had to do two things at once.

First, DIRAG had to expedite its forward movement, cover those ten klicks as rapidly as possible, and hit the Qadiri's column to take the heat off NORTHAG. Major Joan Ward was an experienced, solid combat commander, and she'd be the central core of NORTHAG in Bellamack's ill-conceived assault; but she'd do whatever was necessary to keep things from going to slime. That would give Curt and DIRAG valuable time to cover ground.

Secondly, Curt had to get Sharaf Qazi and the Ahl-i Haqqs involved. Bellamack had insufficient force to take on the Qadiris, especially since Bellamack would probably try to keep the SERVBATT Sierra Charlies of NORTHAG inside their vehicles, which was the worst place to be when taking on irregular infantry units. Zahedan, Namibia, Sonora—all those places had taught the Greys a bitter lesson in that regard.

And where the hell was the Soviet Spetsnaz battalion that was supposed to be operating in support of this Qadiri raid?

"NORTHAG Leader, this is DIRAG Leader! We're going to expedite our movement and close on the enemy from the south as quickly as we can!" Curt reported.

Without waiting for an answer, he called his battalion, *DIRAG all, this is DIRAG Leader! Mount up at earliest opportunity and go into high cross-country travel mode! SCOUT, if you aren't on PTVs, mount anything that will move quickly! We've got to close the ten klicks between us and the Qadiris and do it quickly! SCOUT, when you make contact, form a fire base. Marauder Leader, when SCOUT does that, move forward and attempt to pin down the enemy. Ferret Leader, you're going to get your chance to shine because you'll be the maneuver element when we make contact; I suggest you plan to move flankers left because NORTHAG appears to be making a contact assault on the right. Let's go! Execute!*

Again without waiting for confirmation messages from Adonica, Alexis, and Russ, Curt told his vehicle, "Philip, proceed northward on planned course, press to maximum speed, maintain anti-collision separation with other vehicles, and report any potentially hostile actions!"

He knew he could give this sort of complex instruction to Philip because of the Mod 7/11 artificial intelligence circuity aboard. Philip was a machine that was very "smart" in comparison to other vehicles, but it was still stupid in comparison to a human being. Philip's advantages lay in the fact that it would do what it was told, make simple decisions along the way, and relieve Curt and Edie of the work load of driving it. "Roger, DIRAG Leader!" Philip's artificial voice replied. "Do you want me to monitor the remounting of warbots in the ARTVs and organize the operational column movement?"

"Yes! Make it so! Report verbally to me any problem you run into that you cannot solve!" Curt's statement to the machine was made in language that was as unambiguous as possible.

"Yes, sir! Will do!"

"Edie, how the hell can I find and talk to Hassan?" Curt said to his battalion sergeant major who was also his warbot and communications wizard. He felt Philip wheel around on course. The motion of the vehicle told him Philip was coming up to cross-country cruise speed. A quick glance out of the corner of his eye at the tac display told him Philip was carrying out instructions and organizing the fast-moving DIRAG vehicles column. The company commanders had also gotten their Sierra Charlies and warbots collected and mounted up, and their vehicles were moving out with Curt's toward the north.

"Easy, Major," she told him. "He's got a locator beacon in his helmet and a tacomm unit there, too. Or in his hand if he isn't wearing his helmet."

Curt sighed. "Thank you, Edie."

"For what, Major?"

"For keeping your head and holding things together for me as I try to drain this fucking swamp!" Curt admitted to her, knowing that he'd overlooked the obvious. So had Bellamack. Curt had no reluctance to confess this to Edie. She respected and followed him because he knew he wasn't infallible, was willing to admit it, and was quick to call for the help and support of his top non-com.

"Hell, Major, that's one reason I'm here. Part of my efficient and effective service," she told him with a smile. Checking the tacomm frequency assignments on a terminal screen, she did some magic wizardry with the comm gear and said, "You're set up on Hassan's freak now, Major!"

"You're getting to be as good as Henry Kester," he complimented her.

"Thanks, but that'll be the day! Someone has to keep you officers from screwing things up," she retorted easily. She and Curt had developed an excellent, laid-back way of working with one another. She'd taken her cues from regimental Sergeant Major Henry Kester, the competent top kick who knew everything, was willing to tackle anything, and was available at all times as a staunch shoulder to lean on or stand on. But Edie had brought her own little characteristics into the top battalion non-com slot, as well.

"By the way," she went on, "I'm talking with Henry on another tacomm channel. Don't worry about NORTHAG too much. He and Major Ward know what the hell the score is. They'll do what they can to prevent a total sheep screw without being insubordinate and disobeying direct orders up there."

"Orgasmic! Edie, let Joan and Henry know what we're going to do! I'll depend on you as the comm link with them because the Colonel may be pretty much in outer space at the moment," Curt said to his sergeant major accidentally ignoring military protocol by using first names. He was under pressure—not the immediate, gut tearing fear that always gripped him going into personal combat, but the pressure caused by the nagging concern for the welfare of a large number of people who were also his friends. And possibly giving orders that would send them into mortal danger in the bargain. That hadn't bothered him very much when he was a company commander because he'd been out there in the field with

250

those he commanded; he was very conscious of the fact that now he was running a battalion and couldn't be personally alongside all the people that were in danger.

Curt toggled his tacomm and called in voice mode to Hassan because he didn't know which sort of tacomm unit the liaison officer was monitoring, "Qazi Liaison, this is DIRAG Leader! Hassan, this is Curt Carson! Do you read?" In the heat of action, Curt didn't know whether or not Hassan would adhere to established tacomm protocols or remember call names. Protocol wasn't important right then; communications was.

"Hassan here! Go ahead, DIRAG Leader!"

Curt was partially relieved. At least he had communication with someone who was accompanying the Ahl-i Haqqs. He didn't yet know whether or not he'd be able to exercise any battlefield control over them or not. But he had to try because getting the Kurds to work *with* him in this situation could be the critical factor between having to fight a very tough fracas and conducting a successful operation in spite of Bellamack's strange impulsiveness.

"Qazi Liaison, turn on your helmet beacon! What is your situation?"

A beacon signal suddenly appeared in the tac display about two kilometers to the west of where Bellamack was taking on the Qadiris with NORTHAG. "Qazi is still moving to the south. The Sharaf wants to cross the Tigris before he attacks the Qadiris so he doesn't run the risk of being trapped with the river on one or more flanks. He wants to wait until we get to the open country south of the river."

"Hassan, we've had a change in operational plan. Here's a sit-rep," Curt told him and outlined the situation.

"Yes, sir! Do you want me to ask the Qazi to attack the west flank of the Qadiris?"

"Negatory! No! If you do, you'll run the risk of running into overranged Saucy Cans rounds that overshoot from the east!" Curt warned him quickly. A mobile artil-

251

lery unit firing during the advance has a tendency to overshoot with the assault barrage as the range rapidly closes. The mod 7/11 AI units in the LAMVAs were supposed to compensate for that. But Curt didn't want to risk the possibility that the Saucy Cans would also target the Ahl-i Haqqs because they were without beacons and therefore could be confused with the mass of Qadiris. "GUNCO is pretty good when it comes to targeting, but I don't want to take a chance and trust that the seven-elevens would shoot over you or into you! A seventy-five millimeter Ay-Pee airburst three meters over your head could really screw up the rest of your day! Have Sharaf Qazi wheel his group, move northeastward, and take the Qadiris from the north! We're coming up from the south. NORTHAG is already attacking from the east!"

The Qadiris will run to the west," Hassan guessed. "We can be in their way when they do that."

"No, no, that isn't going to work, Hassan!" Curt objected. "You might take Saucy Cans fire instead of the Qadiris! If you move to the north and the Qadiris retreat to the west, we'll catch them between DIRAG and the Ahl-i Haqqs without the worry about having heavy rounds bursting over us! We're armored and can take any rifle fire the Ahl-i Haqqs accidentally put into us, and we've got good targeting gear so we won't put any of our seven millimeter or twenty-five millimeter stuff into you. I haven't got time to argue, so just get Qazi to turn and move northeast! I'll give you bearings and ranges of the Qadiris as you go so you won't be caught by them if they retreat. Now move it!"

"Yes, sir! I'll try! But do you know where the Soviets are?" Hassan fired back.

"Do you?"

"Negatory, sir! They're involved here somewhere, but we haven't spotted them yet, either!"

"Let me see if RECONCO has a make on them yet from birdbot patrols. Stand by," Curt told him and went to switch channels.

"You have asked Sharaf Qazi to turn around," Sharia

252

Khani suddenly put in. "He won't do that!"

"What do you mean, he won't do that?" Curt asked.

"Sharaf Qazi will think of it as a retreat! He will go directly for the Qadiris instead!"

"Is he nuts?" Curt exploded. "He'll walk right into the Saucy Cans fire that happens to overshoot the Qadiris!"

"I can tell you that is what he'll do," Shariat maintained.

Her guess was confirmed by an immediate call from Hassan. "DIRAG Leader, this is Qazi Liaison! I wish to report that Sharaf Qazi says he intends to turn east immediately and press the engagement with the Qadiris in order to trap them between the assault by NORTHAG and his own attack!"

"Hassan, don't do it! You'll probably be killed if the Saucy Cans aren't dead nuts on target and a round overshoots!"

Chapter Thirty-two

DIRAG Leader, I can't stop Qazi! I believe you, but Qazi's determined to make the assault as I described it! Hassan responded, then added, Sir, with all due respect and with my gratitude for giving me the opportunity to be the liaison officer with the Ahl-i Haqqs, would you mind terribly if I didn't go with Qazi? I'm not a coward, sir, but I'll be damned if I want to voluntarily put myself under a Saucy Cans barrage! I know what a Saucy Cans airburst can do . . .

Curt whirled, thrust a tacomm brick transceiver at Shariat Khani, and snapped at her, "You've listened to what's been said here! You know what's going on! Here! Talk to your Sharaf! Convince him he's walking into a death trap!"

She shrugged in her characteristic fashion. Curt decided it was a fatalistic shrug; he'd seen many people in this part of the world shrug that way. "Once Sharaf Qazi has decided to do something, I can't talk him out of it!"

"Dammit, Shariat, don't be so goddamned defeatist! Try! Otherwise, a couple of hundred good fighters may go to their deaths, and we need every one of them, not more dead bodies to fertilize the Fertile Crescent!"

She shrugged again and took the tacomm brick as Curt advised his liaison officer, Get Sharaf Qazi on the tac-comm, Hassan!

The conversation between Sharaf Qazi and Shariat Khani was short and in Kurdish. Hassan wasn't available to translate. Finally, Shariat said, "I told you I couldn't stop him!"

"Shit!" Curt snarled in anger, then keyed his tacomm

on another channel. *Grey Head, this is DIRAG Leader! I'd like to speak with GUNCO Leader! I have targeting information I need to pass to her.* This wasn't normal tactical procedure in the Greys. Any commander could normally communicate with anyone else as long as the top person was kept informed. But Curt didn't know exactly how Bellamack in his present state of mind might take the fact that Curt wanted to talk directly to Major Joan Ward and warn her of the Ahl-i Haqqs who might be the inadvertent targets of her Saucy Cans if she didn't stay right on top of the Mod 7/11s in the LAMVAs. Soviet tactical doctrine wouldn't have permitted such a straightforward communication because Soviet command structure was linear vertically and not horizontally.

Bellamack acquiesced, and Joan came on the channel.

Curt warned her, and she told him, *Thanks, DIRAG Leader! This is not the easiest targeting job we've ever tackled! Can I get Hassan to do some spotting for us as a forward observer who's on the other side of the enemy?*

Call him and talk to him, Curt advised her. Maybe by serving as a communications node Curt could bring some sanity to this sheep screw before it got going really hot and heavy.

Within minutes, the call came from Adonica Sweet, *Contact! Contact! We have the enemy in visual! Dammit! Trucks! They're in trucks! Not on foot!*

Trucks? What kind of trucks? Since when do the Kurds have trucks? Any armored vehicles with them? Curt wanted to know.

Negatory on armor! Can anyone get a make on the truck type? Soviet maybe?

Steyer-Yugos! Made in Zemun near Belgrade! Yugoslavs sold them to both Greece and Turkey! That was Captain Jerry Allen.

"Shariat," Curt asked his Kurd liaison officer, "Do the Qadiris have trucks? Yugoslav Steyers?"

"No! None of the Kurd tribes have vehicles! Trucks are much too expensive and too hard to keep running in the hills!" she replied quickly.

"Then is the enemy column made up of Qadiris? Or

someone else?"

"They're Turks posing as Qadiris!"

"Are you sure?" Curt persisted.

She shook her head. "No, but every time we've run into people in those trucks, they've been Turks coming across the border and making trouble for us!"

"Holy shit!" Curt breathed. This whole operation now took on an entirely different aspect. It had gotten international in a way that wasn't expected. "Then where are the Qadiris? And the Soviets? Would the Soviets follow the Turks?"

"I didn't think there was any love lost between the Russkies and the Turks," Edie Sampson interjected. "They've hated each other for centuries. Fought each other a couple of times, too."

"Hell, Edie, everyone around here has been fighting everyone else for a hell of a long time!" Curt reminded her. "So I'm going to make the assumption our adversaries aren't Qadiri Kurds but Turkish guerrillas. The Turkish army wouldn't send regular troops down here on a raid, not when we're likely to catch them at it. The Turks are still part of the western forces in NATO."

"Yeah, officially," Edie growled. "But in case you haven't noticed, Major, no one seems to have very much loyalty around these parts."

DIRAG Leader, this is Marauder Leader! Alexis reported on tacomm. *We've made contact! These bastards are armed with Em-twenty-sixes . . . surplus You-Ess Army rifles! The old high-velocity bee-burners!*

Marauder Leader, how are they reacting to the Saucy Cans fire from NORTHAG? Curt wanted to know.

It's busted up a few trucks! Some of the guerrillas are on the ground!

You know what to do! Make it so! Curt told her. He could hear the sounds of the battle through the walls of his ACV now.

Roger! Mary Anns targeted on the soft-skinned vehicles! Jeeps and Novias targeted on guerrillas in the open! We're going to ground with the Sierra Charlies ASAP! I was at Zahedan, too,

256

remember?

Curt did indeed remember. That was the campaign where the Robot Infantry took it in the chops because the Jehorkhim Muslims simply overwhelmed the warbots and the warbot brainies by sheer numbers using Mongol mass assault tactics thousands of years old. That fracas had caused the United States Army to rethink its warbot doctrine and permit the Washington Greys to develop the mixed human-warbot tactics of the Special Combat or Sierra Charlie doctrine.

But at this point, if the Sierra Charlies were coming out from behind the armor of their vehicles, he felt he needed to see what the hell was going on. Really see it. He didn't like relying on the ACV sensors. It was too much like being a warbot brainy and running your warbots by linkage, but not being able to get good downlink data from the bot. And having no uplink capability to change things. So he dilated the hatch in the turret and carefully poked his head up into the real world.

His ACV was atop a slight rise on a rolling hill, and he could see for perhaps three or four kilometers in all directions.

The growing battle was out there before his very eyes. "Jesus Christ!" he breathed to himself.

For the first time in his military career, he witnessed what the military theorists called "the haze of battle."

Curt was used to fighting in Sierra Charlie style, but the Washington Greys hadn't fought in open, rolling country like this since Namibia. And there it had been a matter of the Sierra Charlies and their bots against native troops without vehicles. In Namibia and elsewhere, Curt had also been intensely involved in close personal combat with his horizons extending outward to perhaps three hundred meters at the most. Now he had an overview.

He already knew the awful smell of death and burning things. He knew the sounds of explosions and the screaming of wounded men. But he had rarely seen much of a total battle. Now the scene before his eyes was

257

partly hidden and obscured in a pall of dust and heavy smoke punctuated by flashes from the bright explosions of Saucy Cans air bursts. The landscape was dotted with burning vehicles and hordes of dun-uniformed soldiers running in all directions.

To his right, he could see the vehicles of NORTHAG moving slowly in their ill-conceived advance, the LAM-VAs with the fire-belching Saucy Cans bringing up the rear ranks and firing over the heads of the lead vehicles. Several jeeps were out in the van, drawing fire from the guerrillas. But Bellamack hadn't put his Sierra Charlies on the ground yet; they were still in their light-skinned vehicles. Curt expected that was because NORTHAG was made up mostly of the support troops of SERVBATT.

On the left was a horde of guerrillas charging across the rolling hills, firing rifles. The Ahl-i Haqqs were attacking the Turkish(?) guerrillas in the classical Kurdish method of mass human wave assault. As he watched, he saw some of them hit by fire from the guerrillas who were under attack and returning fire.

Down in a draw and spread over a few of the hills was the dispersing guerrilla force of both trucks and dismounted men. They were trapped between the Ahl-i Haqqs, NORTHAG, and his own DIRAG forces. The only direction that might provide relief was a retreat to the north. But the guerrillas — Turks, if Shariat was right — didn't choose to retreat. They were on the attack against NORTHAG because they were willing to take the chance of carrying out an assault on the soft-shelled vehicles of the Greys rather than come up against hand-to-hand combat with the Ahl-i Haqqs.

Eight of Cal Worsham's Harpies circled overhead. One of them was blowing down a thin line of smoke from one of its lift slots; it had either taken a Golden BB or a Wasp. But none of the Harpies were engaged in tacair support. Curt knew why. The melee out there was too confusing. Cal wasn't about to take the chance of laying ordnance on his own forces; he was circling his aircraft, waiting for a clear shot. He could do nothing else.

Curt overcame a strange compulsion to go to ground with his DIRAG Sierra Charlies. It was strange because he was always scared shitless when he had to go into combat and expose himself to enemy fire, even though his body armor would stop almost any projectile less than 10 millimeters in caliber. It was strange because now he *wanted* to get out there in the thick of it with his comrades. He knew he shouldn't, that he should instead remain in his ACV where he had communications, computer power, big tactical displays, and all the other technology of modern "C³I" — command, control, communications, and intelligence. It was up to him as a battalion commander to direct the battle.

If he could. He remembered the Battle of Longliku on Borneo where he also led a battalion and where the flow of the battle quickly got beyond his control. Because all the tactical manuals and all his military education stressed the need for battle control, he'd had trouble rationalizing the Battle of Longliku. And he'd been forced intellectually to listen to the "voice of experience" that emanated from the War College, the Command and Staff School, and the United States Military Academy when he and Bellamack were reorganizing the Washington Greys after Brunei. He was *supposed* to lead from the rear at this level of command. All the books said so. That's what field command was all about and what made it different from unit command. Or so he was told. He didn't like it right then.

It was obvious that Battalion Sergeant Major Edie Sampson didn't like it either. "Major, the Colonel's going to get creamed if he keeps his Sierra Charlies in their vehicles! And we might get creamed ourselves! When the hell can we go to ground, sir?"

Nor did Shariat Khani. "How do I get out of here? I must be in the battle! It is not right for me to stay here in safety when my people are fighting and dying out there!"

"Both of you!" Curt snapped at them, then was sorry he'd done so because he was frustrated himself. He knew

259

he had two good outfits out there—Morgan's Marauders and Frazier's Ferrets—plus SCOUT with its capability for rapid movement. He had to count on Alexis, Russ, and Adonica. They were on the ground; they knew what was going on. And he'd heard no calls for help. So he also knew they had things in hand. "This is where we're supposed to be! Shariat, you've got an important job as our comm link with Qazi!"

"He's fighting! He isn't talking to me!" Shariat insisted. "It is time to fight, not time to talk!"

"Major, this is a fairly simple engagement," Edie pointed out to him. "Our job is mostly communications. I can patch up the comm and display nets so that we can do just as good a job out there."

"Do as you're told!" Curt snarled at both of them. This was no time for either of them to question orders.

What broke the dam of frustration was a sudden call from Bellamack: *DIRAG Leader, this is Grey Head! NORTHAG needs relief! We're being assaulted by massive waves of human infantry! Move your DIRAG forces to your right flank and give me some relief!*

Grey Head, this is DIRAG Leader! My forces are committed and in action at this time! Curt replied quickly, then suggested, *I might suggest, Colonel, that you put some of your Sierra Charlie forces on the ground to work with your Jeeps in handling the guerrilla assault. Warbots can't do it alone worth shit. They've got to be supported by Sierra Charlies, sir!*

Then why aren't you out there with your Sierra Charlies, Major? was Bellamack's terse reply. *I see your beacon still merged with that of your ACV!*

Sir, by the tactics I understand, I am told that my place is where I am at this moment! Curt fired back.

I see you in the rear of your battalion! I thought you were fit to lead!

Bellamack might be behaving irrationally, but that was the most rational thing the regimental commander had said today. It wasn't a direct order, but it gave Curt the obvious option of doing what he knew he should be doing. If this fight was lost, he might or might not hang for doing what he was supposed to be doing, leading his battalion. But if by doing what he knew he should be doing and the battle was won as a result, it wouldn't make any difference. And then he'd have some leverage to get the goddamned manuals rewritten the way they should be.

"Fuck the books!" Curt snarled. Everyone else was.

Bellamack's sharp remark was stepped on by a call from Alexis: *Curt, the Marauders need some help! Princess, can you swing SCOUT to your right and lay some fire on this bunch I've just enhanced on the display?*

Negatory, Big Allie! SCOUT is fully engaged at this time! was the reply from Adonica.

Allie, this is Cal! I'm waiting for an opening to support NORTHAG, but I can put some ordnance in your area if you'll indicate it on the tac display for me! came the call from Cal Worsham aloft in one of the Harpies.

Here it is, Cal! Do it! Do it!

Tacomm communications protocol was thought to be important to prevent misunderstanding, but Curt was suddenly beginning to realize that it was going to hell in this fight, just as it had when the going got tight at Longliku. People under pressure reverted to nicknames. He found himself following suit. "Make those patches and power up the Jeeps, Edie! Load and lock! We're going to ground ASAP!"

As Curt bailed out of the top turret hatch in his typical Carson Roll to ground, he was aware of the awful din of the fight. His own Jeep, Bucephalus and Edie's Jeep, Delilah, were already on the ground. Edie and Shariat were with them.

Two Harpies rolled in on the attack and chewed up the ground with bursts from their 25-millimeter guns. One of them launched an M100 rocket as well.

"Edie, Shariat, head for that sector!" Curt told them via tacomm, using NE for Edie and verbal for Shariat who didn't have a tacomm helmet. "Shariat, I want you to stay with me!"

"No!" was the brief reply from the Amazon.

Curt bristled. But he knew Shariat wasn't directly under his command. She didn't have to do what he told her. And she didn't. But fortunately whatever she intended to do and wherever she intended to go, she was right alongside Bucephalus.

They made contact with the rear of Clinton's Conquerors. *Kitsy, don't panic! DIRAG Leader is coming up in your minus-x!*

Good! I can use your fire support! The Conquerors were at that moment under frontal assault by about fifty frantic Turks who were trying to break through rather than be forced into the dishonor of retreat.

Before Curt could do anything to stop her, Shariat Khani broke into a run from the cover of Bucephalus and dashed toward Kitsy.

Shariat had her M22 assault rifle in her hands. It was an old and heavy weapon weighing about 3.5 kilograms. The Kurd woman warrior, knowing that Kitsy's body armor would stop most assault rifle rounds, took the M22 by its barrel and swung it back around her shoulder.

Using the heavy old rifle as a club, Shariat Khani swung it at Kitsy so that its heavy steel shoulder stock hit Kitsy with the full force of its momentum at the back of her neck just below her helmet.

Chapter Thirty-three

As Lieutenant Kitsy Clinton pitched forward on her face from the force of the blow, Shariat Khani threw up her arms. The M22 rifle went flying in the air. Shariat also pitched forward as a little red hole suddenly appeared in the back of her loose garment. A red spray erupted from another, larger hole that also appeared in her chest.

Curt heard no rifle report. However, the noise level of the battlefield was very high and the muzzle blasts of many rifles was all around him.

What he did hear, however, was the shout that came from Battalion Sergeant Major Edie Sampson who had her Novia rifle pointed at Shariat Khani: "You bloodthirsty Amazon bitch! Medic! Medic!"

"Sergeant! What the hell did you do? Did you shoot Shariat Khani?" Curt yelled.

"Goddamned right I did! Did you see what she did to Lieutenant Clinton? Medic! Dammit, Ginny, where the hell are you?" Edie slung her rifle and kneeled down beside Kitsy's prone and very quiet form. "Lieutenant? Lieutenant? Can you talk to me?"

Kitsy Clinton didn't answer.

The air was full of snapping things that went past Curt. *Bucephalus, this is Companion Leader!* he called to his Jeep on tacomm. *Cover us! Shoot at anyone who shoots at Sergeant Sampson or me!* Then he yelled to Edie, "Sergeant, get Delilah to cover us, too!"

"Delilah always covers me, Major! I got a real low pucker factor! Goddamit, Kitsy's in trouble!"

Curt tore his attention away from the conflict for a moment and got over to her. He paid no attention to the prostrate form of Shariat Khani. "Is she alive?"

Edie was over Kitsy but hadn't touched her, following the battle injury procedures drummed into all the Greys by Dr. Ruth Gydesen: except to clear an airway or other such emergency action anyone wearing body armor who was wounded or otherwise fallen on the battlefield wasn't to be touched until a bio-tech got there. That saved Kitsy right then. "Breathing! Just. Pulse weak and thready. Maybe shock. Shariat hit her pretty damned hard. Might have broken her neck. Which is another reason why I haven't tried to move her," Edie remarked.

Curt turned his head to look at Shariat Khani who was bleeding through a large bullet wound in her abdomen and had started screaming in pain as she lay on the ground.

"What happened, Edie?" Bio-tech Sergeant Ginny Bowles was there.

Edie started to explain. Although Curt was deeply concerned about Kitsy, he had other responsibilities at the moment. Kitsy was in the best of hands. Curt had to get this fight under control. Or at least get the situation flowing so that the Greys would win it.

Bio-tech Sergeant Juanita Gomez from Frazier's Ferrets appeared through the smoke and dust. Curt just indicated Shariat Khani to her and turned his attention to the fight. *Bucephalus, follow me! Shoot anyone who seems to be ready to shoot at me!*

He found Sergeant Jim Elliott of Morgan's Marauders but didn't find Alexis. Since Elliott had previously served with him in his company before the recent reorg, Curt merely waved recognition then called on tacomm, *Allie, this is Curt! Where the hell are you? Ident your beacon! I'm joining you with my Jeep! Kitsy's down! I'll take her platoon!*

I saw her beacon flash trouble! Kos has her platoon!

Where do you need my help?

I don't need it, but the Colonel sure as hell does! These bastards have NORTHAG under a lot of pressure! Alexis's neurophonic tacomm voice sounded in his head.

As if on cue, Bellamack's tacomm voice sounded in his head almost on top of Alexis's, *NORTHAG, this is Grey Head! Change front forward! Retrograde! Execute!*

Curt couldn't believe what he just heard. *Grey Head, this is DIRAG Leader! Are you really executing a retrograde maneuver?*

Affirmative, DIRAG Leader! This will give you more room to maneuver and allow your advance to put pressure on the rear of the Turks as they follow me and continue to maintain contact!

That was one hell of an excuse, Curt thought. Why would Colonel Wild Bill Bellamack stage a retreat when he had massive firepower available to him and more than fifty Sierra Charlies? The man was acting irrationally at this point. *Grey Head, this is DIRAG Leader! If you can hold your positions for another five minutes, we should be able to give you some relief!*

I can't chance it! These Turks are too close for me to use the Saucy Cans! They're right on top of us! We're taking heavy warbot losses!

Curt noticed that Bellamack hadn't mentioned Sierrra Charlie casualties. Maybe he had none. Or maybe Bellamack thought he was still commanding a regular Robot Infantry regiment. In any event, something was definitely wrong. *Colonel, you've only got six Jeeps to start with!* Curt reminded him. He'd objected to Bellamack undertaking this pincer movement with so few warbots and 69 Sierra Charlies, most of whom weren't active combat troops but support personnel from SERVBATT. *Get your Sierra Charlies in defilade behind your vehicles and then let them put Novia fire into the attackers! And use the firepower you've got in the fifteens on the vehicles!*

Dammit, Major, I'm running this show! Shut up and do as you're told, by God! Or I'll have you up on a court martial when this is all over!

That certainly didn't sound like Bellamack! Now Curt knew the man was in some sort of serious mental difficulty. *Alexis, move it in on these bastards! Let's get some of the pressure off Bellamack!*

Doing the best we can, Major! was the terse and almost formal reply from Alexis Morgan who was undoubtedly in serious trouble herself. This was the first time that the Washington Greys had come up against this sort of enemy since they'd gone Sierra Charlie. It reminded Curt of the sheep screw at Zahedan. Except it was worse because the Regiment had been a full warbot outfit then without Sierra Charlies out in the field taking fire.

Something broke on the battlefield. Curt didn't know what it was at the time. But the heavy incoming rifle fire from the Turks decreased and the pressure on the Marauders and Ferrets was suddenly relieved. *SCOUT! Adonica! Can you disengage and do some recce to find out what's happening?* he called.

DIRAG Leader, this is RECONCO Leader! Major John Gibbon cut in. *We've still got birdbots up. I can give you a quick sit-rep.*

Also from AIRBATT Leader! Cal Worsham added. *Curt, what the hell's wrong with our regimental commander? Why is he retreating? He was in a good position from what I could see! I can't see over there now, even on i-r! Too much activity stirring up too much of a dust cloud!*

Cal, stand by a sec! John, give me that sit-rep! Curt insisted.

The Turks swung all their force strength to NORTHAG just now when they detected the Colonel's turnabout retrograde movement, Gibbon reported. Curt knew the man was in linkage with his birdbots because his voice had that detached, dreamy quality about it. *I've lost visual and i-r contact with the Colonel's OCV because of the dust cloud our retrograde move has stirred up; we're going back over the same ground we just tore up in the advance. Hassan evaluated my recon data almost before I could, and he's apparently succeeded in convincing Qazi to take advantage of it by increasing the intensity of the Ahl-i Haqq attack from the west!*

Curt, if the Colonel will now do another turnabout, he'll catch the Turks with the knickers down! Cal Worsham added.

Grey Head, this is DIRAG Leader! Are you on the net? Did you read that last exchange? Curt called out.

Silence.

Grey Head, this is DIRAG Leader! Do you read me? Curt repeated. It was inconceivable to him that Bill Bellamack had left the tacomm channel. However, the Colonel's behavior in this fight had been so bizarre that Curt really didn't know what to expect next.

More silence.

GUNCO Leader, this is DIRAG Leader! Do you read me? Curt called to Major Joan Ward.

Ready you five-by, Curt! I've lost tacomm with Bellamack, too! came Joan's reply.

Curt made an instant decision. Loss of communication with the regimental commander at this critical point meant that the Washington Greys were leaderless unless Curt assumed command at once. He was Bellamack's second-in-command; this had been part of the longstanding contract between the two men. If Bellamack resumed tacomm contact, Curt would relinquish command to the Colonel at once. So Curt toggled the multi-band channel switch on his helmet tacomm, trusting without doubt that Edie had set the comm gear up properly in the ACV before they'd gone to ground. *Greys all, this is DIRAG Leader! We have apparently lost communication with Grey Head! DIRAG Leader is assuming regimental command!*

He paused, collecting his thoughts in order to issue distinct, unambiguous orders. This battle had gone on too long. Short, violent, decisive fights meant fewer casualties and lower loss rates of equipment. Such quick, vicious fights expended lots of ammo, but Curt knew that ammo was supposed to be expendable in battle; people weren't. Then he continued, *Let's win this sheep screw fast! GUNCO Leader, assume NORTHAG command now! Reverse the NORTHAG retrograde movement and bring all weaponry to bear on the enemy! All NORTHAG Sierra Charlies go to ground now! Seek the protection of your vehicles if necessary! Put lots of Novia fire into the Turks! Use three-round bursts! You've got the regimental ammo supply with you, so don't worry about running out of ammo! And you don't have to shoot to kill, but shoot to scare the shit out of them! Make them go for cover!*

Acknowledge!

Roger, Curt! Will do! Joan's voice replied. Command had shifted so much now that standing code calls were meaningless. As had happened within DIRAG, people went to first names and nicknames instead of codes.

Hassan, keep it up! Push the hell out of the Turks from the west! Be advised the Ahl-i Haqqs may run into fire from NORTHAG! Tell Qazi not to fire into NORTHAG vehicles when they come into sight!

Roger! I'll continue to monitor the tactical display and advise Qazi of closure range to NORTHAG as we advance!

Adonica, move to the right on recon and see if you can locate the Colonel's OCV!

Roger! Disengaging! Moving! And just when we had 'em by the short hairs! Adonica rarely used profanity, preferring to direct all her energy and concentration into the fight when it was going on.

Alexis, hold your ground and secure the south flank of the enemy! Russ, if you're in position to do so, attempt to join the south flank of the Ahl-i Haqqs!

While Alexis acknowledged with a brief roger, Frazier came back with, *We've got them in contact now! Hassan, tell them to stop shooting into us! Otherwise, I'm sure as hell going to waste a lot of Alley Hacks! If they shoot at us, the Ferrets will goddamned well shoot back!*

Russ, Hassan work it out! Coordinate, for Christ's sake! Curt insisted. *Cal, can you see any targets well enough to lay ordnance on them?*

Negatory! Want me to take a chance and use the sand blasting stuff on coordinates? Do you trust the Seven-elevens?

Shit, we've got to trust them until they turn out to be fucked up, Cal! Stay in close comm! Everyone, be aware the Harpies will be laying ordnance on enemy coordinates instead of sight targets. If you start catching sky ordnance, holler! Now get busy and let's bring this thing to a fast, screeching halt! Execute!

Curt knew he couldn't "control" or "manage" the battle now. He'd just done his best to set it up so that it might flow as he wanted it to. The "business management" techniques of Secretary of War Elihu Root first foisted on the Army at the beginning of the twentieth century and completed by McNamara in the 1960s might be highly touted in the texts and field manuals, but Curt now knew that when it came right down to the fight itself, he had to follow the Patton formula and let his troopers use their own brains to accomplish the commander's final objective.

But this didn't mean that he could ignore what was going on. He had to keep his overview, his situational awareness, so he could head off potential disasters and respond quickly to calls from unit commanders who'd gotten themselves into trouble.

But once he had made the critical decision to assume command, even he was surprised at how fast things moved.

Then a very garbled, scratchy, almost unintelligible call came over the straight audio tacomm, *"Nyet! Nyet! Yah Amerikahnyets! Puhchehmoo? Ya nyeh mahgoo dvee-noot nahgoy! Suvehzeetyeh myeh-nych gawspeetahl!"* This garbled shout was immediately followed by what sounded like gunfire from an automatic weapon.

Curt immediately recognized it as Russian and he didn't understand a word of it except "nyet" and "Ameri-kahnyets" and "gawspeetahl." An American was hurt and wanted to be taken to the hospital.

But he did recognize the man's voice. It unmistakably belonged to Colonel Wild Bill Bellamack who spoke fluent Russian.

Then the tacomm channel went dead again.

Chapter Thirty-four

The cryptic and garbled transmission in Russian from
Colonel Bill Bellamack meant only one thing to Major
Curt Carson: somehow, some way, Bellamack and those
with him in his regimental OCV had run into the enigmatic and chimerical Soviet Spetsnaz battalion that had
been encountered only once by the Washington Greys
but never located for certain.

Spetsnaz battalions were as covert as anything the Soviet Union did; Western intelligence agencies didn't know
if the Spetsnaz units were part of the Red Army, the
GRU, or the KGB ... or even any of those. Soviet
military literature occasionally made reference to "desant"
units in contexts that combined both "landing" and "assault" terms. Some Soviet military analysts believed the
Spetsnaz personnel were drawn from the *Vozdushno-De-
santnyye-Voyska* or airborne regiments. Others believed they
were organized and deployed as *Vysotniki* or *Raydoviki,* the
Soviet equivalents to the old British SAS or American
Rangers. But no one knew, and that's probably just what
the Soviet High Command and the Politburo wanted.

But whatever and whoever they were, the Spetsnaz
troops were elite forces and just about the sneakiest in
the world.

Curt guessed that a Soviet Spetsnaz unit could have
easily remained hidden to the east of the fight and targeted Bellamack's OCV for capture when the Colonel
began his retrograde maneuver and was out ahead of his
countermarching NORTHAG unit. The attention of
those in the OCV would have been directed toward the

west where the action was. If the 7/11 unit hadn't been warned ahead of time to be on the lookout for other troops—and Bellamack probably had no inkling that anyone was to the east of him—the artificially intelligent computer running the vehicle wouldn't have even blinked when the Spetsnaz troops came out of their hidden holes or maneuvered into a position to take the OCV in a blind spot. Thus, only the OCV's Mod 7/11 might have been watching where the OCV was going. The Spetsnaz battalion could easily have bushwhacked Bellamack and those with him in the regimental OCV—probably only Regimental Sergeant Major Henry Kester and Regimental Staff Sergeant Georgina Cook since the OCV version of the ACV, the M660B, could carry only three people because of its concentration of comm and computer gear.

Curt wondered what Henry Kester was doing or had tried to do to convince Bellamack to shape up; Kester wasn't one to meekly give in, and he had his own persuasive little ways of doing what was needed while dancing around the matter of flat-out insubordination. Curt was worried. Either Kester had been unsuccessful in convincing Bellamack or the old soldier had been hurt in the engagement. Curt didn't like to think about the latter.

So he tried to do something about it instead.

RECONCO Leader, this is DIRAG Leader! Curt unconsciously dropped back into formal tacomm protocol. He always had a tendency to do that when communicating with Major John Gibbon who, as commander of RECONCO, was the only full warbot brainy officer left in the Greys. That made John Gibbon somewhat of an oddball, but that was John Gibbon in any event, almost the ultimate technerd obsessed with the birdbots and their technology. In a way, he was out of place commanding RECONCO, but when the reorg had been carried out he turned out to be the senior qualified officer. Captain Ellie Aarts, the actual CO of BIRD, was a far better leader than John, and Ellie was actually the one who ran the company.

Go ahead, DIRAG Leader!

Get some birdbot recon over to the east of NORTHAG! The Colonel has dropped off tacomm and I just picked up a rather garbled message from him that makes me fear he's tangled assholes with the Spetsnaz boys!

I heard, Curt! Ellie has her two birdbots heading in that direction now! I'll let you know if we spot anything!

The Spetsnaz battalion may have bushwhacked the regimental OCV.

I suspected that. I'm on top of it. Gibbon was cool and detached. He was sequestered in his ACV in linkage with his birdbots. Adrenalin might have been pumping through his bloodstream as through the Sierra Charlies out there being shot at, but Gibbon maintained the cool demeanor of a warbot brainy running a very complex warbot while trying at the same time to communicate with his commander. Curt knew that a major personality change had occurred in the man since he'd lost the birdbot in linkage over Kerguelen Island several years before; he'd come back from KIA therapy with all his mental marbles back in place, but like several other warbot brainies Curt had known, he wasn't quite the same as before. Being intimately linked to a warbot of any sort while it was destroyed was a little like dying. Curt knew. He didn't like to think about that, either.

Okay! Make it so! Adonica, can you get SCOUT remounted and move quickly to the east of NORTHAG? If the Colonel did get jumped by the Spetsnaz, the quicker we can get some recce on them, the quicker we'll be able to break some Greys off of this fight and go after the Russkies!

Curt, I'll put SCOUT on PTVs. We can move fast, she suggested.

That's dangerous. No armor.

I know. A moving foxhole attracts the eye. But we're wearing body armor, sir, she reminded him. *And we're on our way already! Dyani and Harlan are out in front already! Dyani has her Jeep with her, and so do I!*

Cal, if you can take a moment away from blasting a lot of sand around on top of the fucking Turks, would you kindly veer off to the east and see if any Russkies take a shot at you? Curt called to his tacair compatriot aloft in his Harpie.

Be happy to do it, Carson! I've just about depleted the ammo for my twenty-fives, but I've got a passle of Smart Farts I'd just love to run up a Russkie's ass! A little recce would be a nice change of pace right about now!

The battlefield was suddenly no longer covered with the sounds of automatic weapons. Instead, the warbling sound of Semitic war cries filled the air.

Another call came for him on the tacomm. *DIRAG Leader, this is Hassan! We've creamed the Turks, caught them between the hammer and the anvil! But I'm afraid I can't get the Ahl-i Haqqs to take prisoners! I can't stop them from slaughtering the Turks! They're even killing off the wounded!*

Curt sighed and slung his Novia. "That's no fucking way to fight a war!" he growled to Edie Sampson beside him. He knew the Gurkhas and the Bruneis fought that way, giving no quarter and taking no prisoners; it had sickened him when he'd first seen it. And he knew that the peoples of the Mideast fought that way too, a total commitment to slaughter because an enemy spared is an enemy who will probably come back and try to kill you again. Curt and the other Washington Greys had a different tradition of warfare stretching behind them, one they had originally learned from both the Greeks and the Arabs. The former had spared captives to sell as slaves while the latter had treated prisoners with the respect of one valiant warrior to another. The desert sheiks and even their holy men honored valor when they encountered it; even the fanatic Imam Madjid Rahman, leader of the Muslim Jehorkhims in Zahedan so many long years ago, had spared the lives of both he and Edie Sampson because they'd fought to the last of their abilities on that rooftop in Zahedan.

But there had been no real hatred in Zahedan.

The Kurds *hated* the Turks.

It made a difference.

These people would go on fighting each other until one group was annihilated by the other. There could be no such thing as "world peace" while such bitter hatred flowed out of the minds of people.

Alexis, Russ! Take Turk prisoners if you can! Keep them from being slaughtered by the Ahl-i Haqqs! We might be able to get some information out of them by interrogation! he called to his assault company commanders.

Doing the best we can, Curt! Alexis fired back.

Can we shoot some Alley Hacks if we have to? Russ Frazier wanted to know. That was pure Frazier, of course.

I'd rather you didn't unless they start shooting at you, Russ. After all, they're supposed to be allies . . . and Qazi still has Hassan with him, Curt reminded his assault company commander.

Uh, yeah, come to think of it, I wouldn't want to lose that man. Hassan's a smart cookie! Russ decided.

Thanks, Captain! My ego thanks you, too. I'm doing a lot of fast talking to Qazi, was Hassan's comment. The young Baluchi officer was indeed picking up a sense of humor that indicated he was beginning to feel at home in the Greys. Of course, having been through a fight such as this also helped.

And Curt suddenly realized that it had been one of the most intense and protracted engagements the Greys had been through since the relief of Windhoek in Namibia. Usually, small unit combat was very short even when it was intense. In fact, the most intense it was, the shorter it usually was because of the enormous expenditure of both personal energy and material. The Greek hoplites had never engaged in protracted battles thousands of years ago, and neither had the Israelis and Arabs a hundred years in the past. When the fights got long and drawn out, high-tech usually lost and it became a matter of whose manpower could remain standing the longest.

Another sound accompanied the warbling battle cries of victory: the screams and moans of the wounded, the living dead of the modern battlefield.

Curt suddenly toggled his tacomm, *Medic, any medic! Anyone have any information on Lieutenant Clinton or Shariat Khani?*

"Major, this is Lieutenant Devlin of BIOTECO," was

the verbal tacomm reply. Helen sounded busy, stressed, worried. "I'm in the mobile surgical unit. Not much time to talk. Quick report. Kitsy has a broken neck. She may be paralyzed from the neck down. We don't know yet. Shariat Khani is in surgery; that Novia round took her in the lung and collapsed it. May have nicked the heart going past, too. Wish I had better news, Curt."

Curt sighed. "Thanks, Helen. Please keep me advised. Any other casualties?"

"Nothing serious at this time, Curt. Couple of ranks from SERVBATT got pretty bruised from taking rounds because they weren't wearing their body armor correctly taut. Couple of cuts and bruises from sheer accidents. Everyone except Kitsy can be returned to duty later today once we can get to them. Got a little log jam here right now. Can you give the Greys a little talk about triage? We take the serious ones first."

"Yeah, I know, Helen, but when you're hurting, you've always got a hurt far worse than the next Grey," Curt reminded her. "I'm real concerned about Kitsy. And Shariat Khani, too; her boss could get pretty pissed at us for this."

"Curt, they're both in the best of hands. Talk to you later. Busy here."

Curt knew Helen was reporting the best news and trying to leave out the things that would worry him. The two knew one another very well from warbot brainy days when she'd been his assigned bio-tech; when the Regiment had gone Sierra Charlie and required trained bio-techs to deal with actual battle wounds, Helen Devlin had been one of the first bio-techs to get her R.N. and be commissioned among the first combat nurses. Helen was a good trooper who was trying to look after Curt's well-being as she always had. Well, he decided, maybe he didn't need to know all the gory details at this point.

But the fight was over now. No further firing sounded over the tilled fields along the Tigris River. Curt didn't know how many Turks and Kurds had been killed, but probably enough to help keep these fields fertilized as they had been by the bodies of dead warriors for fifty centuries. He only knew that the Greys had fought well and with honor, as usual. Except he still couldn't get a handle on Colonel Bellamack's bizarre behavior. And he didn't know where Bellamack, Kester, and Cook were. He couldn't go looking for them on his own. He was commanding the Regiment now. He had to depend on the Greys to find out if those three were hurt or even dead.

He got his answer very quickly.

DIRAG Leader and RECONCO Leader, this is BIRD Leader! Ellie Aarts reported in via tacomm from her situation in birdbot linkage. *I have a make on the Colonel's OCV! It's in a draw and out of view of your line of sight. Bearing zero four five, range two-six-zero-zero meters. I'll try to enter it on the tac display if I can, but I've got my hands full of birdbots at the moment! Tracy, can you pick up my NE signal and do the posting for me, please? I don't want to lose these birdbots and maybe go KIA at this point. Spasm mode I don't need, not after a hard day over a hot warbot.*

Curt saw the target come up on the tac display of his helmet visor. *Ellie, see if you can get a closer recon of the area! Any personnel there? Cal, will you mosey on over and have a look, especially for any Russkies. Anything moving out there on visual, i-r, or whatever?*

I don't see anyone moving. In fact, I don't see any human i-r signatures. But it's hard to get a make on a motionless target against this hot ground background, Ellie Aarts told him, an unmistakable hint of excitement suddenly in her computerized vocal reply. *The OCV is hot on i-r, but it isn't on fire. Seems to be cooling down, as a matter of fact.*

Dyani here! Got it! I'm on it! A solid visual make! Harlan, join up with me! Roaring Bull, join me and keep your weapon at the ready! That was Dyani Motega far out in front of everyone else, scouting and calling to her fellow scout while giving orders to her Jeep, Roaring Bull.

Curt knew he had to get over there fast. He was almost three klicks away. So he called to his ACV, *Philip, home on my beacon for pickup! Maximum speed! Shortest route!*

Execute! As an afterthought, he added, *Edie, Alexis, any medic who can join me, converge on my beacon! We need to check this out right now!*

When Philip came roaring up through the dust and smoke, Edie, Alexis, Jerry, Ginny Bowles, and Juanita Gomez joined him clambering up the stirrups on its side as it paused for them. Curt gave Philip the go order, and they took off cross-country riding on the outside of the ACV like Russian tank riders of old.

It took them only minutes to reach the OCV, but it seemed like hours to Curt.

As Philip slid to a stop, everyone piled off.

Dyani Motega and Sergeant Harlan Saunders were already there.

Dyani was giving Henry Kester a drink as the old soldier lay on the sandy ground. Saunders was ministering to Georgina Cook.

Both were conscious but had obviously been beaten very badly. Kester looked the worst, but it was obvious that Cook was hurting badly.

The motionless, blood-covered body of the Colonel's Kurd guide, Mustafa Sahag, lay sprawled on the ground nearby.

When Kester saw Curt, he muttered a quick sit-rep, ignoring his own pain, "Russkie bastards shot everyone but the Colonel. Got Mustafa. Our body armor saved our ass, so they tried to club us to death. Georgina and me both played dead or we woulda been dead. The Russkies took off with the Colonel, sir. I couldn't stop em."

Curt knelt by his old NCO. "How do you feel, Henry?"

"I been beat worse in bars. But I'm gettin' too old for this sorta crap. I think the bastards knocked out a couple of my teeth . . . and I been real attached to them since I was a kid, too." There was a touch of humor in Kester's voice, just enough to tell Curt that the man had been hurt badly but was too goddamned proud to give up.

So Curt replied, "Henry, goddammit, you've gotta stop

277

getting in these brawls or I'll stop giving you overnight passes into town. You'll be a bad example to the rest of the troops."

"Hell, Major, if I was him, I'd be asking how to get out of this chicken outfit," Sergeant Harlan Saunders put in.

"Major, don't make him talk any more," Ginny admonished Curt. "He'll be all right, but we've got to evac him to BIOTECO and check for internal injuries."

"They took the Colonel with them?" Curt asked. The sound of hovering aerodyne came to his ears. One of the Chippies was overhead, prepared to get Kester and Cook back to the medical vans.

Kester didn't shake his head but replied, "Yeah. He was chattering away like crazy with them. They musta thought he was an NIA spook or something from the way they acted."

"Oh, shit!" Curt breathed.

"We gotta get him back, Major," Kester insisted. "I don't think he deserted or anything, but when Georgina and I questioned his order to retrograde, he laid his Novia on us. Sir, I think he toggled over somehow. He wasn't like the Colonel I've gotten to know. We gotta get him back, sir!"

"You're right, Henry! And we will!" Curt assured him as two bio-techs prepared to put the old sergeant on a litter and load him on the aerodyne. "Not only is the Colonel an ex-warbot brainy who knows a lot about everything *and* our new Mod Seven-Elevens, but the Washington Greys never abandon their own . . . !"

Chapter Thirty-five

"Okay, General, that's my sit-rep," Major Curt Carson said into the comm gear of his ACV. The equipment in the regimental OCV had been pretty well gutted by the Soviet Spetsnaz troops except for those modules that Kesler and Cook had destructed before the Sovs could get them. Curt was working with a typical Edie Sampson make-do set up. He had no visual, only poor quality audio. But the link was intelligible. "I'm reporting to you first rather than General Pickens. I don't know how the hell he would take this news, but I know how *you* will react."

Major General Belinda Hettrick was half the world away at Fort Huachuca, Arizona. She didn't comment on Curt's observation. The two of them had indeed worked together a great deal in the past, and both of them knew exactly how the other would behave in most situations—professional, social, and personal. She'd been his company commander, then his regimental commander. The contract between the two of them had never been vocalized; it was just there and had been from Day One. Her first reaction was professional. "Four casualties? Who and how bad are they?"

"Six, if we count them all," Curt admitted sorrowfully then enumerated them, a job he always hated. It was easier to be a warbot brainy running warbots via remote linkage. You were never killed because the warbot took it in the pan instead, and the worst fate that might befall you was to be KIA when you didn't get out of your

279

warbot's computerized mind fast enough. But the Sierra Charlies had discovered the hard way that you can actually get killed, really killed, on a battlefield. It put a bit more excitement in things, if you liked that kind of excitement (some people do), but sometimes Curt detested what he had to do afterward reporting about the killed and wounded. He ticked them off for Hettrick. "Colonel Bellamack missing in action, presumed to be held captive by a Soviet Spetsnaz battalion; his actual condition unknown although he was acting irrationally before he was captured. Regimental Sergeant Major Henry Kester and Regimental Staff Sergeant Georgina Cook were severely beaten and left for dead by the Sovs; Major Gydesen reports that their condition is stable, they suffered no internal injuries, they will recover fully in a day or so, and most of the external damage can be repaired with biocosmetics. The Colonel's Kurdish guide, Mustafa Sahab, was killed; too bad, because he was a nice old guy, and I could sure as hell use a guide right now. Lieutenant Kitsy Clinton is in serious condition with a broken neck; she's totally paralyzed from the neck down and has been airlifted to Mosul with Doctors Tom Alvin and Larry McHenry accompanying her. The other casualty was our Kurd liaison officer, Shariat Khani; she took a seven-millimeter in her chest and has been airlifted with Lieutenant Clinton to Mosul in serious but stable condition."

"Oh my God! How did Kitsy get hurt? Broken neck you say?"

"A Kurd hit her from behind with the full swing of a rifle butt," Curt explained. He didn't want to muddy the water right then, but he knew damned well that Shariat Khani had been exacting revenge. And Curt didn't want to cast a cloud over Edie for reacting as she had; he probably would have done the same except that Edie had been quicker to react. Best to leave all of that for the final report. The bio situation might have stabilized by then. However, Curt was feeling like hell. He couldn't imagine what it might be like to face the rest of her life completely paralyzed. She was too much of a bright star in the Washington Greys constellation! But, then, all the Greys ladies were special insofar as the men were concerned. This was one of the bitter consequences of permitting women into combat situations, however, and Curt would have to live with that. But it didn't make him feel any better about it.

"Henry will recover; he's too mean to die," Hettrick observed, then pointed out, "Georgina may need some help from Henry and her other friends. I'll try to keep her assigned to Gydesen and not evacced to a stateside hospital. Ruth and her surgeons learned a lot of biotechnology from the Bruneis while you were there. Sorry about your guide. And I'm not worried about the Kurd woman. But Kitsy's another matter . . ."

"Yeah, I agree. I hope you'll help me see to it that she gets the best," Curt requested. "If her spinal cord is severed, maybe Colonel Willa Lovell and Captain Owen Pendleton at McCarthy Proving Ground have some way they're thinking about to put neuroelectronic jumpers across the break."

"I'll get on the horn about it," Hettrick promised, and Curt felt better. She would. And she'd pull rank, swing clout, and do anything humanly possible for the Greys. This didn't halt Curt's worry, but he did feel a little better. Kitsy would be in good hands, and he had a job to do in which he probably wouldn't have time for a lot of worry. Hettrick went on, changing the subject, "I presume your recce and scouts are out and keeping track of the Sovs?"

"Yes, ma'am." Although comm protocol had disappeared among the Greys during the Battle of Asi, Curt wasn't about to let his own protocol with his commander get personal. Not at this point.

"You just told me they'd crossed the border into eastern Turkey. They must move pretty fast."

"Yes, ma'am, they do. But you should keep in mind that we're only fourteen klicks from that border ourselves. But we can track them and stay with them. With our airlift capability, we can leapfrog them," Curt pointed out as the tactical plan began to come together in his mind.

"Are they still on foot? Or did you locate some Sov vehicles?"

"They were on the ground until they got back across the Turkish border. Then they rendezvoused with their vehicles—mostly BTR-218 Armored Personnel Carriers supported by MAZ-800 four-by-four light trucks."

"They didn't bring their vehicles into Iraq?"

"Not that we could see. They probably didn't want to hassle the Turkish and Iraqi border patrols. Easy as hell to penetrate the borders here because nothing's marked and the Kurds move back and forth across them daily in large numbers because they figure it's their territory regardless of what the official maps say."

"Okay, I can visualize that. But how in hell did the Sovs manage to operate in Turkey and get all the way from the Soviet Union down into northern Iraq? That's a long trek through Turkey! So how did they pull it off? Are the Turks looking the other way?" Hettrick wondered aloud. "Or are the Turks playing games with the Soviets again?" She was referring to the continued Turkish commitment to NATO but the nation's refusal to join the European economic community, plus the historical fact that after World War I and the October Revolution, the Turks were the first nation to receive Soviet military aid.

"General, these little ethnic and tribal wars create even stranger bedfellows than politics. I'm not ruling anything out. First place, I don't know anything about the Turks we whupped today. Some of the survivors are eager to talk but don't seem to know much. Those who might know something won't talk. The interrogation is still going on. As for how the Spetsnaz unit got here maybe without the Turkish government knowing anything about it—General, take a look at a topo map," Curt suggested. "Pretty damned rugged country along the Iran-Turkey border. I suspect the Sovs moved southward to the west of that border, behind the Turkish border patrols which are mostly on foot. The Sovs may even have used the

Turkish roads. . . ."

"Okay, I can buy that, but some of the Pentagon types might not, especially if they're old warbot brainies and have never fought on the ground. In addition, Turkey has no bitch with Iran at the moment, just an agreement not to shoot into each other's goal," Hettrick mused. "The Sovs might have used the roads if they moved quickly and had good recon to stay clear of Turkish patrols. Hell, we could do that sort of thing with the Greys! But getting a full Spetsnaz battalion covertly across the Turk-ish-Soviet border could be another problem!"

"Look at the topo map again, General. The land stands on end around there."

"Yeah, it does. Too bad they don't make better use of it by farming both sides of the same hectare."

"Besides, these Spetsnaz boys are real sneaky. We didn't even know they were to the east of us. Never even picked them up on i-r!"

"Think they might have some i-r stealth uniforms?"

"Do we have such things?"

"Uh, Curt, I can't discuss that. But, sorry, you haven't got them. None of the Iron Fist does. We're not 'special' forces. Even when I was on the OSCAR desk in the COS office, I couldn't swing that one. That's all I can talk about," Hettrick told him with some bitterness in her voice. "Okay, I'm not going to touch the international diplomatic aspects of this with a three-point-five-meter pole. You say you're tracking the Sovs. That means your birdbots are in Turkish airspace."

"I didn't report that, but your inference is correct, General."

"How about your scouts?"

"The Greys are tracking both in the air and on the ground, General. But I had no authority in the orders for Operation Sturdy Spectra to cross any borders." Curt paused for a moment, then admitted, "So, to do what must be done, and acting as the temporary regimental commander, I've activated Operation Iron Fist. We in-tend to follow those Sovs right into the basement of the

Kremlin if we have to! But we intend to nail their balls to a boulder long before that, whenever the situation is just right for getting Bellamack safely out of their hands. Since the Sovs made the mistake of taking him captive, and since we're not in a state of war with the Soviet Union at the moment, I am assuming that the Colonel is being held as a hostage. Therefore, I'm invoking the Treaty of Karachi and going after him."

The Treaty of Karachi gave national military forces the right to cross into any territory in limited force to carry out the release of hostages, provided the country involved was notified and did not take immediate action to apprehend the hostage-takers. "I sort of figured you would. The Turks and the Sovs won't like it," Hettrick said.

"Screw the Russkies! And the bloody Turks! The Spetsnaz battalion shouldn't be down here anyway! And if those really were Turkish guerrillas today, what the hell were they doing inside Iraq anyway?" Curt snapped. "American forces are here under the eyes of international monitors under a UN resolution! The Soviets aren't! And the Turks sure as hell weren't if those were really Turks! Besides, General, my heavy heartburn isn't with the Sovs. We'll nail them before they can get to their borders. I am indeed worried a little bit about the Turks. We will be on their turf, and the Turkish army's got a reputation almost as nasty and mean as the Gurkhas because of the way Turkish soldiers fought in Korea. I guess what I'm saying is that I need some high-level support. Like someone in Washington to notify the Turks and give them the chance to tell us to piss up a rope so I can officially go across that border in Operation Iron Fist—the name, by the way, not being generated from a computer but from my own jellyware because I'm tired of those goddamned ridiculous computer-generated operational codes! But in the long run if I'm going to keep my ass out of a sling somewhere, I need to get some legitimacy for Operation Iron Fist."

"Legitimacy has never stopped you in the past, Curt," Hettrick reminded him.

"If you're trying to tell me in a nice way that I'm one of the most illegitimate officers in the Army, I will take that as a compliment, General!" In spite of the serious nature of the situation, Curt knew that Belinda Hettrick had a sense of humor that permitted her to maintain perspective on things. Then he got serious again. "Having notified you of my intention to implement Operation Iron Fist, I will upload my ops plan to you as quickly as I can work it out . . . even if it's after we recover Bellamack and return to Mosul; I may not have time to gin up an official ops plan by the book. However, by the book, this is my first report to you, and I need to inform you that my birdbots and ground patrols are already across the border into Turkey. My tacair will be up and looking as soon as they replenish in Mosul."

"Report received and noted, Major. I commend you for your timely response to the situation and for following doctrine by maintaining contact," Hettrick told him. "I'll forward your information through normal channels to higher authority. That should take a while and allow some things to be decided where you are. So in the meantime, I don't think we can afford to wait for a reply or an official approval since the life of a senior officer is possibly at stake. At any rate, that is my opinion as the division commander. Now that we've got that little detail out of the way for the record, the monkey's on my back, Curt, so don't sweat it. I've got the staff here to compound the confusion with commotion, then confuse 'em if I can't convince 'em. A year at a Pentagon desk taught me a great deal! If you think you need me, I'll jump on a utility transport and get there fast."

"General, some day I hope to command this Regiment," Curt admitted. "With all due respect and with gratitude for your offer of on-the-spot help, I think I'd better screw this one to the wall myself because I think I can do it."

"I think you can, too. I've always thought you could," Hettrick confided in him. "But one of the first things you've got to learn as a regimental commander is to quit spending so much time talking to the high brass. So get your ass in gear, go out there, and do it! Shut up and soldier, soldier! Make your names to shine!"

Chapter Thirty-six

"We have no problem with the Russians! They may even give us rifles! You won't! Maybe I can deal with them! So let them go back north! Why should I try to follow and attack them?" Sharaf Qazi confronted Major Curt Carson, his head held high with his chin thrust out.

Curt suspected he'd have trouble with this Kurdish tribal warlord. In spite of Hassan's presence as a Greys liaison officer with the Ahl-i Haqqs, Curt had had no effective control and very little coordination with Qazi's headquarters during the Battle of Asi and the events leading up to it. Qazi was a loose cannon insofar as Curt was concerned; he needed the chieftain's help, but it had to be carefully coordinated with the movements of the Washington Greys or Colonel Bill Bellamack would end up dead.

So Curt had called a Papa brief shortly after he conferred via telecon with Hettrick and as quickly as he could get Sharaf Qazi to come to the ACV. In fact, the mopping up operations following the Battle of Asi were still under way; the Greys were having a hell of a time keeping the Ahl-i Haqqs from shooting all the wounded and surrendered Turks.

If an Orders meeting was an OSCAR briefing, then Curt figured that a planning conference had to be a Papa briefing. Edie Sampson managed to get off a terrible pun on that one, suggesting that Papa briefs should be kept short. Curt deliberately ignored her, although he realized that she was trying to help him maintain his sense of perspective on the situation. Which was difficult. Curt was under pressure. Again, he'd had the regimental command dumped on his shoulders as a result of combat. It wasn't as bad as the first time in Namibia, and there he'd fortunately had Hettrick to talk to for a few hours. Here, the second time, his regimental commander wasn't with him at all.

And he had a rebellious Kurd warlord to deal with, a man who wasn't used to joint operations much less cooperative command situations.

"Believe me, Sharaf, dealing with the Russians would be as bad as dealing with the Turks," Curt tried to convince him. "Or trying to. Look at it another way: the Turks and the Russians both have kept you from getting Kurdistan, your own country. What makes you think they're going to change their minds now? The only reason the Soviet Spetsnaz battalion is down here is to probe the situation. The foreign policy objectives of the Soviet Union and Czarist Russia are the same! They tried to break out to the south for centuries. The Armenians, Turkey, Iraq, Iran, and Afghanistan have all stood in their way—*and so have the Kurds!*"

Qazi waved his hand. "I care nothing for this sort of international scheming! Our enemies are the Iraqis, Iranians, and especially the Turks! Let the Turks chase the Spetsnaz battalion!"

Curt gritted his teeth in frustration and picked up his tacomm brick as if he were about to make a call. He was going to try to bluff this through and be ready to act in case Qazi called his bluff. "Okay, Sharaf, if that's the way you want to play this game. We're going after the Soviets. But I cannot afford to have you operating in my rear with the sort of attitude you have."

Qazi laughed. "So you want to fight us here and now?"

Curt shook his head. "No, you're not my enemy. I don't want to fight you, so I won't. I'll just take you prisoner here and now."

Qazi roared at this statement from Curt. "You are surrounded by Ahl-i Haqqs!"

"Without a leader or his second-in-command, I'm not

worried about how they'll fight," Curt continued his bluff. "You've got no communication with your men, Qazi! You can't even order them to start fighting! Even if you did, are you so sure you want to fight us now? You've just seen our new warbots at work; they'll cut you up with automatic weapons fire and spit you out like bot flush. Wouldn't you rather be on the winning side for a change?"

Qazi suddenly had no retort to that. Curt was out-maneuvering him. Qazi knew he'd verbally taken on a worthy adversary in an attempt to get what he wanted, and he also knew he really didn't want to fight this new warbot unit. Twice he'd seen them in action. They didn't fight like the American Robot Infantry he'd known. In fact, they fought more like his own irregulars, but with a lot better and more deadly weapons.

Curt sensed that Qazi's silence meant a breakthrough in the discussion. Now he had to be very careful to give the Sharaf the easy way out without causing the warlord to lose face among his own troops. But Curt couldn't afford to ease up yet. So he pressed forward to take the high ground of the conversation without giving Qazi time to interrupt. "Sharaf, I'm through screwing around. Time's running out. The Soviets are putting ground between us even as we talk. I'm going to move. And you and I are either going to work together on this thing, or you'll sit on your ass in Mosul until we get our commanding officer back. You'll be treated better than the British treated your forefathers under the same conditions, but things will end up just like they did back then: you won't gain a goddamned thing by being hard to get along with. On the other hand, if you work with us and show us that you've got something more than a horde of undisciplined irregulars, if you show us that you can be trusted, then your chances of getting additional American support will improve a great deal. We've gotten damned tired of trying to help those who won't or didn't fight for their freedom. But we've sure as hell helped a lot of people like the Afghans who did."

Curt paused for a beat, then said, "So, what's it going to be, Sharaf? You going to help me chase the Soviets out of your homeland? Or are you going to continue a centuries-old tradition of losing by trying to do it alone?"

Sharaf Massoud Qazi, chieftain of the Kurdish Ahl-i Haqqs, haughtily looked at Curt, and that look almost caused Curt to give the signal to seize the man and his six lieutenants with him. But Qazi said in a firm voice, "What is your plan? How do we work with you? Show me what you want us to do."

Curt mentally breathed a sigh of relief. But he didn't have time to gloat or rejoice. He had work to do. He got to his feet and indicated a flat topo map taped up on the side of his ACV. If he'd had his druthers, he would have liked to use a 3D holographic chart projected with Georgie's help, but there wasn't room for everyone in the ACV, he didn't have a snake pit briefing room available, and even Georgie didn't have the power to burn a holographic projection bright enough to be seen in the brilliant sunlight of the Tigris River valley.

"Here's what we're going to do. Sharaf, you and your Ahl-i Haqqs are very good on the ground, and you know the territory. You'll stay on the ground, and we'll support you logistically with ammo, food, fuel, and water by airdrop. We will also provide reconnaissance to help you stay in contact with the Soviets. You'll have to move fast to stay with them using the Turkish vehicles captured here at Asi."

Qazi shrugged. "We do not think trucks are useable in the mountains."

"The Soviets are using trucks," Curt pointed out. "If they can, you can. It's important that you stay in contact with them, push them, harass their rear guard, keep them occupied, but *don't attack them!*"

"Don't attack? Why is this?" Qazi was attuned only to the assault, the ambush, and quick strike. That's all he'd ever known, and that's all he'd ever tried. Most military commanders, even the most sophisticated ones from the highest of high-tech countries, suffered from this innate conservatism; Curt was considered to be a maverick who'd try anything that might work, and he was proud of that because his innovative techniques and willingness to consider new approaches had won a lot of fights.

"The reason is simple to understand," Curt told him, also addressing his own subordinates gathered around. "The Washington Greys will leapfrog the Soviets using our airlift capabilities. When we see where they're going, we'll jump ahead of them and set up a defensive line. The Soviets will be driven into us by your forces. Then we'll smash them between us. This tactic is known as the hammer and anvil doctrine. Do you understand what I have been telling you?"

Qazi did, but it was a complete turnabout for him. Pursuit was something he thought he could do, but he was the one who usually did the ambushing. "How do I get messages to you? And how do I get messages from you?" The man was quickly learning twenty-first century military operations, especially the need to communicate.

"You'll have a hand-held radio," Curt told him, indicating his own tacomm brick on a belt clip.

"Uh, Major, aren't those classified?" Major Pappy Gratton brought up.

"We've lost so damned many of them since we converted them from rear echelon comm units that no one really pays too much attention to that these days, Major," Edie Sampson pointed out. She saw that she was going to have to fill the shoes of both Regimental Sergeant Major Henry Kester and the communications slot of Regimental Staff Sergeant Georgina Cook. "The only thing that's really classified now is the programming modules in the ACVs, the gear that sets up the skipping programs and then uploads those programs into the tacomm units themselves. We can give one to Sharaf."

"Can you run it, Sharaf?" Curt wanted to know.

A subtle change had come over the Kurd warlord. "I will learn. Please give me two in the event that one stops working."

"Can do," was the comment from the regimental S-4,

291

Captain Harriet Dearborn.

"If you can handle your own communications with us, Sharaf, that will allow me to put Lieutenant Hassan Mahmud back in command of his platoon. Otherwise, for this sort of thing, I'd probably have to assign both Mahmud and Captain Allen to you as liaison." Curt knew he was going to have to use every one of the Greys on this one. He didn't want to have a loose liaison officer flopping free out there. In the back of his mind, he was thinking that he'd try to maintain surveillance on the Kurd unit J.I.C.. Qazi might change his mind in mid-operation, and Curt didn't want to be caught short by that possibility. He'd need all his troops for Plan B. "Your main job will be to check in with me regularly and to inform me of what's happening." With the tacomm transmissions, Edie could nail down the location of Qazi by d-f procedures. And he'd ask her to slip a beacon module into both tacomms so Qazi would show up on the Regiment's tactical displays. Curt wasn't taking chances.

"Good! We will follow the Russians. But if we run into Turkish soldiers, we will have to stop and fight them," he pointed out.

Curt turned to his AIRBATT commander. "Cal, how quickly can you get a couple of Harpies over a target to lay some ordnance on them?"

"Depends on where the fuckers are and how far we've got to fly," Worsham replied, his moustache bristling. "We can sit cockpit-ready if we can use our ground support equipment to provide standby aux power and keep from burning up fuel on the pad. But Mosul is about a hundred klicks south of the border, and that's about twenty minutes we'll use up even before we get out of Iraq."

"Hell, Cal, you don't need an aerodrome, do you?" Curt reminded him. "If you've got logistical support, you can operate a millimeter inside the border, can't you?"

"Damned right! But our logistical requirements could soak up a lot of SERVBATT capability."

"We had some people take incoming fire here at Asi,"

292

Captain Harriet Dearborn pointed out, "but we're not below our critical manpower level with them on temporary sick call in Mosul. With ASSAULTCO provisioned-up and standing ready, we've still got the manpower to support you in the field, Major."

"Okay, Harriet, you keep us fed and fueled, and we'll operate anywhere," Cal advised her then turned to Curt. "Okay, so you're going to send Sharaf Qazi and his troops to maintain minus-x pressure on the Sovs. Jolley's Rogers are going to stand by to provide any tacair rock pounding that's necessary. I hope to God you don't have the bright idea that Jolley and I are expected to bore boring holes in the air up there on recce. That's a drag when we're loaded. I'd just as leif not entice any goddamned Wasps up to bother me, either, which happens on recce."

"John, how much of that sort of full-time surveillance can your birdbots provide?" Curt asked Major John Gibbon, commander of RECONCO.

"Uh, Major, that depends on how far beyond the border the Sovs go before we decide on a good place to bushwhack them," Captain Ellie Aarts of BIRD company put in. "Major, BIRD company wasn't intended to perform surveillance. And as for the range we have on the birdbots . . . Well, as you know, that's sort of classified information—burn before reading, and all that," Captain Ellie Aarts put in.

"Yeah, we aren't even authorized to inform the regimental commander of that number," Major John Gibbon added. Everyone knew that that birdbot range was restricted because those flying warbots were designed to provide close-in battlefield reconnaissance, not long-range long flight time surveillance. "Let's just say that if we can see 'em, we can control 'em."

"Thanks, that gives me some indication," Curt told him. "Things haven't changed very much in the linkage department since we were all warbot brainies five years ago."

"And even if we had unlimited range, I can keep only

one birdbot up at a time if you expect twenty-four hour surveillance," Aarts admitted.

"Joanne," Curt told his chief of staff, "note that surveillance and recce are a problem for Operation Iron Fist. We'll get the obvious, easy aspects of the mission laid out first, then go to work on solutions to the problems."

She nodded, taking notes on the keypad in her left hand.

"What is your overall operational plan, Major?" That came from the regimental S-3 Operations staffer, Major Hensley Atkinson, the one who would be burdened with most of the details.

In spite of his early stint as temporary regimental commander, Curt had almost forgotten that he had a regimental staff to take care of the details of running and fighting the Regiment. During the final phase of the Namibian Operation Diamond Skeleton, a lot of staff planning and coordination hadn't been necessary; it had been a matter of finishing off something that had already started and then taking care of all the mop-up stuff.

So he figured he'd better start acting like a regimental commander.

Curt looked back at her and told her, "Thank you for reminding me that I've got a staff to help me, Major. Very well, this is a Papa brief to develop the overall plan. When we finish, I want a staff and operational command estimate of how quickly we can do the OSCAR brief? But I want to emphasize that time is of the essence. The quicker we get the operation fully organized and under way, the sooner we'll be able to nail the Sovs and recover the Colonel!"

Chapter Thirty-seven

"Major, look who just checked back in!" Platoon Sergeant Dyani Motega interrupted Major Curt Carson's spartan breakfast of field rations in his ACV.

The Crow Indian girl entered Curt's ACV, removed the blue Sierra Charlie tam from her dark hair, and saluted. She had a young Kurd in tow. He looked very sheepish and submissive.

Curt glanced up from the waffles and syrup which was hot but never as tasty as the real thing made while you wait in a restaurant or in your own quarters. He returned her formal salute and then got to his feet. It was a deliberate move on Curt's part. He was a big man, and now he towered over the young Kurd. Many powerful people liked to remain seated while addressing those who came before them, but Curt decided to stand because of the height advantage. This portrayed the image he wanted: a big man who was a leader, not a small man who ruled. "Ah, Haji Somayeh! *Naharak said!*" Curt greeted his errant native guide in Arabic, noting the boy's bandaged arm. "Are you all right now?"

"*Efendi,* I am sorry!" Somayeh tried to apologize. "I was frightened by the shooting! I do not know what happened. I started running." The young man was obviously embarrassed.

Curt knew Somayeh had made a difficult decision to come back after he'd shagged out of the battle down in the Tigris River bottom and then been shot by Shariat Khani. The young man might have some guts and honor after all, and Curt wanted to encourage that sort of person. "It happens to all people at the start of their first battle, Somayeh."

"But you do not run from battle. Even your women do not run from battle."

"We've been trained not to run, but that doesn't mean we don't want to run sometimes," Dyani Motega admitted in a rare expression of her inner thoughts.

"You're a Kurd who doesn't like fighting?" Curt asked him. "If so, you're the first I've met."

"The Shakaks fight only when we must."

"Well, I wish I could teach Sharaf Qazi and his Ahl-i Haqqs not to be so gung-ho about fighting at the drop of a hat," Curt muttered. "The unwillingness to fight is often a good thing."

"Some of my people have made fighting a way of life," Somayeh admitted, not really understanding the Americanism Curt had used. "Major, I am back to continue my work with you. That is, if you will have me."

"Let's put it this way: you were wounded in the river bottom fight and have just been returned to duty by our bio-techs," Curt told him and toggled his tacomm unit. "Captain Allen, report to the regimental ACV. I've got a talker to help spell you and Hassan with the Qazi comm link."

"You are not going to use me as a guide?" Somayeh suddenly asked, looking very much like a little boy who'd been spanked.

"We won't need you as a guide," Curt explained to him. "But you can be very useful by talking by radio with the Ahl-i Haqqs." That relieved Curt a little. He was worried about burning out Jerry and Hassan in the communications and translation task when he'd probably need them in combat when they nailed the Soviets between the anvil of the Greys and the hammer of the Ahl-i Haqqs.

Jerry Allen stuck his head into the ACV and popped a quick, casual salute. "You called, Major? Oh! I see our errant native guide returned!"

"He's yours, Jerry. Plug him into your comm translation schedule," Curt told him briefly.

Jerry grinned. "Good! Another warm body to chatter in Arabic! Come on, Haji!" And he lapsed into rapid-fire Arabic with the young Kurd as they left the ACV.

Dyani didn't leave. Curt resumed his seat and asked, "Had chow yet, Sergeant? Want to help me eat some of this sumptuous repast? It's too much for me."

"Thank you, Major, but I had something to eat before I went on sentry duty at oh-four-hundred," Dyani told him. "But if you have a moment, I'd like to talk to you. I know that you're under a lot of pressure right now. Catching the Soviets at just the right time is pretty important. If you want me to come back later, I'll understand."

"Sit down, Dyani," Curt told her, motioning to one of the bench seats along the wall of the ACV. "About the only time I can't talk to a member of the Washington Greys is when we're being shot at or some other required thing is going on . . . like muster or Retreat. What's on your mind?"

"Sir, I've already spoken to Lieutenant Sweet and Major Gibbons. When this is over and we get back to Mosul, I intend to ask you to recommend me for Officer's Candidate School and give me a leave of absence from the battalion to try to become commissioned."

Dyani Motega was always up-front and straightforward in her relationships. She said what she was thinking but in a highly disciplined and formal way; she wasn't the impulsive type. In fact, Curt knew from experience that she had a very strong sense of personal discipline, and this made itself felt in the outward discipline she exhibited in the Greys. To some Greys, she'd become known as mysterious and almost unapproachable. Because she was also a very pretty woman, she'd had ample social opportunities in the Greys, but Dyani Motega remained staunchly loyal to a strangely semi-Victorian sense of values and code of conduct.

"I think that's a hell of a good idea, Dyani," Curt told her honestly. "As your batt commander, I will indeed put in a rec for you. I don't know if I can do so as temporary regimental commander, but we'll see what Colonel Bellamack thinks when we get him back to Mosul. But tell me, why OCS? You could enjoy a fine NCO career."

Dyani Motega looked at him strangely. She was gazing directly at him. He had never seen that look on her pretty face before. "Because I have plans, Major. Plans that did not mature until I had joined the Greys. Plans that a young girl just entering the Army didn't have. When I joined up, I just wanted to serve as my family has for generations. Now I understand there's more to a military career than just service. I wish to become the first member of my family to be commissioned."

"A worthy goal, Dyani. What caused you to change your plans?"

Curt was unprepared for the answer.

"You did, sir."

"*Me?*"

"Yes, sir." She was somewhat hesitant about talking this way and apparently searched hard for the right words. "Although Army rules and traditions have eased a lot, a gulf still exists between NCOs who *do* and officers who *lead*. I intend to eliminate it for personal as well as professional resons. It's up to me to do what's necessary to bridge the gap between us." Dyani was agonizingly frank, and it caught Curt completely off guard.

Ample and frequent opportunities had presented themselves for Curt and her, including a very cold night in a tent in the antarctic weather of Kerguelen Island. Dyani had spoken then about her family code of conduct and morality. Now was the first time she had even intimated that she had any attraction to him.

"Is that all, Dyani?" he wanted to know.

"No, sir. I might admit that I have dreams and desires. But it would be impertinent and improper for me to discuss them further with you at this time and under these conditions." Dyani was holding herself under tight control, and the strain showed on her face.

"Dyani, all that isn't really necessary. You know by

now that those of us in the Washington Greys are part of one big family and some of us care very deeply about one another," Curt told her.

"Sir, perhaps the relaxed morals of some of the Greys suits them, but not me. I have a different background and a far more stringent personal code in spite of the old stories about Indian squaws. I don't intend to allow those fabrications to affect what I've been taught." She straightened up. "Sir, I've said far more than I intended to say when I asked for a moment of your time. But I just . . . I had to . . . Never mind! May I be excused, sir?" She perched the blue Sierra Charlie tam on her head and saluted.

For the first time since he'd met her in her personnel interview, Curt realized that he had completely underestimated this young woman in many ways. She was one of the outstanding female Sierra Charlies—disciplined, competent, dedicated, loyal; in fact, she possessed all the qualities a commander dreamed about in a model subordinate. Now he knew there was far more to Dyani Motega, and most of it was tightly bottled up inside, demanding to get out and find expression as she matured.

Curt returned her salute. "You're dismissed, Sergeant. However, you did *not* say too much! You didn't say enough! Some day when things quiet down a bit, I hope you'll say more. You might be surprised."

"Yes, sir!" And she was gone.

The tacomm demanded his attention. Gibbon reported that Qazi was still in contact with the Soviets and that they'd crossed Turkish Highway Number 6 shortly before dawn and then gone to cover. When Curt checked the map, he could see that the Spetsnaz gang was indeed sharp, getting over that highway before the daily traffic began and lying doggo during daylight hours when they could easily be detected by low-tech Turkish militia. It also appeared from their position and general direction that they were intending to pass to the east of the town of Van, the ancient capital of the ancient kingdom of

Van. They were heading right up the Iranian-Turkish border for the USSR.

Curt knew he had to get them soon. Today. At the rate they were traveling, the Spetsnaz battalion would be across the border into Soviet Armenia by tomorrow. He stood before the map, knowing that he'd have to make a decision quickly. Time was running out. The distance between him and the Spetsnaz battalion was growing. Qazi's irregulars couldn't possibly be expected to maintain their forced march pace through those mountains. But where was the best place along their projected route to stop them?

He knew he needed help, but he didn't realize that he needed help in making a tactical decision. He'd never had that problem before. However, he knew what to do when he was faced with an apparently insoluble problem. He stepped outside his ACV into the long shadows of the Iraqi dawn.

And then he almost wished he hadn't. The battlefield of yesterday had begun to stink. No one had bothered to bury the dead Turks, but each of them had been carefully and thoroughly stripped of all clothing and equipment during the night by local scavengers. Vultures wheeled in the sky already, waiting for their chance to get to the unburied dead.

Major Alexis Morgan came around the corner of the ACV, her hand over her lower face. When she saw Curt, she exclaimed, "How long are we going to stick around this pest hole, Major?"

He looked at her and nodded. "Come on inside. At least the life-support system gets rid of the odors."

Once back in the ACV, Curt sat down. "I tried to take a break and get a breath of fresh air. I got neither one," he admitted.

"You're kind of beat, aren't you?"

"You noticed."

"How could I help but notice? I notice a lot of things about you."

"Reciprocal. Still."

"Things change, Curt," she admitted quietly. "Oh, that we could recapture those halcyon days when we were both junior company officers! You've got the Regiment now, and I've got my company."

"Are the Marauders giving you problems, Allie?"

She shook her head while her corn-colored hair bounced. "Not a bit! Love it! But it does mean more work and less free time."

"Yeah, we haven't had much of that lately, have we?"

"We never do."

"And when we do, Colonel Mahathis shows up from Brunei in his personal hypersonic Sabredancer." Curt observed.

"Usually bringing the Sultana Alzena with him, I might add," she replied somewhat caustically.

"I gave up getting jealous a long time ago, Allie. You do what you wish, and I will never try to stop you."

"Thank you," she told him honestly. "Although a girl shouldn't be flattered when a man tells her he no longer gets jealous of her other acquaintances."

"Well, I recall we agreed to that. You don't get your brass green, and neither do I."

"Right. Which is why I dropped by to let you know that I'm really feeling pretty badly about Kitsy. No one should have to face what she's up against right now." It was very unusual for Alexis to admit such a thing to Curt, and it was his second surprise this morning.

"That's quite charitable of you, Allie. And even more so that you came to tell me so."

"Charitable, my ass!" Alexis exploded. "She's a Washington Grey!"

Curt held up his hand. "Okay, let's let it go at that. Thank you for thinking of me."

"Just don't forget that I do indeed think of you often," Alexis reminded him. "Now, Major Curt Carson, it is utterly unlike you to sit on your ass for eight hours without taking action! Goddammit, how long are you going to wait to hit the Sovs? Or are you planning to bust the Soviet border in the process and stage your own invasion of the Soviet Union?"

"Allie, this has *got* to work and work right the first time! If it doesn't, we won't get a second chance! We'll be in Turkey with a bunch of goddamned mad Turks on our ass very fast, and risk the possibility that the Sovs could kill Colonel Bellamack when we hit them. It's got to be right!" Curt told her firmly.

Alexis shrugged. "So? As I recall, you are the same Major Curt Carson who led the First Tac Batt into Kalimantan to rescue me and fifteen other Greys! I think you're the same Carson who handled the operation at Casa Fantasma in Mexico's Sierra Madre mountains. And the same man who was in charge of operations at Strijdom and Windhoek in Namibia. Let's sit down with the troops, figure out what to do, and go do it!"

"I am not the same man," Curt replied quickly, "just as you're not the same young woman I first knew as a chocolate-bar lieutenant fresh out of West Point and assigned to my company."

"Gone chicken on me?"

Curt might have bridled at that question coming from anyone but Alexis. "No, but I do detect that I'm being a tad more careful these days."

"Screw it!" she told him then reminded him, "Colonel Bellamack is out there being held as a captive, maybe as a hostage. *The Washington Greys never abandon their own!* Now, dammit, Curt, do I have to call the Greys together for an OSCAR brief."

Curt realized that he'd been in somewhat of a blue funk brought about by Kitsy's injury, Bellamack's irrational behavior and capture, and the general concern about Qazi rolling around like a loose cannon. Regardless of the size of the unit he led, a combat commander *must not* act that way, he told himself. "No, you don't. You can't," he reminded her firmly.

Reaching over to grab his tacomm brick, he called, "Major Wilkinson, this is Major Carson. Acknowledge, please!"

"Wilkinson here, sir!" was the smart reply from his

chief of staff.

"OSCAR brief in ten minutes! Call 'em up!"

"Roger! Consider it done, sir!"

Without another word to Alexis, he looked at the map, then checked the tactical display. As if to himself, he said, "The Sovs are about one-eighty klicks to the northeast. They're lying under cover during the day. They'll move at sundown. By dawn tomorrow, they'll be tired from the effort of a night march through the mountainous terrain. We can move during the day today, get set up, and be waiting for them when they reach their destination tomorrow morning. That's when we'll hit them! And that's likely to be . . ." He studied the map for a moment, made a mental calculation, measured roughly with the span on his hand, and finally poked his finger at the map. "Here! Where the Bendamahi River forks! We'll hold the high ground at the fork, a place called Caldiran!"

Chapter Thirty-eight

Hauler Leader, this is Fancy Nancy! We're being painted by Turkish and Iranian air defense radars! came the computer synthesized "voice" of Lieutenant Nancy Roberts, the pilot of the Chippie in which Curt was riding.

Roger, Fancy Nancy! Haulers all, this is Hauler Leader! was the reply from Captain Roger Hawley, commander of TACAIRCO. *Keep your Level Four stealth up! We can tuck down real close to these hills because we aren't leaving any downwash trail! AIRBATT Leader, this is Hauler Leader! Did you read that we are being painted?*

Roger, Hauler Leader! AIRBATT Leader and Jolley's Rogers are activating Level Two stealth now! Executing Foxtrot! Cal Worsham's message was the signal for the tacair flight of AD-40C Harpies to lower their observability and activate ECM equipment that would make the smaller attack aerodynes appear to be the big airlift Chippies.

Curt and Cal knew that both Turkish and Iranian air defense radars would likely spot the Washington Greys on their airlift flight to Caldiran in the late afternoon. But it was Lieutenant Hassan Mahmoud who knew the mind of the Middle East and convinced Curt in the OSCAR brief to utilize deception.

Hassan pointed out that the Harpies could mimic the Chippies' radar signatures and, unless air defense cover was necessary on the inbound flight, the Harpies could then proceed to a location over the Ahl-i Haqq irregulars chasing the Soviet Spetsnaz battalion. This would cause both the Turks and the Iranians to believe that the Harpies were Chippies carrying out the normal air reprovisioning flights for Qazi's contingent. The Chippies carrying the Greys could then proceed to Caldiran with less chance of being detected. Even if the Turkish radars—which were the latest Raytheon FPS-717s allocated to all NATO partners and whose performance characteristics were therefore well-known to the Greys—happened to pick up a squiggle from the Chippies, chances are the Harpies would be tagged as the major target. The Turks manning the FPS-717s would tend to concentrate on the Harpie returns and report them as non-threatening logistical flights in support of the Ahl-i Haqqs. The errant signals would be dismissed as bird returns.

Curt was riding in his usual seat to the right of Lieutenant Nancy Roberts. He wasn't in linkage with the aerodyne as she was, so he had a real view of the terrain below and, because they were flying so low, on both sides as well. That didn't bother him; he knew Nancy was one hell of a good pilot and could fly this sort of terrain even at night; she'd done so before. But what did impress him was the rugged nature of the mountains that was thrown into even sharper relief by the low sun angle which cast long shadows and emphasized slopes.

As Roberts lifted the Chippie up and over a ridge line, just clearing its top by scant meters, Curt suddenly saw ahead on the north horizon about 70 kilometers away the distinctive twin peaks of the legendary Mount Ararat, the most unique and conspicuous feature of the region, rearing up 5,165 meters into the blue sky.

This is Hauler Four! Deployment zone in sight!

Roger from Hauler Leader! Haulers all, disperse to deployment coordinates!

The Chippies hauling GUNCO and the Saucy Cans settled down on the ridge to the northeast of the fork in the river, carefully following the close-in charts prepared by computerized topography of high resolution satellite images. Nearly every rock that was larger than a hundred centimeters had been plotted on those charts and fed into navigational and tactical computers. Every tree and bush had been spotted. Suitably large landing zones just beyond the ridge to the east had been picked out, and each Chippie had an assigned landing point within the DZ. Without computers, it would have taken days or even weeks to do that sort of highly detailed planning.

The two ASSAULTCOs and SCOUT platoon were deposited on the ridge to the south of the river fork and the tiny village of Caldiran.

Okay, Major Carson here you are, right on the data point! Nancy Roberts's computer enhanced voice came through Curt's helmet tacomm as she set the Chippie down on the south ridge.

Curt looked around through the cockpit bubble. As they'd descended, he'd noted with satisfaction that the landing point was about a hundred meters south of the ridge crest where he and his ACV's sensor suite could have a clear view of the valley downstream of Caldiran as well as the two valleys above the fork. *Close enough for government work,* he told her, then passed the command to his staff and Gibbons's Goblins, the RECONCO, *Okay, Grey Staff and Goblins, unload and take up your positions on the military crest north of the ridge line. Move it out but don't rush it! Get it right the first time!*

That went without saying. The Sierra Charlies and their warbots debouched from the Chippies fast but not frantically. No one was shooting at them . . . yet. They had hours to get into positions for the ambush. And everyone knew that they had to do it right the first time because there would be no second time — one chance to shine, and many chances to have it all go to slime if it wasn't done right. When it hit the impeller, there'd be no time for second thoughts or second guessing or remembering something you'd forgotten.

Stick around, Nancy, Curt told her, also unnecessarily. The Chippies were staying in the DZ this time, which was an unusual maneuver. Curt wanted them available *fast* in case he had to move units around quickly. *We've got about twelve hours until dawn light, so you can go idiot mode and relax.*

Thanks, Major. A hot and a cot would be right good right

now. But make sure the crew gets the ghilly in place, she replied. *I'm going physical starting now.*

We're D-O-T-B! was the comment from First Sergeant Tracy Dillon, signifying that he was Definitely On The Ball supervising SCOUT in a job. In fact, the personnel of SCOUT were already at work doing something warbots couldn't do because the warbots hadn't been designed to do it; they spread camouflaging ghilly nets over the Chippie. Elsewhere in the Deployment Zones around Caldiran, the Greys were also doing the same low-observable bit with ghillies over the other Chippies. If a Chippie had to spool-up and get the hell out of there in a hurry, the blast from the lift slots would rip the ghilly nets apart and blow them clear. The Chippies weren't invisible, but they were now very hard to pick out from their background.

Grey Sierra Two, how's Pugachev? Curt asked Major Pappy Gratton.

Surprisingly, damned cooperative, Grey Leader! He follows orders, was the reply from the regimental adjutant who was guarding the captured member of the Soviet Spetsnaz battalion.

Good! Sierra Three, make sure someone spells Pappy at twenty-four hundred hours.

If I haven't got someone available, I'll do it myself, Grey Head, Major Hensley Atkinson promised. She'd be plenty busy until then making sure that all operational forces were in the right place and that Operation Iron Fist was proceeding according to plan.

I want to be sure Pugachev's in good shape and ready for a possible trade for the Colonel, Curt reminded them all.

He's not about to try anything, Pappy Gratton advised Curt. *As I pointed out, he's typically Soviet in his subservience to authority.*

Grey Comm, are all the comm nets up and active? Curt was worry-warting this operation to a much greater extent than ever before. This was the first time he'd been forced to split his forces, and he didn't like that idea. At both Longliku and Strijdom where he'd commanded the Regi-

307

ment before, he'd been able to operate with a consolidated regiment. However, the terrain around them in the mountains required that he split the Greys to achieve maximum results from minimum available forces. Communications were therefore critical.

Grey Head, Grey Comm has everything up and fully tactical! In the absence of Georgina Cook, Edie Sampson had taken over that slot in addition to being temporary regimental sergeant major in Henry Kester's shoes. *Major, just keep a cool stool and a hot pot! Any of us will report to you ASAP if anything starts to go to slime, sir!*

Yeah, well, let's just make sure. The last couple of real fur balls turned into real sheep screws and there was no command control at all, Curt reminded her.

Grey Head, Marauder Leader here! If that happens, it happens . . . and there isn't a damned thing any of us can do to stop it! It's set up rationally right now. Even if it starts its own flow, we can go with it. We've done it before! That was unusual! Alexis Morgan was trying to calm Curt's pre-combat jitters, a far cry from the days when he'd done the same thing for her as a new second looie in his old company! That caused Curt to decide to settle down and admit to himself that he was running a bunch of very good and responsible people who could be counted on to do what they were supposed to do when they were supposed to do it. That would give him more time to fret over what Sharaf Qazi would do . . . and how the Soviets would react to the welcome that was being planned for them at dawn.

The Marauders and Ferrets were in their proper positions according to the data on the tac display in Curt's ACV which had debouched from the Chippie and was stationed on the military crest north of the ridge line.

Ellie Aarts had the preliminary birdbots checking the progress of the Soviets as they began to fire up their BRT-218s and MAZ-800s, getting ready to resume their stealthy nighttime move toward the Soviet border to the north. There were, of course, many paths they could take through the mountains, but Curt and his Greys had decided—with some help from Georgie, the 17th Iron Fist Division computer back in Arizona—that the Sovs would most likely follow the best beaten path through this terrain if for no other reason than to keep from becoming lost.

The probe force made up of SCOUT and accompanied by Hassan and Jerry moved quickly down the south ridge and into the town. Their task: clear the Kurdish civilians out of there—preferably without a fight—and move them out of harm's way up the east ridge and behind the Saucy Cans where they could spend the night in one of the Chippies grounded there. Curt didn't anticipate having to airlift the big LAMVAs around by air during the engagement; the LAMVAs were mobile enough by themselves so they could change positions quickly if necessary.

By 2400 hours, the Greys had the area secured and ready to bushwhack the Soviets as they came through shortly before dawn. BIRD reported that the Sovs were moving as anticipated. Joan Ward had the GUNCO Saucy Cans in position and laid in for three potential targets—the downstream road, the upstream road, and the now-empty village of Caldiran.

The Jeeps and Mary Anns of the Marauders and Ferrets were deployed, powered up, and in sentry mode. They would keep unsleeping watch all night while the Sierra Charlies got a few hours' rest.

Back down at the Turkish-Iraqi border, Cal Worsham and the Harpies were standing by, ready to be on station at T-minus-30 minutes, ready to lay ordnance on the Sovs if necessary. Major Ruth Gydesen and her BIOTECO was also standing by there, ready to handle any wounded who had to be airlifted out—and the wounded would be on the first Chippies lifting out of the Caldiran area.

His regimental staff had grabbed sleeping bags and dossed-down outside under the incredibly starry sky. Curt found himself alone in his ACV with the regimental chaplain, Captain Nellie Crile.

Curt had noticed that Crile had seemed to hold back so he could be with Curt alone. So Curt straightened up and told him, "Nelson, go get some sleep while you can. If we have casualties tomorrow, you'll be busy."

"Not solely comforting the wounded and giving last rites, Major. Don't forget Longliku. Sometimes I'm useful for emotional hurt as much as for physical reasons," the chaplain reminded him. "But I thought I'd stick around because maybe you might need me this evening."

"I've never been a very religious man, Nellie," Curt admitted in what was almost an apology. "I know that many of the Greys are. But maybe I've seen too much fighting and its consequences. I get scared, sure, but I've learned how to handle it."

"Have you, now? Don't forget: I came aboard before Namibia, and I've seen you lead the Regiment before," Crile pointed out gently. "Maybe you're no longer frightened about what might happen to you. But I've noticed today that you do seem to have a great deal of concern about what happens to others. This wasn't quite as obvious before."

"Well, Father, maybe I've seen some people hurt badly because of what I did or didn't do that could have prevented it."

"Curt, I'm no military historian or expert on leadership," the chaplain admitted. "But I know of only one individual who's been able to shoulder the responsibility for all people and die for them, and He was someone far more special than you or I, regardless of your beliefs. In short, it takes a far greater individual than either of us to do what you've been trying to do today."

"Nellie, one of the ladies of the Washington Greys was hurt very badly today because of something I should have anticipated."

"That was yesterday, Curt. It's fifteen past midnight," Crile pointed out, checking his watch. "And you had no way of knowing how the Kurdish woman would react or that she'd carry a grudge of that intensity. You can't know everything in advance. You can't plan for every-

310

thing. You don't have total control over people's lives. . . ."

Curt sighed. Even Kitsy, and especially Alexis, often let him know they had their own lives to lead and would do so. "But I may be responsible for their deaths . . ."

Crile shook his head. "You must order men and women into battle. But they aren't like the warbots who will obey orders and follow only the programs put into them beforehand, then go to their destruction without having a personal purpose for doing it. On the other hand, the Washington Greys do it willingly, and each of them does it for their own intensely personal reasons. You lead them only by their willing acquiescence, Curt. You may think you're ordering them into the cannon's mouth and that they'd willingly go, and I suspect they would. But I also suspect they'd ask you, 'Major what kind of armor do you want us to wear while we're doing it?' "

"You're right, Nellie, but maybe it goes deeper than that. When my regimental commander decided to do something totally insane, I should have taken action to relieve him," Curt admitted. "I should have seen it happening. I should have—"

"I don't know what happened to Colonel Bellamack," Crile admitted, interrupting Curt, "but that was also beyond your control. And, as I recall, you did what you could to dissuade him. If you had done more under the circumstances, you might indeed have been insubordinate. Curt, you did the right thing. And you're doing both the right and the honorable thing now. The Washington Greys know this. And they're willingly following you. And they'll look out for themselves, do their assigned jobs, figure out how to get themselves out of their own troubles, and come through winning."

"I've inherited a great group of people to lead."

"No, Curt, you didn't inherit it. You are part of this group and you helped make it what it is. Now you have the enviable job of leading it, and I hope on a permanent basis, although I do not wish any bad luck for our

311

legitimate commander. The Colonel has been our rallying point and the man who is responsible for us. But you are our leader and have been for some time now. Everyone knows it. Even the Colonel knows it."

Curt recalled long conversations with Colonel Wild Bill Bellamack, some of them quite personal. He recalled their mutual agreement, their contract. And he realized he was doing just exactly what he'd promised Bellamack.

"Nellie, I think I'll go catch a few hours of sleep while I can . . . and I think I can do that now. Thank you for being perceptive and giving up your sack time to stay and chat with me," Curt said frankly to the regimental chaplain. "I may not be a religious person, but I know you do a good job serving the spiritual needs of the Greys. I wasn't totally aware that you're also such a useful person when it comes to personal matters other than the spiritual."

Crile got up and smiled. "Oh, just part of my job, Major! And don't be so sure that our chat didn't touch on the spiritual side of your personal life."

Chapter Thirty-nine

"Grey Head, Grey Head, this is RECONCO Leader! Acknowledge! Acknowledge!"

Major Curt Carson came quickly out of a fitful sleep in the cold interior of his ACV. He hadn't slept well in spite of his chat with Captain Nellie Crile. He knew he had the pre-combat jitters. The red display of the master battle clock on the bulkhead told him it was 0423. "Philip!" he shouted to the artificial intelligence unit running his ACV. "Activate my voice reply to tacomm!"

"Good morning, Major! Philip here! You've got it!"

"RECONCO Leader, this is Grey Head! Go!"

"Alpha point unit is now ten kilometers downstream of Site Charlie and crossing the river!"

The Soviets were a little ahead of schedule. They must have begun to move faster during the night. Curt asked his recon company chief, "John, are they maintaining the same sort of deployment and road formation that you observed yesterday?"

"Affirmative! Two BTRs in the lead. The second one appears to be the command vehicle in accordance with Soviet doctrine!"

Good! Curt told himself. In spite of the fact that a Soviet Spetsnaz unit was classed as a *desant* outfit capable of working in very clandestine fashion deep in unfriendly territory, they still tended to follow regular Soviet procedures when they were out of covert mode. Hassan, who'd been so knowledgeable about the peoples of the Mideast, also showed himself to have a real understanding of the Soviet mind. The new officer had told Curt last night,

"Major, the Russians may be European and Byzantine in their culture, but they've got a lot of Oriental blood mixed in because they've been on a major invasion route from the East. I may not understand their language, but I think I can understand how they think. When they're in a retrograde maneuver as they are, they'll revert to what's known to be tried and true. That's simple: a commander always leads his forces while a first class sonofabitching sergeant brings up the rear as a file closer who has no compunctions about shooting down a straggler. That's the way the Red Army has always worked, and they got it from the Mongols, among others."

"Grey Major! Grey Sierra Leader! Grey Sierra Three! This is Grey Head! All Greys to Zulu Alert status now! Activate Plan Iron Fist Alpha!" Curt yelled at the ta-comm pickup. "Edie, get with Worsham! Get his Harpies up and coming!" He was out of his hard bunk at once, having sacked out four hours before still dressed in battle gear with the exception of his helmet, harness, and weaponry. Clamping his helmet on his head, he ran its check list as his body heat provided the energy to run its systems. With his Novia slung over his shoulder, he cracked the top hatch on the turret and looked around.

It was cold outside. He noted that it should be cold. They were more than 2,000 meters above sea level here. The sky was absolutely clear, which had accelerated the heat radiation of the previous day. He had never seen so many stars in his life. But he had other things on his mind than astronomy right then. *Marauder Leader, you ready?*

A brief response came from Alexis Morgan, *Roger from Marauder Leader!*

Ferret Leader, ready?

Ferrets good to go!

Warriors?

Warriors on target! Flare rockets ready! Airburst rounds loaded and ready!

Scout?

Scout ready!

314

Grey Sierra One, is the exchange person ready?

Affirmative from Grey Sierra One! was the response from Pappy Gratton.

Okay, Ferret Leader, you're the one who punches the start button on this one! Keep me advised! Curt told Russ Frazier who, from his position in the village of Caldiran, would be responsible for stopping that first BTR-218 and putting the command BTR under the gun.

Grey Head, this is Grey Major! Jolley's Rogers are airborne and inbound! E-T-A zero-four-four-eight! Edie Sampson reported.

RECONCO Leader what's your best estimate of how long it will take the lead Sov vehicle to reach Site Charlie? Curt wanted to know, checking the timing.

RECONCO Leader estimates two-one minutes at present speed, John Gibbon reported tersely.

That was going to make it close! Curt needed the Harpies to make a low pass right at the start. The Soviets didn't have air support, and Curt needed to impress upon the Soviet commander that the Greys did. All in all, it was a tricky operation. It called for suddenly blocking the road with an ACV and four Mary Anns, all primed and ready to open fire on the soft-skinned BTRs with AT rounds from the 25-millimeters on the Mary Anns and the 15-millimeters on the ACV. Additional Mary Anns, Jeeps and ACVs were tactically deployed around Caldiran. The warbot weaponry wasn't as heavy as the single 73-millimeter on each of the BTRs, but Frazier had more muzzles deployed. However, the objective wasn't to shoot and destroy; it was to halt the Sovs and arrange a transfer of Bellamack for Pugachev.

"Edie, stay in the ACV and handle the comm! Maintain that channel with Jolley's Rogers in case my link fails!" Curt told her.

"And miss this fight? Aw, Major . . . !" Edie began to complain, disappointment on her face. She liked to be where her Major was in a fight. That had been her place since Zahedan.

"Rank hath its privileges, including not being shot at!

315

FIDO, Sergeant!"

Edie sighed. "Yessir! On the bounce, sir! I thought I was a combat soldier not a communications tech-weenie."

It was time for Curt to begin moving with SCOUT, Gratton, and Pugachev down the steep hillside toward the little creek at the valley's bottom and the cover of the sparse, stunted trees and bushes there. "Philip, stand by because you may have to come down to Caldiran to get us," Curt told his ACV before he bailed out of the top hatch and went to ground. "And you will stand by to provide fire support from your fifteen-millimeter on my command! You will also listen to and follow commands, instructions, and requests from Sergeant Edie Sampson. Understand?"

"I understand and will comply, Major," the ACV's aritifical intelligence computer told him. "And I will monitor your tacomm channel for additional orders."

It wasn't an easy trip down the steep slopes, even for Curt and his support elements, the Sierra Charlies and Jeeps of SCOUT Platoon under Adonica Sweet. Pappy Gratton, not being a combat soldier, had a bit more trouble. And some of the Jeeps took longer to descend than their human masters because warbots, no matter how cleverly designed or how powerful their AI circuitry, could never really compete with human beings when it came to traversing rough terrain.

Curt and his unit reached the creek and its vegetation in time to see the first BTR rumble into Caldiran.

Lights from warbots and vehicles flashed on, bathing the town and the approaching road in a glare of light. An ACV and four Mary Anns were in the rough primitive road ahead of the Soviet armored personnel carrier.

Frazier's tacomm was patched into the 17th Iron Fist Division's megacomputer, Georgie, via Curt's ACV, and then back to loudspeaker hailers on several ACVs surrounding the Soviets on the road, thanks to the knowhow of Edie Sampson. Curt heard Frazier's announcement in English about two seconds before it boomed forth in Russian from the loudspeakers: "Soviet

316

soldiers! Halt at once! We are American warbot troops! You are surrounded by warbots and enveloped by air support! We do not wish to fight you! We wish to speak with your commander and to exchange one of your soldiers for the American colonel presently with you!"

In response, the lead Soviet BTR-218 swiveled its 73-millimeter gun not toward the warbots and ACV blocking the road, but toward the buildings and shacks where the Ferrets and Marauders were stationed.

Grey Head, the Sovs are sweeping us with i-r targeting! was the sudden call from Russ Frazier.

Captain, set fire to the building! That will blend our i-r signatures into a hotter background! This comment was from Hassan. Curt could recognize his voice.

As if on signal, three of the battered, ancient shacks of Caldiran began to erupt in flame as the Ferrets fired their surroundings.

Grey Major, give me the loudspeaker voice! Curt told Edie.

You've got it, Major!

"Soviet commander! This is Major Curt Carson, United States Army! We are strong enough to win if we have to fight! But we don't want to fight you to find out who is the stronger. We are here only to rescue Colonel William Bellamack, our commanding officer! If you will agree to open your turret and allow Colonel Bellamack to come out, you can come with him for discussions under a flag of truce. I will come forward with Kondrati Stephanovich Pugachev. I give you my word that we will not shoot at you! Please signal me by flashing the convoy lights on your vehicle!" Curt's voice boomed out over the burning town, his words translated into Russian by Georgie.

Grey Head, this is Warhawk Leader! We have you on sensors! Don't ask me where the fire is! I see it now! Got some trouble? Want some ordnance on it? Cal Worsham's computerized voice boomed in Curt's NE tacomm.

Negatory! Negatory! The Ferrets and the Marauders are in there! Just give me the prearranged flat hat! Roll it in, head to tail! Curt ordered. He needed that show of strength at this precise instant. And he needed to add to it to convince the Soviet commander that the Greys had caught him flatfooted.

Black holes appeared in the starry sky to the east as the lightless Harpies, operating in stealth, topped the Saucy Cans' ridge, and ducked down into the gorge. The thunder of their passage overhead at ten meters shook the ground.

GUNCO, this is Grey Head! One Saucy Cans salvo, parachute flares, break fifty meters over Caldiran! Commence firing!

The sky lit up on signal.

Curt knew from past experience with a Soviet Spetsnaz battalion on Kerguelen Island that they respected a show of force and would talk when they were convinced they were up against something more than a pushover.

Curt stood up, slung his Novia, and pulled from his harness pack something that had become a piece of standard battle gear for him: a white flag that signified not surrender, but a willingness to talk and negotiate before assaulting and killing.

He hoped to God that the Soviet commander didn't fire that 73-millimeter at him. He'd become meat if that happened. His body armor wouldn't stop that sort of incoming. . . .

The convoy lights on the second BTR flashed, and the top turret hatch slowly opened.

But Bellamack didn't emerge from the top turret hatch. A Soviet colonel did. A smaller hatch on the side of the BTR opened and Bellamack came out. He was obviously hurt. He hobbled on a crude crutch, his right leg swathed in bloody bandages. He was helped by two Soviet NCOs in cammies, carrying a new and heretofore unknown short assault rifle, and wearing the soft brimmed campaign hats of Soviet troops in the southern regions.

A very frightened Pugachev was suddenly with Curt under the escort not only of Major Pappy Gratton but also Lieutenant Adonica Sweet and Sergeant Dyani Motega. Gratton had his Novia slung; the two women car-

318

ried theirs at the ready.

The two groups approached one another in the yellow light of the parachute flares and the flickering flames from the burning shacks and hovels of Caldiran.

The Soviet officer wore cammies and a red beret. His collar tabs held the low-visibility combat version of a full colonel's insignia—two red stripes with three gold stars.

Bellamack looked hurt, tired, confused.

Curt saluted. It was as much a salute to his own regimental commander as to the higher-ranking Soviet officer. "Colonel, I am Major Curt Carson, United States Army," he introduced himself in English, hoping that Bellamack would be able to translate if the Soviet colonel didn't speak English.

But the man did, and replied by returning the salute and saying, "I am Colonel Pavel Ivanovich Savkin, Red Army of the Union of Soviet Socialist Republics. I speak English. I was surprised that your Colonel Bellamack speaks Russian; that is unusual for an American."

"Colonel Bellamack, how are you?" Curt asked his regimental commander.

Bellamack was breathing heavily. With his right hand, he returned Curt's salute. "I'm alive, Major, but Colonel Savkin doesn't have the bio-tech facilities to treat my leg, and it's not a good wound. . . ."

"I was hurrying to get your Colonel to our medical facilities," Savkin put in.

Of course, Curt didn't believe that statement for a moment, but it allowed the Soviet colonel to have an excuse, transparent as it might be. Bluff was a way of life for the Russians. "We've given your Sergeant Pugachev medical treatment," Curt explained, "and we're ready to take Colonel Bellamack from you and return him to our own medical facilities. If we can agree on a friendly exchange of personnel here, I'll return my units to Iraq at once and you may continue back to the Soviet Union."

"Not until you get the Kurd terrorists off my rear, Major," Savkin insisted.

319

"They're part of my forces, Colonel Savkin. I will recall them, too," Curt promised.

It was obvious to Curt that Savkin didn't like the idea of having to give up a valuable captive such as Bellamack, a man who undoubtedly had a great deal of knowledge about the American military establishment and could be made to spill his guts quite easily under the persistent techniques developed by the KGB for whom he worked.

On the other hand, Savkin knew very well that he was probably facing a very strong combined force of American warbot troops and the pursuing Ahl-i Haqq Kurds who'd been hounding him from the rear since he'd left Iraq.

Savkin was tired. He'd gotten no logistical support as promised during his foray into Iraq to help stir up the Kurds and probe the American Army there. His battalion was running out of supplies. Food was difficult if not impossible to obtain in this part of Turkey. And none of his superiors would even know for sure that his captured American colonel hadn't died of wounds on the trek to Soviet Armenia; it would be easy to alter the records to show Colonel Bellamack's death . . . and Savkin already had enough of Bellamack's personal effects in the way of uniforms and insignia to claim he'd stripped the body before burying it. He could get away with it, and he could keep Pugachev from talking, too.

Faced with the alternative of fighting a very expensive battle with short-supplied, tired, campaign-weary troops or getting off as easy as this stupid American Major was proposing, Savkin didn't have much trouble making a decision. He spread his hands and shrugged. "It is a fair exchange, Major. And it is better to negotiate and go in peace than to be forced to fight a defensive battle with you. The Soviet people are committed to world peace, and this can be one example of the extent to which we are willing to negotiate to be sure that peace is maintained."

Savkin might have believed it—or not; Curt didn't

care, but personally he didn't buy that for a moment. "Peace" in terms of Marxist-Leninist doctrine still meant that condition which prevails when the enemies of socialism are finally defeated. It hadn't changed in over a century, just as Russian foreign policy hadn't changed, either.

Curt put out his hand. "Then we agree."

As Colonel Pavel Ivanovich Savkin put out his hand, the sound of heavy rifle fire suddenly broke out all around them.

Chapter Forty

Grey Head, this is Marauder Leader! We're under attack from minus-x up the hill on the north ridge! Major Alexis Morgan's voice was urgent over the tacomm in Curt's helmet.

Her transmission was almost stepped-on by a call from Sharaf Qazi on voice-only tacomm that also sounded in Curt's helmet, "Major Carson, this is Qazi! We have encountered Turkish patrols on our left coming down the hill to attack us! We are attacking them!"

Grey Head, this is RECONCO Leader! came Major John Gibbon's voice in Curt's tacomm, again almost on top of Qazi's report. *We have just detected a large and well-dispersed force of ground troops, identity unknown, on the ridge line to the north of the valley and strung out for several kilometers. They appear to be assaulting the Ahl-i Haqqs as well as those of you at Caldiran!*

Grey Head, this is Warhawk Leader! We have Gibbons's targets on i-r, radar, and lidar! I'm in a position to bust a few heads coming down the ridge north of you! was Major Cal Worsham's input from his position aloft in a Harpie.

Colonel Pavel Ivanovich Savkin was apparently also getting radio inputs from his Spetsnaz unit. In between the excited traffic on the tacomm channels that was sounding in Curt's helmet, he could hear Savkin's walkie-talkie brick chattering in Russian.

"Colonel Savkin," Curt said quickly to his Soviet counterpart, "it looks like we're both under attack. I suggest we get our exchange people back to safety and that we coordinate our response to this attack!"

But Savkin was suddenly obstinate, his new Soviet assault rifle now unslung and held at the ready. "You have tricked us! You have planned to attack us after getting your Colonel back! I made a mistake to trust you!"

Small arms fire was now snapping past them in the open. In spite of his condition, it was Colonel William Bellamck who snapped something at Savkin in Russian. Edie Sampson obviously had the circuit to Georgie still open for translation purposes, and Georgie's translation sounded in Curt's helmet tacomm in English, *Goddammit, Savkin, those are bullets going past us, not turds! You're not stupid enough to open fire on your own forces, and neither are we! I'm hurt, and Carson is my second-in-command! Listen to him! Or we're so much dead meat!*

Without waiting for Savkin to do anything, Curt gave the order both by NE tacomm and verbally so that Savkin could hear it, "Marauder Leader and Ferret Leader, reverse your front! Turnabout! Bring all fire to bear on the assaulting troops! Warrior Leader, shift your targeting point to targets designated on the tac display! Gibbon, goddammit, get us some Saucy Cans targets posted on the displays!"

Carson, the Warhawks are on most of those targets! Cal Worsham cut in. *In addition to our usual orgasmic service as sand blasters and rock busters, we'll do a little forward observing and artillery spotting for Joan! Here you come, Joanie! Latest hot spots to put some hot AP rounds! I'll move a little bit west and see if I can't help the Ahl-i Haqqs unless you think you need me here, Curt.*

"Qazi, this is Carson. I've got some air support coming for you! Don't shoot at anything that's flying!" Curt warned his Kurdish ally.

"We do not need your air support, Carson, but it might help!" Qazi fired back. "These are only Turkish troops! We can handle them! We have been fighting them for centuries! We can beat them!"

"Turkish?" Curt wondered aloud.

"They are Turkish!" Qazi replied quickly. And what he then told Curt convinced the American officer that this sort of war was the sort he'd seen before, and didn't

323

exactly enjoy being part of because it wasn't war but the squalid butchery that grows from hatred. "I have just killed two of the detested Turks! Before I killed one of them, he told me what I wanted to know. Sometimes Turks do not want to talk, but we have learned ways to convince them to tell us. And at the last he did not need to keep it secret any longer because he knew I was going to kill him anyway. . . ."

Pappy, get the Colonel out of here! Take whatever help you need to provide fire cover, but get back to Philip! Curt told the regimental adjutant.

Curt, I don't think I can get the Colonel that far! Gratton reported. *He's in bad shape. I'm no bio-tech, but that leg of his looks God-awful to me!*

Medic! Medic! Curt called out. *Adonica, did Al Williams come down the hill with us, or is he standing by to handle Ellie's birdbotters?*

Major Carson, this is Williams! I'm coming! And I'm bringing a PTV with me to haul the Colonel back up the hill to Fancy Nancy for evack if necessary.

Savkin had seen the American soldiers and warbots quickly swing their focus of action from his battalion to the forces attacking them from the north down the hill. He didn't need to be told at that point he was wrong about the intentions of the Americans. He'd also heard Qazi's message to Curt. And he saw and heard the Saucy Cans fire erupting on the ridge above them to the north. A quick command from him on his own tactical radio brick caused men to erupt from the BTR-218s and MAZ-800s while those vehicles themselves turned sharply left and proceeded to move off the primitive road in an attempt to negotiate the steep slopes of the ridge, their 73-millimeter cannons now firing into the oncoming Turks.

"My apologies, Major!" Savkin yelled over the bedlam of the battle. "We will fight with you. We will attack! That is the best defense!"

The Soviets were either riding the vehicles or were plunging up the hillside in the growing light of dawn that was interrupted only by the bright flashes of the Saucy Cans fire and an occasional parachute flare shell that Joan Ward lobbed over the battle center.

Bio-tech Sergeant Al Williams showed up, loaded the Colonel on a PTV—not without some objection from Bellamack who insisted that he was feeling well enough to stay with the fight. Williams was insistent, however; Bellamack was not in any shape to command troops at this moment, nor did he know the ops plan. The standing orders were that everyone obeyed the orders of a bio-tech or a member of BIOTECO if an injury was present. Bellamack was injured but was refusing to admit it, although his voice and eyes said otherwise. The Colonel was obviously in pain.

On Curt's part, he felt he might have used Bellamack's help because it was quickly becoming apparent to Curt that he'd lost control of this fight, too. It was now fluid and flowing and taking on its own course of action. As he glanced at his helmet's tac display, he saw that his people were doing their jobs. He didn't have positive makes on the disposition of all the Soviet forces or the Ahl-i Haqqs, but it appeared that the Soviets and the Kurds were meeting the Turks head-on with the cooperative heavy firepower of the Greys' Jeeps, Mary Anns, and Saucy Cans. He made small tactical suggestions here and there, but there really wasn't much time because, like most combat, it was incredibly intense and wouldn't last very much longer.

In the middle of all this, Edie Sampson called, *Grey Head, this is Grey Major! You've got a Priority One from Iron Fist Head!*

Dammit, put it on hold! I've got a fight on my hands right now!

Yes, sir, I know that. But it's the General. What shall I tell her?

Tell her that I'm up to my asshole in alligators and I'll get back to her once I've drained this swamp, unless she wants to micromanage the Washington Greys. . . .

Uh, I won't tell her exactly that, sir. But I'll tell her! Follow-

325

ing a brief pause while Curt saw to it that Williams had moved Bellamack to a relatively safe place down by the river in a ravine out of the way of incoming, and was administering to the Colonel, Edie replied, *Major, I hate to use the language the General just used, but she told me to tell you in these exact words: Get your fucking ass out of the goddamned FEBA and haul your butt back to where you won't get your balls shot off, or she'll court martial your buns for abandoning your post after she pins the Distinguished Service Cross on your hairy chest. In short, she asks what the hell do you think you are, a goddamned hero or something? Sorry sir, but she told me to use those exact words. She also says she's authorized to talk to you like that because you are in charge of the Washington Greys until Colonel Bellamack recovers from that leg wound and has had a complete evaluation.*

She's right, Edie. So I'm going to rejoin the ACV. Curt considered the order he'd give, then called, *Philip, this is Grey Head! I am identing my beacon! Proceed down the ridge to my location as shown by my beacon.*

Uh, Major, isn't it possible that the ACV could be overrun if you move your cee-pee down to Caldiran? Edie wanted to know.

Sergeant Major, that is entirely possible. General Hettrick herself used to locate her cee-pee right up at the FEBA when she was our regimental commander. So I learned from her. I have to locate my cee-pee where I believe it has to be so I can control the action! Curt didn't tell her that he'd probably lost control of this fight, too. But he was damned if he was going to run back up the hill while his comrades were fighting down here.

Yes, sir! I should have known better than to assume that you'd take slack from a fight. I'm on my way down with Philip! Edie had an upbeat tone in her voice that told Curt she was grinning. She understood him very well.

Curt double-checked his CP position in the creek bed. He had about thirty meters between the creek and the burning village of Caldiran. Cover along the edge of the gully was good, and the terrain between the gulch and the village was reasonably open grassy turf. When he checked his helmet visor tac display for SCOUT which should be with him, he found the beacon plots almost merged. Adonica Sweet was doing what she was supposed to be doing with her scouting platoon, Sweet's Scouts: guarding the regimental CP.

SCOUT Leader, this is Grey Head, Curt called to her. *Philip and Sampson will be joining us shortly. The only direction from which we might get an assault is from the north if the Turks happen to break through the Marauders.*

Unlikely, sir, but correct. Do you want me to extend SCOUT as a line of skirmishers along the creek here? Adonica wanted to know, her tone of voice telling him that she'd come to that conclusion herself and was merely asking for a confirming order to execute.

Make it so, Lieutenant!

Roger, sir! Motega on the right flank upstream. Saunders on the left flank downstream. Twenty meters between. I'd suggest siting our Jeeps at the center, sir.

I requested that you make it so, Lieutenant. You do not need my further permission, Curt reminded her.

A few minutes later, a call came to Curt, *Philip and Grey Major are fifty meters in your minus-x, Grey Head, coming up on you.*

The sound of the battle, which resembled a sporadic fireworks display of the sort they'd been treated to on Borneo, continued around them—the popping of the small arms and 7.62-millimeter automatics, the sharp reports of the 25-millimeter guns on the Mary Anns, and the concussions of the Saucy Cans rounds barraging the Turk positions up on the north ridge.

Another sound came from a new direction: automatic rifle and submachine gun fire from Curt's right.

Grey Head, this is Motega! We've got a Turkish infiltration unit on our right coming down the creek!

Damn! They outflanked us by sending a unit down the valley from the right flank! Curt exploded. The air was suddenly full of snapping rifle and 9-millimeter submachine gun rounds.

Cole! Watson! Pull it back toward the cee-pee! GUNCO, I

327

need some heavy fire support here! Lay your guns on my beacon!

Dyani, this is Adonica! Get the hell out of there before the Saucy Cans start coming or you're dead meat!

Lieutenant, Major Ward doesn't know where to shoot unless she has my beacon!

Something hit Curt's helmet—hard. A Sierra Charlie's helmet is designed to protect the head against any high-tech round of nine-millimeters or less. Curt didn't know what clanged him, but he figured it might have been an old 7.62 NATO round, far more high-powered than modern Novia rounds. The impact shook him, but it did more than that to his helmet electronics; the round must have hit in a critical place. His visor tac displays were gone, and so was his helmet tacomm.

Joan Ward responded with her Saucy Cans, diverting perhaps two LAMVAs on lab AP airbursts on Curt's right flank along the creek. He heard the bursts. They must have been right over Dyani.

Curt grabbed for the hand-held tacomm brick on his harness, his standby. "Motega! Dyani! Report! Are you all right?"

There was no response.

Chapter Forty-one

Adonica Sweet dashed past him from the left, running up the creek bed. The creek was a swiftly flowing mountain stream that spilled over and around through the rocks and boulders that had been deposited there eons ago and worn by the rushing waters. Adonica paid no attention to the water but ran right up the stream. Ten meters beyond Curt, she stepped into a deep pool and almost went under, but came up the other side and kept forging on.

"Philip is here and reporting in!" Curt's ACV announced through the little loudspeaker on his tacomm brick, since the neuroelectronic tacomm unit in his helmet was now inop. "I have identified incoming small arms fire from your right flank, Major. Do you want me to shoot my fifteen millimeter gun at its source?"

"Philip, this is Grey Head! Affirmative! Open fire! But don't shoot at any of our beacons!" Curt told his ACV verbally via tacomm. "Sergeant Motega! Report!"

"Sweet here, Major! I'm looking for her! That Saucy Cans barrage took care of the Turks sneaking downstream toward us! It was also right on top of her beacon signal!"

"Oh, shit!" Curt growled. That was one hell of an act of bravery to call down artillery on yourself in order to stop a flanking assault on your outfit, but he knew it was something that Dyani Motega was capable of doing. If she'd survived—and Curt found himself earnestly hoping that she had—he would write up one of the most glowing recommendations for doing that. If she hadn't, he'd write it up anyway, but he didn't want to think about that possibility right then.

Curt discovered at that moment that his respect and con-

329

cern and — yes, he now had to admit it — even his love for her had slowly and inexorably grown from the very moment he'd first interviewed the young Crow Indian girl more than two years ago. There was no nonsense about Dyani; she wasn't coy or playful or devious, only direct and straightforward and honest, although Curt now knew that she had been holding many things inside her because of her background and training. Dyani Motega was indeed someone special in a way that was different from Alexis or Kitsy — damn Shariat Kahni's vengeful act! — or any of the other women in his life.

Curt couldn't just stand there and passively direct a battle that was all but over. There comes a time when a leader can only stand back and let his people carry through to victory if he's chosen and trained them well; if he hasn't, there's also nothing he can do. So he said to hell with protocol and command responsibilities. He took off up the stream bed, following Adonica and managing to keep from falling in the deep pools she stumbled into.

"Major Carson, Sharaf Qazi is reporting!" his tacomm brick squawked. "My Ahl-i Haqqs have routed the Turks! We've broken them and have them on the run!"

"Let them run, Qazi!" Curt instructed him.

"Yes, of course!" Qazi's excited voice came back. "I have learned some new things about fighting from you, Major Curt Carson! I understand a lot more things about war now! I will let them report back that they were defeated by thousands of excellent Kurd soldiers under the command of a very strong and smart chieftain who had led them to victory!"

"Now you're getting the idea, Qazi! Victory by intimidation!" Curt told the Kurd chieftain. "It will make your next battle easier!"

"I intend my next battles to be big ones with many more Kurds!" Qazi maintained, then added, "You are right, Major Carson! My people need a strong leader who knows how to fight in modern ways to get our own homeland! Thank you, because you have shown me that I can be that man!"

"You've got a long way to go, Sharaf!"

"Yes, but no matter how long the journey may be, we now know that we have begun!"

Curt's tacomm brick picked up the tactical channel as he forged his way upstream through the bounders and brush.

330

"Joan, this is Alexis! We're on the north ridge! We've broken the Turks! Knock off the Saucy Cans!"

"Roger, Alexis! Our Saucy Cans are getting a bit hot now. Did we do you any good?"

"Damned right you did!" was Russ Frazier's voice. "Those fucking Turks are scattering! We broke them! We greased their skids!"

"Grey Head, Warhawk Leader, and Jolley's Rogers Leader have TACAIRCO over the Turk retreat! I don't intend to bring any unexpended ordnance back to Mosul with us! The weight will cut our range too much, if you understand the technology of these aerodynes."

"Cal, you've been running your own damned show here and doing an outstanding job of it!" Curt exclaimed to him between breaths. The high altitude and the exertion of running up a creek bed full of running water and lined with rocks and boulders would have clobbered anyone except a Washington Grey Sierra Charlie in top physical condition, which all of them were. "You've got the high view. Keep those Turk bastards running! But don't let them pot you with a Wasp or an Em-one-hundred if they have them."

"Oh, we made them use those up a long time ago," Worsham replied. "But we have lots of ammo and rockets left."

"Use up your rockets if you want, Cal, but don't forget that you may have to fly air cover for the Chippies shortly when we pull out of here," Curt reminded him.

"Oh, we see Turkish and Iranian interceptors up, but they're keeping a respectful distance. They probably don't know what the hell is going on. We'll keep it that way for them."

Curt got to a spot where he had to climb out of the stream bed. Looking to the northwest, he could see up the valley to where the first light of dawn was striking the twin peaks of Mount Ararat. Pretty, but he was worried sick about Dyani Motega.

He shouldn't have been. Two forms in soaking wet cammies crawled up between some boulders. They were guarded and assisted by Saunders and Cole. Both of the wet forms still carried Novias but only one wore a helmet.

One of them was Lieutenant Adonica Sweet.

The other was equally wet, and Curt experienced a wave of

great relief. It was Dyani Motega, and her cammies were not only soaking wet but ripped and torn in places.

"Lieutenant, I'm fine, thank you," Dyani was saying to Adonica. "I'm just cold from that water!" She was shivering. She tried to straighten up and salute as she saw Curt approach. "Major Carson! I'm all right! Couple of scratches, that's all!"

"Scratches? Dyani, I thought you were dead when I saw you in the water under that rock with all that blood in the water around you!" Adonica told her.

"Lieutenant, a lot of that blood was Turkish blood from those flankers who got caught in the open under the Saucy Cans barrage," Dyani pointed out. "But I knew it was coming! And do you know of any better protection against overhead airburst AP rounds than to duck under a rock *and* under water, too?"

"But you got hit anyway," Adonica pointed out.

"Uh, yes, a couple of bits of shrapnel nicked me, but I'm wearing my body armor just like the Major wants us to! So I didn't get penetrated, only nicked in a couple of places where the shards did manage to breach the armor. It's not bad. The damned cold water has kept them from bleeding." Dyani was being typically stoic.

Curt toggled the tacomm brick. "Medic! Medic! We're about a hundred meters upstream of the cee-pee site. We have superficial wounds and two cold and wet Sierra Charlies!" He put the tacomm back on his webbing and grabbed for his field survival pack. Without looking because he knew by feel where everything was, he pulled out the tightly packed survival blanket, ripped the package seam, and shook it out. Harlan Saunders did the same.

As Curt wrapped it around Dyani, he found that his concern included a little bit of anger at her for pulling that risky stunt. He forced himself to use her formal military address. "Dammit, Sergeant Motega, you could have been killed!"

Dyani stared at him with that strange look in her eyes again and managed a wan smile for the first time. "Yes, Major, but I knew what to do. I wasn't killed. And I wasn't about to get killed. I have too many things left that I want to do!"

"Grey Head, this is Fancy Nancy!" came the call from

Curt's highly regarded Chippie pilot. "I've got you on my display, and I'm coming down for pickup! It's time to get Dyani and the Colonel and the rest of the wounded back to Mosul. I'd like to run a full load, so I'll take as many of you and as many vehicles as I can. I'm light, and I brought my shoehorn in case we need to cram a few things in tight!"

"Wounded," Curt muttered to himself. There should be no wounded, but Curt knew it was inevitable in such a fight. "Grey Sierra One, this is Grey Head! Pappy, have you been tracking wounded?"

"Affirmative, Grey Head! That's my job! I don't know about Motega's injuries, but the only other injured Greys are suffering the usual contusions and bruises from taking bullet impacts and shrapnel."

Alexis Morgan reported in, "Grey Head, this is Marauder Leader!"

"Grey Head here! You okay, Alexis?"

"Why shouldn't I be? I had a good Sierra Charlie combat instructor, remember? So where the hell are the Sovs?"

"What do you mean, where the hell are they? They should be up on that ridge with you and Russ!" Curt told her.

"Well, they're not!"

"John, do you have a make on the Soviet Spetsnaz unit?" Curt asked his recon company chief.

"Looking, Curt!" After a short pause, Gibbon replied, "Ellie has a make on them now! Looks like they moved north along the ridge and came back down into the valley behind and to the north of that Turk patrol that got upstream of you, best I can tell. They're all moving up the road to the northeast, going like hell for the Soviet border at the moment!"

"Bastards!" Curt growled. If Savkin had really been cooperative, he would have come in behind the Turk patrol and eliminated the need for Dyani to call down the Saucy Cans on herself. He realized that Savkin had been behaving normally; he'd only wanted to get his own ass out of a sling and beat it back home since he'd been caught flatfooted in both Iraqi and Turkish territory.

Curt sighed and slung his Novia. "Okay, let's break this thing off! Is anyone in Caldiran? Is anything left of it?" In the early morning light, Curt looked down the valley in the direction of the little village. All he saw was a cloud of smoke.

Well, he told himself, at least he'd gotten the noncombatants out of the way before the fighting had started; he'd saved their lives, but he hadn't been able to save their homes. He regretted allowing Hassan to set the fire to keep the Soviets from picking off the i-r targets that were Morgan's Marauders and Frazier's Ferrets.

"Damned little left!" came the report from Joan Ward up on the east ridge with the Saucy Cans. "I've got it under surveillance at this time, and those old buildings burned like hell except those made of mud and bricks. Not much left, Curt!"

"Damn! What the hell are we going to do with the people of Caldiran?" Curt wondered.

"Uh, Curt, Haji Somayeh has been up here with me keeping them company and talking with them since he speaks their language." Joan replied. "He says they're Kurds. Caldiran wasn't their home village; the Turks forced them to stay here. Typical of the way the Kurds are treated, he claims. Anyway, these people want to come back to Iraq with us so they can be with the other Kurds down there. The Iraqis treat them somewhat better."

"Dammit, we can't do that!"

"So what are we going to do, Curt? Leave them here so the Turks can tear them up because they cooperated with us? Or maybe shoot them if they follow us?"

"They can't follow us. We're leaving by air," Curt pointed out. Then a potential solution came to him. "They're Kurds, so they're Qazi's people. They can go with him."

"Grey Head, this is Hassan. I've been listening to this," Lieutenant Hassan Ben Mahmud broke in on the tacomm. "Major, these people don't even like one another very much. I'm not sure Qazi will have them or even if they'll go with him!"

"I'll talk with Qazi," Curt promised. "You talk with Haji Somayeh and the Caldiran people. If they don't start working together, they'll spend another fifty centuries trying to get their own homeland . . . and they'll continue to fail. Look, it's not our job to save them or give them what they want. They've got to do it themselves. Every time we've tried to go in and fight for someone else's freedom, we've gotten our fingers burned. I think we'll help the Kurds if they show that they'll help themselves, but that isn't my decision to make! Jerry!

Captain Allen! Grab a Chippie and go get Qazi! I want to talk to him and the other Kurds up on the Saucy Cans ridge. As for the rest of the Regiment, get the Chippies in position and start loading up! We're going home!"

As if in response to that command, the huge shape of a Chippewa was suddenly overhead with Lieutenant Nancy Roberts carefully guiding it to a landing in a very restricted space between the creek and the primitive road. As it touched down, the huge cargo doors gaped open, an invitation to load up, fly out, and go home.

Chapter Forty-two

Major Curt Carson disliked visiting wounded comrades in the hospital. He didn't like seeing them hurt. Instead, he liked to carry with him the images of what they'd been before they were wounded. But he knew that visiting wounded comrades was a duty, and duty always had priority over personal feelings. Especially now.

And also because it would be a little easier on him to visit Lieutenant Kitsy Clinton because Major General Belinda Hettrick had flown in, was waiting at Mosul when the Regiment returned, and stated unequivocally that she would accompany him the next day. Hettrick understood. It was easier when friends and comrades went along.

Which is why Hettrick had apparently but covertly arranged for the two of them to be accompanied by Alexis Morgan, Jerry Allen, Edie Sampson, and the now-mobile Henry Kester—all former members of Curt's company, Carson's Companions, as Kitsy had been.

Henry Kester and Georgina Cook were both ambulatory, although Henry still limped a little bit and showed the bruises he'd taken when the Soviets had left him and Georgina for dead.

On the other hand, Kitsy was bedridden. She lay covered in a bed in a pleasant room in the Army Hospital in Mosul. Her appearance shocked Curt more than he thought it would. Although Kitsy was covered with a sheet, it was obvious that she was wired up with electrodes and tubes. Her head was firmly and rigidly held in a metal frame that was pinned both to her shoulder blades and into her skull with screws. It immobilized her head and held her neck in tension as well.

Her face was pale and drawn, and she was breathing only because of neuroelectronic stimuli from a bedside computer complex that also kept her heart beating. Doctor Ruth Gydesen had told them all prior to entering Kitsy's room that Kitsy's neck had indeed been broken and that she was totally paralyzed from the neck down. She was being kept alive only with the help of neuroelectronic stimuli at this point. Ruth admitted that she didn't know as yet whether or not Kitsy's spinal cord had been totally severed or just badly damaged; the hospital at the Mosul casern wasn't fully equipped like Walter Reed.

Only fifty years before, the sort of injury suffered by Kitsy would have killed her within hours because her brain had effectively been disconnected from the rest of her body.

Kitsy knew it, too.

But she did smile as she moved her eyes back and forth to see everyone in the room gathered around her bed.

And Curt noticed that the pixie expression on her face was still there. Furthermore her eyes were bright.

But, because her breathing was under regular control of the computer, she spoke only when she exhaled. This tended to break up her sentences. But she could speak. And she did.

"Well, to what do I owe this visit . . . from the stellar assembly?" Kitsy said, the brightness still in her voice.

It really bothered Curt to see the perky little Lieutenant in this condition. She'd always been such a lively girl who put the bounce and enthusiasm of youth into everything she did. Her injury wasn't something that could be chalked up to the fortunes of war; this was the result of a vendetta caused by Kitsy defending her turf and not suspecting the savage reprisal. She knew it, and so did the rest of the Greys assembled around her bed.

"We just wanted to see how you were and find out when Doctor Ruth is going to let you out," Hettrick opened the conversation.

"It will be a few days. . . . I've got to grow a new neck . . . and maybe some new nerve channels. . . . But I'll do it . . . Don't count me out. . . . I'll be back in the Club with you all . . . before you know it," Kitsy breathed.

"Well, I don't think Doctor Ruth told you," Alexis spoke up, "but I've been talking with Colonel Mahathis in Brunei.

Remember him?"

"Sure! Who could forget . . . that magnificent hunk?"

Alexis touched a black and yellow ribbon that was on the lower left bottom of her two rows of decorations. Although it was probably worth more to her than anything except the Congressional Medal of Honor which she didn't have, it was a foreign award. Protocol dictated that it be worn below and to the left of all American decorations. "Few people realize that the award of the Sultan's Star of Brunei — with which both Curt and I were honored — means the recipient is a member of the royal family of Brunei. So I called my family. Colonel Mahathis will be landing at Mosul as quickly as he can get here. He's bringing three of his top biotechnologists — and you know how advanced the Bruneis are in that area!"

Kitsy managed a smile. "As I remember, you were wounded in Brunei, Alexis . . . and they did right well for you."

Alexis grinned. "In a very embarrassing place, too, I might add! Right across the left bun! But I don't even have a scar there now. When I told Colonel Mahathis what had happened, there was no hesitation on his part. He told me exactly what he was going to do for you because, of course, he remembers you well."

"Allie, is the Army going to allow someone else to come into this hospital and treat a wounded officer?" Adonica asked. "Isn't that a bit non-reg?"

"Lieutenant, suppose the Bruneis had called and told us of a terrible accident. What would we do? Now, if you recall, we have a bilateral trade and defense agreement with Brunei," General Hettrick reminded her. "Seems it also includes provisions for humanitarian aid and technology transfer. But when we were slogging it out in Brunei during the Greys, little sojourn down there, none of us really imagined that the tech transfer could go from Brunei to America! Believe me, the Army will have a little heartburn about it because the Chief Surgeon is a little bit jealous of his prerogatives and suffers from the main malady of all science-types in Washington, the Not-Invented-Here Syndrome. But Major Gydesen is excited about it; she knows when she needs help, so she okayed it. And, most important, I approved it. Not totally on your account, mind you. I want to meet this man that Alexis seems to be so interested in and disdainful of at the same time."

"Oh, that's good!" Kitsy looked even brighter. "You'll get to see the other side of the Brunei equation, General. . . . I'll bet he's bringing his twin sister with him. . . . The Sultana Alzena always comes along . . . to see Curt, of course! I'm jealous. . . . But I'm in no position to compete right now. . . . However, regardless of the biotechnology . . . I'm not going to let *this* . . . stop me very long! . . . So keep that slot in the Washington Greys . . . open for me, please."

"Hell, Lieutenant, none of us figure you'll be out of action for very long. We'll cover for you," Edie Sampson assured her.

"Yeah, Lieutenant, don't worry. We've got ways to get our way," Regimental Sergeant Major Henry Kester agreed.

Everyone in the room knew what was meant:

The Washington Greys always take care of their own.

"Curt, you've been very quiet," Kitsy observed. "Now that I look at you . . . do my eyes deceive me . . . or has that gold oak leaf on your collar tab . . . faded into silver?"

"Field promotion, Kitsy," Curt admitted. "Purely temporary."

"Temporary, my ass!" Hettrick exploded gently. "Curt, you will be a Lieutenant Colonel permanently as soon as I can turn some screws on the Deputy Chief of Staff for Personnel . . . and I know where a few bodies are buried in that shop after a stint in the Pentagon!"

"I wish I could shake your hand, Curt . . . Hell, I wish I could kiss you . . . to congratulate you! . . . You deserve it!" Kitsy breathed.

"I'll give you that chance," he told her. Leaning forward over her, he gently kissed her on the lips. She might have been paralyzed from the neck down, but her face wasn't. She responded with fervor that surprised Curt because of her condition but which was in the tradition of Kitsy Clinton's philosophy, *Anything worth doing is worth overdoing!*

When Hettrick interjected, "Okay, Congratulations have gone on long enough, about three times long enough unless you want me to start using a calendar instead of my watch. Curt, the perks of regimental command go only so far, you know!"

"Regimental command?" Kitsy wasn't exactly sure of the meaning of what she'd just heard. With concern, she asked,

"You got Colonel Bellamack back. . . . You did, didn't you? . . . . He's alive, isn't he? . . . . Is he all right?" She turned her attention to a concern for her commanding officer.

"He's here in the hospital," Hettrick assured her.

"He has a minor wound in his leg that got practically no medical attention from the Soviets," Adonica Sweet added. "Ruth can pretty much handle that. She's a little out of her league with the rest."

"When he went into linkage with that Soviet Spetsnaz sergeant in an attempt to get some information," Jerry Allen explained, "he got locked into some kind of split personality, schizoid problem. He talks part of the time in English and sometimes in Russian. Sometimes he's Colonel Bellamack, sometimes he's someone else. It's some sort of mix-up that's probably like rapid delinking from a warbot or a warbot brainy being KIA. At any rate, he's in semi-spasm mode."

"Colonel Willa Lovell is on her way here from McCarthy Proving Ground," Curt added. "I called her as soon as we got back to Mosul. She's bringing some specialists in this area—she calls it Neuroelectronically Induced Psychotic Syndrome or something. She and her experts may be able to work with Ruth here, but they're probably going to have to transfer Colonel Bellamack to a special hospital in the ZI. They think they can get his circuits straightened out again."

"Ahem! What Colonel Carson is so carefully dancing around with great skill," Henry Kester put in gently, "is that I'm going to be his nurse maid again. Colonel Bellamack may be out of it for a while."

"And anyway it's time Bill Bellamack was kicked upstairs to the OSCAR desk in the Pentagon anyway, because General Calhoun intends to retire as soon as his replacement is found, and we need a Sierra Charlie there to keep an eye on the warbot brainies who still think they run the Army," Hettrick added. "What this old banty rooster is saying, Kitsy, is that I've given command of the Washington Greys to Lieutenant Colonel Curt Carson!"

"God! It's about time!" Kitsy breathed.

"I second that!" Jerry Allen said.

A cautious, hesitant knock on the door interrupted the chorus of agreement from the old members of Carson's Companions.

Dyani Motega walked in.

"General! Colonel! I'm sorry I'm late," she apologized. "I had a difficult time finding both a uniform that would fit and the proper insignia to wear on it."

Alexis and Adonica were grinning from ear to ear. When she saw Dyani Motega, Kitsy Clinton grinned, too.

On Dyani's collar tab was a single gold bar.

Curt cleared his throat. "General, if this is your doing, I should like to submit a complaint!"

"About what, Colonel?"

"About the fact that you haven't kept your new regimental commander informed," Curt replied. "Apparently, the ladies of the Washington Greys are in on this, so I'd like to request some equal treatment of the male side of the house, please. Naturally, I'm delighted at what this appears to be, but would you care to explain, ma'am? If I'm supposed to be commanding the Washington Greys, don't you think it's a good idea that you keep me informed of what you're doing with my personnel?"

"Colonel, you rarely kept me informed of what you were doing with them and I had to learn about it from Rumor Control, but that was discrete behavior and is as it should be." Belinda Hettrick was smiling. It wasn't often that she managed to pull one off on Curt Carson, but she'd succeeded this time. And none of it was because of the secrecy of the so-called "Inner Amazon Circle" of the Greys which didn't really exist; and it never would because they'd all met an Amazon now and didn't like the reference at all.

The commanding general of the 17th Iron Fist Division went on, "Lieutenant Clinton is likely to be on official medical leave for an indefinite time while modern biotechnology performs a miracle. Therefore, it occurred to me while I was reading Colonel Carson's recommended citation for Sergeant Motega's Distinguished Service Cross that she should be rewarded beyond a mere Purple Heart for wounds received in action and perhaps the DCS if confirmed, as I believe it will be. So I exercised my powers as commanding general of the Seventeenth Iron Fist Division to authorize a direct appointment of Lieutenant Motega on the basis of her outstanding record, her demonstrated valor, her continuing computer-net educational program toward her baccalaureate degree, and her demonstrated abilities. That will be validated by DCS-PERS, too, because there are a *lot* of bodies buried in the Outer Ring of the Pentagon! And, if I run out of bodies there are lots of skeletons in lots of closets, too!"

Hettrick paused to let that all sink in, then went on, "Besides, Curt, you'll need Dyani to fill a vacant officer's slot while Kitsy is recuperating. Afterward . . . Well, that's your problem, sir!"

Curt couldn't be more pleased. He knew Hettrick was enjoying this, so he figured he ought to do the same. When the fighting was over and the work was done, the Washington Greys were indeed one big family, and it was the pride of the unit that helped make the Regiment what it was. Part of the legacy of the Greys was a sense of humor; if you didn't have it when you came aboard, you developed it soon as a means to maintain a perspective on an otherwise violent and often capricious world. "Yes, ma'am, it is my problem, all right! But, considering my own outstanding record of handling the ladies of the Washington Greys, I believe I'm probably up to it!"

The reply was a series of low hoots and whistles and laughter from the ladies present.

"I'm glad to see that I have the confidence of my subordinates," Curt remarked lightly.

"You always have . . . and you always will," was the response from Kitsy Clinton. "Now you have given me additional motivation . . . to get the hell out of this goddamned iron frame! Fast!. . . . Dyani, good luck! I'm very happy for you!"

"On this auspicious occasion," Curt added, "and as my first official order as commanding officer of the Washington Greys, I decree a mandatory Stand-to at the Club at eighteen-hundred hours! The first round is on me, of course." He paused, then added, "Kitsy, the first toast after toasting the Greys will be to you."

"Oh, I'll be there, Curt," Kitsy told him seriously but with that twinkle in her eyes that told him she hadn't quit, not by a long shot. "In spirit at first . . . but in person in a few months or so! . . . After all, I can't let my friends down . . . or the Washington Greys!"

Ruth Gydesen didn't want them all to remain too long.

Kitsy was tired and she needed all her seemingly boundless personal energy to handle the situation she was in . . . and winning, according to Ruth, although the doctor didn't really understand why. Curt could have explained it. So, as they left the hospital and headed back across the compound, Curt remarked to Alexis and Dyani, "Major, Lieutenant, please see me at your convenience so I can discuss the Lieutenant's assignment to the Marauders' first platoon. But no rush. We're in sort of a post-operational stand-down for a few days here. But will one of you please let me know when the aerodrome receives words of the E-T-A for the Brunei Sabre-dancer? I'll be in quarters."

Alexis looked at him and remarked, "I may drop by."

"Please do! I need a chance to make some points before the competition shows up," Curt replied in a joking tone. He couldn't do otherwise. He was too devastated about Kitsy Clinton to do anything more than joke at this point. Otherwise, it hurt too much.

Alexis picked it up but apparently didn't catch Curt's pain. "Not used to competition, are you?"

"Neither were you, remember?" was his quick rejoinder. He enjoyed joking with Alexis. He did have very serious thoughts about her and had often in the past two years kicked himself in the ass for not suggesting matrimony earlier. Now, with the son of the Sultan of Brunei actively courting Alexis, maybe it was too late. The best he could possibly do was to laugh at it and at himself. "You told me it wasn't serious!"

"That was two years ago!" Alexis told him. "Besides, as I said, he's rich and he outranks me. And I might as well have fun while I can."

"Well, I qualify on one of those counts," Curt observed.

"Excuse me," Dyani Motega put in, "but is this an inside joke or something?"

Alexis laughed. "Some days I think it's a joke, some days I don't!"

"Surely you've been plugged into Rumor Control, Dyani," Curt said.

"I've never placed much credence in it," the new officer admitted without humor. Lieutenant Dyani Motega's sense of humor had developed a little bit since she'd joined the Greys, but Curt knew it would take some time yet before she really came out of what seemed to be a shell. The field promotion had apparently initiated it, but he was sure that the full implications of a commission hadn't yet dawned on Dyani.

Curt was relaxing in his quarters a few hours later, content to be able to take the afternoon and just unwind, when the door chimed. He was attired in only a pair of baggy cammies, his favorite relaxing dress, so he called out in cadet slang because he was expecting Alexis, "Bounce and rest!"

The door opened. "May I come in?" Dyani Motega asked.

"Uh, yeah, I wasn't expecting you, Dyani."

"Alexis sent a message," she said, closing the door behind her. "The plane from Brunei arrived. Alexis went to meet it because Colonel Mahathis was aboard. But the Sultana Alzena couldn't come this time."

"Thanks, Dyani."

She didn't move. "Disappointed?"

He nodded.

"She's a beautiful woman. But don't be disappointed." She walked over to him. "Things have changed."

"Things always change, Dyani."

"Some things change for the better." Dyani had never been a chatterbox. Sometimes she didn't need to be. This was one of those times.

She stepped up to him, removed her cap, tossed it casually on the desk, shook her dark hair free, and looked up at him. Curt noticed for the first time that she was much smaller than he thought. She had always seemed to be a taller person because of the way she projected herself as an individual of integrity, honor, strong morality, and strong purpose.

And Dyani now seemed to glow, to radiate, to glisten, and shimmer. What she projected penetrated Curt's mind something like person-to-person linkage. He got a sensation, a mental image of walls coming down, doors opening, or a dam suddenly breaking.

Without a word, she reached up, put her arms around his neck, and kissed him.

Curt was suddenly awash in waves of caring, loving, passionate affection that poured forth over and around and through him from this soft, warm young woman.

He could do nothing but respond. When he did, he discovered his own pent-up emotions spilling forth in strange new

344

ways as if drawn out by her.

"Dyani," he whispered softly. "we have to be at Stand-to in two hours."

"That's a very long time from now, dear." Dyani said smiling.

Appendix I

ORDER OF BATTLE

OPERATION STURDY SPECTRA

17th Iron Fist Division (R.I.), Army of the United States
Major General Belinda J. Hettrick, commanding officer

3rd R.I. "Washington Greys" Special Combat Regiment
Colonel William D. Bellamack, commanding officer

Regimental staff:
    Major Joanne J. Wilkinson, chief of staff*
    Major Patrick Gillis Gratton, regimental adjutant (S-1)
    Major Hensley Atkinson (S-3)*
    Captain Nelson A. Crile, regimental chaplain
    Regimental Sergeant Major: Sergeant Major Henry G. Kester
    Regimental Staff Sergeant First Class Georgina Cook (communications)*
Tactical Battalion (TACBATT) (Carson's Companions):
    Major Curt C. Carson
    Battalion Sergeant Major Edwina A. Sampson
    Reconnaissance Company (RECONCO) ("Gibbon's Goblins")
        Major John S. Gibbon (S-2)
        First Sergeant Tracy C. Dillon

Bio-tech Sergeant Allan J. Williams
Scouting Platoon (SCOUT) ("Sweet's Scouts")
1st Lieutenant Adonica Sweet
Platoon Sergeant Dyani Motega
Sergeant Harlan P. Saunders
Sergeant Thomas C. Cole
Sergeant Joe Jim Watson
Birdbot Platoon (BIRD) ("Aarts's Avians")
Captain Eleanor S. Aarts
Platoon Sergeant Emma Crawford
Sergeant William J. Hull
Sergeant Jacob F. Kent
Sergeant Christine Burgess
Sergeant Jennifer M. Volker
Assault Company A (ASSAULTCO Alpha) ("Morgan's Marauders")
Major Alexis P. Morgan
Master Sergeant First Class Carol J. Head
Bio-tech Sergeant Virginia Bowles
First Platoon: ("Clinton's Conquerors")
1st Lieutenant Kathleen J. Clinton
Platoon Sergeant Charles P. Koslowski
Sergeant James P. Elliott
Sergeant Paul T. Tullis
Second Platoon: ("Pagan's Pumas")
2nd Lieutenant Lewis C. Pagan
Platoon Sergeant Betty Jo Trumble
Sergeant Joe Jim Watson
Sergeant Edwin W. Gatewood**
Assault Company B (ASSAULTCO Brave) ("Frazier's Ferrets")
Captain Russell B. Frazier
Master Sergeant Charles L. Orndorff
Bio-tech Sergeant Juanita Gomez
First Platoon: ("Clock's Cavaliers")
1st Lieutenant Harold M. Clock
Platoon Sergeant Robert Lee Garrison
Sergeant Walter J. O'Reilly
Sergeant Maxwell M. Moody
Second Platoon: ("Hassan's Assassins")
2nd Lieutenant Hassan Ben Mahmud
Platoon Sergeant Isadore Beau Greenwald

Sergeant Victor Jouillan
Sergeant Sidney Albert Johnson**
Gunnery Company (GUNCO) ("Ward's Warriors")
Major Joan G. Ward
First Sergeant Nicholas P. Gerard
Bio-tech Sergeant Shelley C. Hale
First Platoon: ("Allen's Alleycats")
Captain Jerry P. Allen
Platoon Sergeant Forest L. Barnes**
Sergeant Andrea Carrington**
Sergeant Jamie Jay Younger**
Second Platoon: ("Ritscher's Rascals")
2nd Lieutenant William P. Ritscher #
Platoon Sergeant Willa P. Miller**
Sergeant Richard L. Knight**
Sergeant Louise J. Hanrahan**
Air Battalion (AIRBATT) ("Worsham's Warhawks")
Major Calvin J. Worsham
Battalion Sergeant Major John Adam
Tactical Air Support Company (TACAIRCO) ("Jolley's Rogers")
Captain Robert Jolley
1st Sergeant Clancy Thomas
1st Lieutenant Paul Hands
1st Lieutenant Gabe Neatherly
1st Lieutenant Bruce Mark
1st Lieutenant Stacy Honey
1st Lieutenant Jay Kennedy
Flight Sergeant Zeke Braswell
Flight Sergeant Larry Myers
Flight Sergeant Adam Adams
Flight Sergeant Grant Brown
Flight Sergeant Sharon Spence
Airlift Company (AIRLIFTCO) (Hawley's Haulers")
Captain Roger Hawley
First Sergeant Carl Bagwell
1st Lieutenant Ned Phillips
1st Lieutenant Mike Hart
1st Lieutenant Timothea Timm
1st Lieutenant Dorothy Peterson
1st Lieutenant Nancy Roberts
1st Lieutenant Harry Racey

Flight Sergeant Kevin Hubbard
Flight Sergeant Jeffrey O'Connell
Flight Sergeant Barry Morris
Flight Sergeant Ann Shepherd
Flight Sergeant Richard Cooke
Flight Sergeant Harley Earll
Flight Sergeant Sergio Tomasio
Flight Sergeant John Espee

Service Battalion (SERVBATT)
  Major Wade W. Hampton
  Battalion Sergeant Major Joan J. Stark
  Vehicle Technical Company (VETECO)
    Major Frederick W. Benteen
    Technical Sergeant First Class Raymond G. Wolf
    Technical Sergeant Kenneth M. Hawkins
    Technical Sergeant Charles B. Slocum
  Warbot Technical Company (BOTECO)
    Captain Elwood S. Otis
    Technical Sergeant Bailey Ann Miles
    Technical Sergeant Gerald W. Mora
    Technical Sergeant Loretta A. Carruthers
    Technical Sergeant Robert H. Vickers
  Maintenance Company (AIRMAINCO)
    Captain Ron Knight
    First Sergeant Rebecca Campbell
    Technical Sergeant Joel Pruitt
    Technical Sergeant Richard N. Germain
    Technical Sergeant Douglas Bell
    Technical Sergeant Pam Gordon
    Technical Sergeant Clete McCoy
    Technical Sergeant Carol Jensen
  Logistics Company (LOGCO)
    Captain Harriet F. Dearborn (S-4)
    Chief Supply Sergeant Manuel P. Sanchez
    Supply Sergeant Marriette W. Ireland
    Supply Sergeant Lawrence W. Jordan
    Supply Sergeant Jamie G. Casner
  Bio-tech Company (BIOTECO)
    Major Ruth Gydesen, M.D.
    Captain Denise G. Logan, M.D.
    Captain Thomas E. Alvin, M.D.

Captain Larry C. McHenry, M.D.
Captain Helen Devlin, R.N.
1st Lieutenant Clifford-B. Braxton, R.N.
1st Lieutenant Laurie S. Cornell, R.N.
1st Lieutenant Julia B. Clark, R.N.
1st Lieutenant William O. Molde, R.N.
Bio-tech Sergeant Marcela V. Jolton, P.N.
Bio-tech Sergeant Nellie A. Miles, P.N.
Bio-tech Sergeant George O. Howard, P.N.
Bio-tech Sergeant Wallace W. Izard, P.N.

NOTES

* — The revised TO&E for a Ghost-style Special Combat Regiment has no slots for these individuals who were formerly in Headquarters Company in staff positions. However, it is traditional in the Washington Greys to find new slots for persons who lose slots in any reorganization. No slots were available for these individuals in the new TO&E, but they are being retained in the Regiment in staff capacities until they either retire, request transfer to other units, or become casualties. "The Washington Greys always take care of their own," and an administrative or tactical reorganization does not change this tradition.

** — The revised TO&E eliminated many slots when the Headquarters Company disappeared in the reorganization. These individuals were given the choice of transfer to another unit or reassignment within the regiment, including restraining for a new and different Rated Position Code.

— In accordance with the Army policy and regimental tradition of promoting from within a regiment where possible, these outstanding former NCOs were chosen and accepted merit combat promotions and field commissions including 12 weeks at OCS. Other NCOs may have been offered this opportunity but declined to accept because of their high relative rank as NCOs; acceptance of a commission by these NCOs would have resulted in a lower pay rate and/or reduced military benefits.

All Warbot Technicians formerly assigned to combat companies have been reassigned to a smaller, more streamlined

Warbot Technical Company whose mission is to perform Level 2 maintenance and repair of the Mod 7/11 Warbots. Because of the greater simplicity of the Mod 7/11 warbots with their modular plug-in equipment, Level One maintenance and repair are carried out at the platoon level.

To increase unit morale, combat platoons are now allowed to adopt individualistic and motivational names in addition to their alpha-numeric designators.

APPENDIX II

THE ORGANIZATION OF THE ROBOT INFANTRY SPECIAL COMBAT REGIMENT

(Excerpted from United States Army "Handbook of Military Training," TM-105-8, Revision 3.1.2, Department of Defense Open Network Data Base DODON-DB.)

BACKGROUND:

As a result of actual field combat experience in Operation Steel Band (Trinidad), Operation Diamond Skeleton (Namibia), Operation Black Jack (Sonora), Exercise Happy Abode (Brunei), and other operational experience of the 3rd Robot Infantry Regiment, "The Washington Greys," following the adoption of revised war robot doctrine that put human soldiers back into the field alongside advanced warbots (the Special Combat or "Sierra Charlie" doctrine), regimental organization slowly evolved from that of the standard Robot Infantry Regiment to that discussed herein.

Successful implementation of the Special Combat doctrine demanded greater flexibility than that possessed by a regular Robot Infantry Regiment because of the higher mobility, improved firepower, and wider versatility that had been exhibited by the 3rd Robot Infantry (Special Combat) Regiment in actual operations under a wide variety of circumstances in the above campaigns.

Robot Infantry (Special Combat) Regiment

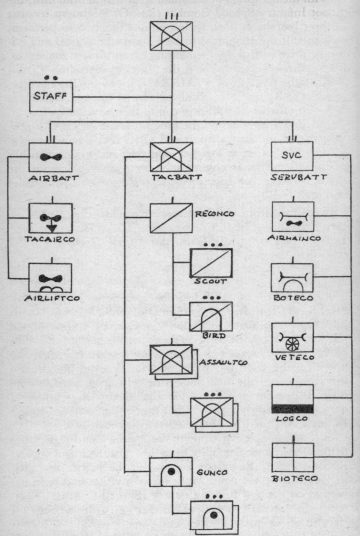

THE ROBOT INFANTRY SPECIAL COMBAT REGIMENT:

With the exception of the small Regimental Staff unit, the Robot Infantry Special Combat (RI/SC) Regiment consists of three battalions, each with a unique function to perform, that permit the Regiment to be a complete tactical and administrative entity while remaining a basic unit of maneuver. These three battalions are the Tactical Battalion (TACBATT), the Air Battalion (AIRBATT), and the Service Battalion (SERVBATT). Total personnel in an RI/SC is 137—40 officers and 97 non-commissioned officers.

TACBATT operates on the ground, while AIRBATT provides tacair and air transport and SERVBATT handles service functions such as logistics, biotech, and maintenance.

Each Battalion is commanded by a field officer of the grade of Major or Lieutenant Colonel assisted by a chief battalion NCO with the rank of Sergeant Major or Master Sergeant.

STAFF UNIT:

A Special Combat Robot Infantry (SC/RI) Regiment requires a smaller administrative and support capability than a standard Robot Infantry Regiment. Hence, the SC Regiment no longer contains a Headquarters Company. All administrative activities have either been concentrated in a small and highly versatile Regimental Staff or broken out and assigned to battalion and company commands. An increased and improved level of automation and computerization permits this to be done without placing additional administrative loads on active operational units. The administrative use of artificial intelligence was extremely helpful in allowing computers to handle repetitive, everyday paperwork with a minimum of attention from company and platoon personnel.

THE TACTICAL BATTALION (TACBATT):

TACBATT is the Regiment's primary ground fighting unit capable of ground maneuver, ground-launched firepower, warbot reconnaissance mostly in the form of remotely operated aerial robots (birdbots), and human-warbot scouting and patrolling.

TACBATT contains a Reconnaissance Company (RE-CONCO) commanded by a Major or a Captain who is assisted by a lead NCO with the rank of Master Sergeant or First Sergeant.

The RECONCO Scouting Platoon (SCOUT) is led by a platoon-level officer with three NCOs accompanied by a minimum of four M33A2 General Purpose Warbots and transported on the ground by M92 Personal Transportation Vehicles and, if necessary, an M660 Airportable Command Vehicle configured to transport the additional M33A2 GP warbots. Its function is to perform regimental reconnaissance and scouting on the ground.

The RECONCO Birdbot Platoon (BIRD) is the second platoon-size unit in this company and is the only neuroelectronic warbot unit in the RI/SC. Its platoon officer and five NCOs are all highly qualified NE warbot operators. BIRD equipment includes 24 M20 Aerial Reconnaissance Bird Robots with Mod 7/11 artificial intelligence modules. The BIRD platoon is responsible for covert tactical reconnaissance over the Regiment's area of operations out to a classified range. Birdbots are used in the same manner as in a standard RI Regiment, especially in operations where a high level of enemy counter-air activity is present or suspected and which would lead to an unwarranted high level of risk for manned tacair recon.

TACBATT has two Assault Companies (ASSAULTCO), each led by a Major or Captain with the lead NCO being a Master Sergeant or First Sergeant. A Bio-tech Sergeant is attached to each ASSAULTCO to provide immediate field medical attention to casualties. Each ASSAULTCO contains 2 platoons. An ASSAULTCO platoon is commanded by a Captain or Lieutenant with a Platoon or Lead Sergeant and two Sergeant NCOs as squad leaders. The ASSAULTCO is the maneuvering and shock element of the Regiment and is organized so that it can act either as an assault unit or a maneuvering unit in order to provide the regimental commander and the TACBATT commander with the maximum field flexibility. The warbot assault power of an AS-SAULTCO is made up of 24 highly-mobile M60A Airportable Mobile Assault Warbots, familiarly known as "Mary

Anns," equipped with Mod 7/11 artificial intelligence modules and mounting the variable-fire M300 25-millimeter cannon. Additional warbot support comes from 18 M33A2 General Purpose Warbots ("Jeeps") with single M133A 7.62-millimeter heavy automatic guns. Ground transportation is by a mix of M660 Airportable Command Vehicles (ACV) and M662 Airportable Robot Transport Vehicles (ARTV).

The heavy-fire base of TACBATT is the Gunnery Company (GUNCO) with the same personnel complement as ASSAULTCO but equipped with 8 M457 Light Artillery Mobile Vehicles (LAMVA or "Lamb") capable of airtransport and directed by Mod 7/11 AI modules. Each M457 mounts a single M500 75-millimeter automatic, self-loading cannon capable of firing subcaliber saboted ammunition (SSA) as well as full-caliber ammunition (FCA). A variety of rounds are carried in each LAMVA — high-explosive antivehicle rounds (HEAV), fragmenting anti-personnel rounds (FAP), anti-riot concussion rounds (ARC) — which may be either "smart rounds" or "dumb rounds" with integrated rocket propulsion (IRP) or variable velocity propulsion (VVP). Because of the versatility of the M500 cannon and its M457 LAMVA mounting, it may be fired at quadrant elevations between -15 degrees and +80 degrees with respect to the LAMVA longitudinal axis, thus permitting it to be utilized as a gun, a howitzer, or a mortar.

THE AIR BATTALION:

The Air Battalion (AIRBATT) is commanded by a Lieutenant Colonel or a Major with a Sergeant Major or Master Sergeant as the lead NCO. The AIRBATT commander also flies as the lead combat pilot of the Tactical Air Support Company (see below). All personnel of AIRBATT have Rated Position Codes of RPC 15 or RPC 71. The AIRBATT is made up of two companies.

The AIRBATT Tactical Air Support Company (TACAIRCO) has a complement 7 pilot officers, including a commanding officer with the rank of Major or Captain, and 7 NCO crew chiefs who man 8 AD-40C "Thunder Devil" Tactical Assault Aerodynes, each armed with two M300A 25-millimeter cannon, the airborne model of the weapon carried by the M60A Airborne Mobile Assault Warbot. Also carried internally are 12 M100A anti-tank/anti-aircraft tube rockets, the same weapons carried by the personnel of TACBATT. The AD-40C is a small, highly stealthed, heavily armored assault aerodyne developed from the Aerospace Force and Navy AD-40 "Sky Devil" and "Sea Devil" assault aerodynes. The AD-40C is operated by a single pilot in neuroelectronic linkage with the craft's Mark 35 autopilot utilizing Mod 7/11 AI modules.

The AIRBATT Airlift Company (AIRLIFTCO) consists of 8 officers and 8 NCO crew chiefs, including a Major or Captain as commanding officer. AIRLILFTCO is equipped with 8 UCA-21C Chippewa Assault Transport Aerodynes, each capable of a maximum payload of 10 metric tons, speeds up to 250 km/hr, and ranges out to 11,000 kilometers (untanked for additional range). The function of AIRLIFTCO is to provide rapid response mobility in tactical situations as well as to assist in providing long-range strategic airlift of the Regiment.

THE SERVICE BATTALION:

The Service Battalion (SERVBATT) is commanded by a Major or a Captain assisted by a Master Sergeant or First Sergeant and consists of 5 companies: the Vehicle Technical Company (VETECO), the Warbot Technical Company (BOTECO), the Aircraft Maintenance Company (AIRMAINCO), the Logistics Company (LOGCO), and the BioTech Company (BIOTECO). The function of SERVBATT is to provide backup technical and supply services to TACBATT and AIRBATT.

VETECO is commanded by a Major or a Captain with 3 NCOs, all possessing an RPC 91. The VETECO provides the expertise and additional equipment for Level 2 ground vehicle maintenance in the field. Level 1 maintenance is carried out at the Company level in TACBATT.

BOTECO is commanded by a Major or Captain with 4 NCOs, all with RPC 91, and provides Level 2 warbot maintenance while Level 1 maintenance is carried out at the Company level within TACBATT. The exception to this is maintenance and repair on the complex M20 Aerial Reconnaissance Neuroelectronic Bird Robots and their associated linkage equipment which is highly classified; only BOTECO is authorized to perform any maintenance or repair work on the M20s.

AIRMAINCO is commanded by a Captain or Lieutenant supervising 7 NCOs, all with RPC 71. The job of AIRMAINCO is to perform Level 2 maintenance and field repair on the aircraft assigned to AIRBATT.

LOGCO is commanded by a Major or Captain with 4 NCOs, all with RPC 70. They operate the various M664A Airportable Command Support Vehicles—the M664A1 fuel and potable water tankers, the M664A4 commissary vehicles, the M664A3 ammunition carriers, and the M664A4 parts supply vehicles. It is their function to provide 100 hours of logistically independent operation of the Regiment in the field under combat conditions.

BIOTECO is a medical or bio-technical company staffed by personnel from the Medical Corps. It is commanded by a Major or Captain qualified as a doctor and is staffed by three additional doctors who are Majors or Captains, 5 professional bio-technicians who are certified Registered Nurses with the rank of Captain or Lieutenant, and 4 NCOs who are licensed Practical Nurses or Bio-technicians. BIOTECO has a complete mobile field hospital with surgical capabilities in 3 M660E Bio-tech support Vehicles.

APPENDIX III

REGIMENTAL EQUIPMENT
Brief Descriptions
(Including Warbots & Vehicles)
Sierra Charlie Ghost Regiments

M33A2 General Purpose Warbot, ("Jeep") mounting a single M133A 7.62mm heavy automatic gun with variable fire rates up to 3,000 rounds per minute. Mod 7/11 artificial intelligence circuitry and programming allow self-direction in the field to avoid obstacles and automatic response to preprogrammed situations.

M20 Aerial Reconnaissance Neuroelectronic Bird Warbot ("Birdbot") with new 7/11/AB artificial intelligence circuity allowing internal self-control of routine reconnaissance functions.

M60A Airborne Mobile Assault Warbot ("Mary Ann") mounting a single M300 25mm automatic cannon with variable fire rates up to 3,000 rounds per minute. Mod 7/11 artificial intelligence installed to allow field independence, obstacle avoidance, and selected responses to numerous combat situations.

M457 Light Artillery Mobile Vehicle, Airportable (LAMVA or "Lamb") mounting a single M500 75mm "Saucy Cans" automatic self-loading cannon capable of firing subcaliber saboted ammunition (SSA) as well as full caliber ammunition (FCA) with high explosive anti-vehicle rounds (HEAV), fragmenting anti-personnel (FAP) rounds, and anti-riot concussion (ARC) rounds. Rounds may be selected to be "smart rounds"

(SSR) or "dumb rounds" (/DR). Propelling charges may be integrated rocket propulsion (IRP) or variable velocity propulsion (VVP) to suit the combat requirement. The M457 is capable of firing at quadrant elevations between -15 degrees and +80 degrees and may be used as a gun, howitzer, or mortar.

M92 Personal Transportation Vehicle (PTV or "Trike") capable of carrying one combat-ready human soldier and one M33A2 General Purpose Warbot ("Jeep") at speeds up to 50 km/hr over most terrain with slopes of less than 45 degrees. Propelled by energy cells for silent running of up to 4 hours at full power. Similar to a civilian "all terrain recreational vehicle" and derived from the antiquated side-car motorcycle.

M660 Airportable Command Vehicle (ACV) capable of carrying up to six human soldiers plus a single M33A2 Jeep and serving as a command and transport vehicle for units of platoon size and greater. Capable of sustained cross-country speeds up to 50 km/hr for 24 hours without reprovisioning. For regimental command purposes where greater tactical information must be processed with the regimental computer and combat data and instructions communicated, a modification, the *M660B Operational Command Vehicle (OCV)* is used and can carry only three persons. The regimental BIOTECO uses three *M660E Bio-tech Support Vehicles*.

M662 Airportable Robot Transport Vehicle (ARTV) capable of carrying eight M60A Mary Anns, twelve M33A2 Jeeps, twelve M92 PRVs, or a single M457 LAMVA. Armored only in critical areas of the turbine propulsion system, fuel tanks, and running gear. Capable of speeds up to 50 km/hr cross country for 24 hours without reprovisioning. Operated by self-aware Mod 7/11 artificial intelligence circuity utilizing inputs from visual and infrared sensors.

M664A Airportable Command Support Vehicle (ACSV) utilized by the SERVBAT to provide logistical support in the form of the M664A1 tanker, M664A2 commissary, and M664A3 ammunition carrier. Utilized to provide the regimental "tail" capable of maintaining a regiment in independent field combat conditions for up to 100 hours.

M33A2 "Ranger" Assault Rifle is a 7.62mm hand-carried, semi-automatic, self-loading, clip-fed, laser-ranged, visually aimed personal combat weapon weighing 2.45 kilograms and carried by all personnel. The latest modification permits variable velocity firing pioneered by the unsuccessful Hellcat rifle and thus permits its use in a wide variety of combat situations. The Ranger rifle is an American development of the Mexican M3 "Novia" rifle and is manufactured in the United States.

M44A "Black Maria" Assault Shotgun is an 18.52mm (12-gauge) hand-carried, semi-automatic, self-loading, clip-fed, visually aimed combat shotgun carried by combat personnel and weighing 2.62 kilograms. It is capable of firing scattering pellet rounds, solid slugs, rubber bullets, or the M3A1 plasti-cex grenade while still in its casing.

M100A (FG/IM-190) Anti-tank/anti-aircraft (ATAA) Tube Rocket is a 100mm. shoulder-fired, tube-launched, rocket-propelled, self-guided, "smart" missile with a 250-gram warhead capable of penetrating the equivalent of up to 300 millimeters of hard steel armor plate on impact or activating as a linked-rod explosive fragmentation warhead when triggered by its smart target sensor within its kill-distance of an aircraft. It weighs 2.35 kilograms at launch and is contained in a launch tube weighing 1.23 kilograms.

UCA-21C Chippewa Assault Transport Aerodyne is the Army's primary assault transport aerodyne capable of lifting 10 metric tons (10,000 kilograms) of payload in the form of personnel, warbots, and/or vehicles at speeds up to 250 km/hr to ranges of 1000 kilometers (untanked) at altitudes up to 3500 meters. The latest Chippewa C is flown by a human pilot in neuroelectronic linkage with a Mark 26 autopilot utilizing mod 7/11 artificial intelligence circuity to relieve the pilot of routine loads allowing him to become a "systems manager" rather than a continuously directing activator.

AD-40C Thunder Devil Tactical Assault Aerodyne is a small, highly stealthed, armored assault aerodyne developed from the Aerospace Force and Navy A-40 Sky Devil attack aerodynes for Army tactical air support use by "Ghost" Sierra Charlie regiments. It is flown by a single human pilot operating a Mark 35 autopilot with Mod 7/11 artificial intelligence circuitry. Speed, range, and service ceiling data are classified. The Thunder Devil is armed with two M300A 25mm automatic cannons capable of fire rates up to 3,000 rounds per minute with selectable ammunition — anti-tank, anti-vehicle, anti-personnel, riot-suppression concussion, or tracer rounds. The AD-40C also carries 12 internally mounted M100A Anti-tank/anti-aircraft (ATAA) Tube Rockets. The Thunder Devil utilizes the same fuels, computers, artificial intelligence units, and ammunition as the regimental ground forces it supports.

APPENDIX IV

GLOSSARY OF ROBOT INFANTRY TERMS AND SLANG

ACV: Airportable Command Vehicle M660. See Appendix III, Regimental Equipment List.

Aerodyne: A saucer-shaped flying machine that obtains its lift from the exhaust of one or more turbine fanjet engines blowing outward over the curved upper surface of the craft from an annular, segmented slot near the center of the upper surface. The aerodyne was invented by Dr. Henri M. Coanda after World War II but was not perfected until decades later because of the predominance of the rotary-winged helicopter. See Appendix III, Regimental Equipment List.

Artificial Intelligence or AI: Very fast computer modules with large memories which can simulate some functions of human thought and decision-making processes by bringing together many apparently disconnected pieces of data, making simple evaluations of the priority of each, and making simple decisions concerning what to do, how to do it, when to do it, and what to report to the human being in control.

Bio-tech: A biological technologist once known in the twentieth century Army as a "medic."

Bot: Generalized generic slang term for "robot" which takes many forms, as warbot, reconbot, etc. See "Robot" below.

Bot flush: Since robots have no natural excrement, this term is a reference to what comes out of a highly mechanical warbot when its lubricants are changed during routine maintenance. Used by soldiers as a slang term referring to anything of a detestable nature.

Cee-pee or CP: Slang for "Command Post."

Check minus-x: Look behind you. In terms of coordinates, plus-x is ahead, minus-x is behind, plus-y is to the right, minus-y is left, plus-z is up, and minus-z is down.

Creamed: Greased, beaten, conquered, overwhelmed.

Down link: A remote command or data channel from a warbot to a soldier.

FIDO: Acronym for "Fuck it; drive on!" Overcome your obstacle or problem and get on with the operation.

Fur ball: A complex fight, battle, or operation.

Go physical: To lapse into idiot mode, to operate in a combat or recon environment without neuroelectronic warbots; what the Special Combat units do all the time. See "Idiot mode" below.

Golden BB: A small caliber bullet that hits and thus creates large problems.

Greased: Beaten, conquered, overwhelmed, creamed.

Humper: Any devise whose proper name a soldier can't recall at the moment.

Idiot mode: Operating in the combat environment without neuroelectronic warbots, especially operating without the benefit of computers and artificial intelligence to relieve battle load. What the warbot brainies think the Sierra Charlies do all the time. See "Go physical" above.

Intelligence amplifier or IA: A very fast computer with a very large memory which, when linked to a human nervous system by nonintrusive neuroelectronic pickups and electrodes, serves as a very fast extension of the human brain allowing the brain to function faster, recall more data, store more data, and thus "amplify" a human being's "intelligence." (Does not imply that we know what "intelligence" really is.)

Jeep: Word coined from the initials "GP" standing for "General Purpose." Once applied to an Army quarter-ton vehicle but subsequently used to refer to the Mark 33A2 General Purpose Warbot. See Appendix III, Regimental Equipment List.

KIA: "Killed in action." A warbot brainy term used to describe the situation where a warbot soldier's neuroelectronic data and sensory inputs from one or more warbots is suddenly cut off, leaving the human being in a state of mental limbo. A very debilitating and mentally disturbing situation. (Different from being physically killed in action, a situation with which only Sierra Charlies find themselves threatened.)

LAMVA: The M473 Light Artillery Maneuvering Vehicle, Airportable, a robotic armored vehicle mounting a 75-millimeter Saucy Cans gun used for light artillery support of a Sierra Charlie regiment. See Appendix III, Regimental Equipment List.

Linkage: The remote connection or link between a human being and one or more neuroelectronically controlled warbots. This link channel may be by means of wires, radio, laser, or optics. The actual technology of linkage is highly classified. The robot/computer sends its data directly to the human soldier's nervous system through small nonintrusive electrodes positioned on the soldier's skin. This data is coded in such a way that the soldier perceives the signals as sight, sound, feeling, or position of the robot's parts. The robot/computer also picks up commands from the soldier's nervous system that are "thought" by the soldier, translates them into commands a robot can understand, and monitors the robot's accomplishment of the command action.

Mary Ann: Slang for the M60A Airborne Mobile Assault Warbot which mounts a single M300 25-millimeter automatic cannon with variable fire rate. Accompanies Sierra Charlie troops in the field and provides fire support. See Appendix III, Regimental Equipment List.

Novia: The 7.62-millimeter M33A3 "Ranger" Assault Rifle designed in Mexico as the M3 Novia. The Sierra Charlies still call it the "Novia" or "sweetheart." See Appendix III, Regimental Equipment List.

Neuroelectronics: The synthesis of electronics and computer technologies that permits a computer to detect and recognize signals from the human nervous system by means of nonintrusive skin-mounted sensors as well as to stimulate the human nervous system with computer-generated electronic signals through similar skin-mounted electrodes for the purpose of creating sensory signals in the human mind. See "Linkage" above.

Orgasmic!: A slang term that grew out of the observation, "Outstanding!" It means the same thing.

Pucker factor: The detrimental effect on the human body that results from being in an extremely hazardous situation.

Robot: From the Czech word *robota* meaning work, especially drudgery. A device with humanlike actions directed either by a computer or by a human being through a computer and a two-way command-sensor circuit. See "Linkage" and "Neuroelectronics" above.

Robot Infantry or RI: A combat branch of the United States Army which grew from the regular infantry with the introduction of robots and linkage to warfare. Replaced the regular infantry in the early twenty-first century.

RTV: Robot Transport Vehicle, now the M662 Airportable Robot Transport Vehicle (ARTV) but still called an RTV by Sierra Charlies. See Appendix III, Regimental Equipment List.

Rule Ten: Slang reference to Army Regulation 601-10 which prohibits physical contact between male and female personnel when on duty except for that required in the conduct of official business.

Rules of Engagement or ROE: Official restrictions on the freedom of action of a commander or soldier in his confrontation with an opponent that act to increase the probability that said commander or soldier will lose the combat, all other things being equal.

Saucy Cans: An American Army corruption of the French designation for the 75-millimeter "soixante-quintze" weapon mounted on the LAMVA. See Appendix III, Regimental Equipment List.

Sheep screw: A disorganized, embarrassing, graceless chaotic fuck-up.

Sierra Charlie: Phonetic alphabet derivative of the initials "SC" meaning "Special Combat." Soldiers trained to engage in personal field combat supported and accompanied by artificially intelligent warbots that are voice-commanded rather than run by linkage.

Sierra Hotel: What warbot brainies say when they can't say, "Shit hot!"

Simulator or sim: A device that can simulate the sensations perceived by a human being and the results of the human's responses. A simple toy computer or video game simulating the flight of an aircraft or the driving of a race car is an example of a primitive simulator.

Sit-guess: Slang for "estimate of the situation," an educated guess about your predicament.

Sit-rep: Short for "situation report" to notify your superior officer about the sheep screw you're in at the moment.

Snake pit: Slang for the highly computerized briefing center located in most caserns and other Army posts.

Snivel: To complain about the injustice being done you.

Spasm mode: Slang for killed in action (KIA).

Spook: Slang term for either a spy or a military intelligence specialist. Also used as a verb relating to reconnaissance.

Staff stooge: Derogatory term referring to a staff officer. Also "staff weenie."

Tacomm: A portable frequency-hopping communications transceiver once used by rear-echelon warbot brainy troops and now generally used in very advanced and ruggedized versions by the Sierra Charlies.

Tango Sierra: Tough shit.

Tech-weenie: The derogatory term applied by combat soldiers to the scientists, engineers, and technicians who complicate life by insisting that the soldier have gadgetry that is the newest, fastest, most powerful, most accurate, and usually the most unreliable products of their fertile technical imaginations.

Tiger error: What happens when an eager soldier tries too hard.

Umpteen hundred: Some time in the distant, undetermined future.

Up link: The remote command link or channel from the warbot brainy to the warbot.

Warbot: Abbreviation for "war robot," a mechanical device that is operated by or commanded by a soldier to fight in the field.

Warbot brainy: The human soldier who operates warbots through linkage, implying that the soldier is basically the brains of the warbot. Sierra Charlies remind everyone that they are definitely not warbot brainies whom they consider to be adult children operating destructive video games.